THE
DUCHESS
OF KENT

THE
DUCHESS
OF KENT

The Troubled Life of
Katharine Worsley

MARY RIDDELL

SIDGWICK & JACKSON

First published 1999 by Sidgwick & Jackson

an imprint of Macmillan Publishers Ltd
25 Eccleston Place, London SW1W 9NF
Basingstoke and Oxford

Associated companies throughout the world

ISBN 0 283 06329 7

3 5 7 9 8 6 4

A CIP catalogue record for this book is available from
the British Library.

Typeset by SetSystems Ltd, Saffron Walden, Essex
Printed and bound in Great Britain by
Mackays of Chatham plc, Chatham, Kent

Contents

✤

Contents

Acknowledgements

Some of those whom I interviewed in the course of researching this book preferred to remain anonymous. I thank them for their invaluable help, together with many others who were generous enough to agree to long, and sometimes multiple, interviews. My thanks, for assorted assistance and in no particular order, to Lord Coggan, Lord Bridges, Lady Lothian, Professor David Dilks, Jill Dilks, the Right Reverend Michael Mann, Robert Smith, Kenneth Rose, Professor Simon Wessely, Dr Peter White, Dr Martin Deahl, Father Vladimir Felzmann, Professor Leslie Findley, Freddy Burnaby-Atkins, The Very Reverend Michael Mayne, Lady Sally Greengross, Lady Elizabeth Anson, John Studd, Sarah Bradford, Dr Charles Shepherd, Mavis Moore, Martyn Lewis, Carol Bellamy, Reggie Purbrick, Sir David Willcocks, Basil Keen, John Hamill, Helen Storey, Jane Procter, Stacey Adams, Debbie Buckenham, Valerie Gorringe, Anne Fancourt, James Whitaker, Christopher Wilson, Clifford Longley and Maureen and Michael James.

I am also grateful to Dee Nolan, editor of *YOU* magazine, who first commissioned me to travel with the Duchess of Kent and Unicef, whose work I have had the privilege

Acknowledgements

to cover over a number of years; to the Royal College of Obstetricians and Gynaecologists, members of Runton Hill Seniors, the Kingswood Centre for opening its archive, Stuart Clarke for help with the pictures, the British Olympic Association and the office of the Duke and Duchess of Kent and Buckingham Palace Press Office for their assistance. Thank you to my editor, Susan Hill. And, last of all, thanks to John, Jack and Joe Shute, without whose technical help, patience and support this book would not have been written.

Prologue

BOMBAY, INDIA, 1996. In her suite at the Taj Mahal Hotel, the Duchess of Kent was preparing to leave for home. There was one last official engagement of the kind she always dreaded – an after-dinner speech in the hotel's Crystal Room – before her overnight journey to London.

A plane of the Queen's Flight, which had carried her from Calcutta in the north to Madras in the south, loaded with cream teas and the royal 'blood fridge' – containing type-matched transfusion bottles in case of medical emergency – would take her party back via Luxor in Egypt. The Duchess herself was booked on British Airways flight 138 to London Heathrow, under the name of Mrs Mills, the pseudonym chosen by her office to protect her identity when she travels.

In the adjoining room, her maid was packing away the designer wardrobe selected by the Duchess for her ten-day tour as royal patron of Unicef. The public role was over, and Mrs Mills would require only leggings, a jumper and a greatcoat for her anonymous journey.

Throughout her tour, the Duchess – elegant as always – had been greeted by those she met as the Maharani, the

Queen. Now she was sitting on her hotel sofa, in a crushed linen skirt and straw sandals, reflecting on what she had achieved.

By any standards the tour – arranged to mark the fiftieth birthday of her favourite charity – had gone well. She had comforted the old and embraced children. She had demonstrated all the empathy that makes her the warmest member of the royal family. She had witnessed the seemingly hopeless: gravely ill babies and little boys condemned to roll cigarettes for a few rupees a day. She had seen the hopeful: improved schools, feeding centres and light industries set up and run by women.

In the hours before her departure, it seemed natural that she would be both satisfied with a job well done and exultant at the thought of a family reunion. This time she had a particular reason for relief. Unbeknown to all but a handful of confidants, the Duchess was ill. On the eve of her departure for India, she had been notified of the cause of her recent bouts of exhaustion.

She had been told that she had Epstein-Barr Virus – a form of glandular fever and a precursor to the ME she was to announce later that year. It was an unusual diagnosis. Ninety-eight per cent of the British population are immune to EBV by the time they are sixty. The Duchess was sixty-three.

Two years later, she was herself to cast doubt on the origins of her ailment, claiming that her wretchedness might have been caused by a food allergy. For now, she had no option but to accept the advice she had been given. Coming on top of her long battle with illness and serious depression, it had proved a devastating blow. Nonetheless, she could congratulate herself that, in sticking to her schedule and behaving so valiantly that no one guessed how ill she felt, she had achieved a notable success. Now it was over. She could look forward to rest, to seeing her family and to sleeping in her own bed in her grace-and-favour apartment at York House.

It was clear, instead, that the prospect of returning home appalled her. 'I dread it,' she said. 'When I get back to England, I feel very lonely to start with. The first few days are very tough. I might talk about what I've done with a few friends . . . but friends who will understand what I'm trying to say.'

On one level, her feelings were explicable. The people she had met – the poor and the sick – had, of course, inspired in her a wish to make their lives better in any way she could. They had also inspired a sort of envy. 'What I find here, in these dark, dark eyes is an acceptance of life's destiny,' she said. 'We are never satisfied. I just passionately love these people. They accept their destiny, and it's more peaceful in a way.'

The picture she painted of her own life did not immediately suggest peace or passion or love. Instead she sketched out the image of a driven perfectionist, tormenting herself with reminders that she could somehow have done the job better. Of an isolated woman, strolling through Green Park or sitting on a park bench, alone with her thoughts.

She made little mention of her own family – three children, four grandchildren – and none of the Duke of Kent, cousin of the Queen, eighteenth in line to the throne and her husband of thirty-five years. That was not in itself unusual, for members of the royal family are not given to delivering cosy insights into domestic life, blissful or otherwise.

But Katharine Kent was born not into royalty but into a family which, though of the establishment and utterly loyal to it, placed human values first. As a plain 'Miss', she was the first untitled woman in more than a century to marry into the Windsor firm and to discover what losses and sacrifices that privilege would bring. In every sense she was the torch-bearer. By the next generation, arranged matches with obscure but blue-blooded scions of European royalty were entirely out of vogue.

The Duchess of Kent watched as Prince Charles married Lady Diana Spencer and as Prince Andrew exchanged vows with Sarah Ferguson, little knowing that one union would end in tragedy and the second in the vulgarization of whatever shreds of mystique still clung to the monarchy. What she did know about, from bitter experience, were the pressures applied on outsiders like herself by the job, by a flawed marriage, by a machiavellian household and by a royal family struggling to devise a new and popular role for itself in the fading years of the millennium. The Duchess of Kent has never publicly complained of such pressures.

She has neither carped nor been carped about, even by those who question the usefulness of 'major' royals and can find no merit at all in 'minor' ones. From Kerala in India to KwaZulu Natal in Africa, the Duchess is welcomed – frequently by those without television or tennis racquet – as 'the wonderful lady who gives out the prizes at Wimbledon'; a radiant and gracious figure, always ready with praise for those who win and condolences for those who lose.

Those Centre Court appearances, along with her work for numerous charities, epitomize the public face of the Duchess of Kent – untroubled and full of easy charm. It is not, of course, the complete or even a tolerably accurate picture. The truth, both more tragic and more courageous, was nearer the surface on the February afternoon when she sat in her hotel room in Bombay, marvelling at what she had seen and fearful about what would come next.

She did not look forward to being back, she said constantly. Indeed, she dreaded it. She would be sad and confused – or, as she put it, 'like a zombie'. Part of her anxiety hinged on the problems she would again confront from the moment she arrived. But another part hinged on a sense of loss and nostalgia. She had, or so she felt, seen a kinder, more courteous and less privileged world; a peaceful existence in which ambition is never over-prized and destiny never challenged.

Earlier on in her trip, the Duchess had vaguely aired her preference for Indian values as opposed to western ones, and the British press had picked it up. Did the Duchess of Kent really mean that Indian families living in penury had a better deal than the relatively privileged of the first world? Faxed newspaper cuttings were hastily forwarded from her office so that she could see the tenor of the reporting.

Although the interpretation exaggerated what she had meant to say, she did not alter the admiration she professed for a simpler life, far removed from the trappings of royalty. As plain Mrs Mills might have told herself, on the long flight home, that was how it had all begun.

CHAPTER ONE

The Captain's Child

❧

It was only a short walk. The Palladian façade of Hovingham Hall overlooks a sweep of North Yorkshire pastureland. The back entrance, opposite the village pub and next door to the Saxon church, abuts the main street. Like its inhabitants – and, in particular, the child born on 22 February 1933 – the Worsley family residence spans a borderline between the grand and the ordinary. Villagers, bearing small gifts of jam and preserves to celebrate the birth, made their way to the rear entrance.

Inside the hall doctors reassured Captain William Worsley that his wife and her fourth child were doing well. Although it was only breakfast time, the baby's grandfather, Sir William Worsley, ordered a bottle of champagne so that he could toast the new baby. 'To my grandaughter – to the baby, to her long and happy life.' Outside, feudal Hovingham prepared to deliver its gifts.

The birth of Katharine Mary Lucy Worsley was not an event to shake worlds or, for that matter, villages. Hovingham, nonetheless, was politely excited on behalf of Captain Worsley – heir to the estate, cricketing hero and popular local figure – and his wife, Joyce. The Worsleys already had three sons, and the arrival of a daughter was naturally viewed with approval by a small community whose lives were intertwined with those of the local squirarchy.

The baby's older brothers were similarly intrigued. Marcus, aged ten, was away at prep school. John, four, and Oliver – who had woken that morning to his sixth birthday presents and to the sight of the snow coating the parkland – were taken from their nursery at the back of the house to see their new sister, blonde-haired and sleeping in the firelight of her mother's bedroom, while their father telephoned relations with the news and composed his brief announcement for *The Times*: 'On February 22nd, at Hovingham, Yorks, to Joyce, wife of Captain W.A. Worsley – a daughter.'

Like her sons, Joyce Worsley was pleased by the birth of a girl to complete her family. A member of the Brunner dynasty – a clan noted for its entrepreneurial drive, philanthropy and involvement with politics – she had, in the nine years since her marriage, abandoned all pretensions to be a Liberal Party campaigner and instead embraced a life dictated by the demands of small children and wifely duty. Hovingham was in every sense conservative. Old Sir William, a widower, had only three years left to live by the time his granddaughter was born, and Joyce was already preparing for her role as wife to the fourth baronet. Hers would be – was already – an existence steeped in the minutiae of village life – church, Women's Institute, ministering to the sick and the old. Part social worker, part regal presence, Joyce's particular brand of community involvement and hauteur would be regarded by those in her fiefdom with some fondness and a great deal of wary respect. 'She was very kind, but you never forgot she was Lady Worsley,' says one villager.

Katharine was to be brought up in the same tradition of public service. 'She is my deputy,' Joyce Worsley would say in later years, while the child's father showed his daughter off to visitors with pride. Of all those who bent over the baby's crib on her first day, it is hard not to imagine that, even then, William Worsley was the most entranced by Katharine's birth.

As she grew up, he would forge her happiest memories of childhood. Even as a widely travelled royal Duchess, Katharine would tell friends that her favourite place in the world was 'Scarborough, where I played on the sands with my father'. Later, when she agonized over whether she should become engaged to Edward Kent, cousin to the Queen, her father would advise her: 'Marry him.' When royal life grew intolerable, she would flee back to Hovingham and her father in tears and leave, reassured and attempting to smile. When Sir William died, she would confess to being haunted by 'anxiety and despair'.

But, for now, there was no inkling that this child – a direct descendant of Oliver Cromwell, whose great-granddaughter, Mary Frankland, married a Worsley forebear – had any destiny beyond the enclosed county world she was born into. The Worsleys were, in Yorkshire terms, a very grand family. Hovingham was a very small stage.

In the wider world, Europe was already becoming a crucible for war. Adolf Hitler had been appointed Chancellor of Germany in January, and, four days after Katharine's birth, the Reichstag was swept by fire. As Berlin citizens likened the charred building to 'the funeral pyre of German democracy', Nazi Storm Troopers intensified their campaign against socialists and others. 'We shall show no mercy,' said Hermann Goering. 'Every Communist must be shot on the spot.'

In Britain too, the talk was of war. A few days before the Reichstag fire, the Oxford Union debating society carried, by 275 votes to 153, a motion that 'this House will, in no circumstances, fight for its King and Country'. In the ensuing uproar, a patriotic invading party stormed the debating hall and ripped to shreds the record of the offending motion. This lapse in security deeply offended Prince Leonid Lieven, a former Union official, who asked the current president: 'Sir, even if you are not prepared to defend your King and Country, might you not have defended the minute book?'

The Worsley family, reading of this furore in their copies of *The Times* and the *Yorkshire Post*, would probably have sided more with the raiding party than with a few misguided student peaceniks out of kilter with the spirit of the times. In an era when the British establishment was serenely omnipotent, whatever dissent faced the twin gods of King and Country was unlikely to find any echo at Hovingham Hall.

Like Starkadders at Cold Comfort Farm, there had, it seemed, always been Worsleys at Hovingham. Pillars of the community and upholders of the establishment, they forged careers in parliament, in the law and in the armed forces. A Lancashire family, the clan first moved to North Yorkshire during the sixteenth century and thirty years into the reign of Elizabeth I. The original manor house stood until 1750 when Thomas Worsley, the grandson of Oliver Cromwell and known as 'the Builder', inherited the estate at the age of thirty-nine.

An equerry to George II and appointed by George III as Surveyor-General of the Board of Works, he gained overall responsibility for royal buildings in an age when regard for grand architecture was close to a religion. Neighbouring

Castle Howard was the work of Sir John Vanbrugh and Nicholas Hawksmoor – a former pupil of Sir Christopher Wren – and Thomas Worsley had similarly grand plans for the new-look Hovingham, commissioning Robert Adam to design an exterior. In the event, Thomas, hampered by lack of cash, undertook the work himself, including a riding school incorporated into the main body of the hall, where he, an accomplished horseman, could train his horses as the household looked on from the gallery above.

In 1961, two centuries later, phalanxes of European royalty, including three queens, were to travel to Hovingham to re-establish the links Thomas had forged with the monarchy. They would pass through the old riding school and watch, at the end of the reception, as Katharine Worsley – the new Duchess of Kent – drove off for her honeymoon. A few who took their eyes off the bride saw the unshed tears in her father's eyes.

Although Katharine's was an improbably grand marriage, the Worsleys had retained some bonds with royalty. The grandson of Thomas the Builder was created a baronet in Queen Victoria's coronation honours list. By the time *his* grandson, Katharine's grandfather, inherited the title, the culture of the house where she was to grow up was established.

For old Sir William and his wife, Mary Chivers Bower, life revolved around church, music, cricket and the upbringing of their five children – Winifred, Isabel, Victoria, Edward and Willy – heir to the title and Katharine's father. Willy Worsley was born into privilege. Charm and humour allowed him to capitalize on it. Educated in the conventional manner of the upper-crust Englishman (Eton and Oxford), his chief claim to brilliance was on the cricket field. A captain of Yorkshire in 1928 and 1929, he became president of the MCC after instilling in his daughter not only the ability to play a reasonable innings but his own passion for the sport.

He endured a punishing First World War, first wounded and then reported missing. Several months elapsed before his family learnt that he had been taken prisoner-of-war. Six years after he returned home, a party of Hovingham villagers travelled to London to watch Cosmo Lang, the Archbishop of York, marry Captain William Arthur Worthington Worsley and Miss Joyce Morgan Brunner at St Margaret's Church, Westminster. The guests, including two ex-prime ministers, Stanley Baldwin and Herbert Asquith, and the reception – a champagne 'crush' or cocktail party at the bride's home – indicated a high society sophistication rarely replicated in the Worsley social diary, which was more geared to roast beef dinners for the county set and visiting worthies.

At the time of her marriage, Joyce Brunner had little experience of the world of the country squirarchy. Her grandfather, John Brunner, the son of an immigrant school-teacher from Zurich, had begun his life as a Liverpool clerk before co-founding, with Ludwig Mond, the Brunner Mond chemical firm that was to evolve into ICI. Brunner used his personal fortune to underpin a second career, devoting his considerable wealth to building schools and endowing professorial chairs at Liverpool University. Driven by politics and philanthropy, he became a Liberal MP and later a baronet. His granddaughter Joyce – Katharine Worsley's mother – was to inherit much of his £900,000 estate and his love of politics.

Joyce's father, John, was attempting to get himself selected as a Liberal candidate when she was born at 23 Wetherby Gardens in London, a mecca of Edwardian stylishness in comparison with staid Hovingham. Joyce Brunner's milieu, prosperous and fashionable, was one of improvement and reform. The Brunner family – both her distinguished grandfather and her less successful father – were devoted to improving the lot of the ordinary citizen. The Worsleys would have applauded this respect and concern for the common man; while nonetheless expecting him to know his place and doff his cap.

Joyce's parents, by contrast, supported egalitarian organizations such as the National Trust and garden suburbs in Hampstead and Liverpool. Winston Churchill would drop in at their home for afternoon tea, along with the Asquiths and the Stanleys. Joyce and her only brother, Felix, grew up steeped in politics at a time when support for the Liberal Party was dying. Her father was heavily defeated in the postwar 'khaki election', and Joyce, who had campaigned for him, was both shocked and disillusioned. By 1923 Liberal fortunes had ebbed further.

In the same year, Winifred Colegate, William Worsley's sister and married to a Brunner Mond employee, became friendly with Joyce. She and William were introduced at Winifred's Northwich home and engaged several months later. At a time when Joyce's old world – that of Liberal politics – was collapsing, marriage to William Worsley offered a seemingly charming alternative. The affluent of North Yorkshire, accustomed to good county marriages, would never quite welcome Joyce as one of their own. They were, however, both approving of and intrigued by the match linking the Worsley squirarchy and the *nouveau riche* Brunners, who had contributed so much to their adopted country.

Having departed on her Italian honeymoon, wearing – as *The Times*'s fashion correspondent noted – 'a dark blue alpaca dress with a cerise and blue cloche hat' – the new Mrs Worsley settled into a home on her father-in-law's estate. The Cottage, a modestly sized and unpretentious stone house, lay on the south side of Hovingham Hall, then still occupied by Sir William and his younger, bachelor son, Eddy. The Yorkshire county set, hospitable and curious, threw so many dinner parties to welcome her that old Sir William reopened the dusty Hovingham ballroom and held a party of his own. Joyce, it was noted, sat out most of the dances. Perhaps, a contemporary commentator observed, this was 'through demureness'.

That seems unlikely. Joyce Brunner, though dignified, was not a prim woman. Confident to the point of autocracy after moving in the smartest circles of London society, she could also be shy and so ill-at-ease in large groups of people that Yorkshire neighbours describe her as an almost spectral presence, even as hostess at her own functions. Much later in her life, there were whispers of a shyness bordering on neurosis.

If Joyce's reserve contrasted with William's bonhomie, that was only one aspect of the mixed genepool they would pass on to their daughter. William, though born into aristocratic life, had a charm that seduced ordinary people. Joyce, the child of well-heeled Liberal thinkers, paradoxically developed the skills of a bred-in-the-bone conservative wife. A paragon of good works, deeply attuned to the needs of the citizens of Hovingham and always on hand to celebrate a village birth or mourn a death, she was, nonetheless and deliberately, never quite on their wavelength. The interests of her past life – politics, social policy and the London social scene – would re-emerge in her daughter, mingled with Sir William's warm manner.

The backdrop to the life of Katharine Worsley has always

been painted as an untarnished idyll, in which she was brought up in a storybook setting, cherished by her three older brothers and adored by happily married parents. Certainly the window-dressing suggests that this was so.

Hovingham, although only a short drive from York and a stroll from Castle Howard, is a secluded place. Particularly in summer, when roses ramble over the stone cottages, the village – and Hovingham Hall itself – represents the epitome of chocolate-box Britain; the sort of dreamscape nostalgically conjured up by prime ministers from Stanley Baldwin to John Major. Cricket on the lawn, spinsters cycling to communion – all the essence of charming rural England might have been distilled from Hovingham.

That did not necessarily make it an ideal milieu for a small and rather isolated girl; destined to be separated in term-time from her brothers, all of whom were sent away to boarding school, and brought up virtually alone in a large and draughty house, made distant from the rest of the community not by geography but by the gulf of class and status. Though the squire's daughter might play with village children, there would always be a divide.

It seems likely that fissure would have been emphasized by Joyce Worsley. For all her Liberal leanings and despite – or more likely because of – her 'trade' background, Joyce was, even in the respectful account of villagers, a woman prone to snobbery and aloofness. Although she would be Katharine's constant, and frequently only, companion in her early years, no lasting closeness would develop between mother and daughter. From choice of school to choice of husband, the decisions taken by Joyce on behalf of her youngest child would make Katharine bitterly unhappy and resentful.

There is no suggestion that Joyce Worsley set out

deliberately to make her daughter's life more difficult. There is, however, evidence that she was a rather unhappy, and possibly unstable, woman who never wholly settled into her grand role as a country squire's wife.

Although an impeccable performer – adept at good works and resolute at fulfilling her chatelaine role – Joyce eschewed the social side of her husband's life, preferring to remain at home while he was out and about with the Yorkshire county set. William, by contrast, was a charming extrovert, who liked his cricket, relished the public commitments that increased over the lifespan of his marriage and enjoyed the company of pretty women. While there is no hint of infidelity or any overt wrangling between the Worsleys, there were vast character differences dividing amiable Sir William – who was widely liked – and his withdrawn, colder and less popular wife.

That gulf was to have a great effect on Katharine. The one profound and enduring relationship of her life was to be with her father, who bestowed on her almost dangerous quantities of love and admiration. There was nothing insidious in William's affection, apart from one element. Katharine, born into a hermetically sealed, big house environment, would have less contact than most young children with her peers or with other adults. From the outset, her bond with her father would be the benchmark for all other relationships. In contrast with such perfection, friends, siblings and partners would, throughout her life, be found flawed and wanting.

But all of that was in the future. In the 1920s and 1930s William and Joyce Worsley were ostensibly the ideal couple – cosseted by privilege but possessed of a strong communitarian streak and a burgeoning family.

*

The first son was named for his father. William Marcus John, now the fifth baronet, was born on 6 April 1925, the day after Captain Worsley's thirty-fifth birthday. Oliver, two years younger, was called after his ancestor, Cromwell. John arrived a year later. At his christening, his maternal grandfather, Sir John Brunner, had talked hopefully of standing in a by-election at Cheltenham, a place where friends and connections should offer him a favourable chance. Instead he failed. Shortly afterwards he died; broken and disappointed. He was sixty-three.

Joyce Worsley, devastated by her father's death, decided that the time had come to alter her own lifestyle. Possibly reasoning that the upheaval of a move would be useful therapy, she announced that she wanted to leave The Cottage – cramped with three small boys – and settle into Hovingham Hall, still the home of her elderly father-in-law, who would remain in situ if no longer in control. 'Do change things around,' he said, and Joyce did. Out went the battered dining-room chairs, to be replaced with a Chippendale set from the ballroom. Adam chairs were shifted from drawing-room to ballroom, and the portraits of Worsley ancestors were reshuffled through the newly painted rooms to Joyce's satisfaction.

Katharine, alone of the Worsley children, was born into the refurbished elegance forged by her ambitious mother from the dusty artefacts of a male-dominated establishment. As Europe edged towards war, Hovingham Hall, spruced up and redecorated, remained a tranquil oasis, far removed from international or national crises. In the year of Katharine's birth, thousands had marched on Hyde Park, protesting about unemployment.

On the day of her christening, the staff of the hall – a butler, a clutch of maids, a cook and the children's minder,

Nanny Mist, were primed to ensure that all went graciously and smoothly. The service itself was a simple affair. Carried from the hall to the next-door St Peter's, with a flock of family godparents in tow, she was baptized, in the spring of 1933, in the church's rose-marble font. The vicar, the Revd John Jackson, described the baby undertaking her first public engagement as 'well-behaved and seraphic'.

If so, Katharine Mary Lucy Worsley was already demonstrating that she was her father's child, blessed with his equanimity and optimism. She was also her mother's daughter.

CHAPTER TWO

From Cradle to Grave

❀

IT IS NOT recorded whether His Royal Highness Prince Edward George Nicholas Paul Patrick, the current Duke of Kent, cried during his christening at the private chapel at Buckingham Palace. Certainly he wailed throughout the baptism of his sister, Alexandra, two years later. Visitors calling on the Duke of Kent and his wife, Princess Marina, were quick to point to the fractious nature of their firstborn son. The diarist Chips Channon, invited to inspect Coppins – the Kents' newly acquired country home – and their baby, was clearly more favourably struck by the former.

'The result is charming, and the rooms now glow with luxe and gaiety,' he wrote. 'It is entirely Prince George who has transformed it, and he now thinks of little else. We had a massive tea, and then the besotted father carried in the pièce de resistance, the curly-haired, very red, howling Prince Edward. He had fine blue eyes, golden curls and looked like all four Georges rolled into one.'

'Little Edward became bumptious, and knocked over a table, spilling a kettle of hot water over his little pink legs, and he bellowed,' Channon noted after a return visit. Tea, he recorded, therefore ended in 'tragedy'. As it transpired, genuine tragedy awaited Prince Edward, orphaned at the age of six by the mysterious death of his father. When Edward was born, in the early hours of 9 October 1935, another life was drawing to a close. The health of his grandfather, George V, was fading fast.

'Saw my Kent grandson in his bath,' the old King noted in his dairy, during Christmas at Sandringham. A month later, he was dead, and the monarchy was veering towards one of its greatest crises. In the following twelve months Edward VIII would succeed to and abdicate the throne of England.

At Hovingham Hall, the King's dereliction would have been greeted with the deepest sadness. The arrival of the infant Prince Edward, some months earlier, would by contrast have been noted with loyalist pleasure. In London, the Royal Artillery fired a forty-one-gun salute in honour of the child born fifth in line to the throne.

At 3 Belgrave Square, the Kents' London home, neither public rejoicing nor the cloud gathering over the monarchy altered the fact that this was a very modern birth. George, Duke of Kent, insisted on staying with his wife, Marina, throughout her labour, leaving her side only to assure waiting reporters that hot coffee would be sent down to them. 'I do hope it will be over soon. I don't think I could stand much more of this,' he said.

Edward's birth was greeted with suitable eulogies. His parents, and in particular his mother, appealed to the British people. Like Princess Diana, Marina – the most glamorous royal of her generation and a leading scion of the Greek and Russian royal familes – was a moulder of style and a fashion icon; skilled at juggling frivolity and public service. Unlike Diana, Marina could never fairly have been described as 'a people's princess'.

Marina was a princess of Greece. In truth, there was nothing of Greece in her pedigree, barring a quite Olympian grandeur. Early in her marriage, Marina described her sister-in-law, Queen Elizabeth the Queen Mother, as 'that common little Scottish girl' and constantly advised her own children that 'breeding will out'.

If anyone had told Marina that her newly born son would choose as his bride a plain 'Miss' from Yorkshire, her blood, distilled from the royal houses of Denmark and Russia, would have run cold in her veins. Her mother, Grand Duchess Helen, was a first cousin of the Tsar, assassinated with his children – past playmates of Marina and her older sisters, Elizabeth and Olga – in the Bolshevik Revolution of 1917. Her father, Prince Nicholas, was the son of George I of Greece, born Danish but shifted to be King of his adopted country after Greece failed to find a suitable English candidate.

King George was assassinated by a madman in 1913, and his successors – rocked by internal unrest and war in the Balkans – were driven out. Marina, brought up in the luxury of a palace given to her mother by the Tsar and fussed over by her Norland nanny, was twice exiled from Greece. She was fourteen when her family ended up in Paris, ousted for good.

Marina's teenage years are routinely painted as impoverished and bohemian. In a very relative sense they were. Her mother looked after Russian refugees, and her father painted to earn a living. Marina herself learned to beg for and alter designer clothes, modelled for Pond's face cream and travelled by public transport. But she also went to the finest schools and maintained close links with the British royal family, and in particular her formidable godmother. It was seen as entirely fitting that Queen Mary's favourite god-daughter should, in due course, marry her favourite son.

George and Mary produced six children: Edward (VIII, known as David, in 1894), Albert or Bertie (the future King George VI, born 1895), Mary (1897), Henry (1900), George (1902), and John (1905), handicapped, an epilepsy sufferer and destined for an early death. George, an irascible disciplinarian and Mary – described by the King's biographer, Kenneth Rose, as 'rigid as the buckram on which rested her diamond parure' – were emotionally ill-equipped parents.

Of all Mary's children, only George had the cleverness, charm and cultivation to melt her reserve. When he served in the Navy, she – knowing that he was miserable and perpetually seasick – fussed over him from afar. 'Be an angel,' she wrote to her husband's equerry, 'and find out for me whether any ship is likely to go to Malta before Christmas, as I have two or three largish parcels for Prince George.'

Marina and George had known each other vaguely since childhood, playing croquet together when she was four years old. For a time Queen Mary had sized her god-daughter up as a suitable bride for her oldest son (and thus a future Queen), but David's preference for married women pre-empted any such match.

Instead, late in 1933, George and Marina sat opposite one another at the lunch table of Emerald Cunard, the London society hostess Queen Mary would grow to hate for her encouragement of David's affair with Mrs Simpson, the woman for whom he would renounce the throne. Emerald's lunch, the first serious encounter between George and Marina, was to change their destiny and that of Katharine Worsley. She was then seven months old.

Whatever the attraction between the English prince and the Greek princess, it seems to have fallen short of love at first sight. Some months elapsed before a second meeting at Claridge's. But, the following summer, George altered his plans and travelled to meet Marina during her holiday with her sister Olga and her husband, Prince Paul, at Bohinj in the Yugoslav mountains. Their engagement followed a few days later.

Queen Mary was suitably gratified. As she explained: 'No bread and butter miss would be any help to my son, but this girl is sophisticated as well as charming, and she will be. Theirs will be a happy marriage.' George himself spoke about his fiancée with a curious lack of passion that would be echoed, years later, by Prince Charles. Asked, on his engagement to Lady Diana Spencer, whether they were in love, he said: 'Whatever that means.' Although their attachment proved far deeper, George was almost as cavalier when tackled on his romance with Marina. 'We laugh at the same sort of things,' he told a friend. 'She beats me at most games. And she doesn't care a damn how fast I drive when I take her out in a car.'

Even so, it seemed an ideal match. Marina, rigorously slimmed down by her mother as a prelude to finding a suitor, was – at least by the lumpen standards of the British monarchy – a considerable beauty and so impeccably blue-blooded that no arranged marriage could have been more suitable. There was only one drawback. On any reading of his lifestyle, George was deeply unsuitable husband material. A philanderer and a bisexual, he had a string of past affairs with men and women. As one friend is said to have observed: 'I was told no one – of either sex – was safe with him in a taxi.'

George's conquests were wide-ranging. In his later years,

Noël Coward used to speak of his flirtation with the Prince, but George did not confine his attentions to society stalwarts. '*Pourri de charme*', as one friend described him, he trawled low-life nightclubs, firing rumours of encounters with an Argentinian diplomat and an Italian aristocrat. On one occasion he was found with a homosexual in the Nut House club and deposited in police cells until his identity was discovered. On another, according to Bruce Lockhart, a scandal erupted over letters he wrote to a young man in Paris. 'A large sum had to be paid for their recovery.'

There were also strings of aristocratic women eager to charm the King's most attractive son, slim, dark-haired and handsome. Two, Poppy Baring and Lois Stuart, came close to marrying him. Another, an American called Kiki Whitney Preston, introduced him to cocaine, widely available at more louche royal haunts and so indispensable to the Prince that David, his brother and soulmate, shut him away in his country house in order to wean him away from his addiction.

As the Chilean Ambassador remarked: 'For extra-curricular activities, baccarat, roulette, double whisky sodas and ladies with pasts were his favourite.' The wild days, so it seemed, were over when George brought Marina, his future bride, home to England. 'Everyone is so delighted with her,' George wrote to Prince Paul of Yugoslavia. 'Cos when she arrived at Victoria Station, they expected a dowdy Princess, such as unfortunately my family are. But when they saw this lovely chic creature they could hardly believe it … and shouted: "Don't change. Don't let them change you."'

If the Worsleys of Hovingham knew anything about Princess Marina prior to her engagement, they were better informed than most. The public caught on quickly. From the start Marina was a style-leader, responsible for a populist fervour for pillbox hats at half-a-crown, 'Marina blue', the colour of the moment, and fairytale weddings. The residents of Hovingham Hall had a particular interest in the marriage of George and Marina, held at Westminster Abbey on 29 November 1934. The celebrant, the Archbishop of Canterbury, Cosmo Lang, had – as Archbishop of York – married Katharine Worsley's parents. Though there was little comparison, in terms of grandeur, Marina injected into the occasion the demotic spirit she would be lauded for, announcing that she would sooner see people give their money to the unemployed than to buy expensive wedding gifts for her. (Her mother, Princess Nicholas, redressed the balance, letting it be known that unless the invitations were reprinted to include the title 'Her Imperial Highness' she would be boycotting the whole event.)

In fact, Marina's altruism was thrown into question by the British Treasury. Secret government papers, released in 1998, revealed disapproval that she had chosen a trousseau costing £202 (or £8,000 at today's prices) in Paris, rather than supporting the British fashion industry at a time of depression. A letter from Sir Warren Fisher, Permanent Secretary to the Treasury, to George V's private secretary, read: 'I am not, of course, an authority on women's attire, but I am assured by some of the best-dressed women I know that there is nothing that cannot be bought in London that does not compare favourably with clothes purchased elsewhere.'

The scandal of Marina's unpatriotic wardrobe was soon to be overshadowed by more pressing worries affecting the royal family. Within two years of Prince George's marriage to Marina, his son Edward was born, his father died, and his favourite brother, David, renounced the throne of England to marry the American divorcée, Wallis Simpson and live in exile. In the aftermath of the abdication there were rumours that George would be made King in favour of his lacklustre older brother, Bertie, who was eventually crowned George VI. Such a plan was never viable, given the constitutional difficulty of tampering with the line of succession and George's scandalous past. Nevertheless, Marina – the grandest of royal Duchesses – might have thought herself within a hair's breadth of becoming consort to the next King of England. No doubt she, never a doubter of her own self-worth, would have taken on the task with equanimity.

The unswerving confidence of Marina was to have a great impact on Katharine Worsley, still a toddler at Hovingham. In the years to come, Marina would have the prescience to see that her prospective daughter-in-law – a woman with much less self-esteem (and in Marina's eyes infinitely inferior breeding) – would find her own foray into a royal existence to be hard and daunting. Marina would also have the autocracy to make icily plain her resistance to a marriage between Katharine and Edward, thereby rendering Katharine's task in coming to terms with the life she had chosen even more difficult.

Although Marina would not meet Katharine for many years, the foundation stone for their relationship was cast in the lead-up to the older woman's wedding. Marina was an effortless royal, a natural performer and an instinctive autocrat. She had no doubts concerning her charm, her influence or – although her looks fell well short of perfection – her beauty. Her common touch, which was sure, was tempered always by belief that her pedigree placed her on a plane far aloft of the masses and some distance above most of the Windsors.

Katharine Worsley – a far more fragile and self-doubting character – was never destined, through upbringing and temperament, to become a Duchess of Kent in the imprint of Marina. Once it had become clear that Marina was to be saddled with this less-than-satisfactory daughter-in-law, she would try to shape, or manipulate, Katharine into what she deemed a passing resemblance to the real thing. The experiment was not to prove successful.

As for George, he met his future daughter-in-law only once. When Katharine was three years old, the Duke of Kent – on a visit to Yorkshire – dropped in at Hovingham Hall on a courtesy visit to the local squire. George would probably have had a word or two for the pretty blonde child, held in her father's arms, for by then he was an attentive father himself, no doubt eager to return home to his baby son, Edward – Katharine Worsley's future husband.

George's heir, the current Duke of Kent, had not – unlike his bride-to-be – started life in a climate of apparent tranquillity. A child descended from the royal families of Romanov and Hanover, Saxe-Coburg-Gotha, Mecklenburg-Strelitz, Denmark, Greece and Britain, he was born in the immediate wake of the abdication and into a clan exhibiting every symptom of family dysfunction and seismic upheaval.

For all that, Edward's early childhood was remarkably blessed. George V's children had scarcely produced a glut of royal births, and Princess Margaret found her new cousin such a novelty that she prodded him in his crib and asked: 'Is it real? Will it break?'

George doted on his son. As soon as he could walk, Edward was encouraged into the garage to tinker with his father's cars. At one, he could say 'car'. At four, allegedly, he could rebuild an engine. When he went into hospital to have his tonsils removed, he waited eagerly for his father to take over from Marina at his bedside. According to one story, the small Prince demanded to know how many bricks there were in the hospital, and – having got no answer from his mother or his nurses – finally told the matron: 'I know how many bricks there are now. My father told me. My father knows everything.' By distanced royal standards, the Duke was an extraordinarily attentive father, buying his son the latest toys, such as a yellow plush cat with battery-lit eyes.

Other children arrived: Alexandra on 25 December 1936 and Michael on 4 July 1942. Charming as Alexandra was, it seems clear that Edward – diffident, tearful and awkward – forged a particularly close relationship with his father. With the outbreak of war, those ties inevitably slackened. Armed with a set of suitcases capacious enough to contain clothes for an invading army, Queen Mary set forth for Badminton with her Kent grandchildren in tow. Marina, meanwhile, as an arbiter of British taste, had taken to wearing cheap and unfashionable cotton frocks, in the cause of drumming up trade for the Lancashire mills. The nation duly wore cotton. She had personally killed off a current craze for chrome-plated furniture and lavishly patterned curtains. 'I should not like my home to look like a bar,' she said. The nation, cured of its lapse in taste, thought minimalist.

Menus, flowers, paintings, antiques and the redecoration of Coppins she left to the artistic eye and spendthrift nature of the Duke, concentrating on establishing herself as a royal performer and a devoted mother and wife. Marina may indeed have been besotted by a husband who – always flighty and weak-willed – proved himself perfectly capable of betraying her. Alternatively, she may have made the personal choice of trading off her husband's imperfections for the glamour and status that now attached to her.

Certainly Marina was not allowed to forget George's past. On one occasion, a well-known homosexual approached her in a nightclub and told her: 'You don't know me, but I was your predecessor.' Marina, however, had been accustomed all her life to withstanding potential humiliation and reversal of fortune. Probably her love, and indisputably her pride, ensured that the Kents entered the war as exemplars of married bliss and public service.

Marina, at the King's urging, became commandant of the WRNS, paying particular attention to the design of the hats. 'No woman wants to wear a hat which makes her look unattractive, war or no war,' she said. 'The right sort of hat is most important if we are to get recruits.' She also served as a nursing auxiliary at University College Hospital, working incognito under the name of Nurse Kay. (Whether by coincidence or deliberately, her future daughter-in-law, Katharine, was to adopt the same pseudonym, almost thirty years on, when she became a volunteer tending the sick and cleaning rooms at Lourdes.)

The Duke of Kent, meanwhile, had flown over 60,000 miles in twelve months in a punishing schedule of wartime inspections and quasi-diplomatic duties. In 1941 he crossed the Atlantic in a Liberator and toured Canada and the US. On 25 August 1942, three weeks after his younger son's christening, the Duke drove himself from Coppins to London, where he took a train north. His destination was Invergordon and a secret fact-finding mission to Iceland. It was the last such tour that he, hoping for less onerous duties, planned to undertake.

The Sunderland flying boat took off down the Cromarty Firth in good light and in the afternoon. It was dusk when a Highland crofter heard an explosion and saw, above the mountainside, a sheet of flame. The bodies, thrown clear of the wreckage, were found at dawn the next day. One crew member lived; the rest had perished. His Royal Highness, the Duke of Kent, was instantly identified by his name-tagged wristband.

Even now, speculation about the crash persists. The Duke himself had been at the controls, according to one rumour. In another version, British Intelligence were alleged to have killed him; a story based on the fact that he and Marina – she with one Nazi-sympathizing brother-in-law and another, Prince Paul, later denounced as a quisling – were pro-German prior to the war. The report of an official inquiry blaming pilot error mysteriously disappeared from the Public Records Office. Subsequent expert opinion advanced faulty instrumentation as a more likely cause.

The news was phoned through to Coppins that night, as Marina slept in the room next to Michael, her seven-week-old baby. By the next day the nation would be in mourning. Hovingham sorrowed over a Duke they felt they knew (without, of course, having the slightest familiarity with his track record as a bisexual drug-user). His picture, taken on the day he visited the Hall and lifted Katharine, the squire's daughter, in his arms, still hung in their village hall.

Queen Mary, the first to hear of the tragedy, prepared to comfort her daughter-in-law. 'I must go to Marina,' she said. Amid the grief shared by an icy matriarch and a despairing young widow, it is not recorded how Edward, the only Kent child old enough to absorb what had happened, reacted to the news.

To him, his father had been a hero. He was mourned as such. Five monarchs – King George VI, King Haakon of Norway, King George II of the Hellenes, King Peter of Yugoslavia and Queen Wilhelmina of the Netherlands – stood over the coffin, decorated with a wreath of garden flowers. With them was a small boy clinging to his memories. The toy car the Duke had bought him for his birthday.

The Duke chasing his nieces, Elizabeth and Margaret, over the Coppins lawns at his tea party.

The new Duke of Kent was sufficiently schooled in protocol to behave calmly in public. He was six; too old to let the scars of loss show and too young to guess how they would affect his life.

CHAPTER THREE

Prisoner of War

KATHARINE WORSLEY WAS also six years old when her peaceful life was shaken, albeit in less tragic fashion. War came slowly to Hovingham. The Prime Minister, Neville Chamberlain, stood in the House of Commons at noon on 3 September 1939 and announced: 'This country is now at war with Germany. We are ready.' The Worsley clan, out at in church for the morning service, missed the formal declaration but swiftly made up for lost time.

The local air-raid warden travelled to the hall to fit its inhabitants with gas masks. Sir William Worsley (now a baronet, following the death of his father) rejoined his regiment, the Green Howards, and his wife prepared to direct operations on the home front. If patriotism could be measured by weight of jam and acreage of needlework, Hovingham would not be found wanting.

It was decided too that the time had come for Katharine to have at least a semi-formal education. A governess, Miss Evelyn Brockhurst, thin, wan and too old for the call-up to the war effort, was imported to Hovingham Hall to supplement the efforts of the music tutors and riding instructors bussed in by Lady Worsley to teach her daughter. Although the earliest pictures of Katharine's life – portraits of a solemn-faced child carrying a miniature watering-can and following her mother round the Hovingham gardens – reinforce the bucolic image of her childhood, the notion of a six-year-old taught in solitary confinement by an ageing governess offers a desolate tableau, suggesting that, even by the anachronistic standards of the country gentry, this was an odd life for a small girl.

During the war years, when her parents were preoccupied with their own projects and the staff at the hall was pared down to an elderly butler, a cook and Miss Brockhurst, Katharine seems to have had such remarkably little contact with the outside world that even the Hovingham villagers thought her situation strange. As one of them says: 'The hall was a lonely place for a child.'

Not that Katharine was wholly starved of company. She saw her slightly older cousins – Joy and Isabel Colegate, the daughters of Sir William's sister Winifred – but she appears to have formed no great bond with them. When, several years later, she was sent to the same small boarding school as the Colegate sisters – both higher achievers than their younger cousin – there was no suggestion of any residual friendship. Katharine also, sometimes, joined in activities with the village children, their numbers increased now by busloads of evacuees with gas masks and the basic survival kit stipulated by government – spare clothing, a comb, a toothbrush and a handkerchief. Katharine, however, had little rapport with the incomers. Instead she was baffled both by their Durham accents and their townie ways. 'He says he's never seen a cow or a sheep,' she said, uncomprehendingly, of one child.

Her brothers, of course, were around during holidays. Although she never formed a close bond with Marcus, the oldest, the two younger Worsley boys – John, and, in particular, Oliver – encouraged their sister to join in their games, teaching her to ride ponies and helping her to climb trees. Both John and Oliver would later play a significant role in her life, remaining allies and supporters during her teenage years and early adulthood. But even those links were not to last. As a royal Duchess, Katharine would sever close contact with her old home and with her brothers, who came to regard her, according to one friend, as 'high-hatty' and distant.

It seems likely that a sense of isolation and a difficulty in forming enduring relationships – a thread running through the life of the Duchess of Kent – was inculcated in her early years at Hovingham. Indeed, with hindsight, it appears as if Katharine was almost cloistered away; a novice already being groomed for the lonely vocation she, the future royal bride, was to take on. Certainly the Worsleys were always ambitious for her, and the upshot of those still unformulated hopes was a regime in which Katharine grew up in an unusually introspective climate.

If the rhapsodic country house childhood was, in large part, a chimera, then Katharine herself appeared to have absorbed that myth. Throughout her life she would struggle to recreate what she saw as the Hovingham ideal of happy families. The reasons she would fail so spectacularly in her efforts may be that the idyll was always flawed. Her early reliance on family suggested a dependency, dictated by the fact that her existence was ring-fenced by the boundaries of the Hovingham estate.

Whatever the restrictions on Katharine's life, there is no doubt that the most cheerful note was provided by her father, idolized by his daughter and admired by his staff.

'Such a busy man,' says the woman who used to be his secretary and 'backroom girl' for part of the war. 'He was colonel commandant of the Army Cadet Force and the colonel commanding the North Riding Home Guard. He was great as a boss. He knew exactly what he wanted, but he also had the ability to do it himself. He didn't mind you taking that extra bit of time, but it had to be right.'

Katharine's own perfectionism – 'homework' done rigorously before royal engagements, official outfits scrapped if she spots a speck of grime – was learned at her father's side. Sir William dictated his letters fluently and verbatim but refused to sign them unless the spacing and alignment were impeccable. 'Always keep a tidy mind,' he cautioned those who worked for him.

But he was also relaxed and generous, pressing staff to take leave to visit injured relatives and reluctant – though it was made eminently clear that he was in charge – to stand on dignity. When a servant of the hall inadvertently locked him into his office over a lunchtime, he was amused rather than furious. The servant in question was merely grateful that he had not accidentally imprisoned Lady Worsley. As he says: 'She was rather different from Sir William – a presence. I don't think she suffered fools gladly or lightly, and she knew exactly what she wanted. Informality did not go with the late Lady Worsley.'

If Joyce Worsley had known that her daughter was destined to marry into royalty, then she – paradoxically the child of Liberal free-thinkers – could not have provided a more regal example. On one level she was utterly in tune with her village – dropping in small gifts whenever a baby was born; an attentive visitor at the sickbeds of the old and dying. To the bereaved, she would write kind letters, expressing not only condolences but messages showing that she understood the depth of family bonds. Lady Worsley could be deeply compassionate. She could also be glacial.

Less obviously she, like her daughter, was shy. A Yorkshire peer remembers Sunday lunches at Hovingham as a talking shop for the distinguished and worthy and a dull ordeal for a child. She recalls also jollier evening functions, at which Sir William would shine while his wife remained in the background, so unnoticed and unnoticeable that 'you never really saw that she was there, even at her own parties. I don't think she liked parties. She wasn't really grand – just retiring. Didn't like being in the limelight. I always got the impression that when, later on, Sir William was doing something as Lord Lieutenant, she didn't go if she could avoid it. She didn't like public life.'

This deep reserve would re-emerge in Katharine, who has never lost her terror of working a roomful of strangers at an official function. So, at times, would the autocracy of Joyce Worsley occasionally be revealed. Long after the war, Sir William announced to a local newspaper correspondent that a new stained-glass window was being fitted to the church, in memory of his sister Winifred Colegate and his wife's mother, Lucy Brunner, and that the news could be passed on to the local press. The following day he returned, abashed, to report that Lady Worsley was furious at this snippet being made public before she had given permission and to ask if the exclusive could, after all, be suppressed.

Certainly Joyce Worsley was a woman of contradictions – charming and frosty, gracious and reserved in equal part. Equally certainly, her relationship with Katharine was not always an easy one. Lord Coggan, the former Archbishop of Canterbury and one of the Worsley family's dearest friends, confirms it. 'There's no vision of Lady Worsley in my mind. I mean she was there, but Sir William was the chap who chivvied it all along. Her mother was no comfort to her [Katharine], but he was.'

That charge of coldness suggests the gravest of rifts between mother and daughter; one prompted by several factors. Undoubtedly Lady Worsley would have felt to some extent excluded and made envious by the strength of the bond between her husband and her youngest child. She would have been fearful that her daughter – who resembled her closely in appearance and, in some aspects, in tempera- ment – might become, like her, withdrawn and increasingly reclusive. When Katharine, later in life, was to express misery over the grand marriage Joyce had helped engineer for her, her mother would prove incapable of offering compassion – perhaps less because she failed to understand Katharine's problems than because she, emotionally frail, understood them too well.

But the time when Katharine would crave her parents' comfort was in the future. For now, Lady Worsley had a good war and Katharine, her daughter and lieutenant, joined in her efforts. As president of the local Women's Institute, Joyce asked local women to her sewing parties, run along the same lines as those held by Queen Elizabeth in the Balcony Room at Buckingham Palace.

'Do you mind if she joins us?' she would ask her volunteers, as Katharine hovered outside the Tapestry Hall at Hovingham, filled with classical sculptures. The hall kitchens were given over to jam manufacture – Hovingham plum, mixed, on one occasion, with a bar of yellow carbolic soap which had slipped unnoticed into the boiling pan. Katharine's old clothes, and those of her brothers, were parcelled up for a village clothing exchange founded and run by her mother. In any remaining spare time, Lady Worsley instructed the ladies of the village in lampshade-making.

The fulfilment of the Worsley family motto – the greatest good to the greatest number – was extended in particular to the many villagers living in the estate's tied cottages. At Christmas, Sir William would visit each home with a brace of pheasant. If he was ill or otherwise occupied, Katharine would deliver them instead; a familiar, unremarkable little girl with beautifully brushed hair and scruffy tomboy clothes; accepted as part of a community she had barely left, apart from trips to Scarborough with her father and summer holidays spent with her Brunner cousins in Selsey.

In the outside world, the war wound on. The Battle of Britain. Dunkirk. At Badminton, Queen Mary instructed her grandson, Eddie Kent, in ivy-clearing, taught his sister Alexandra to curtsey and insisted on saving petrol by riding through the estate in a horse-drawn farm cart. Told by the Duchess of Beaufort that she looked as if she was riding in a tumbril, Her Majesty replied: 'Well, it may come to that yet. One never knows.'

Hovingham maintained a more optimistic outlook. War had transformed the village – population 400 – into a more cosmopolitan place. Nissen huts sprang up by the park. Canadian troops were installed down the road. The village hall was given over to picture shows and weekly dances. Though too young for such entertainment, Katharine Worsley had reached her tenth birthday. It was finally decided that the time had come for her to go to school.

St Margaret's was hardly a change of culture, merely a move from one splendid backdrop to another. Castle Howard, just down the road from Hovingham, was fire-ravaged, palatial and a newly designated girls' boarding school. The setting was familiar to Katharine. Before the Howards vacated their stately home for the duration of the war, she had sometimes played with the children of the family in their perfectly equipped gym, complete with wall-bars, vaulting horses and ropes.

Now it had been sequestered, with Lady Georgina Howard's gold and yellow bedroom turned into a girls' dormitory full of iron beds. The blend of grandeur and utilitarianism was a novelty to most of the thirty girls who joined the school in 1943. Although Katharine knew the place well, she – used to being alone – considered herself an outsider. A day-girl among boarders, she asked to be dropped some distance from the school, so that she could arrive inconspicuously. Later, she would persuade her parents to let her make her own way, riding her pony, Greylegs, across the fields. She made one good friend, Diana Hynes – a girl gifted, as Katharine was, at music – but there were no signs of any natural gregariousness as she emerged from the confinement of Hovingham.

At Castle Howard, in 1944, Katharine Worsley saw her future in-laws for the first time. The King and Queen, paying a visit, along with Princess Elizabeth, after inspecting troops in the North Riding, paused to exchange a few words with the older girls. Katharine remained a background figure; as ever, not a child who demanded or attracted notice. Good at music, poor at Latin, pleasant, eager and an amiable girl to have in class, her reports noted, as her stint at St Margaret's, and the war, drew to a close.

On VE day, Britain's rejoicing was reflected in the flags, bunting, red school cloaks and blue summer tunics hung over the façades of Castle Howard. Katharine danced with her schoolfriends, roasted potatoes in the embers of the bonfire and went home to Hovingham.

If Katharine's childhood was not the fairytale of legend, it still compared favourably with that of Edward Kent – two years her junior. At his prep school, Ludgrove, he was punished for drilling holes in a lavatory cistern, causing severe flooding. At home, he took every opportunity to escape from the house and spend hours in the garage, listening to the one man prepared to regale him with anecdotes about his dead father.

Frederick Field had been Prince George's chauffeur. Now he was full of stories about the adventures undertaken by his glamorous employer. Given George's waywardness and sexual proclivities, these would have needed careful editing for the ears for the young Edward. Even so, there was plenty of material. As a naval officer, factory inspector, King's emissary and putative Governor-General of Australia (a posting deferred with the onset of war), George had been a truly charismatic, and in some ways an admirable figure. Even so, Edward's appetite for Field's stories of derring-do was both insatiable and rather sad.

Few others were eager to fuel his childish memories, awakened constantly by his home environment. Marina had left Coppins as a museum to her late husband. As Chips Channon wrote: 'The Duchess has rearranged her sitting room, kept the Duke's just as it was and has shut up the music room . . . I was haunted by the spirit of the Duke. Every room and object is so inspired by him . . . The house still vibrates with his vivacious personality.' Though his ghost lingered, the Duke was so little spoken of that Marina's staff do not remember her ever mentioning him in her children's presence. While her reticence may have been a by-product of personal sorrow, there was a wider move to relegate George to the shadows. To this day the royal family remains tight-lipped about a wayward, bisexual prince whose personal papers have never been disclosed to historians.

To Edward, bereft of a father, this climate of silence was the worst possible therapy. The vacuum created not only by George's death but by the fact that his memory was excised from all family conversation was obvious to all who met him. Marina, concerned about the lack of male influence on her son, engaged as tutor and holiday companion a young Eton schoolmaster, Giles St Aubyn. Edward clung to St Aubyn – hardly more than a boy himself – as if desperate to find a surrogate father.

Though sometimes stubborn and often difficult, Edward was more tempestuous than ill-tempered. Where both his father and his grandfather had been irascible men, Edward expressed his feelings differently. Prone to wild fits of tears, he was, by the rigid standards of the English public school-boy, emotionally uncontrolled. His tutor-cum-equerry struggled to understand and control his moods as he accompanied him everywhere: to the dentist in London, to Birkhall (the Queen Mother's Scottish residence), frequently leaving Marina and her younger children at home with her Coppins clique. If Marina seemed happy to devolve the responsibility for her oldest son on a glorified nanny, the King was less sanguine.

George VI, the father of the current Queen and a man oppressed by anxiety and the rigours of public duty, still spared an extraordinary amount of time for the child he regarded almost as an adopted son. He made it clear that the boy should be taught to hunt, shoot and fish, country pursuits beloved of royalty.

And, unbeknown to Marina, he contacted Eton – after Edward had embarked on a short and unhappy career there

– to ask that letters should be sent to him regularly, reporting on every aspect of his nephew's progress. Each behavioural lapse and poor mark was duly noted and passed on to Buckingham Palace. At the same time, the King would ask Marina for news of her son, listening, without comment, to her glowing accounts of high achievement and brilliant grades. Very slowly it dawned on her that George VI was not only getting two separate versions. He also knew more about Edward than she did. The Eton masters who had obeyed the King's command were subjected to the full brunt of Marina's icy hauteur, but the practice continued.

George's dutiful interest in his nephew failed to make Edward's childhood any happier. Not only did Edward greatly fear his uncle – probably for his status rather than his personality, for George was far from being a tyrant – but he loathed the lonely, enforced, country sports holidays in Scotland, during which he was supposed to prove himself as a person imbued with royal machismo.

After the King died, in 1952, a newspaper reporter commented on how unprepossessing the young Duke of Kent appeared at the funeral. 'In his mourning clothes, he looked diffident, shy and incapable of making contact with the foreign royalty and personalities who had come to London,' he wrote. Certainly the Duke was an awkward and gauche figure. He was also a seventeen-year-old, compelled, once again, to mourn a paternal influence. Although he had not loved the King, his death awakened, once again, the unassuaged loss of his own father.

To be a male child born into royalty is rarely the route to emotional literacy. In Edward's case, the chances of him emerging as the sort of man able to offer understanding and empathy were particularly low. For male role models, he had a king, a chauffeur and a part-time tutor-cum-nanny. For parental support, he had his mother.

Although Edward adored Marina, she was less a doting maternal figure than a public presence – still one of the most dazzling stars on the royal circuit and mistress of a glittering salon, a small outpost of foreign glamour in the dull shires. The mystique of Marina was to be picked over and revised for years to come. In 1998 a Northern Irish academic called William Lloyd Lavery published a fantastic and unsubstantiated claim that he was the illegitimate child of Marina and Tsar Nicholas's grandson, Alexei. While there is no evidence for such an exotic liaison, the life Marina constructed for herself was certainly not that of a rusticated widow.

Visitors to Coppins included Noël Coward – her husband's alleged former lover – Sir Malcolm Sargent and Danny Kaye, whose impersonations so convulsed the young Prince Michael with laughter that he almost had to be removed from the dinner table. But the lustre of Marina and her circle – many of them older, gay men, whom she found charming, unthreatening and adoring – was not expressly geared to the needs of unsure and unhappy adolescents like Edward.

When the stars were absent, Marina would turn to her female companions. In particular she liked to sit and smoke with her dearest friend, Zoia Poklewska, a Polish refugee to whom she had loaned a cottage on the Coppins estate, and the only person allowed to insult the Duchess or to treat her as an ordinary person. Neither the death of her husband nor changing circumstances had dented Marina's belief in her own grandeur; a certainty bolstered by the public rumour machine.

Marina, it was hinted, would emigrate to America, or

become a Hollywood star, or marry the King of Norway. In addition, accounts of affairs were rife. Douglas Fairbanks Junior, even Noël Coward and Cecil Beaton, were all whispered, without proof, to be her lovers.

In fact, according to her biographer, Sophia Watson, Marina's enduring love was her personal private secretary, Philip Hay, beautifully educated, handsome, and possessing the blend of faint pomposity and tact essential to those in royal service, a discretion so complete that Edward may not have been aware of the attachment.

Hay's ostensible role was more prosaic. A rigorous comptroller of the Coppins accounts, he insisted that those employed (at Marina's notoriously frugal rates) to mind the children paid all expenses up front and out of their own pockets. On inspecting the bills and finding them suitably modest, Hay would then arrange reimbursement.

If money was not a problem at Hovingham – thanks to Sir William's estate and Joyce's inheritance – it was deemed to be at a premium at Coppins. Despite her royal duties, Marina had none of the £25,000-a-year Civil List income her husband would have commanded, while George, profligate in life, had left everything that remained in trust for his children. Marina therefore took her economies seriously. According to Sophia Watson, she once removed the card from a bunch of roses sent to her by Sir Malcolm Sargent and dispatched then, under her own name, to Princess Marie Louise. Certainly, she held grand versions of a car boot sale, disposing of furniture, art, porcelain and silver worth more than £90,000. A second sell-off of the family silver raised £12,000 more.

It is unlikely that Marina was ever dangerously near the breadline. Allowances from Queen Mary and George V to her and her three children, along with the gift of a London base in Marlborough House, rendered her moderately secure. Edward, however, was brought up in a climate where grand aspirations were rarely matched by generosity or largesse. One summer, Marina announced that her whole retinue – children, their minders and staff – must pack for a stay in Greece, where they would revisit the splendour of her youth. The day of departure came, and Edward – along with the rest of the party – was told that the destination had altered. The Duchess had plumped instead for Bognor and a small rented house.

There seems little doubt that Marina, while reconciling the death of a husband she both adored and mistrusted, did not neglect her children or fail to love them. It is equally clear that Edward's home life – glamorous, bohemian, dictated by strict economies and overseen by his mother, the ultimate *grande dame* – was not designed to turn a troubled and bereaved small boy into an emotionally literate man, capable of building a secure family of his own.

Edward's future bride, Katharine Worsley, was thirteen when she was thrust out of her almost cloyingly secure family existence. The war over, Joyce had finally decided that her daughter could no longer stay at home and would be sent to the boarding school where her cousins were enrolled. Joy Colegate, the older, was regarded as 'brilliant and eccentric' by her schoolfriends. Isabel, though deemed less talented, was to emerge as a successful novelist whose books include *The Shooting Party*.

Here, in Joyce Worsley's opinion, was a school where Katharine would flourish academically and spend a happy adolescence. On both counts she was wrong.

CHAPTER FOUR

Lessons in Loneliness

Runton Hill, near Cromer in Norfolk, was the last bulwark between rural Britain and the North Pole. Today, following a merger with another private school and eventual closure, its windswept buildings have been converted into a holiday camp and labelled with upbeat American names. If the Duchess of Kent were to revisit 'The White House' and 'The Hollywood Diner', inhabited now by teenagers enjoying a summer break, she might feel more favourably disposed to her Alma Mater.

When she arrived there, shortly after the war ended, her reaction inclined towards horror. Although previous biographers have claimed that Katharine Worsley spent a happy four years in secondary education, her old schoolfriends are puzzled that she has never dwelt on the Runton years. As one of them says: 'When she became engaged to the Duke of Kent, there was nothing about Runton. It was all junior school and what happened afterwards. We wondered: did she hate it so much that she didn't want anything said about it?' The answer appears to be yes.

To Katharine, arriving with her new uniform – airforce

blue gymslip, tweed coat, pudding basin hat and navy gym knickers (the outer layers hand-me-downs from her Colegate cousins) – Runton Hill seemed an exceptionally cheerless place. The school, just reconvened after being exiled to the Cotswolds for the war, was naturally in a state of upheaval. Its indomitable head, Miss Janet Vernon Harcourt, an acquaintance of Sir William Worsley, a former pupil of the pioneering school Wycombe Abbey, and one of the first prophets of an academic and liberal education for girls, strove to create for her pupils conditions of tolerable comfort. She was not assisted by the weather.

Before Katharine's arrival, one old girl summarized Runton's bracing climate. 'The games field in winter was like a Siberian plain with the wind blowing straight from the North Pole, and we were grateful for the pointed woollen caps designed by Miss Harcourt and copied from caps worn by the Andean fishermen on Lake Titicaca.' During Katharine's second year, a correspondent for the school magazine – the *Runton Hill Gazette* – detected no shift towards global warming. 'The tradesmen made heroic efforts to keep the school running smoothly, for the butcher walked out from Cromer with 62 lbs of meat on his back, in order that we might not go dinnerless. The postman also brought the letters on a sledge, and the baker struggled through with the bread. Altogether, everybody combined with commendable self-sacrifice to keep the school going.'

The sacrifices demanded of Katharine Worsley were, on the face of it, small. She was not bullied or persecuted. She was not friendless. She was not even subjected to the head's formidable wrath. Other pupils, bereft of 'favourite' status, were summoned to her study for a telling-off combined with a string of orders. 'Find my glove, girl,' Miss Harcourt would roar, watching as some hapless child sifted through untidy heaps before discovering the missing item in a drawer or wastepaper bin.

But Katharine, though never a model pupil, was the child of a friend. Miss Harcourt personally – and, by her standards, indulgently – watched over her progress, or lack of it. The root of Katharine's discontent was in part practical. Though she never flaunted the fact, her background was grander than that of most of her contemporaries, in the main the clever and ambitious daughters of doctors or lawyers accustomed to the privations of wartime. She, by contrast, was attuned to Hovingham Hall – Poussins on the wall, cricket on the lawn, music in the ballroom and, everywhere, the smack of aristocratic privilege. More relevantly, since Katharine was not a snobbish child, she found herself suddenly bereft of the insulation of a cloistered life overseen by her parents, and in particular by her indulgent father.

In attitude, as in fabric, Runton was an altogether less cosy place. On Katharine's first day she moved into a five-bedded dormitory in the school's older North House, where she was provided with a camp-style bed, a hanging rail for uniform and a plain deal chest of drawers, on which she might stand a family photograph. Her temperature was taken by Matron – standard procedure to check for the onset of any infectious illness – and her name placed on the list of duty rota: fire-lighting, tidying the kitchen and ringing the morning wake-up bell. Bathing, she was warned, was rationed and hair-washing permitted in strict rotation, owing to the post-war shortage of coal.

Though conditions were bleak, Runton had many compensations. In an era when well-off families were content to settle for their daughters being lightly educated, JVH, as she was always known, prized individualism and, where possible, high achievement. Having, in the early days of her tenure, outlawed 'stays', or corsets, which she derided as 'armour-plating', she moved on to dispense with less tangible restrictions.

Girls were never expected to walk in crocodile or to submit to more than a minimum of enforced group activities. Pupils might cycle to any local church of their choice, knowing that the headmistress would occasionally dispatch staff to check that no one was flouting the rule, sacrosanct at low-church Runton, that Sunday worship was obligatory. Lessons apart, there were few other formalized rituals. Exceptions included an annual school picnic at nearby Blakeney Point and JVH's pre-Christmas reading to the assembled school of *A Christmas Carol* – a nod to the festive spirit combined with a wish to instil in her charges a love of the classics.

An inspectors' report, published just after Katharine's departure and JVH's retirement, paid tribute to what the well-heeled got in return for their £126 annual fees (plus extras including pianoforte lessons at 17s 6d for seven classes). 'Most of the girls are extremely able intellectually ... though there are some whose intellectual progress is slow. During the last three years, from a total of 75 girls who left ... no less than 23 went up to universities, mainly the older ones, or to medical school. There is clear evidence the school has given its pupils the opportunities they need to build careers appropriate to their abilities.'

Lady Worsley concurred with the inspectors' plaudits. If she was aware of her daughter's difficulty in settling in, she certainly laid no blame on Runton Hill. Asked to make a speech at a school function, she praised an establishment whose liberal inclinations echoed the tenets of her own upbringing and which offered an education that was 'varied, humane and individual'. Almost half a century after Katharine left, her old schoolfriends still echo that approval. The majority enjoyed their schooldays. Though Runton is defunct, many still keep in touch through the 'seniors', or old girls' association. Katharine Worsley, who refused to join this organization, shared neither her mother's views nor those of most Old Runtonians. It is possible that she, never eager to display her feelings, did not confess to her parents how homesick and miserable she was. Certainly she hid it from all but her closest friends at school. A few years ago, Judith Ryland, two years her senior, was reintroduced to her at a charity lunch. Their conversation was brief, but the Duchess of Kent confided that she had been bitterly unhappy at school.

Would she have sent her own daughter to Runton? Mrs Ryland had asked, simply as a conversation-opener. The Duchess shuddered. 'No way,' she said. 'I wasn't at all happy there.' The curious thing was not so much that Katharine – a sheltered child from a protective home – was appalled by the rigours of Runton and its communal life. It was, instead, how very well she hid her problems.

Some of her old classmates barely remember her at all – although she never forgets the faces and names of Runton old girls she still meets by chance in her official duties. Others recall her as a deeply unexceptional girl – 'plain, dumpy, straight-haired and shy; not this wonderfully elegant woman you see now'. Certainly she never let her teachers or her associates know her real state of mind. To a limited extent, she joined in school activities: playing for the lacrosse team and appearing in school plays, including *Twelfth Night*, staged for visiting parents in the Dell – a natural outdoor theatre in the grounds.

Then, and indeed now, she hates being the focus of public scrutiny, and her role as Sebastian cannot have been a particular joy to her. Even centre-stage, she proved unremarkable. A school magazine reviewer referred to her performance only in passing: 'The castaway twins, N. Harter, as Viola and K. Worsley as Sebastian, had not much chance of being mistaken for each other, but then the last thing we are meant to do is to believe in the plot . . .'

But there was another side to Katharine. She had a few close friends, and those who did break through her reserve liked her enormously; pointing to the sense of fun and mischief still apparent to those who best know the Duchess of Kent. At the age of fifteen, she was moved out of austere North House into West House – a small 1930s semi on an estate adjoining the school playing field. Valerie Gorringe, one of eight girls sharing this overspill accommodation, remembers her as 'very human; a great friend to have and absolutely smashing. Even then, she had a sympathy for people. She would know what other people were thinking.

'She made the best of her time there. We all have times when we're not happy and she just made the best of it. She said she had a wonderful home relationship, and probably she did miss Hovingham. But she didn't seem unhappy as one knows unhappiness. It wasn't depression or anything. But she was very much a family person at that stage. She adored Sir William, and he adored her. Family and music and cricket – all the things that went on at Hovingham – were definitely her; far more than school.'

In the academic subjects that interested her, Katharine applied herself vaguely. But, in the main, her homework would remain undone or dashed off at the last minute. 'Oh, damn,' she would say, warned that an exercise was due to be handed in. 'I'll have to do it quickly.' Opinion is divided over whether she could have carried on at school, like her clever cousins, to take her higher certificate. A later Runton headmistress believes from conversations with retired staff that Katharine was quite capable of doing the exams but that her unusual 'sensitivity', and resulting unhappiness, meant she longed to get away from the school. Her own close friends think she simply was not academically bright enough. 'She'd never have done it,' says one. 'She was not very high up in her form. She just muddled along in the middle somewhere.'

Katharine herself had a low opinion of her talents; a view that may have been based on realism but which also grew out of a general lack of self-esteem. Though she has never, unlike Princess Diana, berated herself for being 'as thick as a plank', she frequently tells friends that her two clever sons 'certainly didn't get their brains from me'. But, despite her self-denigration, it is more likely that any wish to further her studies was far outweighed by the burdens of a closed community she disliked.

Not that Runton was inward-looking. While struggling to feed her girls in the years of rationing (the fresh meat quota was reduced in 1947 from 1s 2d per person per week to one shilling, and bacon, eggs, fish and wheat remained in short supply), Miss Harcourt took pains that they should be conscious of the less basic realities of post-war Britain. Although Katharine and her friends might have missed the appointment of Lord Mountbatten as the last Viceroy of India or the arrival of Dior's sensational 'Hour Glass' look – condemned by Cabinet newcomer Harold Wilson as 'irresponsibly frivolous and wasteful' – they would certainly have been aware of the engagement of Princess Elizabeth to Lieutenant Philip Mountbatten of Greece on 9 July 1947 and of a royal wedding scarcely greater in pomp than Katharine's would be.

Equally, while the birth of the NHS might have passed

them by in the following year, the arrival of Prince Charles made such an impact at Runton that the school radiogram was dusted off, a dance held and a song composed by the sixth-form in the baby's honour. The lyrics, sung to the tune of 'Oh, No John', began as follows.

> A little Prince so young and tender,
> Born to be a king is he,
> Bringing great delight and pleasure,
> To our England fair and free.
> Chorus: Oh welcome, welcome, little Charles.

Katharine, joining in this saccharine verse, could scarcely have foretold how close her links with Charles would become or how a schoolgirl's dutiful obeisance to the future monarch would turn, one day, to bitter disapproval of his treatment of Diana.

Most probably she wished only to get away to her own music. Runton schoolgirls of her time, even those who barely remember Katharine, recall her brilliance at the piano and her ability to play by ear any tune they could name. For hours, when her strain and loneliness became too great, she would disappear to practise her pieces over and over. Although she quickly reached Grade Eight exam standard, that was not the prime objective.

For her, music was both a safety valve and a survival mechanism. When school life became too much for her, she used the piano as a refuge, an escape into her own world. In later years, overwhelmed by unhappiness, she continued to retreat into her music. In later years too, she would withdraw totally into herself – placing a barrier, just as she did at Runton, between herself and the unpleasant reality of the outside world.

But if her schooldays in some ways sowed a seed of the depression she would later experience, they also implanted the strength she would need to deal with it. None of those who watched Katharine Worsley playing the piano for hours on end – even her closest confidantes – realized how isolated she felt. To them, she was simply a talented classmate indulging her favourite pastime. That was how she – private, strong-willed and unwilling ever to let her unhappiness show – wished to be seen.

In the summer of 1949, at the age of sixteen, Katharine got her school certificate exam results. Passes in English Language, Geography, Biology and – a disappointingly low mark – Music. Credits (one grade higher) for English Literature and French. Her schooldays were over and a cab for Cromer waited. It was less of a graduation than a release.

Edward Kent, meanwhile, was about to begin his second year at Eton. Like the Worsley brothers, he had attended Ludgrove, the feeder school of choice, before moving on. Unlike Marcus, Oliver and John – gone, before his arrival, to Oxford or the Army – his schooldays were not particularly joyful or successful. Despite the best efforts of his tutor, Giles St Aubyn, Edward had never quite overcome the easily shed tears and lack of emotional equilibrium of his early years. Part of that was attributable to the loss of his father, part to his own temperament and part to the fact that he had been brought up in a female-dominated, exotic home out of kilter with the macho culture of establishment Britain in which his new classmates had been reared. Edward's sister, Alexandra, cheerful and well-balanced, wrote him strings of encouraging letters. Even so, he settled in with difficulty. Possibly he counter-balanced insecurity with superficial boorishness. Perhaps he, never noted for overt charm, simply had difficulty making close friends.

Either way, a contemporary claims that he was the only boy of that time 'swiped', or given a beating by the Head Master, for a very serious offence. The nature of the crime was never disclosed, but a close friend of his says that 'it wasn't any gay activity or anything of that nature. Purely bad behaviour.' Although she was not the most attentive of mothers, Marina appears to have been more sensitive to her son's unhappiness than Joyce Worsley was to her daughter's.

Just before Edward's sixteenth birthday, he was removed from Eton by Marina. No explanation was vouchsafed to his classmates, but it was reported that he had been suffering from 'severe chronic allergic sinusitis and rhinitis', exacerbated by the damp and low-lying situation of the school. While that was correct, it was also true that Edward had been miserable.

Although their upbringings had been vastly different, both Katharine Worsley and Edward Kent had, by their mid-teens, similar histories of unhappy schooldays. They displayed their lack of contentment in different ways, but the inference, even then, was that neither had the sort of equable temperament indicative of an untroubled future. The solution, in Edward's case, was deemed by Marina to be a stint at an exclusive Swiss finishing school, Le Rosey, where the future Duke of Kent, reprieved from the rigours of Eton and the misery of blocked sinuses, began to enjoy himself.

There is a footnote to Edward Kent's Eton career. Shortly before his departure, he was introduced to a new and glamorous addition to the school staff. Andrew Burnaby-Atkins was a war hero, a double-holder of the Military Cross and a former aide-de-camp to General Montgomery. His new job, Adjutant to the Eton Corps, was an army posting intended to round off a glittering military career.

In the next year, Burnaby-Atkins was to meet Katharine

Worsley and embark on a relationship that would change her life and drastically alter his whole future. But for now his attention was focused on the Queen's cousin, a gauche boy who dreamed of the day when he too might be an Army legend. At fifteen, he had some way to go. Even under the tutelage of the glamorous new adjutant, Edward Kent experienced some difficulty in putting one foot in front of the other.

As Burnaby-Atkins reported to his friends: 'The Duke of Kent marches like a duck.'

CHAPTER FIVE

Love, Loss and a Broken Heart

THE ASSUMPTION THAT Katharine Worsley had no serious suitor before meeting the Duke of Kent is not true. Among several less serious relationships, there was a great love affair that came close to destroying the life of the man involved.

Though some time was to elapse before their first meeting, Katharine – once released from the repressive confines of boarding school – had stipulated for herself a more diverting life. She wanted, she said, to follow her brothers to Oxford. Both her school exam results and the fact that well-to-do families saw little need for their daughters to be excessively educated rendered her the odd one out. Marcus, eight years her senior, had already finished a history degree at New College and joined the BBC. Oliver, doing a second degree in agriculture after a stint in the Army, and John were both at Trinity.

Katharine was installed at Miss Hubler's finishing school at 22 Merton Street, previously vetted by Lady Worsley and found to be ideal for a daughter who had shown little academic prowess. The town house, off the High Street and under the shadow of Magdalen Tower, combined all the scenic charm of Oxford with a fraction of the work required by more conventional students. 'I had no staff for teaching,' Miss Hubler explained, years later.

But study was not really the point of the establishment. Her eight pupils – all well-connected and several the daughters of peers – would, as their parents knew, be admirably guided through the transition between home life and partial independence. Of course the girls did some work. Apart from outside lectures, Miss Hubler herself taught French history, literature, art and architecture, along with household management and current affairs. Visiting tutors advised on antique furniture and dressmaking and couture. Most afternoons were free.

Katharine booked in for lessons with a piano tutor and continued to apply herself to improving her music. In a recent interview, she told the *Daily Telegraph*: 'I passionately wanted to have a career in music, but I wasn't good enough. I failed to get into the Royal Academy of Music – my own fault entirely.'

Whether or not she was sufficiently able, the interviewer's claim that 'she went on to study music in Oxford for five years' sounds slightly enhanced. Katharine's stay in Oxford was a brief interlude, followed by a period of shuttling between Hovingham and London; between social work and social life. These were among the happiest years of her life.

The climate of the early fifties was one of post-war euphoria. In London, crowds gathered on the South Bank of the Thames to watch the King and Queen opening the Festival of Britain. Staged a century on from the Victorians' Great Exhibition, the festival provided what its director called 'fun, fantasy and colour'. Few, in a generation emerging from the bleakness of the war years, had more fun than

Katharine Worsley. Those who knew her in her Oxford and London days unfailingly describe her in those terms. 'Good fun . . . terrific fun.' The shyness, reserve and capacity for loneliness and unhappiness she had shown during her schooldays had not been excised from her character; but in her late teens and early twenties they were in abeyance. The transition from schoolgirl to city sophisticate was easily achieved. Her Runton school photographs show her as a dishevelled, mousily blonde, almost plain child, and villagers at Hovingham remember her as a scruffy teenager, wandering out to the shops in old skirts and trousers. But they also recall seeing her out with her father at parties or the occasional fancy dress ball, carefully made up and stunningly dressed when the more chic events in the Yorkshire social calendar demanded it.

Katharine would only devote herself to becoming an ardent shopper, spender and style-setter after her engagement to the Duke of Kent. It would take much longer before she, an averagely attractive young woman, would become a middle-aged beauty, her bone structure the product of rigorous dieting and her radiance made more luminous by years of pain.

The Katharine Worsley who first arrived at Oxford was not yet an arresting woman. More soignée than in her schooldays, she was still an apple-cheeked country girl with thick, wavy hair tamed now, rather than hacked. She had, even then, the capacity to dazzle.

Her first escorts were her two brothers, John and Oliver, who took her to parties, theatres and concerts. Sometimes she would skip meals at Miss Hubler's and queue up with Oliver for a British Restaurant two-course lunch at 1s 3d. Frequently she would join them for dinners and balls full of charming and eligible young men; some of them students, some Army officers learning to forget, in the bright social round, the horrors of war.

Many admired Katharine Worsley. One fell deeply in love. Andrew Burnaby-Atkins had served in the King's Royal Rifle Company, the same regiment as Oliver Worsley, but their experience of war was very different. Burnaby-Atkins was born in Lincolnshire in 1922; one of a distinguished military family whose forebears included Colonel Fred Burnaby, described by his contemporaries as 'the bravest man in the world'.

His descendant was twice awarded the Military Cross – the first time in March 1945, when he was serving in the North-West Europe Campaign. The citation for the initial award recorded that 'on three occasions in five days, during which his platoon was almost continually in action, Lt Burnaby-Atkins displayed outstanding initiative and devotion to duty in the face of the enemy'.

On the third day, Burnaby-Atkins established the first contact between the American Ninth and the British Second Armies, almost sacrificing his life in the process. In the words of the citation: 'Without awaiting orders, in full view and fire of the enemy, this officer made a banner from the fluorescent panel of his carrier and with one Rifleman walked some 600 yards to contact the American tanks. Immediately he reached the leading tank he came under intense and accurate Nebelwerfer fire. Lieutenant Burnaby-Atkins was badly shaken and knocked over by two bombs which burst beside him. He continued his mission.'

In fact, he suffered nothing worse than a nosebleed, but his heroism made headlines in the *News of the World*, which described him as 'an absolutely mad Eton boy'. His second Military Cross was won in more tragic circumstances. His company, forced to withdraw from the damaged Twente Bridge at Delden, was being mown down by enemy fire when he 'took a Bren gun and two magazines, crossed 30 yards of open ground swept by Spandau fire and, in full view of the enemy, fired from the hip . . . to cover the withdrawal of the forward platoon. It was his initiative that made the withdrawal possible.'

Bill Deedes, his company commander, was awarded the MC with him. 'A survivor's medal', he called it, rather bitterly, in his memoir, *Dear Bill*, adding that: 'A week later . . . the last subaltern who had left England with me (except Andrew Burnaby-Atkins) was killed.'

Burnaby-Atkins clung both to life and reality, regularly writing to his elderly mother to assure her he was well and to advise her on caring for her chickens. But, by the war's end, he had seen swathes of his comrades and fellow officers perish. Most could not have avoided death. One chose it. Years later, he told friends how a soldier, learning that he had been abandoned by his girlfriend, drove recklesly into fire with his bare head clear of his armoured vehicle. He was duly shot.

By the time Burnaby-Atkins met Katharine Worsley, he was rather more than a charming and incredibly handsome officer nearing thirty and looking for a casual relationship and a good time. He had seen and endured events that would leave scars for ever. But, before their paths crossed, one more stint of glory awaited him. Field Marshal Montgomery, newly appointed Chief of the Imperial General Staff, was looking for an ADC and invited Burnaby-Atkins round for tea with a senior officer, in order to see whether he would do. He was appointed that evening. In the next two years he and Monty travelled round the world two and a half times.

As Katharine Worsley awaited her last exam results at Runton, Burnaby-Atkins, looking young and carefree, was pictured sitting with his older brother, Freddy – then ADC to Field Marshal Lord (Stuart) Wavell – on the steps outside the Viceroy's residence in India. Not long afterwards he moved, in 1951, to become adjutant to the Eton College Cadet Corps. If the fifteen-year-old Duke of Kent, callow and unsophisticated, made little impression (other than his propensity to 'march like a duck') on the glamorous new master, then Burnaby-Atkins would certainly have made a profound impact on the Duke – bent on an Army career of his own and now under the instruction of a hero.

But Burnaby-Atkins's mind was not entirely on his young charges. Having spent some time settling into his new life, he announced to the young masters sharing his 'colony', or teachers' house, that he would be inviting a girlfriend over to have dinner with them all. Her name, he said, was Katharine Worsley. His colleagues were impressed. 'We thought she was very nice and very pretty,' says one. 'We didn't see the serious side of her, which came out later. To us, she was just a good-fun girlfriend of Andrew's.' But, from the start, Burnaby-Atkins regarded her as more than that.

Theirs was, according to one of the closest members of his family, 'a great love affair. He was definitely quite affected by her and very much in love with her. It was clear that it was a great romance.' Burnaby-Atkins, a popular man with any number of casual girlfriends, began to devote more and more time to Katharine. Years later he told friends how he got into the habit of arriving back at Eton in the early hours of the morning, on his motorbike and sidecar, feeling 'jaded and tired and guilty' after driving her home. He was a frequent visitor to house party weekends at Hovingham

Hall, where Joyce Worsley was scrutinizing potential husbands for her daughter, and he invited Katharine to Winchester, his regiment's home base.

In later life he told one of his family how he had 'put her to bed' in his own accommodation and gone off to stay at a hotel. The inference was that he slightly mourned his gentlemanly behaviour, but there was not the slightest suggestion that there was anything in the relationship to alarm the Worsley parents. Katharine was a dutiful daughter, a devout young woman, and besides – as one of Burnaby-Atkins's relatives says: 'People behaved so much better in those days.'

Certainly, beautiful behaviour was a Burnaby-Atkins hallmark. In addition to his wit and good humour, he was also accustomed to rubbing shoulders with Katharine's future in-laws. His closest friend was equerry to Princess Margaret, who would later appoint his older brother Freddy as her private secretary, and Burnaby-Atkins was used to moving in royal circles. Perhaps more relevantly, he shared Katharine's love of children and humanitarian instincts and involved himself in bringing the scouting movement to inner cities.

Despite her sense of social duty, it was obvious that in the three years after she left school Katharine had established no clear idea of what she wanted to do with her life. Instead she embarked on a butterfly existence, leaving Oxford to return to Hovingham, where she organized one of the hall's frequent music festivals, and later working in St Stephen's, a York orphanage operating under the patronage of Lady Worsley.

Her stint there – which included being on duty throughout a Christmas Day – was the foundation stone for her lifelong empathy with children and the needy and a precursor of the work she would do, many years laters, during her pilgrimages to Lourdes. Her duties at St Stephen's included bathing the youngsters in her charge, mending their clothes, shopping, cooking and cleaning up if a child was sick. 'Someone's got to do it,' she said. She was, according to a member of the permanent staff, 'always happy, singing about the place; almost like a child herself'.

Selfless volunteer or girl-about-town: which was she? The Duchess of Kent has always been a person of great contradictions, and there was then no obstacle to the young Katharine Worsley having it all. Her parents rented a London flat for the months of her 'coming-out', and – still seduced by the amusements of the capital – she returned there as a nursery teacher.

Despite her lack of any qualifications (a drawback outweighed by her compassion and connections), she was hired, at £12 a month, as a kindergarten helper at the exclusive nursery run by Patricia, Lady Eden – sister-in-law of Sir Anthony Eden. Her ground rules for a worthwhile education – kindness, cleanliness, tidiness, manners, deportment and a ban on frozen vegetables – were explained to Miss Worsley, who helped out cheerfully, just as the future Princess Diana would do in her career as a nursery helper.

Yorkshire neighbours were, nonetheless, slightly perplexed – disapproving even – that Katharine, now heading towards twenty-one, had never quite severed the umbilical cord with home and found herself a 'proper job'. Most girls, according to a prominent North Riding peer, went abroad or got regular employment in London to see them through until they were married. 'She kept going back to Hovingham. I'm not saying she didn't work, but she didn't have a job like the majority of girls did in those days. It was unusual, to say the least.'

The reasons for Katharine to cleave to Hovingham were both practical and emotional. Her secluded childhood and the affection lavished on her by her father had made it difficult for her to thrive in an inimical environment, such as Runton Hill. Even after her schooldays, at a time when her life was more pleasing, she seems to have felt a frequent need to bolt for the security of her father's house. During these spells, she was the trainee chatelaine, assisting her mother – increasingly frail and suffering from arthritis – in the duties of a hostess, more onerous since Sir William's elevation to be Lord Lieutenant of the North Riding in 1951.

But Lady Worsley's physical frailty was not the only factor. Neighbours talked of a woman growing increasingly withdrawn, possibly neurotic, and certainly disinclined to spend her time at her husband's side at official functions. It would have been hardly surprising for Sir William to welcome, or to prefer, his charming and beloved daughter to take on the role of occasional consort and hostess. For Joyce Worsley, described by visitors as such a phantom presence that they were barely aware of her impact, even at her own soirées, the value of a stay-at-home daughter must have been a mixed blessing. Possibly envious of Katharine's close relationship with her father, Joyce was certainly eager, for other reasons, that she should finally leave home. In contrast to the Worsley circle, who paint a mousy and silent Lady Worsley, Katharine's male friends remember a pushy and socially ambitious woman who made no secret of the fact that she was assessing male friends who dropped in at Hovingham as potential husband material.

Joyce wanted her daughter married, and she wanted her married well. She herself had acquired, in Sir William Worsley, a husband who had offered her enhanced social status. Though she was an heiress, the cachet of the Brunner family – enriched by new money – lay principally in its links to political movers. When the Liberal Party lost its lustre, Joyce had instead embraced, through her marriage, the world of the English landed gentry. The fact that she was viewed in Hovingham as immensely grand suggests that she had also embraced all the snobberies of her adopted class. The fact that the Yorkshire upper crust deemed her chilly and lacking in personality confirms, by contrast, that they had never bought the notion of Joyce Worsley, child of a chemist's family, as a self-invented *grande dame*.

In finding an even grander marriage for Katharine, Joyce would conceivably enhance her own status, assure her daughter's future and – whether or not as a conscious objective – get her out of Hovingham Hall for good. But, for the moment, Katharine's focus remained Yorkshire and home. From that vantage point, her eyes – like those of all of Britain – were also on the royal family. On 15 February 1952 King George VI was laid to rest in the vault of his ancestors at St George's Chapel, Windsor. As the cortège bearing the oak casket passed Marlborough House, Queen Mary appeared from behind a half-drawn blind, her face bowed in homage and grief. He was her third son to die.

Those gathered in the chapel included the Duke of Kent, impassive, awkward and newly returned from Le Rosey to mourn the uncle who had treated him like a son. A year later he would again join a funeral cortège; this time to grieve for Queen Mary.

In deference to the national mood and the new Queen he served, Sir William Worsley cancelled a dance planned to celebrate his daughter's birthday. There would be time for parties later. In June 1953 Elizabeth II was crowned, following vast quantities of planning and much anxiety on behalf of aspirant guests. One peer approached the Duke of Nor-folk, vice-chairman of the Coronation Commission, to explain that he was nervous he might be excluded from the list because he was recently divorced. 'Good God, man,' said the staunchly Catholic Duke, impatiently: 'This is a corona-tion, not Royal Ascot.'

Sir William and Lady Worsley were never in doubt of their invitation. They watched from the Westminster Abbey congregation as the Duke of Kent, a coronet on his head, knelt to swear the oath of fealty. 'To become your liege man of life and limb and of earthly worship; and faith and truth I will bear unto you, to live and die, against all manner of folks. So help me God.'

Then he walked up the steps to the Crowned Queen and sealed his act of homage; a hand on the crown and a kiss on his cousin's left cheek. Katharine Worsley saw the ceremony on television at her brother's flat. If she registered the young Duke's performance at all, she might have noticed that he had forgotten, in the drama of the occasion, to remove his glove.

It would be three years before they first met. For now, she remained the object of another man's affections. It is not clear – mainly because Andrew Burnaby-Atkins sedu-lously avoided discussing his love affair, even with his closest family – when he first met Katharine and when they parted. Her decision to end the romance may have been before she met the Duke of Kent. It may have been just afterwards.

Certainly they remained in touch and on such good terms throughout her engagement that Katharine invited him to her wedding. Despite this surface cordiality, her decision to abandon him and marry the Duke left Burnaby-Atkins with a near-obsessional interest in her and with scars that would last a lifetime. His reaction was all the more surprising because he was not, in his youth, a man of enduring emotional attachments.

His brother, Freddy, says: 'He had a lot of girlfriends in his life. He wasn't a chap for making his mind up very quickly about whom he wanted to marry. But he had great charm – an enormous amount; and integrity. They were very fond of each other, I think. When she married, she didn't keep up with Andrew, really. Friendships are pushed away when you marry.' Other friends put it less tactfully. Burnaby-Atkins, indomitable hero, was, they said, so 'gutted', torn apart and devastated that he may never fully have recovered. In the words of one: 'She had a lot to answer for.'

To accuse Katharine of deliberately colluding at the collapse of someone else's life seems unfair. She, eleven years younger than her boyfriend, might not have been ready to commit herself to a man whose horrific experience of war had, on one level, rendered him older than his years. She might have lost patience with his inability to decide on a lifelong commitment. She may have hoped for the grander match she eventually achieved. She may not have loved him, or she may simply have fallen out of love. One thing remains certain. Andrew Burnaby-Atkins would not have measured up to the specifications of Lady Worsley, in whose eyes the Eton Adjutant would have been a second-ranker, deficient in wealth and in social prestige. Joyce would have been aware of her daughter's friendship, just as Katharine – heavily influenced still by her strong-minded mother – would have been aware of her hopes. The fact that Sir William sided with his wife on this matter, also dreaming of a glorious match for the daughter he adored, may have proved the final influence on Katharine when she decided to terminate her love affair with Burnaby-Atkins.

His friends saw a great and instant change in him.

Though still charming and adored by everyone in his circle, he found it increasingly hard to make decisions and commitments. He was in his forties before he married a well-connected woman called Caroline Dalgety. She, almost twenty years younger than he was, later joked that even she would not have persuaded him to get engaged, had she not pursued him to Africa on the pretext of meeting a friend there. More seriously, she wondered if his relationship with the future Duchess had made him frightened to commit to any of the host of women who had fallen in love with him in the intervening years.

Caroline, a great beauty, was as charming and courageous as the man she had married. Though hers was a loving marriage, and friends describe them as 'a magic couple', she was to need all her bravery. Burnaby-Atkins left the Army to join the brewing company Whitbread, known as 'the fifth battalion' because of the numbers of officers from the 60th Rifles on its staff roll. From hop-picking in Kent, he rose to become a director on the main board before being made redundant in his early fifties. Devastated by this fresh blow, he succumbed to depression and a dependency on prescription drugs – nightmares that the Duchess was also reportedly to endure in later life.

Though he got a new job, as director of the Burghley Horse Trials, he became more ill. In his mid-fifties, he was diagnosed as having Parkinson's disease. His wife, Caroline, nursed him devotedly, prepared his horse for him to hunt and suggested, without success, diversions such as bee-keeping and fishing on the lake near their Rutland farmhouse.

But, although his charm survived, Burnaby-Atkins became more ill and distant, retaining an interest in few aspects of the outside world. One was the Duchess of Kent.

While he was still fit, he met her once more, at a society wedding, and they chatted – alone and animatedly – about their lives and their families: his two children and her three. Through his long illness, he was fascinated by any photograph or news item that appeared about her in the papers. Though he rarely spoke of the Duchess to Caroline, whom he loved, she knew him well enough to understand that the affair would haunt him for all his years.

He had few left to live. Andrew Burnaby-Atkins died, aged seventy-two, in 1995. When his wife went through his papers, she found an invitation to Katharine Worsley's wedding to the Duke of Kent and – scattered through his files and drawers – dozens of photographs.

They were all identical: black-and-white passport-sized snapshots of the future Duchess, plumper-faced than now and with the bobbed hair worn by fashionable fifties girls. Caroline Burnaby-Atkins wondered vaguely why the photos had been taken. Had they, perhaps, been skiing together?

Whatever the initial purpose of the snaps, they had enabled Burnaby-Atkins to keep a sort of faith. Though their lives had separated, he had ensured that – through his own happy marriage and through disappointments and illness and decline – he could see Katharine Worsley's face everywhere.

His widow kept one picture and threw away the rest.

CHAPTER SIX

Pride, and Prejudice

Katharine's reprise of life at Hovingham was an anachronistic existence more appropriate to a Jane Austen heroine than to an intelligent and popular young woman in post-war Britain. She was barely twenty-one when she went home for good, certain that she would find plenty of projects to occupy her time as she settled back into her parents' home but aware too that there was no obvious future for her beyond a good marriage.

A few months previously she had flown out to Montreal for the wedding of her brother, John, to Carolyn Hardynge, the daughter of a British viscount turned Canadian entrepreneur. After a round of parties and the wedding itself – Katharine, in white grosgrain and crimson velvet, was a bridesmaid – she travelled back to complete her last months as Lady Eden's nursery assistant and to celebrate her twenty-first birthday with two parties: one with the children and a second organized by her brothers. Shortly afterwards, she returned to Hovingham.

On the face of it, the life she had chosen was stultifying. She gardened – a passion she shared with her mother – played the church organ, learned something about catering from Mrs Hackett, the Hovingham cook, walked her poodle, Charles, and continued to help organize the hall's music festivals.

A second brother married. Marcus – soon to be Conservative MP for Keighley – announced his engagement to Bridget Assheton, daughter of Lord Clitheroe. Again, Katharine was a bridesmaid. 'You will be next,' friends told her. It was hardly a startling prediction, given the lifestyle she had chosen. The hermetically sealed world of Yorkshire high society provided, for women in Katharine's position, an endless calendar of diversions. Cricket, music, house parties, hunt balls, York races, tennis with friends like the Earl of Scarborough's youngest daughter, Serena. But, much as Katharine liked the social round, she was not by nature a dilettante.

Her decision to help her mother and her father was based on a respectful daughter's allegiance to both. It was also, more disturbingly, linked to the fact that Katharine had never acquired the self-confidence to be out of her father's ambit for long. The people the Lord Lieutenant now entertained, with his daughter at his side, were not only a dull procession of mayors, aldermen and corporation luminaries. Sir William, a devout Christian, counted among his friends a string of erudite churchmen who would help shape Katharine's future life. Gordon Wheeler, a convert to Catholicism who later became Bishop of Leeds, was responsible for influencing and guiding her conversion. Donald Coggan, the future Archbishop of Canterbury, was to guide her through several of the great crises of her life.

In the summer of 1956 a quite different lunch guest was ushered in. Sir William, always with a weather eye on the movements both of royalty and the local army barracks, announced that the Duke of Kent had been posted to Catterick. According to her early biographer, Helen Cathcart, Katharine – entirely uninterested – asked: 'Oh. What regiment's he in?' Her knowledge of the Duke, Cathcart claims, barely extended beyond the awareness that his background was Sandhurst and Army.

Even given that Hovingham was not at the leading edge of London gossip, it is likely that Katharine was better briefed than that. Certainly Edward had graduated creditably from Sandhurst, passing forty-fourth out of 220 and winning the Grierson prize for modern languages before joining the Royal Scots Greys. But the Duke, at twenty, was not best known for his prowess at square-bashing or linguistics.

Princess Marina had ensured that her son was beautifully schooled in royal duty and protocol, taking her with him on an extended tour of South East Asia when he was sixteen. Even on such occasions, the Duke was prone to erratic behaviour. At his seventeenth birthday dinner, organized by the governor of Singapore, Eddie flourished the curve-bladed dagger, or kris, provided to cut the birthday cake so violently that he managed instead to slice his mother's face.

Despite the blood pouring down her dress, a quick inspection showed that no real damage had been done. By a millimetre or two, the blade had missed her eye, and the party went on. The episode, however, was an accurate omen of a youth marked out both by revelry and by accidents.

The accidents were chiefly the product of the Duke's obsession with cars, fostered by his long hours absorbing the wisdom of Field, his father's chauffeur, by his old tutor, Giles St Aubyn, and an Eton friend, Nicky Gordon-Lennox. And, of course, by the memory of Prince George, the Duke's late father. It is doubtful if Eddie remembered much of the engine-building lessons given to him as a toddler, but he would certainly have learned since about his father's charm and flaws.

Though lacking his public charisma, Eddie bore an almost uncanny resemblance to George. A little more angular, not as handsome, a trifle balder but unmistakably his son. The legend of George was wide-ranging. As his son would have gradually learned, he was remembered as compassionate, devoted to public service, profligate with money, prone to affairs with unsuitable partners of both sexes and a lover of fast cars.

Of this mixed package, Eddie had inherited his father's sense of public duty and his motoring mania. One of the Duke's frequent crashes made a splash in the *News Chronicle* on 21 June 1954. 'Duke Of Kent: Concussion', the headline said, over a story announcing that Princess Marina was waiting at her son's bedside as leading surgeons assessed him for possible brain damage.

The Duke quickly recovered consciousness. Mr R. H. Higton, the motorist unfortunate enough to be travelling the other way on the Penzance to London road when Edward's car ploughed into him, eschewed any hint of recrimination. 'The car's smashed,' he told his wife over the phone. 'But the worst of it is – the other fellow's the Duke of Kent.'

Rather worse was the shock dealt to Marina, whose nephew, Prince Nicholas of Yugoslavia, had been drowned in a ditch at Datchet six weeks previously when his car overturned. But, even if he was in general a compliant son, Eddie was not designed for restraint. His name was continually linked with wild escapades and frequently with girls, possibly captivated by his manner (certainly made more urbane by his Sandhurst stint) and indisputably by his status.

Edward Kent certainly deployed all his acquired charm when, after lunch in the pleasant surroundings of the Hovingham dining-room (Hepplewhite, Chippendale and pastel-washed walls), he was taken by Katharine Worsley to inspect the oil-paintings of past scions of the dynasty and a portrait – the first of many – of her. 'Ah, Miss Worsley,' the Duke of Kent is supposed to have said. 'It doesn't do you justice.'

This innocent first encounter was far from impromptu. While Sir William Worsley may only have been fulfilling a social duty in inviting the Duke to visit, Lady Worsley's agenda was less disingenuous. Her daughter, at twenty-three, must be steered into a grand marriage. Edward Kent, the best hope so far, was an exceedingly good catch.

At the hint of an incipient romance, life at Hovingham changed. In the preceding years Andrew Burnaby-Atkins and other, far more casual, male friends of Katharine's were used to being welcomed to the weekend house parties at which Joyce Worsley would scrutinize her daughter's acquaintances. The invitations stopped abruptly. As one male friend was heard to say: 'The moment royalty hove into view, she was shut away from the rest of us. The thinking seemed to be that we might contaminate or spoil or destroy it. That decision was made by her mother. She was very, very pushy.'

As for Katharine, it is unlikely that the Duke's raw charm alone was sufficient to sweep her off her feet. She, three years older than he, was used to the attention of handsome and sophisticated young men attracted by a potent cocktail of prettiness, wealth and a sense of fun. Edward Kent – though schooled in good manners – was neither particularly handsome nor especially sophisticated. He was, however, very royal.

If the impetus for a love affair was provided by Joyce

Worsley, then Katharine was initially a willing participant. But the Duke himself, emotionally deprived and entranced both by a charming older woman and the warmth of her family, was the more smitten. Shortly after the Worsley lunch, he asked his aunt, the late Princess Royal, to invite Katharine to Harewood House. From then onwards, he became a frequent visitor to Hovingham, frequently driving in by a back route to avoid press or local speculation and, on one occasion, taking a bus for miles when his car broke down.

The national press, by now apprised of the relationship, carried pictures of them at a Yorkshire fancy dress ball: Katharine dressed fetchingly as a pink and white Dresden shepherdess and Edward gawky and boyish-looking in Tudor garb and foppish velvet cap. On the face of it, the romance was proceeding in textbook fashion. Joyce Worsley was happy, Katharine seemed content, and Edward gave every sign of being in love, as one observer put it, 'in the deep and single-minded fashion of his Romanov grand-uncles'. The first cracks were about to emerge.

Hovingham, its somnolence disturbed, grew restive at the press focus. More relevantly, Marina was beginning to realize that this was not merely another of her son's casual affairs. The Christmas after Edward met Katharine, he spent the holiday at Sandringham with the rest of the royal family but told his mother that he planned to leave on Boxing Day to travel to Yorkshire. She, furious, forbade him to go, not dreaming that, for the first time in his life, he would defy her. Ignoring his mother's wishes, Edward sought permission from the Queen, who said that she was happy for him to leave.

This small act of rebellion crystallized two things in

Marina's mind. The first was the certainty that this was a serious relationship. The second was that she was implacably opposed to it. Just as Joyce Worsley had set her sights on the Queen's cousin as a suitable match for her daughter, so Marina had scrutinized those members of European royal families who might provide a suitably blue-blooded alliance for her impeccably bred son. She was not yet being presented with a *fait accompli*, but the warning signs were there. She, a Princess of Greece who had judged the Queen Mother as too common for her destiny, was facing the unpleasant prospect of having a village girl – albeit a top-drawer one – as a daughter-in-law.

As the first moves were played out in the chess game of Katharine's marriage, it is hard not to see her as a pawn caught between two queenly presences – Marina and Joyce Worsley. Marina, too regal and too clever to betray her feelings, chose her strategy with care. Katharine was invited for the weekend to Coppins, travelling down with Edward in his Sunbeam Rapier, registration K7. On the doorstep was Marina, Russian cigarette trailing from her fingers, inviting Katharine into the house that was soon to be hers. It is doubtful if Katharine found this first encounter particularly alarming. Coppins was less grand than Hovingham Hall. Marina, once the daunting beauty of the royal family, was evolving into the angular, *jolie laide* appearance of middle age. Any hostility was subtly concealed.

Katharine sat silently as tea was served, listening to Marina chattering – in a blend of different languages – to other friends invited round. If the newcomer was humbled by this faint snub, Edward chose to disregard any hint of *froideur* delivered by his mother. The next day he took Katharine to tea with 'Aunt Elizabeth' – the Queen Mother

– and introduced her to his sister, Alexandra, one of the few members of his family who would become a friend and ally to Katharine Worsley.

A year passed. The romance continued. When the royals gathered at Coppins to celebrate Alexandra's twenty-first birthday, Katharine Worsley was the only outsider invited to her dinner dance. To an impressionable young woman the event must have had a surreal quality. Watching the House of Windsor line up for the conga; staring on as her boyfriend danced with the Queen; was this really a foretaste of her future life? The answer was delivered shortly afterwards by her future mother-in-law. Soon after Katharine's twenty-fifth birthday, Edward announced that he wanted to marry her. Marina said no.

The refusal was tactfully couched. Edward was still too young to know his own mind. It would be better to wait. The truth was that, quite apart from her own ambitions, Marina had two legitimate concerns. The first was that her son, rash and emotionally erratic, was indeed too immature to countenance settling down. The second was that Katharine, 'nice and pretty' as she judged her to be, was simply not up to life as a royal. By putting off any engagement, she could reasonably hope that someone more suitable would come along.

By now, and long before any betrothal, the dream match that Joyce Worsley had helped engineer for her daughter was beginning to turn sour. The phone rang constantly at Hovingham Hall, and Sir William suavely informed press callers that Katharine had no plans, beyond organizing another music festival.

That excuse did not suffice. The scrutiny focused on the romance – almost as relentless as the spotlight played, years later, on the young Diana Spencer – stemmed from two factors. Edward Kent, as the most prominent male royal of his generation, was an obvious magnet for media attention. In addition, the press had become attuned to what, even by today's standards, was a lurid cocktail of royal stories.

In the space of a few years a King had abdicated in scandalous circumstances, another had died and a new, glamorous monarch had been installed on the throne. Any notion that the coronation was treated with old-fashioned decorum is nullified by some of the reporting of the time. When the *Daily Mirror* 'revealed', with sketches, the design of the Hartnell dress the Queen would wear under her coronation robes, an American magazine sent the following cable to a leading Fleet Street correspondent: 'Informants in London reveal Lizzie changed dress design as result Mirror story. Stop. What's chance getting publishable declaration this effect from responsible source?'

Having disposed of coronation hysteria and Queen Mary's funeral, the press was primed for more royal drama. Katharine Worsley was in its sights. Speculation presented the Worsley parents with a dilemma. Neither Sir William, desperate to protect his daughter, nor Joyce, who had fervently hoped for an engagement, could be seen publicly – or indeed, privately – to endorse a match that had failed to receive the blessing of Marina and, by extension, the Queen.

As for Katharine, she had secretly shared Marina's worries. Unsure about her feelings for Edward and uncertain that she wanted, or would be able, to fit into a life of royal duty, she had increasing misgivings about whether she should go ahead. The fun of meeting the royal family and the amusements of courtship were already beginning to bleed out into stress and obstruction when Edward learned that his regiment was about to be transferred to Germany for two years.

Emotionally charged and infatuated, he proposed a solution. He and Katharine would marry in Hovingham church, and she would move with him. To the Worsley parents – he a devotee of royal protocol and she hopeful of a marriage and a wedding that would be the envy of well-connected mothers everywhere – this sounded like a nightmare scenario. Whatever the eventual outcome, a plan more evocative of Gretna Green than Westminster Abbey was unthinkable. As the Worsleys pointed out, they were shortly to leave for Canada and an extended stay with their son John. There would simply not be time to fit a wedding in.

The Duke of Kent had one last try. In a family conclave at the Italian summer home of Prince and Princess Paul – Marina's brother-in-law and sister – he demanded permission to marry immediately. The resistance, by now more bitter, was also implacable. Marina's refusal, underpinned by the fact that Edward would need (and fail to get) the Queen's permission, under the Royal Marriages Act, was the final word.

Katharine, presumptuously or naïvely, turned up for the last stage of the holiday after a break of her own with friends on Lord Astor's yacht in the Mediterranean. Part of her was no doubt relieved at Edward's sheepish explanation that they would have to wait. Part of her would be furious. Though uncertain of her own feelings, Katharine Worsley's dalliance with royalty and its whims had crystallized her own strength. In later years she would prove that, if she was a less adept political player than Diana, she was an equally resolute fighter against the system.

Pique, perhaps more than passion, had prompted her to back Edward this far. Now Marina imposed her deal: they must agree to total separation, with no communication, for a year in order to be certain that they wished to marry. This ultimatum, ruthlessly insensitive, may have implanted in Katharine the resentment against the royal family that would emerge again as the years went on.

Rejection, to a woman as sensitive as she is, was a cruel blow. On two separate occasions she had been judged by Marina and deemed imperfect. However great her respect for her future mother-in-law and however tactful the given reasons, such treatment was bound to have an impact. At the very least, the complexity of her dealings with Marina may have fudged whatever attempts she made to sort out her confused feelings about Edward and the marriage, if it was ever to happen.

The press, compounding her misery, had decided that it certainly would. The *Daily Sketch* offered its analysis of 'the girl Britain expects to wed the Duke of Kent', citing her beauty, charm, natural qualities, aversion to chattering or giggling and throwing in – for good measure – a hint of Marina's opposition.

Sir William Worsley, meanwhile, continued to deflect speculation as best he could. 'I certainly have no knowledge of any objection by the Duchess of Kent to the Duke's friendship with my daughter,' he said benignly. The Duke himself lacked such sang-froid. Having paid a final visit to Hovingham, where he celebrated his twenty-third birthday, he left with his regiment for Germany. At the airport, he scrabbled vainly to find his chequebook to pay a £3 14s 9d excess baggage charge, spilling shirts from his suitcases on to the floor until an official spared his embarrassment by proffering a blank cheque form for his signature. Scarcely had he arrived at his new quarters before a reporter got through on the phone. Was the Duke about to announce his engagement to Miss Worsley? 'No,' he said shortly. 'I do not know anything about that. It is complete nonsense.'

In Hovingham, Katharine cancelled her booking to read the lesson at church and stayed at home. At last she had time to think and to recover. Her first refuge was, as so often, in the familiar. She would dedicate herself to organizing another Hovingham music festival. Her parents, newly returned from Canada and realizing that media interest in their daughter would persist, along with suggestions that she had been jilted, had a better suggestion. Katharine should also visit John, his wife, Carolyn, and their children, Willa and Harry, whom she had never seen. Within a few days she was on a plane to Toronto.

Katharine's stay at 306 Vesta Drive, in the city suburbs, would normally have been an adventure and a pleasure. Instead, friends of her brother described her as 'a lost soul' – joining in with family activities but patently distant from what was going on. Whenever possible she remained at home, shunning the parties and social round of Toronto. Once an easy mover in the London high life, she reverted to the persona of her Runton schooldays: unhappy, withdrawn, an outsider.

The simple explanation would be that she missed the man she loved. The reality was more complex. Ever since her sheltered Hovingham childhood, Katharine had remained in thrall to her home. Now, left to her own thoughts, she had to address whether she really wished, or would be able, to substitute the Duke of Kent for her father as the dominant male figure in her life. Sir William, aware of her dependency, also feared that – whatever Marina finally decreed – this marriage might not make his daughter happy. Lady Worsley, so keen on the match, was more concerned that its abortion could blight her daughter's chances of finding another grand suitor.

Katharine, exhibiting, in her withdrawn behaviour at her

brother's home, the first signs of depression, failed to resolve the conflict in her own mind. She made no suggestion that she wished to sever her bond with the Duke of Kent. On the other hand, she continued to be desperately worried about whether she wanted the life a marriage to him would entail.

Back in Hovingham, she worked out a strategy that she would use many times in her life. Rather than submit to the miserable limbo imposed on her, she would break out and find something that would please her. With a friend, Fiona Myddleton – who later married the Queen Mother's Comptroller, Sir Alastair Aird – she returned to Canada, planning to use her brother's home as a launchpad for a trip, by Greyhound bus, to Mexico.

To top up her £50 travel allowance – then the maximum amount a British citizen was permitted to take out of the country – she took a job in a Toronto department store, selling leather goods and souvenirs. It was, as she told friends long after her marriage, a wonderful experience. It was also an illustration of a lifelong contradiction in Katharine Worsley's character. The shopgirl Duchess would, in the years to come, crave the simple life and the grand, in equal parts. The middle ground was always the hardest to find.

Even then, as she served behind her counter, regular letters arrived from Alexandra, passing on friendly, and suitably neutral, snippets about her brother. Freewheeler or Duchess? One day soon, Katharine would have to decide. But for now she could defer the hard choices and revert to the sort of life she really enjoyed.

As she travelled towards Mexico, Edward Kent coped in his own way with separation. A young and beautiful visitor to another Army regiment remembers meeting him at a party and, repeatedly, spurning his invitations to dance until he abandoned his pleas and rejoined his friends. His reluctant dancing partner saw him once more; tobogganing down a staircase on an upturned table while slugging champagne from a bottle clutched in one hand.

The busy social life of a single Army officer did not deflect Edward from his purpose. As Katharine neared the end of her bus tour, a bouquet of flowers was delivered. The accompanying card contained the single initial: E. When he returned home on leave, a year after their parting, Marina agreed, under the terms of her deal, that Katharine should be invited to dinner. The romance of the occasion was marred only by the fact that Edward, apparently in a rush to greet his guest, fell down the stairs and broke a bone in his foot.

By now Marina's excuses were running out. Nonetheless, she had one last card to play. Another royal engagement would be unthinkable until after the wedding of Princess Margaret – superficially recovered from her doomed romance with Group-Captain Peter Townsend and about to marry Antony Armstrong-Jones. On the basis that royal events, like buses, should be staggered rather than arriving all together, even that announcement was deferred until after the birth of the Queen's third child, Prince Andrew.

Even so, it became increasingly clear that the Worsley–Kent marriage would take place. Despite her grave reservations about Katharine's suitability for the rigours of the life to come, Marina began to train her in the art of royal behaviour. Tutorials included hand-shaking and dressing beautifully. A bibliography was provided of royal biographies essential to a trainee.

Previous accounts of the Duchess's life suggest that during this time, she – like a novice absorbing the convent mystique – dutifully prepared herself for the life to come.

Instead, on the threshold of her engagement, Katharine escaped with her friend, Lady Serena Wiley, the youngest daughter of the Earl of Scarborough, for a spur-of-the-moment trip to the 1960 Rome Olympics.

Lady Serena, now living in Virginia, had been a confidante since she and Katharine had met at York races and found themselves on the same county circuit of point-to-points and hunt balls. The excuse for the trip to Italy was meeting up with friends in the British equestrian team, headed by Lieutenant-Colonel Harry Llewellyn. The lure was one last chance of simplicity and freedom. She and Serena travelled on cut-price train tickets, stayed in bed and breakfast *pensione*, ate spaghetti on the grounds that it was cheap and filling, saw the sights of Rome and partied with the Olympic Team.

While it is unlikely that the daughter of the Lord Chamberlain and the future Duchess of Kent had a very orthodox view of what roughing it entails, this was certainly Katharine's last celebration of what she saw as normal life. The press did not know that she was in Rome, Marina's protocol lessons were temporarily shelved, and she could enjoy herself as she always used to and as she never would again. Katharine's final holiday was more, probably, than a sentimental journey. In a pattern that had established itself in her life, she was running away. At times, she had bolted back to Hovingham. At others, she had – always temporarily – disappeared on some grand adventure, as if seeking to prove that she was an independent woman, wholly in control of her own life. The truth was that she had been, and continued to be, manipulated: by an overly adoring father, an ambitious mother and the machinations of Marina. Now, as she returned from her Italian trip – the last dash for freedom – the net was closing.

Katharine was not convinced that she was doing the right thing. To Serena, as to her other friends, she confessed her misgivings about a royal existence and whether she would be capable of fulfilling the demands made on her. In reality, they would be slight. For as long as Marina lived, she would be the *de facto* Duchess of Kent, loved by the nation and a trusted ambassador for the Queen. Katharine would attract, to start with, little of the scrutiny that would fall, years later, on Diana Spencer.

Still, she was not entirely happy with her choice. Perhaps if she could have foreseen how royal life was to unfold, she might have made a different decision. Diana and Sarah Ferguson were both to provide an example of how royalty can tear apart those not bred to its constraints; of how royal marriages were to become less a passport to privilege than a catalyst for unhappiness and tragedy. But, on those points, there was no one to advise the future Duchess or to point out that her worries about an onerous royal life – genuine though they were – might also be a displacement anxiety; a substitute for asking herself whether the Duke of Kent was really the man she wanted to marry. In this uncharted terrain, the only warning signs were her own instincts and emotions. She overruled them, failing to ask herself the one salient question. Did she love this man? Her behaviour, throughout her dogged waiting game and in her last throes of unease, suggested that the answer was No.

But the romance was now reaching endgame. The Duke of Kent, nearing the conclusion of his time in Germany, began to take on a royal portfolio. Appointed an aide to the Queen for the state visit of the King and Queen of Nepal, he also represented her at independence ceremonies in Sierra Leone. Shortly afterwards, he formally requested permission to marry Katharine Worsley.

He proposed on New Year's Day, 1961, in the Hovingham library, offering, for a ring, a mammoth sapphire set in diamonds. Sir William produced champagne. Lunch was served and the secret maintained until the formal announcement in March: 'It is with the greatest pleasure that the Duchess of Kent announces the betrothal of her elder son, Prince Edward, Duke of Kent, to Katharine, only daughter of Sir William and Lady Worsley, to which union the Queen has gladly given her consent.'

The charm of the future Duchess, the length of the courtship and the obstacles along the way suggested a romantic plot of Romeo and Juliet dimensions, albeit with a happier outcome for the star-crossed lovers. The truth was rather different.

Lord Bridges, a friend of the Duke, a school and university acquaintance of the Worsley brothers and former chairman of the Duchess's favourite charity, Unicef, has a more realistic view – one echoed by many others – of the driving forces behind the engagement.

'I suspect she undertook the marriage partly out of a sense of duty. In other words, it wasn't a romantic, overwhelming thing that most people have. I suspect she had no wish to enter into the royal world of protocol. She would have been happier with a good county marriage. I think that might well have been her approach.

'But, after all, if a member of the royal family proposes to you at that age, it's something you have to take seriously – whatever your inclinations may be. Her parents would have said: "Well, my dear, if you marry this nice young man, I think he'll look after you well. It would be a nice position in life, wouldn't it?"'

Katharine Worsley was about to test this theory.

CHAPTER SEVEN

Myth of a Fairytale

❧

After a long and troubled courtship, Katharine Worsley was to marry a man she did not unreservedly love and embark on a life she viewed with fear. That bleak construction does not, of course, tell the whole story. She, a dutiful daughter and a person of strong religious conviction, had not lightly undertaken her decision.

She thought she knew about happy families, for her own – although more flawed than appearances suggested – had been the centrepiece of her life. She had a streak of determination and stubbornness, crystallized by the opposition she had faced from Marina. Undoubtedly the future Duchess's belief that her marriage would be happy and blessed overrode her doubts.

Besides, the die was now cast. Years later, Diana Spencer – still riven with uncertainty in the days before her wedding – was told by her sisters: 'You'll have to go through with it, Duch [her family nickname]. The teatowels are printed.' In other words, the panoply of a royal wedding is unstoppable. Katharine Worsley's was very royal indeed.

The chosen venue was York Minster, hosting its first royal wedding since Edward III, aged fifteen, married

Philippa of Hainault there, 633 years previously. The date was set for 8 June. The invitation list of 2,000 included three Queens: the Queen, the Queen Mother and Queen Victoria Eugenie of Spain. If the grandeur of the occasion daunted Katharine Worsley, her fear was not apparent.

Jean Rook, then women's editor for the *Yorkshire Post*, was eager to point out the graciousness and humility with which Katharine approached her wedding. At a photocall, she had forced the Duke of Kent to pose again for the benefit of one cameraman who had arrived late and distraught after his motorbike had broken down. When she arrived for a wedding dress fitting, she apologized to the cleaner who had just finished washing the steps. 'I am so sorry I have to tread on them,' she said. As young girls spurned the Parisian fashion for Jackie Kennedy tailoring in favour of the future Duchess's off-the-face hats and shoulder brooches, it was clear that Katharine Worsley was already becoming defined by charm, empathy, stylishness and an unforced common touch.

There was also, visible only to those who knew her, a touch of hauteur offering an echo of her mother's manner and commensurate with her new status. Friends had always called her Kate. From now on, she said, she should be known as Katharine.

The planning for the wedding, like the event itself, combined Yorkshire practicality and the lavishness befitting a fairytale. Perhaps in deference to the Duke's salary (as an Army officer employed at the War Office, he was earning £2 18s a day), a fifty-item wedding list was lodged at Fortnum & Mason. Among the gifts specified were two hand-painted toothmugs – one monogrammed K and the other E – at 17s 6d each; two Foley Pink Routland breakfast-in-bed sets with coffee pots; white alabaster lamps, a red leather string box, a large Thermos jug and twelve brandy glasses (8s 9d apiece). At the end of the requests was a heavily underlined plea: No more trays, please.

Clothes were a less mundane business. Katharine took charge of the outfits for Princess Anne, the chief bridesmaid, and the seven others, plus the yellow jackets and white breeches for the three pageboys. Mothers were asked to make an appointment to have their children fitted by Belinda Belville, one of the bride's favourite designers. 'Quite outrageously expensive,' one aristocratic parent complained. Most acknowledged that, county frugality notwithstanding, style must be maintained. Katharine's own gown was commissioned from John Cavanagh, a favourite of Marina and once a designer with Molyneux, the Paris house which had made her wedding dress.

As with all weddings, there were problems. London florists, each convinced they had the commission to fill the cathedral with white roses, were piqued to discover that they had been imperiously summoned to Hovingham by Lady Worsley in order to submit a tender for the job. A council sub-committee specially convened to oversee wedding plans hit on the ingenious scheme of charging citizens to watch the proceedings. It would, it said, build 2,100 seats at £5, £3 and 10s; hastily halving that number when the thrifty of Yorkshire declined to pay up.

The logistics were complex. Princess Marina's office played a part. The Earl of Scarborough, Lord Chamberlain and an old friend of the Worsley family, orchestrated the movements of the royal family, including a train from King's Cross to York. To mark the splendour of the occasion, British Railways Eastern Region issued a silver-edged menu for its special guest service. VIPs were offered a drinks menu boasting three brands of sherry, two of vintage champagne

and an extensive wine list. Luncheon, served on the way up
to York, comprised melon, cold salmon mayonnaise, pineapple glace, cheese, salad and biscuits. Dinner, served on the
way back, included smoked river trout, roast turkey and
trimmings, strawberries with liqueur and whipped cream
and another cheeseboard.

The morning of the wedding was grey. As Katharine
climbed into her bridal gown, made of more than 250 yards
of white silk gauze, the rain beat against the Hall windows.
Pearls – a wedding gift from her parents – were clasped
round her throat, and a long veil, designed to float back
across her fifteen-foot train, was anchored with a bandeau of
diamonds once owned by Queen Mary. One last piece of
veiling was pinned, with more diamonds, to fall down across
her face.

By the time she was dressed, sunlight filtered through
the wet glass, picking out the iridescent threads woven
through her dress. She was ready: a medieval bride gazing
over the familiar fields where she had played, a diffident,
tomboyish child who adored her home and never really
thrived when she was removed from it. Now the wrench was
almost complete.

Her attendants waited downstairs for her, among them
Princess Anne, her Canadian niece, Willa – recovered from
a fever of the day before – and Jane Spencer who, years
later, was to tell her sister, Diana: 'You'll have to go through
with it, Duch...' On any normal day, Katharine, who
loved children, would have been utterly disarmed by her
eight bridesmaids in white organza and pink roses.

Today she was pale and silent as she drove through
Yorkshire lanes in the glass-topped car lent by the Queen.
Beside her, Sir William watched as she fingered her pearls,
his gift, and heard the minster bells grow louder in the

distance. She was late when she arrived at the cathedral door. 'Is it a long walk for a bride?' a journalist had asked the day before, inspecting the aisle.

To Katharine Worsley – who, even as a seasoned Duchess, loathed the stress of public appearances – it was the longest walk of her existence. She had always feared the scrutiny that she, as a royal, would attract. Here, under the television cameras and the ranks of packed pews, was the reality.

On one side sat county Yorkshire, in their summer prints, there to be impressed and proud and, if appropriate, critical. With them were the staff and villagers of Hovingham. (Although Lady Worsley's organizational skills had not been greatly taxed, she had – to her credit – insisted that they must have good seats in the minster.) Across the aisle, the pews were packed with royalty. To the rear, scions of the European royal houses whom Katharine barely knew and would never, in general, much like – Crown Prince Constantine of Greece, Prince Harald of Norway, Princess Margarethe of Denmark, Prince Frederick of Prussia; a smattering of Yugoslav royalty and Spanish nobility.

And, in front, the British royal family, led by the Queen, in lilac silk Hartnell, with Prince Philip and Prince Charles alongside a pregnant Princess Margaret, wearing pale blue, her husband, Antony Armstrong-Jones, and the Queen Mother, dressed in aquamarine. Princess Marina had not allowed Yorkshire, the rain or the royal taste for limp pastels to cramp her style. She had chosen corn-coloured silk organdie, designed by Cavanagh and embroidered with gold, diamanté and topaz. Beneath her matching ostrich-feather hat, tears slipped down her face.

She, the most beautiful royal bride of her generation, wept perhaps for loss: of her title and her home, both bequeathed to the daughter-in-law she had had kept at arm's length for so long. But, in the main, she wept for a deeper loss. The Duke of Kent, standing at the altar in the scarlet and blue ceremonial uniform of the Royal Scots Greys, bore an almost uncanny resemblance to his dead father. 'It could have been George standing there,' Lord Mountbatten said later.

As the moments passed, the Duke – his best man and brother, Prince Michael, at his side – occasionally glanced around anxiously for the first sight of his bride. As he turned for the third time, she entered the west door on her father's arm, slim, statuesque, her face invisible behind the veiling. A shower of hailstones rattled against the closed church door.

The ceremony, of which she had been the chief impresario, had begun. The music, chosen by Katharine, included the Hymns 'Lead Us, Heavenly Father, Lead Us' and 'O Perfect Love, All Human Thought Transcending'. The promise to obey her husband, although not included in the order of service, was – at Katharine's demand – inserted into the pledge she took so earnestly. 'Wilt thou love him, comfort him, honour and obey him, in sickness and in health; and, forsaking all other, keep thee only unto him, as long as ye both shall live?' There was only one other alteration to the planned programme. An anthem taken from Psalm 45 contained the words: 'Forget also thine own people and thy father's house.' Katharine demanded that it be dropped.

It is impossible to know how much of the ceremony she absorbed, conscious of the scrutiny of the cameras and the congregation as she and the Duke knelt before Dr Ramsey, Archbishop of York and Archbishop-designate of Canterbury. By the time she turned again towards the sea of faces, her destiny was set. Katharine Worsley, squire's daughter and one-time kindergarten helper, was the Duchess of Kent; the first Englishwoman to bear the title since the dukedom was revived in 1799 and bestowed by George III on his fourth son, Edward. The previous incumbent, Princess Marina, her tears now dry, was preparing to leave the minster, catch up with her newly married son and have a restorative cigarette.

The new Duchess moved through the aisle. The ordeal was over. She had survived it with dignity and aplomb. All the years of uncertainty were finished; the waiting, the delays, the satisfaction of seeing Marina bend, in the end gracefully, to her will. This, perhaps, was the moment for a smile of exultation that the tensions were past.

As she walked down the aisle, her long veil snagged on a bench, threatening to rip Queen Mary's diamonds from her head. She stood very still as an usher freed it, before stepping forwards to make her deep curtsey to the Queen. From the press enclosure, *The Times*' correspondent watched her progress. 'A short, elbow-length veil partly hid Miss Worsley's face on arrival,' he wrote. 'But, as she finally moved down the long nave on her husband's arm, with the veil thrown back, it seemed at one moment almost as if she was going to faint; so pale and exhausted did she look. But in answer to a pleadingly encouraging smile from the Duke she smiled tremulously back.'

Other faces in the minster caught that expression. The Hovingham staff, who remembered her as the tousle-haired child who played with their own families. Marina, who had wondered whether she would endure the spotlight of royal life. Lady Worsley, who had longed for her daughter's altered status (and who, in the moments after the wedding, quite forgot to curtsey to the new Duchess). Andrew Burnaby-Atkins, who had loved her and been spurned.

If her pallor and exhaustion were any more than symptoms of wedding day nerves, the Duchess of Kent was far too professional – and, no doubt, too relieved – to let it show. She passed through the ceremonial arch of swords raised by the Duke's fellow-officers and stepped into her car for the journey home.

Oliver Worsley had planned a garden party, in which the 2,000 guests mingled on the Hovingham lawns, drinking champagne. There were no speeches but ample chance for the far-flung royal clans to become reacquainted with each other and – if they chose – the Yorkshire squirarchy. Among the meetings was one which would have delighted Princess Marina. Cousin Ena (an appropriate title for the landlady of the Worsley Arms but, in fact, the exiled Queen of Spain) introduced her grandson, Juan Carlos – later the King of Spain – to his future bride, Princess Sofia of Greece.

Queen Elizabeth and the rest of the royal party stayed for the afternoon before departing for York and the royal train home. The Worsleys, hugely relieved that the greatest day in their lives had passed off with great success, embarked on a roast dinner (boar rather than beef, given the magnitude of the occasion) for their friends and helpers.

Katharine chose a pleated white silk dress, with a pattern of royal blue and jade green poppies, and a royal blue silk coat for her going-away outfit. Together with their dogs, Charles and Columbus, she and the Duke left by car for RAF Linton, where a Heron of the Queen's Flight was to take them on the first leg of their honeymoon.

Though the plane and its in-flight menu – champagne and smoked salmon sandwiches ordered by the Queen – were luxurious, the honeymoon was of the rigorous type preferred by the royal family. The Duke had accepted by the Queen Mother's offer of Birkhall; a haunt of his childhood and the place where he spent long summer holidays with George VI, the uncle who had regarded him almost as his own son. Certainly Birkhall is a more charming and less austere refuge than nearby Balmoral, where Princess Diana spent such cheerless holidays in the early part of her marriage.

In addition, the new Duchess, a rural girl herself, could be expected to feel at home, even if the Duke's taste for rugged hillwalks has always been more voracious than her own. At Dyce airport, in Aberdeen, and on the road to Deeside, wellwishers threw flowers and confetti. Once installed, the new Duchess wrote immediately to her parents, telling them of a thunderstorm before landing. The following day, the couple were reported to have driven to Ballater to buy a fortieth birthday card for Prince Philip. The day after that, they came close to scandalizing the local population for failing to turn up for the morning service at Crathie church.

A week later they left for Majorca and three weeks in a borrowed villa; this time by a small charter plane hired by the Duke – cautious of appearing to exploit the British taxpayer and mindful of criticism directed at his own parents' fabulously lavish honeymoon. From the minutiae of their holiday – sunbathing, swimming, tennis and speed-boats – the only detail fed back to the press was that the Duchess had spent too long outside and had sunstroke.

The anxiety of the engagement was over. She had made her decision. There were no omens to suggest that this would be anything but a charmed marriage. Back at Hovingham, life returned to some semblance of normality. In the village, every detail of the wedding was dissected, from dawn to the couple's departure.

The guests had cheered as the Duke and Duchess of Kent drove out of the Hovingham riding school. The couple waved their last farewells. Almost unnoticed among the revellers, Sir William Worsley – the father of the bride – stood on the village main street and watched the car disappear. His back was turned, and only one guest caught his expression. It was one of unutterable sadness.

CHAPTER EIGHT

The Reluctant Duchess

THE PUBLIC HAD followed, with fascination, every detail of a romantic royal wedding and absorbed with interest every snippet leaked from the Kent honeymoon. No one, bar a couple of Katharine's friends – and, no doubt, her father – knew that the myth of the perfect marriage barely survived the ceremony.

As royal guests and villagers mingled on the Hovingham lawns, the bride, according to friends, was found upstairs, weeping in her bathroom. Inconsolable and shocked by the pressure of the occasion and the ceremonial, she had been given her first glimpse of what a life in the public glare would mean. She might not be able to go through with the existence she had chosen, she is said to have told one friend who tried to comfort her. This breakdown implied more than stress. Katharine, married for only a few hours, was already fearful that she had made a terrible mistake. There was no option but to dry her tears, bury her terrors and carry on with equanimity. As the new Duchess of Kent realized, there was no prospect of turning back.

The public had devised for her a fairytale. She had colluded in it. Now she must follow the script. The Duke and Duchess returned from their honeymoon to find the exterior of Coppins transformed. Marina had left, with Alexandra and Michael, to live at Kensington Palace, and staff had strung flags across the façade and hung out a banner, labelled Welcome Home. Inside little had changed.

Some of the six bedrooms had been redecorated, to Katharine's taste, in pink and blue. Marina's collection of art treasures – fans, antique cigarette cases, Czarist silver and Fabergé pieces – had gone, auctioned off at Sotheby's in one last effort to raise some ready cash. In their place were piles of wedding presents: glass, silverware, towels, tea trolleys, saucepans and sheets, as stipulated on the bride's Fortnum's list. There were also more substantial items. A Ford car donated by the manufacturers was parked in the garage. Princess Alexandra's gift – a double bed designed to unzip into two singles – was installed in the master bedroom. Contrary to royal custom and practice, the Duke had decided to use his father's old separate bedroom purely as a dressing-room, saying: 'I can sleep alone when I'm in barracks.'

Bar the wedding presents, the house remained almost eerily unaltered; and not only from Marina's tenure. Coppins had been created by George, the Duke's father. Almost two decades after his death, it remained a temple to him. In his lifetime, the chintzes and satins he loved had transformed a dingy home – bequeathed by his Aunt Victoria, Queen Alexandra's daughter – into a model of gracious living, full of good furniture, books and jazz records and, in the music room, the Ibeck piano George would play before dinner while he drank his favourite cocktail of gin and pineapple juice.

As a young bride in her first home, Katharine was presented with a setting that must have seemed less a monument to faded glamour than a mausoleum whose atmosphere was dictated, in almost equal part, by family allegiance to George's memory and by the frugality towards housekeeping demonstrated by Philip Hay, Marina's comptroller.

The kitchen was ancient and shabby, offering no modern conveniences beyond a decrepit gas stove. The house was so cold that the new Duchess stipulated coal fires in the bedrooms until electric convector heaters could be installed. The fabric was easy to alter. The ghosts were harder to excise. In the old Duke's study, untouched since the day of his death, the last memo he wrote still lay where he had placed it. 'Do not touch anything on this desk,' it read.

And Katharine did not; respecting not only the memory of a father-in-law she never knew but the wishes of a husband she had promised to obey. Like most of his family, the Duke of Kent was averse to wasting money on household fripperies. According to the Duchess's early biographer, Helen Cathcart, he proposed that a malfunctioning television almost old enough to merit a slot in one of Marina's Sotheby sales would do splendidly for the staff sitting-room. More relevantly, his wish to embalm what his father had built – a desire even stronger than Marina's – was undiluted by his own marriage.

Katharine, an avid gardener, was eager to tackle the Coppins grounds, sectioning off a private family area similar to the one her mother had created at Hovingham. Edward, meanwhile, wanted to restore the rose garden his father had planted and rebuild a summerhouse to George's exact specification. Two greenhouses had been added to George's original design. His son ordered that they be knocked down. While there is no suggestion that this nurturing of the past caused any clash, a small marker had already been put down. This was not a marriage like any other. It was, instead, one in which royal tradition, example and protocol would always be present.

Katharine, despite the unhappiness of her wedding day, was determined to adhere to that compact. Although she had embarked on her marriage with no great sense of confidence and, most probably, no great sense of love, she had an almost over-developed notion of obligation and duty. It is likely that, in the post-honeymoon period, major doubts were eclipsed by the daunting task of running her new home according to Marina's traditions and under Marina's exacting eye.

In some respects the Kents lived not so very differently from any other well-to-do young couple. Edward would set off every morning in his white Austin for his desk job at the War Office, returning at 6.30p.m. prompt. Katharine had the garden and the house to organize, with the help of four ancient retainers and the Duke's valet, newly promoted to butler. When the appointment did not work out, an underling to Marina's former steward was installed to impose some order on the household.

It is certain that Katharine's perceived inadequacies and the fact that Marina retained remote control of her old house combined to make life more stressful. Good organization, as Katharine's mother-in-law would have told her, was a prerequisite when her teatime guests included the Queen and Prince Philip, sentimentally attached not only to the Duke but also to Coppins, where Marina had fostered and encouraged their early courtship.

Then there was the village protocol to observe. Iver Women's Institute were quick to invite the new Duchess to join them. Rather surprisingly, given her mother's solid work for the Hovingham branch, Katharine turned down the invitation. A letter from Marina's office informed the

WI committee that Her Royal Highness, the Duchess of Kent, would not be taking up any public invitations 'for the time being'.

Perhaps the haughty tone of the reply conveyed the feelings of Marina, rather than those of Katharine, whose populist instincts have always shown a sure touch. In any case, the Women's Institute – and the wider community – felt duly snubbed. 'They are calling you the reluctant Duchess,' a friend told Katharine, who duly retracted the refusal and presented herself for a demonstration of savoury snacks, appearing ten minutes early.

Much later in her life, chauffeurs became accustomed to driving the Duchess to official engagements on circuitous routes to counteract her habit of eagerly arriving before schedule (and invariably leaving much later than planned, because of her absorption in those she was visiting). On this, her first royal engagement, her premature entrance not only flustered the snack-makers of the WI but resulted in the newspaper headlines she would soon grow to dread.

It was not that the rather scant coverage she attracted was unkind. A few years after her marriage, Jean Rook – a fan in her Yorkshire days – was the first to point out that the new Duchess was revolutionizing the dowdy image of the royal family. 'The Duchess has a got-her-eye-in approach to fashion that we haven't seen since the vintage days of the young Marina,' Rook wrote in the *Sun*.

'She is the only royal girl, apart from Princess Margaret, who changes her hair style as frequently as her hats. She was into a frilly white Viva Maria blouse almost as soon as Bardot. And, with her narrow shoulders and tortoiseshell kitten face, looked almost as good. She even had the courage to go Courrèges . . . In short, the Yorkshire lassie who lived in pants, sweater and headscarf before she married the Duke of Kent is steadily moving up among the fashion leaders. When I knew the former Katharine Worsley, in Yorkshire, she shopped at the local Marshall and Snelgrove – alone, but for two dogs tied with string because she could never find their leads.'

In the early years of her marriage, Katharine had no great pretensions to become a fashion icon. She did, however, have a great nostalgia for the times when she could trawl through a department store with two dogs on a piece of twine. Increasingly, she felt the need to hide. Once a week she travelled up with Edward from Iver to London for a hairdressing appointment, shopping and lunch with a friend. But now she was scrutinized by the curious in Harrods and in Bond Street; so much so that she began to avoid main streets and major stores. On one occasion, she turned up at King's Cross to meet her father so that they could travel to Hovingham together, only to discover him politely answering questions form a newspaper reporter. 'It gave me a sinking, shrinking feeling,' she told a friend.

If the Duchess's public role was still negligible, the strain of feeling herself to be in the spotlight was increasing, just as she had always dreaded it would. Her escape valve then, and in the years that followed, was always the same. According to Lord Coggan, a lifelong friend of both Sir William and the Duchess: 'What Katharine found was that when she took on this tremendous London life, she was able to nip on a train or a plane and get up to Yorkshire and talk to her father. He would chuckle, and she would go off with a load shared. He was that kind of man; and she was devoted to him.'

Back in Buckinghamshire, the focus was also on family. The Duke and Duchess held a dinner party to mark Alexandra's departure for a tour of duty in the Far East. On her return they hosted a dinner to celebrate Marina's fifty-fifth birthday. As always, the Kents decamped to Sandringham for Christmas and attended morning church with the rest of the royal clan.

Half-way through the service, the Duchess felt so faint and ill that she had to leave, accompanied – solicitously but rather curiously, given the number of adult relatives in the party – by the young Prince Charles. Though Katharine quickly recovered, this was her first lesson that any public sign of frailty by a member of the House of Windsor must either be sedulously avoided or, failing that, followed up by a plausible explanation. Later on Christmas Day, she had a friendly talk with the Queen. On the following day it was announced that the Duchess of Kent was expecting her first child in the summer.

Although her pregnancy went well, Katharine – like any royal mother of her generation – faced certain constraints. She wanted to accompany her husband to St Moritz, where, in January 1962, he was to captain the ski team of the Royal Scots Greys. Katharine had not the faintest interest in downhill skiing – a pursuit she always found frightening rather than exhilarating – but she leapt at the chance of a European trip.

Once, she had been able to pack a bag and leave, on a whim, for Canada or Rome. Life at Coppins was, by contrast, quiet verging on dull. Furthermore, she would welcome an escape from the intrusion of the builders engaged to rebuild the kitchen wing. Finally, and following dire warnings of what might happen if she slipped in the snow, she settled instead for a holiday with Marina at Kensington Palace before spending her twenty-ninth birthday at Hovingham, where the Duke joined her for a day at the races.

Whatever her disappointment over her cancelled trip, Katharine was not unduly restless. Her initial terror notwithstanding, this was a time of relative contentment and a sort of limbo. Like his father before him, Edward had regarded marriage as a catalyst to toning down his wilder side. As an antidote to crashing cars, he sat the advanced driving test of the Institute of Advanced Motorists. His passion to be a serving soldier was sidelined, for the time being, in favour of pen-pushing at the War Office and religiously telephoning home during his lunch break. On quiet evenings, he taught Katharine to play chess.

She, meanwhile, was excited even by the standards of an expectant mother. The pressures of being in the public eye naturally diminished as she spent more time at Coppins. Her husband was rarely absent and usually attentive. But, more than that, she was fulfilling one of her greatest ambitions. At almost thirty – relatively old for a first-time mother of her generation – she was starting to create her own family. The rigours of life at Coppins and a homesickness for Hovingham had implanted in Katharine's mind a romanticized notion of family life. All the problems and unhappiness of her own early days, and the pressured years prior to her marriage, seem to have been excised from a vision of perfectly balanced harmony and accord in the Worsley home. That was the model she planned to replicate for her own family. For reasons beyond her control, she was to fail.

On 25 June there were no cheerless omens – only a houseful of relatives summoned by Marina, who had temporarily moved into Coppins, along with the Worsley parents. 'Come at once,' she told Alexandra, who was half-way through dinner with friends. 'Kate is starting to have her baby, and she needs all her family with her.' The announcement was slightly premature. In the absence of any progress, the Duke of Kent departed as normal the following morning for the War Office, only to be summoned back from Whitehall a few hours later. Although contemporary accounts stressed that the Duke was present for the birth, one newspaper insisted that he was still driving home when George Philip Nicholas, tenth in line to the throne, was born at 3p.m. on 26 June, weighing 6lb 4oz.

In Hovingham the church bells were rung for an hour. In Iver Colonel Walter Corfield – a parish council luminary who had, in the face of some opposition, decided to organize a collection for a present for the child – went to the local shop to see what his collecting cans, fashioned from cocoa tins, had yielded. At Coppins, Miss Gwendoline Howell took her latest charge off to the nursery.

Although the Duchess's son was delivered by Sir John Peel, the Queen's gynaecologist, she had departed from tradition in declining one of the stable of royal midwives. Sister Howell, favoured by Princess Marina, whose sister, Olga, had employed her, was fifty-five, starchy, a firm believer in bottle-feeding and famous not only for delivering the babies of the rich and titled but for nursing George Bernard Shaw in his last illness.

Bar the appointment of Sister Howell, all other aspects of the royal birth and christening strictly followed royal protocol. The baby was christened at Buckingham Palace, aged eleven-and-a-half weeks, in a gold lily baptismal font brought from Windsor Castle and installed in the music room. Although he wore the Honiton lace christening gown in which all royal babies were then baptized, George was technically a commoner, following a decree by George V that only children of the sovereign and children of any sons of the sovereign should henceforth be a Prince or Princess or take the title of Royal Highness.

The baby was designated the Earl of St Andrews; his father's subsidiary title. George St Andrews, whose dislike for the unwanted trappings of royalty would greatly exceed his mother's, was never going to mourn his great-grandfather's early nod towards a slimmed-down monarchy. On the day of his christening, however, there was little evidence of retrenchment. The Archbishop of Canterbury performed the service, the godparents included the Duke of Edinburgh and Princess Alexandra, and the Queen, Princess Margaret, the Queen Mother and the Princess Royal looked on.

Katharine, used to counting this circle as frequent companions, though not (except in Alexandra's case) familiars, was about to make her first proper entrance into the charmed circle. It was not, perhaps, the best moment for the Duchess – a nervous beginner and the mother of a very small child – to represent the Queen abroad. Nevertheless, she welcomed her role as dual representative of the Crown, alongside the Duke, at the Ugandan celebrations of independence.

As with all her later engagements, the Duchess focused her attention on two areas. The first was her clothes. Though she let it be known that she was taking sartorial advice from the Queen and her dresser, Bobo MacDonald, it is unlikely that these talks progressed much further than a Ugandan weather forecast. ('It will be warm,' the Queen warned.) In terms of style, the Duchess went back to her own favourite, Belinda Belville, and Marina's couturier, John Cavanagh, for a stylish and brightly coloured wardrobe, so extensive that the press wondered tartly exactly how many pieces of luggage were required for two weeks in Africa.

Though entranced by her clothes and how she would look, Katharine had other concerns. Even in the last days of her pregnancy, she ploughed through briefing papers, teaching herself about the history and customs of the country. 'I'm doing my homework,' she said. Years later, on charity visits to India and Africa, she – once the reluctant student – would say exactly the same thing. 'I always do my homework. No one knows how hard I work . . .' But, back in 1962, she was establishing herself as two things. For the first time, she was forging a role as the serious crusader; determined to bring not only a compassionate dimension but an intellectual one to the work she undertook. Also for the first time, she was relishing her duties. Though the Duchess detests public scrutiny, she adores the grandeur that attaches to it. On one hand, she is her father's daughter; a model of kindness and simplicity. On the other, she was taught by two indomitable women – Marina and her mother; both from vastly different backgrounds, both distinguished by their hauteur.

On this trip, Katharine was given all the privilege attached to royalty. Among salutes and presentations, she was received on to a Britannia airliner of the Queen's Flight and welcomed, on the Entebbe tarmac, by the premier, Milton Obote, and the retiring governor, Sir Walter Coutts. The programme was similar to any royal tour – a few hospital and college visits, coupled with receptions, dinners and a state ball, at which the Duchess shone in gold and cream organza. For a shy Yorkshire woman forced to abandon her four-month-old baby, this might have been more penance than delight. The Duchess adored it.

Lord Coggan, one of her great friends, sat with the Kents at an official lunch and discovered that he and the Duke were both celebrating their birthdays. Amid the toasts and jollity, Katharine was radiant. 'This was really the first big thing where she represented the sovereign,' Coggan says. 'And she did it with such panache.'

The official functions over, the Kents drove to see the Owen Falls Dam, at the head of the Nile, before travelling on to the Queen Elizabeth National Park, where, from their bedroom window at the Royal Safari Lodge, they watched elephant herds traipse past. After a Land Rover safari the Duchess – on her first proper solo engagement – opened a major hospital in Kampala before flying on to Nairobi and from there to London.

However nervous she had been, and however greatly she missed her child, she must have felt that, for the second time that year, she had begun to fulfil a major part of her destiny. To be admired, to be fêted, to be cast in a major role for a small piece of world history; this was only the start of a new career in which, at her husband's side, she could be emissary for her Queen and country. And this, after all the anxiety, was what royal duty entailed.

It was not. Although Uganda was not the last major royal tour undertaken by the Duchess of Kent, neither was it the prelude to a multitude. Several factors decreed that this should be so. A generation of young royals – the Queen's children – waited in the wings. In years to come the Duchess's ill health and nervous breakdown would render a major public role impossible.

Neither was any vision of dual responsibility, in which the Kent team would work side by side through the years, an accurate one. An official who watched them, triumphant in Uganda, remarked – almost forty years afterwards – that he, who knew them both well, had never again seen the Duke and Duchess of Kent share a public platform.

CHAPTER NINE

A Soldier's Wife

❧

THERE WAS, FOR now, no hint of estrangement between the Kents. On the contrary, they were about to embark on a cheek-by-jowl existence far removed not only from the glittering days of the Uganda tour but from any preconceptions Katharine once had of life in the royal cocoon.

The Duke had been posted to Hong Kong as second-in-command of C Squadron of the Royal Scots Greys. The Duchess and their five-month-old son flew out to join him a few weeks prior to her thirtieth birthday. As on the Africa tour, the transport was a Britannia aircraft; not, this time, the beautifully appointed Queen's Flight version but a troop charter given over to Army wives and their children.

Katharine's first stint as an expatriate wife could hardly have started more ominously. The car carrying her, George, and his Scots nanny, Mary McPherson, got so lost in fog on the way to Stansted airport that it became clear that the party would miss the flight. A phone call established that the plane would not, in any case, take off that night because of the weather conditions, and Katharine was driven back to Kensington Palace, arriving late and exhausted to beg a bed from Marina.

The Britannia finally set off the following day, and the Duchess took her turn to change the baby's nappy in a curtained-off booth and soothe him as the plane touched down for refuelling stops at Istanbul and Bombay. An uncomfortable, long-haul flight full of wailing children would have been anathema to most members of the royal family. Katharine, segregated from the rest of the Army wives and helped by her nanny, naturally travelled in more comfort than most on the flight. In addition, her hands-on charity work had made her used to occasional discomforts. Nonetheless, the journey was a prelude to a very different life. The Kents' flat in Kowloon offered a daunting illustration of downshifting. The Duke, who had picked his wife and son up at the airport in his Ford car, drove them straight to the apartment: the upper floor of a stark Army house comprising three small bedrooms, a living-room, kitchen and bathroom, plus a terrace with views towards the sea and a small balcony with a washing-line to dry the baby's clothes.

Despite the lack of comforts, this was one of the happier times in the Kent marriage. With a British nanny, plus local help, Katharine was free to walk with her baby in the park – indistinguishable, in her loose dress and sandals, from any other Army wife – and to sail, water-ski, play tennis and attend the Chinese Opera with her husband.

Throughout her life she maintained her fondness not only for a Chinese takeaway meal but also for the culture of Hong Kong, which she has often visited; retaining close links with the universities. In her years there, no political pressures existed. Another three decades would pass before Prince Charles stood, in driving rain, to watch the colony being handed back to a Chinese government that had come to detest Chris Patten, the last governor. For now, Army life represented a more relaxed version of the sort of existence she had enjoyed, before her marriage, in Oxford and London.

The Duchess mucked in. In addition to picnics, regattas and parties she rode frequently; training one of the Army horses to jump through a blazing hoop at a gymkhana. When the engagement was announced, back in Britain, between Alexandra and Angus Ogilvy, she and the Duke bought tickets to watch the official film at their local cinema rather than opting for a private screening. For now, most pressures had been removed from Katharine. Both those who worked with the Duke and visitors from England who dropped in to her apartment attest to the couple's apparent contentment. Noël Coward, who visited during a Hong Kong holiday, wrote in his diary of 'a really enchanting evening with Prince Eddie and Kathy, who live in an ordinary officer's issue flatlet in the New Territories. [They are] . . . as merry as grigs and having a lovely time untrammelled by royal pomposity. They really are a sweet couple, and it is a pleasure to see two people so entirely happy with each other. I also saw George, who is thirteen months and blond and pink and smiling.'

The biggest measure of how ephemeral this existence was came in April 1963, the date set for Alexandra's wedding to Angus Ogilvy. The Kents flew home for the ceremony and parties; sparkling even by the standards of their own wedding. Once again Marina had been confounded in her wish. Her daughter had been perfectly groomed for a royal life. In addition, her easy manner and charm had endeared her – even more than Edward – to the Queen. The bridegroom she had chosen had an impressive pedigree. His father was Lord Chamberlain to the Queen Mother, and Angus's career, although patchy, included a PPE from Oxford, a spell with the Scots Guards and a seemingly burgeoning

City career that had already notched up for him twenty-nine company directorships. He was, however, a commoner.

Marina's disappointment did not only centre on the thwarted hope that her daughter might be Queen of Greece or of Norway. She worried – as she had with Edward and Katharine – about whether an outsider could withstand the rigours of a royal existence. Though she continued to school her new son-in-law in the protocol of royalty (he was berated for introducing his wife at one dinner party as 'Alexandra' rather than 'Her Royal Highness, Princess Alexandra'), the Ogilvy marriage produced difficulties even Marina could not have foretold. Her son-in-law's business career was to be shaken by his association with the business tycoon Tiny Rowland – involved in tax evasion during his takeover of the mining company, Lonrho, on whose board Ogilvy sat. The Ogilvys' daughter, Marina – named for her grandmother – was to have a child out of wedlock, an unhappy marriage and a divorce. She was also to gain – in lieu of other title – the accolade of 'Rear of the Year'.

Ironically, of all the glittering royal matches of the era, that of Alexandra and Ogilvy was to prove the most successful. Katharine and Edward's union was not to be one of enduring happiness. Princess Margaret's marriage – undertaken on the rebound from her banned love affair with the divorced Group-Captain Peter Townsend – to Antony Armstrong-Jones ended in divorce and, for Margaret, a rather purposeless life, to the minds of many, marked by loneliness, chain-smoking and later a stroke at the age of sixty-nine.

Long before the divorces of Diana, Princess of Wales, the Princess Royal and the Duchess of York, the flawlines in the supposedly concrete bond of royal marriages were about to show. None was apparent for Alexandra's wedding festivities. The Queen and Prince Philip gave a ball at Windsor

Castle, at which the cream of European royalty (and the milk, for Katharine found herself presented to even more distant relatives than at her own wedding) danced to Joe Loss and the pipers of the Royal Scots Guards.

The wedding itself bore familiar overtones. Bridal gown by Cavanagh – this time in magnolia and designed round a length of Valenciennes lace Marina had worn for her wedding. Wedding march – again the Toccata in F by Widor. And, in a reprise of the pallor and exhaustion she had shown on her own wedding day, Katharine – dressed in a coral coat and hat she had commissioned in Hong Kong – watched, stony-faced, while her husband gave the bride away.

Those who caught the Duchess's strangely withdrawn expression as she sat in her pew at Westminster Abbey put it down to misery at being parted from her small son, who had stayed behind with his nanny and a local amah, or nurse. Katharine, in fact, was well used to being parted from George. Not only did she have a small retinue of carers; she had also left him, with no apparent heart-searching, for her tour of Uganda when he was only a few months old. It is possible that Katharine's gloom was induced only by the memory of the nightmare of her own wedding, reactivated by being thrown once again into a massed gathering of the European and British royal clans. It is likely, however, that her anxiety was even more deeply rooted. The schisms in her marriage were, by then, not far distant. Nor was her second pregnancy.

In the outside world, Harold Macmillan's government was fatally wounded by the call girl scandal involving the War Minister, John Profumo (a personal friend of Marina). The Great Train Robbers got away with more than £1 million. In Dallas, Texas, President John Kennedy was assassinated. In Hong Kong the Duchess of Kent realized, in the autumn of 1963, that she was expecting her second child. This time, she would spend most of her pregnancy apart from her husband – due, soon after they left Hong Kong at Christmas, to take up his new posting at Fallingbostel in Germany.

Although Katharine was perfectly fit to travel – in January she accompanied her husband to St Moritz, where he was competing in the Army ski championships – she opted to stay behind at Coppins, letting it be known that, while she would be quite happy to have the baby in a German military hospital, the public might prefer the baby to be born in Britain. There were other compelling reasons to stay. The first was that a royal birth was, in 1964, less an event than a club activity.

The Queen was pregnant with her fourth child, Margaret with her second, and Alexandra was expecting her first baby. But, whatever the bonding process with other royal mothers, Katharine had other links to re-establish. Much as she enjoyed Hong Kong life, she had desperately missed Hovingham and, in particular, the father whose advice she relied on. Not only did she spend her pregnancy at Coppins; she wondered whether she might stay there once the baby was born – explaining that, of course, she would prefer to be with Edward, though she was not sure if married accommodation could be found.

This was both a flimsy excuse and one, seemingly, that the Duke would not countenance. On a day trip to the German base, the Duchess was shown the house that had been earmarked for her before flying back to England to await her new baby. Sister Howell was re-engaged, Marina moved back in, and Helen Marina Lucy was born on 29 April, weighing 7lb 8oz and twelfth in line to the throne. According to the *Daily Telegraph*, the Duke was informed of the birth by his mother 'and will return to England as soon as he can get leave'. In fact, he had arrived home an hour before his daughter was born in the same bedroom, overlooking the Coppins garden, as her elder brother.

In the village of Iver, the baby was treated like any other new arrival, receiving the £1 premium bond offered to the child of a Women's Institute member, to 'start it off in the world'. (Mrs Marjorie Ridgwell, the president, had earlier made plain that no exceptions would apply. The payment would be conferred 'as long as Her Royal Highness remembers to pay her five shillings membership fee on the first Tuesday in January. We make that a rule. Our members must be paid up.')

As a member of an even more tightly regulated coterie, Lady Helen Windsor (the first royal child to take the family surname) was baptized in the traditional Honiton lace gown in the private chapel at Windsor. 'We are delighted with my first granddaughter,' Marina wrote to her sister, Olga. 'Especially as Katharine longed for a girl.' Katharine herself had told a friend that she was relaxed about the child's sex. 'I don't mind whether it's a girl or a boy, because we intend to have more children. Two isn't really a family, is it?'

Years later, the Duchess's wish for a large family would be one of the chief factors driving her to the edge of sanity. In the aftermath of Helen's birth, the slowness of her recovery hinted at a bout of post-natal gloom or depression. Marina had naturally stood proxy for her as godmother to Prince Edward, whose christening coincided with the last days of her pregnancy. But Katharine was still not sufficiently well to attend the baptism of James Ogilvy, Alexandra's son, a fortnight after Helen's arrival. Again, Marina was the stand-in godmother.

Four weeks afterwards, Katharine saw her own child

christened at Windsor. Shortly afterwards, she closed Coppins for the second time and left, with George, the baby and the children's nanny, Mary McPherson, to join her husband in Germany. The family home – one of a line of identical modern houses, custom-built for British officers on a tree-lined street – was, according to a neighbour, 'a glorified council house', offering very slightly more space than the Hong Kong 'flatlet'. There was a living-room, four bedrooms and a back garden just large enough to accommodate the baby's playpen and a few garden toys for George. Standard issue furniture reflected the barracks-style existence that would dictate Katharine's lifestyle for the next eighteen months.

Where Hong Kong had been a cosmopolitan place, full of local colour and, conversely, social butterflies eager to woo representatives of the royal family, Fallingbostel was a less glamorous milieu. The Duchess adapted with her usual smoothness. 'She was a sweet, gentle person; terribly nice to everyone,' says a neighbour. 'She was straight and very natural. She used to sing in the barracks choir and push the children round the base in their pram. She didn't overdo her looks. She could be in an old jersey and a pair of trousers, and she still looked marvellous. She was just an army officer's wife out there.'

At home, the Duchess was a deeply attentive wife, obligingly testing her husband on exam papers for his forthcoming Staff College exams. On nights out, she would join in with local preferences, preparing pâté or a trifle for the 'bring-a-course' dinner parties popular at Fallingbostel. Even on skiing trips, where she fell over constantly and never got past novice status, the Duchess seemed unfailingly cheerful.

As a member of the royal family, she was occasionally

called on to present flower show trophies or gymkhana prizes to soldiers and their families. Her husband's clan – members of the German nobility related to Marina – were eager to have the Kents for country house weekends. There was one major engagement undertaken on behalf of the Queen who, still being relieved of parcels of old empire, asked her cousins to represent her in the Gambia independence celebrations.

But, in the main, Katharine Kent lived very much like an ordinary officer's wife. Though no casual, or even close, observer would have detected it, that life was beginning to chafe. She had certainly not rushed to join her husband in his latest posting. Now she was keen to leave. 'By the end she found it terribly dull, and she was eager to get away,' says one of the officers who worked most closely with the Duke. Although it is unsurprising that she found her life less than seductive, this was a significant turning point for her.

Much as she loved the razzmatazz of royal life, she detested its restrictions and the scrutiny of being in the public gaze. That much she had predicted from the earliest days of her relationship with Edward. Now the simple round of an officer's wife had also begun to pall. Edward, however, was a serious and committed soldier, ambitious to command his regiment. In addition, four years into his marriage, it is unlikely that he – bred to the cool and unromantic ways of royalty – was able or inclined to bestow on Katharine the undivided warmth and attention she had been used to receiving from her father and, to a lesser extent, her brothers.

Where was she to go from here? Back at Coppins, a difficulty in attracting local help meant that she had to shoulder the unaccustomed weight of running a large household. Edward, meanwhile, had started a three-month military science course at Shrivenham, living at college and returning home only at weekends. Katharine, by default or design, had lost touch with many of her old schoolfriends and companions from her Hovingham days. Though there were new, and grander, replacements, the vacuum in her social life was greater than it had ever been. Unsurprisingly, it was filled by the Worsley parents, who visited their daughter often. In 1966 Sir William Worsley, who had been a member of the Leeds University Court and Council for more than a quarter of a century before his retirement four years previously, carried with him an informal invitation. How would Katharine like to become Chancellor of the university?

Unsurprisingly, she jumped at the chance. Not only did this role, as successor to the late Princess Royal, avoid any potential clash in patronage with Marina – still, despite her demotion, the *de facto* Duchess of Kent. It also offered the potential to fulfil her more serious aspirations. Katharine, who had once longed to study music at the Royal Academy, was gradually to become a vicarious academic, establishing close bonds both with Leeds and with the University of Hull – which later bestowed an honorary doctorate on her, in recognition of her support – and fiercely upholding the 'rights' of the young to higher education.

Although her passion for learning was still unformulated, she was eager to take on a more solid commitment than the vapid engagements that currently came her way – opening a footwear exhibition or being the token royal at a ball or a concert. Like most women who veer between trivial and worthy pursuits, the Duchess was ambivalent about her frivolous side, spending a fortune on clothes (an expense probably underwritten by Brunner family wealth, since the Duke's pay did not run to luxuries) but initially deeply wary about a request from the Associated Fashion Designers of London to name her as one of the country's ten best-dressed women.

The Leeds appointment would be the perfect foil for her deeper, more contemplative nature. She was installed on 6 May after a short speech, in which she spoke of 'my' university – laying claim to her first serious role which had nothing directly to do with being a royal consort or Army wife. 'I have the warmest affection for Yorkshire and Yorkshire people,' she said. 'I am always glad to have an excuse to come back. Now I have a very strong reason – to visit my university.'

True to her word, she returned to confer honorary degrees a fortnight later, walking through a demonstration by anti-Vietnam War protesters. Though the Duchess appeared unruffled, Conservative students protested on her behalf to Jack Straw – then president of the union and later Home Secretary. This was the first of many visits.

As the Duchess had suggested, her new appointment had provided a lifeline back to Yorkshire and to Hovingham. It also opened the way for the first steps towards her conversion – one she did not feel able to undertake for another three decades – to Roman Catholicism.

Years later, Katharine would present that conversion as an impulsive switch almost evoking that of St Paul on the road to Damascus and inspired by an unlifting Christmas carol service, at which she stood next to Cardinal Basil Hume, the head of the Catholic Church in England. According to those close to the Cardinal, her spiritual journey towards Catholicism actually began in the mid-sixties, only a few years after she married. The Duchess, trapped by the irksome constraints of a royal existence and the pomp and grandeur attached to the established Church, was – vaguely in those days – already casting around for a

Above: The girls of Runton Hill in summer, 1949. Katharine Worsley is third from left, second row.

Left: Katharine as Sebastian in the school production of *Twelfth Night*.

For better, for worse: portrait of a royal bride. *Camera Press*

Above: Princess Marina offers a regal smile as her husband addresses an audience at Iver, Buckinghamshire.

Right: Andrew Burnaby-Atkins (left) and his brother, Freddy, on the steps of the Viceroy's residence, India 1947.

The young Kent family at Coppins. *Camera Press*

At work for higher
education. *University
of Hull*

For charity, one of the Duchess's favourite roles. *Camera Press*

Pilgrims' progress: Cardinal Hume, the Duchess and a fellow-traveller at Lourdes.

The off-duty Duchess; in casual dress for her work with the homeless. *Max Cisotti & Marco Deidda*

Lady Helen Windsor's wedding to Tim Taylor. Her brothers Nicholas and George are pictured either side of the Duke of Kent. *Camera Press*

simpler system that would offer her both enlightenment and the security of fixed rules. The process of conversion began not at Westminster Cathedral, but in Yorkshire; the home county of her first great spiritual guide.

Gordon Wheeler was ordained co-adjutor Bishop of Middlesbrough in 1964, with right of succession to the elderly incumbent. For his first journey north, from Westminster Cathedral where he was previously the administrator, he was offered a lift by a monk who happened to be returning to Ampleforth Abbey on the same day. The chauffeur was Dom Basil Hume, the priest who was to be the Duchess's second mentor.

Wheeler had every reason to look forward to his appointment. He was facing a new challenge, and he was going home. Descended from a Yorkshire family of wool merchants, he read history at Oxford before studying for the Anglican ministry. Six years after his ordination, he was received into the Catholic Church.

Both his business and ecclesiastical connections meant that he was well known to Sir William Worsley. In 1966 the link strengthened. At exactly the time that Katharine took up her duties as Chancellor of Leeds University, Wheeler became the city's Catholic bishop, and the bond between them was forged.

Wheeler was the sort of man and mentor the Duchess adored. A priest of deep culture, with wide-ranging intellectual ability, he combined theological conservatism with a populist touch. He loved good food and company but never forgot the less privileged in his diocese. Every Christmas Day he was joined in the episcopal dining-room by the homeless invited to share his turkey – a gesture that struck a chord with Katharine, who had already spent one Christmas working with the dispossessed.

In addition, Wheeler shared her love of music, combining his visits to parishes with a musical session in the church hall, at which the audience would demand the latest popular songs and sing to his piano accompaniment. More important, he had undertaken the difficult route from the Anglican to the Catholic Church – a hard road for an ordained Church of England priest and an even lonelier path, as he recognized, for a member of a royal family then tightly bonded to an established Church.

Indeed, it would have been unthinkable for the Duchess to announce her conversion at the beginning of her marriage. It is clear, however, that the spiritual vacuum made more intense by the tragedies she was to endure later was already in place. An eminent priest currently working closely with Cardinal Hume says: 'The desire, the intensity began in the sixties. Wheeler would have started all that off. He was very instrumental. More instrumental than has ever been recorded. There was no desire on Bishop Wheeler's part – or Cardinal Hume's – to convert her. That is the last thing they would do. But they would listen to her. Had she never met the Duke, I think we might have found a very spiritual lady, but perhaps she would not have become a Catholic. Being a member of the royal family probably drove her to intense simplicity in terms of the spiritual life.'

Wheeler, an arch-diplomat, died in 1998, at the age of eighty-seven, without disclosing to anyone the anxieties and doubts the young Duchess had shared with him. Two things remain certain. The first is that, long before her nervous breakdown and depression, she sought a new fulfilment to regulate her life and fill an emptiness within it. The second is that she longed to join the Catholic Church for many years before altered trends within the royal family rendered her conversion acceptable. More than a decade before that,

Wheeler regularly told one priest he regarded almost as an adopted nephew: 'You know, the Duchess would dearly like to be a Catholic.'

Whatever Katharine's inner yearnings, the outer persona had become more assured. Hers, nonetheless, was an almost schizophrenic existence. On one level, she was simply a well-to-do county wife, at ease with the villagers of Iver and careful not to stand on ceremony. One Christmas card to the WI president contained passport-sized portraits of her two children, stuck to a piece of card with a handwritten message: 'With my very best wishes for Christmas and the New Year, Katharine.' Unlike Marina, she was a frequent visitor to the village shops, depositing the children's clothes at the dry cleaner's and chatting as she scooped sweet papers out of their pockets.

Meshed in with the plainer life was an increasing round of royal engagements. The Queen, having made the Duke 'personal aide-de-camp to Her Majesty' – a title he shared with Lord Mountbatten – appointed the Duchess Controller Commandant of the Women's Royal Army Corps, a post that Katharine approached with a seriousness diluted only by her decision to wear her skirt two inches shorter than the regulation length. The disbursement of empire continued, and the Kents represented the Queen at the independence of British Guiana and Barbados. In 1967 they attended the coronation of King Tupou of Tonga, before which the Queen warned Katharine – even now a famously picky eater: 'You must eat up. They may be disappointed otherwise.' As she forced her way through her share of the 1,000 pigs slaughtered for the week's feasting, Katharine was no doubt remorseful that she was missing her son's sports day and his performance as a gnome in the school play.

Even so, her royal duties – still far from onerous –

allowed her plenty of time to devote both to her children and to her wider family. Her brother Oliver had married, aged forty, and she tacked on a further family celebration at the end of the Tonga trip, flying back via Canada for a holiday with John Worsley. Although she was slowly increasing her royal portfolio – becoming patron of the Nuffield Orthopaedic Centre and undertaking a round of engagements in Northern Ireland, the first chapter in a lifelong interest in Ulster – the Kents remained a low-profile couple.

While a dearth of younger royals meant the Duke had a significant role as the Queen's emissary, surveys in Britain suggested that the public had little knowledge of the couple or what they did. In Canada, by contrast, they were fêted like stars. Invited to open the Calgary stampede, they were presented with saddle-cloths embroidered with their titles and cheered by crowds lining a five-mile route to watch the royal visitors, sandwiched between Irish Guards and a procession of Mounties, ride into town. Designated 'Running Rabbit' and 'Pretty Woman' by the Blackfoot Indian tribe, the Kents were cast in the image of a Hollywood double act far removed from the stern confines of the royal image.

This sort of attention the Duchess could take. Though her legendary capacity for amusement had been bruised by the corset of royal duty and the sometimes stultifying routine of Army life, she retained her appetite for 'fun'.

The Duke, not given to bursts of raw enthusiasm, refrained from public comment. The Duchess had no such reservations. 'I'm shaking with delight,' she told her hosts, full of hubris at the attention and the freedom conferred on her. It was a rare example of how carefree her life could still be. It was also the last.

CHAPTER TEN

Death of a Princess

PRINCESS MARINA, DUCHESS of Kent, died in her sleep at 11.40 in the morning of 27 August 1968, as royal doctors and her family watched over her at Kensington Palace. She was sixty-one.

Marina's children had known she was dying. She did not. For years she had suffered from poor balance and occasional falls. 'Oh, I'm so silly,' she would say. 'Always tumbling about.' When her left arm and leg grew painful, in the summer of 1968 – not long after she had, as normal, presented the prizes at Wimbledon – she was admitted to hospital for tests.

Edward was summoned shortly afterwards to be told that his mother had an inoperable brain tumour and perhaps six months to live. The truth was concealed from Marina either because her children felt she could not bear it or because of a wish, ever-present in the royal family, to leave the deepest feelings unarticulated and to sidestep emotional storms.

This was not Katharine's way. On her visits to hospitals – and, particularly, in her later work for the hospice movement – she frequently looked death in the face. She could talk, even joke, with her own beloved father about his mortality and advancing age. If she dissented from the consensus that Marina should be allowed to believe that she was merely suffering from rheumatism, she did not say so. In the event the pretence was short-lived. A month after the initial diagnosis, Marina was dead.

Despite the gravity of her condition, Edward and Katharine had decided it would be safe to take their children on holiday to Sardinia, returning to find her feebler but still cheerful. 'She was in bed and looked very papery,' wrote her old friend, Noël Coward, after one visit. 'I am worried about her. She was very cheerful, however, and we gossiped and giggled.'

Two days after the anniversary of her husband's death, her best friend, Zoia Poklewska – Madame Pok to the Iver villagers – came up from the country to stay overnight. Late in the evening, Marina said: 'I feel very tired. I think I will go to sleep now.' The following morning, Edward urgently summoned Dr Ramsey, the Archbishop of Canterbury, to her bedside. He arrived by taxi just before she died.

Later Alexandra wrote to her mother's friend, Cecil Beaton: 'Thank God my sweet mama knew no pain or suffering. And now she is at peace.' Beaton himself mourned her with ardour. 'Beautiful and romantic princesses are a rare phenomenon today, and their mere existence enhances . . . With Princess Marina's death, that lovely glow has gone from the land.'

Marina would have concurred wholeheartedly with this tribute. Impossibly imperious, improbably grand and still possessed of a common touch that endeared her to ordinary people, she had never been in the slightest doubt about her mesmeric qualities.

Her earliest biographer, Grace Ellison, writing just before Marina's wedding, concluded her interim work with an accolade fulsome even by the hagiographical standards of the time. 'And so we come to the end of the story of the fairy heroine, who met her Prince Charming. And now comes the wedding. May the fairy princess marry and live happy ever after.' Marina, finding the tone entirely to her taste, inscribed her own handwritten comment on the flyleaf. 'I think your biography is charming, and it has my entire approval. Marina, Princess of Greece and Denmark.'

She had not, in the event, succeeded in living happily ever afterwards. Her marriage was brief, her life beset – at least by her standards – by financial constraint. (Her will, published in October 1968, reflected that stricture. She left £54,121, or £17,398 after death duties; a paltry sum for a royal duchess.) Her attachment to her aide, Philip Hay – as recounted by her later biographer, Sophia Watson – was veiled in the utmost secrecy. Neither age nor private diffi-culties had diminished Marina's standing, in the eyes of the British public, as the fairy princess she considered herself to be. She was mourned as such.

Flags flew at half-mast. The Queen, on holiday at Balmoral, ordered court mourning for a week and prepared to travel home for the funeral. A crowd of 1,000 gathered to watch members of the congregation drive to St George's Chapel, Windsor, for the service and for Marina's burial in the royal mausoleum at Frogmore next to her husband, whose remains had been moved, the previous night, from his resting place in the chapel vaults.

Among the mourners was the normal phalanx of Euro-pean royalty, plus the Duke of Windsor, faltering and elderly but determined to fly in from Paris to pay his respects to the woman once mooted as his bride – a future queen – and ultimately the wife of the brother he loved the best.

The Times obituary noted that 'she was greatly admired

for her remarkable personal beauty and respected and loved for her high sense of duty, her modest charm, her dignity in sorrow and her devotion to her family. Princess Marina was the most recent of a long line of foreign princesses to marry into the British Royal house, and none of her predecessors was more successful in winning the hearts of the British people.'

'She was beautiful up to the last,' said the Queen Mother, generously glossing over, in death, the ultra-royal Marina's early, scathing reference to her as 'that common little Scottish girl'. Marina's friend, Kenneth Rose, writing in the *Daily Telegraph*, underlined her mystique. 'In her presence, few other lights shone brightly. Her serene elegance was matched by a down-to-earth realism as sturdy as the huge and unbecoming pair of spectacles she would wear when working at her writing table . . . The most adoring of mothers, she watched over her children with a fidelity that was not wholly maternal. She taught them that their lives belong as much to their country as to themselves.'

This lesson had been well absorbed by Edward, her oldest son, inculcated by a spirit of absolute obeisance to Queen and to country and moulded, from an early age, to put royal duty before all. But he was also human. His father's death had affected him deeply. Even to a married man with two small children, the loss of his mother – dead in middle age – must have been devastating. Edward, schooled to disguise emotion, translated his shock into practical action. For most of her life, Marina had been inseparable from her Russian cigarettes. Although there was no suggestion that smoking had been directly linked to the tumour that killed her, Edward never smoked again.

For Katharine, the impact of Marina's death was more complex. The influence of her mother-in-law had mutated from rejection, in the time before her engagement, to a rigid control under which Katharine's diary, method of running a home and diligence as a wife had been subjected to remorseless scrutiny. From the first time they met, Marina's assessment of Katharine had been straightforward and only loosely concealed. Here, in her view, was a woman of dubious pedigree and a person not up to the task that faced her. Katharine would have been well aware of that verdict. For someone so sensitive and so insecure, Marina's lack of confidence and interference must have been almost insupportable. Although Katharine did not – then or now – deviate from her public line that her mother-in-law had been a comfort and an inspiration in all she did, the reality was very different.

But, in one sense, Marina had been a bulwark. For as long as she lived, she would never let her daughter-in-law – less strong, less beautiful and less accomplished – upstage her. Katharine had Marina's son and Marina's home. She would not have Marina's job. To inherit that portfolio now, far sooner than she had expected, was a double burden for Katharine. Not only did she fear greater exposure, much as she sometimes relished the adulation and perks that went with royal duty. In addition every line of Marina's obituaries and every starry accolade emphasized how adored she was and how hard she would be to follow.

Marina did have charm; such an overload of it that Katharine would, on one level, have been mesmerized by her. No doubt much of her grief was genuine. It was also a sorrow laced by a fear that her husband might not have understood or heeded. Edward is unlikely to have been much help in unravelling these complex emotions. He had never deviated from his love of his mother, from his wholehearted belief that she was correctly sanctified – in life as in death – or from his belief in her credo of duty. Katharine would simply, in the family tradition, have to get on with the task ahead, casting aside any hidden hope that, as Charles and Anne grew up, her relatively small role in the royal family would dwindle further. As for the Duchess herself, she retained an ambivalence about her future. On one hand, the limelight scared her. On the other, her record as an under-achiever troubled her. For much of her adult life Katharine had been encouraged, and had wanted, to be ambitious and to be somebody of import. Marina's early death dictated what that difficult role would be.

If her predecessor had lived longer, the Duchess of Kent might have been spared some of the misery to come. As it was, she could only cope with the burdens as best she might. Prior to Marina's illness, she had told friends that she felt 'the merest beginner' in royal duty. Now the apprenticeship was over. In a series of planning meetings at the beginning of 1969, Marina's portfolio and that of the sick and incapacitated Duke of Gloucester were divided up among other family members. As always, in the disposition of royal duties, no allowance was made for Katharine's uncertainty about how she would cope or to the trauma her bereaved husband might be facing.

It was decided that Katharine should take on eight of the patronages and offices held by her mother-in-law, including the Spastics Society, the first of the many large charity roles that she would adopt in the coming years. Her diary, once sparsely filled, was now packed with work involving at least a five-day week with copious travel thrown in. She opened school buildings, launched ships on Teesside, presented medals, inaugurated old people's homes; always, no matter how punishing the schedule, charming and apparently relaxed.

A decade later, and shortly before he was murdered, Lord Mountbatten explained the function of the Kents to the writer, Audrey Whiting. 'Charles will need the support of people like Alexandra and Eddie. They don't grow on trees, you know. To be a monarch and have cousins like the Kents is of untold value – they are both relatives, friends and, at the same time, bloody hard-working people. I like to think that I helped to make the Kents the people they are today. I taught them how to shake hands faster than anyone else – at least, when pushed, twenty people a minute.'

Though not a graduate of the Mountbatten school of speed-greeting, Katharine had certainly been trained for her new role, both by Marina and by Joyce, her mother, who presided over Hovingham as if running a minor realm. But for all the schooling, and for all her natural warmth, the Duchess was not – nor is still – the natural performer she seems. She has never trusted herself to make an off-the-cuff speech in public, even if that address includes nothing more than a few gracious words to a crowd waiting to greet her in a third world village. More than once she has agreed to visit institutions she loves, on the proviso that she will not speak. Often, long after official programmes are printed, she will arrive bearing a brief address that she has toiled over and say: 'I would like to say something after all. Do you mind?'

That hesitancy, born of her own self-doubting nature and strengthened by the pressures applied by Marina and her own mother, has never faded. Fragility is not a subject much enjoyed or explored by any member of the royal family. In addition, Edward – even if he had been fully attuned to the pressures on his wife – was not a source of constant support to his wife. At the time of Marina's death, the Kent marriage was becoming semi-detached; a consequence both of the Army career he was determined to pursue and of the couple's diverging interests.

Separate agendas of royal engagements inevitably decreed a lack of togetherness. But, even outside that arena, the Kents were moving in different, if not opposing, directions. In 1966 – two years before Marina died – the Duke was named as the new Grand Master of British Freemasonry. In the same year the Duchess took up her Leeds Chancellorship and her spiritual mentor, Gordon Wheeler, moved to the city.

However strong or tentative her first leanings towards the Catholic Church, Katharine's lifelong devotion to Christianity hardly meshed with the tenets of Freemasonry. The Duke's decision to take the post stemmed from a wish, never absent in his life, to honour the memory of his father, who had been Grand Master from the beginning of the war until his death three years later. In 1967 he was installed by the Earl of Scarborough at the 250th anniversary celebrations at the Albert Hall, watched by Freemasons who had flown in from all over the world for the organization's greatest spectacular.

Though precedence decreed that the monarch should be the titular head of Freemasonry, the royal family was far from universal in its support for the Brotherhood. The Queen Mother, a staunch Christian, disapproved. Prince Charles, later to declare himself a 'defender of faiths', was widely expected to take over from the Duke when he reached his twenty-first birthday in 1969. Instead he was utterly dismissive. 'I do not want to join any secret society,' he said.

If the Duchess's private view was similar, the disparity between her husband's new role and her increasing reliance on religion as a source of solace was scarcely sufficient to constitute grounds for rifts in a marriage. It was merely one more small example of how the relationship was shifting.

The greatest pressure on Katharine, in the aftermath of Marina's death, was combining a hectic and demanding royal schedule with the role of being the mother of two small children. Like Diana after her, the Duchess had no intention of allowing her son and daughter to be foisted off on nannies and trained only in the chilly world of royal duty. But of course, Katharine never lacked nursery staff to help out, either in the early, relaxed days of her marriage or now, when she was so busy.

Even so, she regarded being a mother as a hands-on task. It was, she felt, her duty to pass on to her children her spirituality and the code of morality and simplicity she cherished. 'I wanted them to have a sense of wonderment,' she said, many years later. But the Duchess was also an anxious mother. Both George and Helen had been admitted, as babies – according to staff at Great Ormond Street Hospital – to have their ears pinned back, on the grounds that they had inherited the protruberant Windsor variety. Her concern, over all aspects of their development, stemmed from her wish to create the perfect family – a replica of her own childhood (in reality, a claustrophobic one) at Hovingham; idyllic, untroubled and insular; a world in which two devoted parents would focus almost undivided attention on a large and contented brood. But the Duke of Kent, bred to be withdrawn and destined to be frequently absent, was a very different man from Sir William Worsley, the architect of Katharine's dreams.

Furthermore, while Joyce Worsley's idea of a working trip was an annual visitation to the Women's Institute conference, Katharine's new duties meant that she was frequently either away or poring over her research for a job that she treated with the utmost seriousness.

In 1969 the Duke and Duchess were enlisted to visit

Australia, New Guinea, the British Solomons and the New Hebrides, a trip that touched every nostalgic chord the Duke possessed. Marina had toured Australia not long before her death, returning with assurances of how much her son would love this 'other world'. Thirty years had passed since George, the Duke's father, had prepared to take up his term as Governor General, a mission never accomplished because of the outbreak of war.

Just as Coppins was a shrine to his memory, so too was Government House, Canberra, still decked out with the blue satin sofas, swagged curtains and pastel-painted and panelled walls designed to George's specification. The Duchess shared her husband's memories, toured hospitals and schools, moving gracefully from engagement to engagement and from state to state.

In Perth the first real signs of strain began. As soon as she reached the city, a doctor was summoned. The Duchess, he said, was suffering from exhaustion and must rest. There was no question of her carrying out any further engagements that day. By the following afternoon she was working again, brushing off any concerns about her health. 'Of course it's nice to carry on,' she said. 'I feel quite better.'

It was the smallest of episodes, easily explainable – as her retinue said – by over-exertion and a humid climate. Nonetheless, the Duchess's demonstration of frailty, the first public 'lapse' since the faintness that expedited the announcement of her first pregnancy, would have been noted at Buckingham Palace. The royal code demands an ox-like constitution and the acceptance that, if one is not actually dead, then the show must seamlessly go on.

When, almost twenty years later, Diana – torn by misery, famished and in the grip of bulimia – fainted at the Expo '86 exhibition in Vancouver, Prince Charles's response was to upbraid her. 'He said I could have passed out quietly somewhere else, behind a door,' she said later.

In a world where reliability is seen as indispensable to the job, the Duchess had fallen short, however briefly, of the durable standards expected of a royal emissary. She quickly made amends. February 1970 was set aside for her first solo overseas tour. As Colonel-in-Chief of the WRAC, she was scheduled to visit units in Singapore and Hong Kong. Just after Christmas, Dr Saint, her GP in Iver village, confirmed that she was pregnant. The Duchess was adamant. The tour must go ahead. The Army would look after her, and the baby would be fine. The trip was long, and the itinerary planned for her arduous and exhausting enough to tax the strength of the fittest. Katharine survived it with aplomb and without complaint; proving, as she would often prove again, that whatever nervousness or anxieties plagued her, she would endeavour, beyond all reasonable expectation, to prove her capability to measure up to expectations.

She flew back to Britain in time for her birthday – her thirty-seventh – and immediately began working again. Late in March it was formally announced from Coppins that the Duchess of Kent was expecting her third child and was 'very well'. George, aged seven, and Helen, now five, had both been born at home, as Marina and other members of the family gathered.

This time Katharine, out of concession to her age, was booked in to King's College Hospital in London. The Duke had departed in June – two months before the baby was due – to command a squadron of his regiment in Cyprus, where the Royal Scots Greys made up part of the UN peacekeeping force.

There was no question of him returning to see his second son born, a few days early, on 25 July. Messages were sent to the Queen, to Alexandra – on holiday in Sardinia – and to Sir William and Lady Worsley, announcing the arrival of a boy, weighing 6lb 4oz and born thirteenth in line to the throne.

Katharine herself rang her husband in Cyprus, late in the evening, to tell him the news, before cradling the baby she had longed for. She planned to call him Nicholas. Though she adored all her children, he was to be the one on whom she most doted, for whom she would most grieve and on whose behalf she would expend the greatest anguish. He was also to be her last living child.

CHAPTER ELEVEN

Into the Shadowland

❖

SHORTLY BEFORE THE birth of her third child, the
Duchess of Kent was accosted by a wellwisher as she
stepped from an Andover of the Queen's Flight at Manchester Airport. He pressed into her hand a lump of mineral
and told her that this was Cheshire rock salt, designed to
bring her good fortune. The Duchess smiled, thanked him
and dropped the salt into the pocket of her dress. For luck.
As events transpired, she was about to embark on the most
ill-starred period of her life.

The seventies began with no hint of the chronicle of
death and heartbreak that would dominate her existence for
many years to come. Katharine was, as ever, busy. In 1971
she became patron of Unicef, the United Nations Children's
Fund, a departure from Marina's portfolio and the start of
an enduring commitment to the charity she would come to
view as her major commitment and her career.

A year later she gave out honorary degrees at Leeds,
accompanied by her ten-year-old son, George, who was
acting as her page – having renounced a trip to watch Leeds
United play Arsenal in the FA Cup Final – and by the

Duke, accompanying his wife for the first time since she had taken over as Chancellor six years previously.

Coupled with this rare display of domestic unity was a time of domestic upheaval. The Kents had decided to move from Coppins, the home imbued with memories of the Duke's parents. At the time of writing, Coppins stands empty, flanked by builders' skips, its interiors ripped out and grubby net curtains sagging at the windows – a temporary dereliction while the shell is totally refurbished and refitted for its new Arab owner.

When the Kents sold up, the house where two of their children were born had been decorated to the Duchess's taste, and the surrounding grounds – several acres of parkland – provided a safe space for the youngsters to play. Nevertheless, there were good reasons for a move. Katharine may have wished for a home less enmeshed with her husband's past and her dead mother-in-law. More compellingly, there was a sound financial incentive to cash in a major asset in order to supplement Edward's £3,000-a-year Army pay.

Coppins was duly sold to a Mr Eli Gottlieb for more than £400,000, and the Queen offered the Kents a grace-and-favour apartment at York House, St James's Palace, formerly used by the Duke's father, George, and his brother, the Duke of Windsor, and recently vacated by the Duke of Gloucester, following a serious stroke.

The York House residence – which would be the Kents' London home for more than twenty years – was convenient, free and cramped. A thin, vertical slice of a vast building, it contained a minute sitting-room and four bedrooms, reached by a twisting staircase, plus two reasonably sized reception rooms, one on each floor. These were stocked with the Duchess's favourite antiques and hung with family portraits, including – in pride of place on the dining-room wall – a striking portrait of the Duke's father, painted in the romantic style of Philip de Laszlo.

Grand artefacts notwithstanding, York House, dusty and devoid of garden, struck some regular visitors as less than charming. 'Imagine having a door backing on to the main tradesman's entrance,' said one. 'You have vans unloading 600 chairs every day, and all the caterers for major events. One would go mad living there.'

Since there was no suggestion at the time that minor royals should live in anything other than lavish style, the Kents were not permanently confined to these oppressive surroundings. The Queen also offered her cousins Anmer Hall, a two-storey, six-bedroomed mansion, freshly decorated and standing in ten acres on the Sandringham Estate.

Katharine Kent, with her three children and her two new homes, had every reason to feel secure as she approached her fortieth birthday. Newspapers reported the occasion with suitable deference. One, while noting the Duke's frequent absences and the trials of moving house, claimed that 'the daughter of the wealthy Hovingham squire is one of those fortunate girls who, like cognac, improve with age'. The official birthday portrait told a quite different story. Though the tiara and diamond eardrops suggested restrained elegance, nothing could disguise the thinness of her face or the haunted eyes. Friends described Katharine as very tense, preoccupied with the passing of time and the fact that she was growing older.

Her longing for more children was intensified by the personal tragedy about to overwhelm her. Sir William Worsley was ill and, as she knew by then, dying. 'His ill health brought me moments of despair and anxiety,' she wrote, years later in an eightieth birthday tribute to her friend and comforter Lord Coggan. As she recorded, Coggan – then Archbishop of Canterbury – would pray daily in his private chapel for her dying father.

Sir William himself faced his last illness in the relaxed manner he had demonstrated all his life. As the Duchess said in her testament to Coggan: 'He [the Archbishop] would take the time to visit him in hospital and once, on returning from such a visit, he rang me in London to report that my father had said; "What are you doing here? I don't need you yet." I was much comforted by my father's reaction and typical sense of humour. There was a lake in the garden of that particular hospital, and I remember my father saying: "I would willingly throw myself into that lake for that man [Coggan] – I love him so." That was how we as a family all felt.'

Coggan was, as she said, personally close to the Duchess. The godfather of Nicholas, her younger son, he would frequently drop in for tea in the kitchen at York House. The fact that the highest accolade she could pay him was the acknowledgement of how he had helped her father illustrates how deeply she loved Sir William. To lose him was not merely a bereavement. It was, as she had written, a matter for 'despair'. He – the most important and sustaining prop in her life – had always been there to comfort, reassure her and make her laugh when she fled home, to confide the miseries imposed on her by the exigencies of royal life.

In snow and mud, Coggan buried Sir William Worsley at Hovingham on a December morning in 1973, as Katharine looked on, heartbroken. It would not be an exaggeration to say that some part of her had also died. To compound her misery, Lady Worsley was stricken by her husband's loss. There was no hope that she – frail now and frequently wheelchair-bound – would forge a new, independent life as a widow. Yorkshire neighbours who shared the Worsleys' social circle say they never saw her again, from the day Sir William died until her own death six years later. As for Hovingham Hall, Katharine's home and refuge, that was now the fiefdom of her oldest brother, Marcus, the fifth baronet, then the Conservative MP for Chelsea and a formal man, not close to his sister and quite different in style and manner to the ebullient father for whom she grieved.

But the royal calendar accords scant space for mourning, and Katharine's work went on. A trip to Japan and Burma with her husband, now promoted to Lieutenant-Colonel, did little to assuage her misery, and – for the first time – her health began seriously to falter. At first she ignored the gall-bladder infection she was suffering from, before submitting to treatment and a period of rest. It seemed, when she returned to her engagements, that she was fully recovered.

Still, the desire for another child consumed her. If anything, Sir William's death had magnified her longing for a large and mutually supportive family. Logically, the Duchess – never the strongest of women – had ample to cope with: a toddler, two older children, royal duties, a considerable portfolio of charity work and a frequently absent husband. She, remorseless and stubborn in achieving those goals she deems worthwhile, is unlikely to have evaluated her life in such practical terms.

On 30 April 1975, *The Times* ran a single paragraph on a new but minor illness. 'The Duchess of Kent has German measles and will be unable to carry out her engagements for the next few days, it was announced from York House, her London home.' The story that she was also pregnant did not emerge until many years later.

The facts surrounding German measles were stark. Rubella – if caught in the first eight weeks of pregnancy –

was almost guaranteed to infect and damage an unborn child, causing multiple defects to the heart, the brain, the eyes and the hearing organs. In many cases, the mother would suffer a miscarriage. If not, then there was a near-certainty that the baby would be born terribly handicapped. Though the risks diminished dramatically for women who caught the illness later on, the prognosis for those who contracted it early in the pregnancy was chilling.

By the early seventies doctors were well aware of the risks. Many years earlier, the link between the illness and birth defects had been posited, to general disbelief and scepticism, by an Australian ophthalmologist. In the sixties an epidemic in America, which left thousands of babies handicapped, prompted governments – the British included – to launch proper inoculation systems.

By 1974 a programme was under way to screen all women attending ante-natal clinics and to give a post-partum inoculation to those not immune to rubella. Like all such initiatives, this one took several years to get going. It was not until 1988, when the programme was widened to include injecting infants of both sexes before their second birthday, that the illness became extremely rare. Pregnant women of the Duchess's generation were still failed by the system. The majority of victims – Katharine, possibly, among them – caught the illness from their own school-age children.

In the light of the available knowledge, a leading royal doctor told the Duchess that, in his view, she should have an abortion. Torn by her longing for a child and driven by her personal credo – that human life is sacred – she turned, for a second opinion, to those she most esteemed in the Established Church. The advice mirrored that of her doctor.

If medical opinion decreed that she should have her baby aborted, then Katharine would be committing no fault in following it. But ultimately it was her choice.

According to Lord Coggan, a close confidant at the time: 'She had to debate in her own mind whether it should be an abortion or not. It was an abortion, and I think that has quite probably troubled her throughout her life.'

Losing her baby was the loneliest and hardest decision she had taken. So deep and enduring was her unhappiness that when, many years later, one of her best friends alluded to the abortion, Katharine, greatly distressed, temporarily severed all contact with that friend. No doubt she told herself at the time, and on a rational level, that she had done the right thing. Perhaps she wondered whether she – under strain herself – would have had the personal resources to cope with a seriously handicapped child. She might have considered that royal life, difficult enough for healthy young-sters, was particularly inimical to the sick. For all his privileges, the Duke's epileptic uncle, Prince John, had lived a life cloistered away from the world and, in the main, his family, before dying in his teens. Rumours that the Queen, mindful of such problems, put pressure on the Duchess to have an abortion are untrue. Nor is there any evidence that the Duke of Kent attempted to force his wife's hand. The fact that it was her decision, made logically, with the blessing of the Church and in full awareness of a dismal medical prognosis for the pregnancy, did not – then or later – assuage the guilt and anguish she felt.

Even without this additional trauma, the Duchess of Kent had – throughout the seventies – lived an increasingly lonely life. Early in the decade, the Duke had transferred to Northern Ireland as commander of a squadron of the Royal

Scots Greys. Despite Prince Andrew's later role in the Falklands war, posting the Queen's cousin to Ulster at the height of the Troubles seems, in hindsight, a cavalier move.

Though British soldiers were initially heralded as potential protectors of the Catholic population, the honeymoon period for the forces dispatched in the last throes of Harold Wilson's government was brief. A headline in the Derry press – 'Bogside Sings A Welcome To The Troops' – mutated, three years later, in 1972, into the Bloody Sunday disaster, in which thirteen unarmed civil rights protesters were shot dead by law-enforcers. A quarter of a century would pass before a British prime minister, Tony Blair, ordered a new inquiry into an incident that remained, in nationalist eyes, an enduring symbol of the horrors perpetrated by an occupying army.

In the immediate aftermath, outrage filtered from the Bogside to the floor of the House of Commons, where Bernadette Devlin, the Independent MP for Mid Ulster, rushed across the floor of the Chamber and attacked Reginald Maudling, the Home Secretary, hitting him in the face, scratching him, tearing at his hair and calling him a 'murdering hypocrite'.

By the end of the decade, Lord Mountbatten – mentor to the Duke of Kent – would be dead, murdered by the IRA. For now his protégé was part of the war machine, a posting that caused no apparent *frisson* at the Ministry of Defence, or at the heart of the royal family, where Prince Philip – with extraordinary lack of prescience for an altering public mood, let alone the horrors unfolding in Northern Ireland – was pleading poverty. Speaking on an American TV programme, he claimed that the royals might have to leave Buckingham Palace 'if we go into the red', arguing that the Queen's allowance of £475,000 a year was 'based on costs of eighteen years ago. We sold off a small yacht, and I may have to give up polo,' the Duke grumbled.

In Ulster, the Duke of Kent seemed to relish a life away from everyday ties of family and the constraints of royal duty. 'He loved the Army,' says Reggie Purbrick, the officer who gave up his flat in the bachelor officers' quarters for Edward. 'There was a minute sitting-room and a tiny bedroom and bathroom. It was pretty spartan and rightly so. He arrived without a private detective or anything. He was just an ordinary squadron leader. It was one of the times when a member of the royal family can be completely normal.'

But nothing in the Northern Ireland of the seventies was normal. In the winter after the Duke's arrival the rioting in Derry reached unprecedented levels. Internment provoked huge protest, and the military – an extension of the British political will – had the role of flooding the province with soldiers in support of the Protestant RUC. The Duke neither got, nor wished for, any treatment that would single him out from other officers running the crossing points of the border between Fermanagh and Tyrone. 'There were no particular arrangements to keep him out of any personal danger,' says Purbrick. 'If a squadron leader was needed to drive off to Londonderry to take charge of a security operation up there, it could just as well have been him as any of the others.'

For the Duke, an experienced cold war warrior from his time in Germany, this was an entirely new experience. Despite the horrors of the Northern Ireland conflict, it is clear that he was more contented and more relaxed than he ever appeared on the royal stage. Even allowing for some generosity among his peers, he was evidently respected and well-liked. 'You can always judge a squadron leader by the affection and esteem his soldiers hold him in,' says one fellow-officer. 'He was an incredibly kind and caring man, and they adored him. He wasn't a great man to gladhand – not an exhibitionist. Never took the lead in any conversation. Just very pleasant.'

Of course, some royal duty was inescapable. The Duke was frequently invited to dine with the Duke and Duchess of Abercorn. Another officer would drive him out, addressing the passenger hunched in the front seat of a tiny Fiat as 'Edward' until he pulled up at the ducal mansion. Then the car door would be respectfully opened for 'Sir' as the old duchess walked down the steps of her mansion, before performing a deep curtsey to the royal visitor.

The Duchess of Kent, unsurprisingly, never visited. Nor, it seems, was she much spoken of. As one officer says, vaguely: 'The Duchess was not on the scene at all.' But her separation from her husband would not, in the end, be a protracted one. The Army, in some ways less hierarchical and bureaucratic than today, had been slow even to consider the public relations ramifications of allowing the Queen's cousin to chance his fate in the crucible of Irish politics. Eventually, military strategists reassessed the situation and decided that the risks to his safety were too great. In public, the Duke was philsophical about his recall, demanded less on ground of personal danger than – even more humiliatingly – because he was viewed as a potential kidnap victim or hostage. In private, he was both bitter and furious.

That command offered stark proof that the career he loved had effectively been strangled. To be royal, and to be a soldier of the top rank, were mutually exclusive. He would never command his regiment, as he had hoped. His father, in whose memory he had modelled himself, had died serving his country. George, though he perished in a freak accident, had been deemed a hero. Edward was to be insulated from risk; a cotton-wool soldier.

In any marriage the problems now facing the Kents would have been daunting. Edward, despite the blow to his career and esteem, was the minor sufferer. For Katharine, the seventies were proving a litany of disaster. Her father's illness and death, her abortion, her poor health: all of these added up to a dreadful burden of misery.

To compound that, she was worried about George, her older son. He had thrived at Heatherdown, the Berkshire prep school he attended with Prince Andrew, sharing his police security. The Kents' investment in his education (£200 a term in fees, met out of the Duke's £3,000 annual Army wage) had paid dividends. Though neither the royal family, nor the Worsleys, were renowned for academic sparkle, the Earl of St Andrews performed so well at school that his cousins nicknamed him 'Brainbox'.

Not only did he pass the entrance exams to Eton, his father's old school. He entered as a King's Scholar, one of the *crème de la crème*; an achievement that apparently did little to allay the Duchess's concerns. At least one master picked up instantly on her anxiety. 'Normally we sweat our guts out, and the parents aren't the least bit interested, having just got the child off their hands at an awkward time. So it was nice that the Duchess should be so interested. She was a far more concerned mother than most.' The truth is that Katharine's troubles were, through no fault of hers, causing her to focus an almost obsessive anxiety on her children, and, in particular, on her older son. As the Eton master says: 'Maybe the Duchess had a premonition that he would have such problems in the future.'

Whether or not Katharine's anxiety was a contributor to those problems, the evidence of George's troubled secondary school career would not appear until later. For now, the Duchess's seeming awareness that those difficulties were on the horizon simply provided one more piece in a jigsaw of concerns. In March 1976 she entered the King Edward VII Hospital in London, reportedly 'in need of a rest'. A month later it was announced that she had mild anaemia, and her engagements were cancelled for a further fortnight. This spell of illness, undoubtedly presaging the chronic depression she would later suffer, coincided with the Duke's decision to leave the Army. The two events were, naturally, never linked at the time, but the truth was that the Kent marriage – battered by separation, by Katharine's worries over her son's future and by her anxiety over the royal performance required of her – was already in trouble.

Although the Northern Ireland episode had blighted Edward's hopes of having a military career of great distinction, another factor contributed to his resignation. 'I think the Duke would have stayed for longer but for the fact that he had a family,' says a friend tactfully. In other words, Edward seemed to have reconciled himself to the fact that the Duchess's parlous state of health was not conducive to his *modus vivendi* of part-time bachelor and full-time soldier.

Earl Mountbatten, guru and lifestyle adviser to the younger royals, was consulted. What career might be suitable? The Queen, probably briefed by Mountbatten, was sanguine about her cousin's move to civilian life, and Edward found the job that would remain the backbone of his working portfolio until the present day. As the new vice-chairman of the British Overseas Trade Board, he would not have a secure income above an expenses arrangement for foreign travel. But he would have ample scope to fulfil a wanderlust he was loath to relinquish. In 1976, the first year of his appointment, his work included visits to the United States, South America, Scandinavia and Germany.

Nonetheless, he had at last discovered a post that was conducive to something resembling normal family life. If Katharine's problems had suggested that the Kents' existence could no longer be defined in such cosy terms, that gloomy conclusion was about to be rewritten and her dearest hope realized. In 1977, at the age of forty-four, the Duchess of Kent discovered – to her unmitigated joy – that she was pregnant once more.

CHAPTER TWELVE

Countdown to Tragedy

❖

THE DUCHESS'S PREGNANCY seemed ideally timed. George and Helen were teenagers now, and she was said to feel that the new baby would be a playmate and companion for six-year-old Nicholas. In addition, she was close to achieving the large family she had always wanted. The loss of her previous child had left her guilt-wracked and bereft. This baby represented atonement and reparation; almost a signal from God to the deeply religious Katharine that she had acted correctly and that all would be well. In addition – although no one knew of her growing unhappiness – she believed that this child would cement a dying relationship with her husband.

In another year of royal baby boom – Princess Anne and the Duchess of Gloucester were also pregnant – the formal announcement of the Duchess of Kent's pregnancy was issued from her office at York House on 24 June 1977. The timing was curious. If the baby was indeed due at the end of February 1978, as the statement said, the news had been issued when the Duchess was only four weeks pregnant; in other words almost before she herself knew that she had conceived.

She would, a spokeman said, 'be cancelling all engagements outside London until the end of July, on the advice of the Queen's doctors. She is then expected to lighten her duties until the end of September. We are not expecting complications – it is just a wise precaution. The doctors think it will be sensible. If all is well by September, as anticipated, she will resume her normal engagements until a date rather nearer the birth.'

Katharine, it was said, still intended to go to Persia in the late autumn for a four-day visit to open a British Cultural Festival. In fact, that overseas engagement would have fallen at exactly the time she was scheduled to give birth. The baby was due not in February 1978 but almost five months earlier, in October 1977.

This bizarre fudging of dates remains a mystery. The Duchess herself confirmed, many years later, that her last child – who was indeed born in October – was delivered at term. A lady-in-waiting who visited her shortly after the birth confirms her version. Lady Lothian, a lifelong friend of Katharine, thinks the child was premature, but only slightly.

But courtiers, who released the announcement, do not, in general, seek so blatantly to mislead the public. Nor is it conceivable that the Duchess's distinguished doctors, Dr Richard Bayliss, Physician to the Queen, and George Pinker, Surgeon-Gynaecologist, could be five months adrift on dates. The most plausible explanation is that the timing was blurred because of anxieties that the pregnancy would not go well, whether because of the Duchess's age, her previous gynaecological history, her mental and physical frailty or a combination of those factors. It may have been thought that, if any problems were to occur, a mishap passed off, wrongly, as an early miscarriage would be easier to explain to the public and might involve less hurt to the Duchess and her family.

In a relatively unquestioning era, no one appears to have noted the discrepancy in the dates or registered the suspicion that Katharine's doctors may have thought, from the outset, that this pregnancy might not have a good outcome. But the Duchess, unbeknown to almost anyone outside her family, must have been placed under huge additional strain. If her baby was born at term – and there is no reason to doubt her version – then she was, in effect, having to live a lie. To pretend that one is four months pregnant, rather than approaching full term, must, at the very least, impose a huge psychological burden. Whether Katharine willingly colluded in this deception, or whether she was reluctantly persuaded of its doubtful merits, her last pregnancy must have taken on a nightmarish quality in which her age would have seemed the least of her problems.

Nonetheless, it remained a concern. Some risks – notably those of having a Down's syndrome child – do increase dramatically for older women, and the Duchess was the oldest prospective royal mother since Queen Charlotte, wife of George II, gave birth to their daughter Amelia in August 1783 at the age of forty-five years and three months. But this was the late seventies, and fertility was no longer the province only of the young. The Duchess herself, partly through her friendship with the ultrasound pioneer Ian Donald, was an expert on the subject. Many years later, she delivered a long speech on laparoscopy, scanning and test-tube babies to the Royal College of Obstetricians, so detailed and knowledgeable as to beg the question whether she had first-hand experience of early fertility techniques. Sir George Pinker says not. 'The Duchess had no fancy treatments.'

On 6 July 1977 – supposedly two months into her

pregnancy but actually six – she cancelled an engagement to open the 21st British Congress of Obstetricians and Gynaecologists, asking for her speech to be read for her. The address was typical of her style: meticulously prepared, triple-spaced and with the words demanding emphasis carefully underlined. The content was not. This was, instead, the most heartfelt message she had ever delivered.

'Termination of pregnancy, being a controversial issue, was not one I ever intended to discuss today – but as all doctors must find inspiration in respect for the dignity of human life – and compassion for the wellbeing of mother and child – I am sure that you must share my disquiet that this indispensable ideal seems to be increasingly at risk. What particularly worries me is that abuse (under the existing legislation) can easily become the accepted standard. We would like to see these standards modernized, with greater speed, greater enthusiasm and less indifference.

'Human life is sacred and uniquely valuable; every birth a miracle. It is the gift of God, and, as such, never to be taken for granted, much less treated lightly or callously. I honour those who dedicate their careers to its protection; and, by so doing, helping to uphold the traditions of Christian family life.'

The speech was uniquely political – the first intervention by a member of the royal family into the abortion controversy. Her plea for tighter controls was made more significant by its timing; a critical moment in the Commons debate on a contentious Private Member's Bill, sponsored by William Benyon MP, which sought to tighten the existing law by stipulating that termination might not be carried out after twenty weeks.

But the Duchess's words were not only fuel to a moral debate. They were also the *cri de coeur* of a woman whose experience of abortion had been rendered more dreadful by the fact that she believed passionately in the Christian model of family values of which she spoke. Sir George Pinker says her anti-abortion message was certainly informed by her own experience. But more remarkable was a part of the speech never reported, a deliberately cheerful little passage in which Katharine presented apologies for her absence and, in doing so, demonstrated all the implacable courage she would need to sustain her in the months and years to come.

'I doubt whether it would be possible to find a more convincing excuse than I have for not being here in person today. Nevertheless I am deeply disappointed at not being able to overrule the advice of my doctor ... As a woman and a mother – not to mention a mother-to-be – I must declare a special interest in your deliberations. The health of a baby is the most precious asset with which it can be endowed – immeasurably more valuable than any privilege of birth, wealth, or even education. Without health, such attributes are empty mockeries.'

The last two sentences represented both a lament for one lost child and the portent of another tragedy. Though the tone of the Duchess's speech was upbeat and optimistic, she must inwardly have been wracked by anxiety. She did not appear in person, according to her doctor, Sir George Pinker, because 'she was having health problems with her pregnancy'. So the difficulties had already begun? 'Yes.'

Even then, the Duchess did not entirely relinquish her public duties. She was at Wimbledon, as always, later in June, this time for the centenary of the championships; handing out commemorative silver medals to champions ranging from Kitty Godfree and Jean Borotra, the 1924 champions, to the previous year's victors, Björn Borg and Chris Evert.

In the following months, the pregnancy seemed to be progressing normally. Indeed, the Duke of Kent had already left for Iran – on the trip his wife was supposed to have shared with him – when George Pinker was summoned, late on the night of 4 October, to York House.

A brief statement was issued, announcing that the Duchess had suffered complications and been admitted to the King Edward VII Hospital in London, where she was resting quietly 'but still facing the possibility of a miscarriage'. The Duke, summoned home from Teheran, ran up the hospital steps the following evening, leaving his wife's bedside only to summon the one other person she might have wished to see on the bleakest day of her life.

Donald Coggan, the Archbishop of Canterbury, had also been on an overseas tour and was on his way home to Lambeth Palace when the call came through. Katharine, who had seen the solace he had offered her father in his dying months, respected Coggan for his spiritual guidance and warmth; so much so that, according to friends, he was the pastor on whose opinion she had most relied before opting for her earlier abortion. Now, at the Duke's behest, he was summoned to offer comfort after the death of a second child. Unsurprisingly Katharine was beyond Coggan's, or anyone's, consolation. For a quarter of an hour he sat on her bed, attempting to comfort her in her terrible grief, and then left.

The Duke broke the news to reporters as he left the hospital. 'She's lost her baby,' he told them briefly. Few knew then, or for many years afterwards, the extent of the Duchess's bereavement. Officially she had suffered a miscarriage in the fifth month of her pregnancy. In fact Katharine had given birth to a third son, delivered at nine months. She had asked to see him – cradling his body and registering how perfect he looked. She named him Patrick.

To this day, the Duchess mourns her child. 'It had the most devastating effect on me,' she said in a recent interview. 'I had no idea how devastating such a thing could be to any woman ... I suffered from acute depression for a while. I think it would be a fairly rare individual who didn't cave in under those circumstances. The baby was born dead at nine months. It was a horrible thing to happen.'

The only mask the Duchess could apply to her despair was one of courage. Three days later, she left hospital with the Duke, on his forty-second birthday, pausing as she departed to talk to the press. 'Thank you so very much for your concern,' she told them. 'It helped me a great deal.'

To friends she said simply: 'It is God's will.' But behind that resignation lay the unthinkable suspicion that this death, in the wake of her previous tragedy, was somehow more than that. 'The Duchess thought it was God's way of punishing her,' says someone who knows her well. It is actually unlikely that Katharine, the most Christian of women, thought of her heartbreak in Old Testament terms of sin and retribution. On the contrary, God and religion were to become one of the few forces that could give purpose to her life and assuage her loss.

But for now, she gave herself no time to contemplate the enormity of her sorrow. Instead she hurled herself back into a frenzied round of royal duty. At Winfrith in Dorset, she donned protective clothing to move nuclear fuel rods with a remote handling device. At Murton Colliery in County Durham, she spent the morning of her forty-fifth birthday dressing up in a safety helmet and donkey jacket to be lowered down a pitshaft.

She opened cancer centres and old people's homes, unveiled a stained-glass window at Chichester Cathedral, joined the Bach Choir as a soprano – a link that would provide great solace to her throughout her life – attended, as usual, the graduation at the Royal Northern College of Music and demonstrated, official functions aside, that she refused to dwell on her own sadness when others must be thought of.

Shortly after her baby died, she offered public help to Martina Navratilova, the Wimbledon champion split up from her family after she defected from Czechoslovakia in 1975. First Katharine begged the Czechs to allow Martina's mother to come to England to watch her play and, when the request was granted, invited Jana Navratilova and her daughter to tea at York House. 'Next year I hope to entertain your husband and second daughter as well,' she said.

Her wish was granted. The Duchess's lobbying persuaded the Czechs, after years of obstruction, to allow the whole family to join Martina. The champion, still only twenty-three, wept when her mother, father and sister flew out to join her in Dallas, Texas. 'It's the Christmas present I've hoped and prayed for,' she said.

Hope and prayer – the Duchess's great tools of survival – were achieving little for her. In 1978 she went back into the King Edward VII Hospital for a gall-bladder operation, shortly after cancelling a planned trip to New Zealand with the Duke. In the same year, she was unwell for the wedding of her new sister-in-law, Marie-Christine Troubridge, to Prince Michael of Kent.

The new Princess Michael's status – a formerly married Roman Catholic – might not have endeared her to the Duchess. Nor, in future years, might the queenly manner of 'Princess Pushy' or the commercial imperatives seemingly driving the media-labelled 'Rent-a-Kents'. But, of course, in normal circumstances, the Duchess would have enjoyed the civil service in Vienna town hall and the glittering dinner and ball at the Schwarzenberg Palace Hotel.

These were not normal circumstances. The Duke of Kent, best man to his brother, was, as Lord Mountbatten's private secretary, John Barratt, recorded, on splendid form. 'I have never seen the Duke of Kent look so animated,' he wrote, noting briefly the contrast in his wife. 'The Duchess of Kent was unwell.'

Although she never stopped working, stories of the Duchess's ill-health were beginning to dominate. Doctors ordered her to cut short a visit to one of her best-loved institutions, the Royal Northern College of Music, where she had planned to stay for a student production of Wagner's *Das Rheingold*. At a family dinner party, thrown by the Duke and Duchess for a few close friends, she sat, pallid and spectral, throughout the evening – a fabulously dressed but ghostly figure. Towards the end of the evening she rose and drifted silently from the room. She had barely spoken a word.

Despite encouraging noises from those around her – 'She's pitching up well,' said one relative bracingly – it was becoming clear that the Duchess of Kent was seriously ill. If ever she had needed the nurturing family she had relied on in her younger days, it was now. Instead more grief lay around the corner. In January 1979 Lady Worsley died in her sleep at Hovingham Hall.

Although she had never been as close to her mother as to her father, this latest bereavement was crushing. Katharine's brothers were scattered, her children too young fully to understand or deal with her anguish, and the royal family was instinctively, if not congenitally, programmed to be wanting in such a crisis.

In later years Diana, suicidal, bulimic and desperate, would fling herself against that barrier of incomprehension and dearth of understanding. 'There is this barrier of not accepting mental illness,' says a close friend of the Queen. 'Both the Queen and Princess Margaret are brilliant on physical health. At one family diamond wedding party – a small luncheon – one of the elderly guests went purple in the face and looked as if he was going to have a heart attack. The two of them were marvellous. Windows were opened, he was got out and help called with the minimum of fuss. They directed it all.

'But I don't think they have a conception of how to deal with nervous breakdown. I wouldn't call it uncaring. I wouldn't even say it's lack of understanding. They think it's controllable. So, if someone is a bit unpredictable, it's as if they sigh, shrug their shoulders and think: "Oh, I hope nothing awful will happen today."'

Although – or perhaps because – the Queen is rumoured by many in the psychiatric world to have been treated for depression in the sixties, she is a firm believer in the tenet that, if one is demonstrably alive, the job in hand must be tackled without demur. For the Duchess, infinitely respectful of the Queen and desperate not to embarrass or offend her, that demand, always unspoken, merely intensified the pressures on her. For far too long she fought to meet the impossible standard that she had set for herself and which, or so she believed with some justification, others had also marked out for her.

As for the Duke, no stranger to bereavement himself but schooled by his mother – a woman more royal than the royals – always to exhibit fortitude in the face of great sorrow, there is no evidence that, in the bleakest times, he was harsh to his wife or wilfully oblivious to her disintegration. Nor is there much sign that he possessed the armoury to cope with mental illness.

Years later, when the Duchess was still frail, her hosts at

an official dinner were anxious that she had barely eaten a mouthful of the special meal they had prepared for her, having been told that she was currently following a vegetarian diet. 'Oh, don't worry,' said the Duke, audibly and cheerfully. 'She never was a very good feeder.' But in the time following the loss of the Kents' last child, the problems between them vastly exceeded mere differences of personality and style.

Even those who knew of the mounting problems in the Kent marriage do not seem fully to have allowed for the seriousness of the Duchess's plight. Those beyond the inner circle of the royal family – people who knew nothing about the depth of the crisis – were, even so, inexcusably dismissive and unkind. Word got out that Katharine, on holiday in Norfolk and still mourning her baby, had developed a nesting instinct, collecting old birds' nests from the estate and filling them with eggs and scraps of cloth. Her new nickname, whispered at gatherings of the well-heeled, was 'Cuckoo'.

The insouciance or misunderstanding of some of those who surrounded her, coupled with the sheer cruelty of others, must have had a devastating effect on the sensitive Duchess. By now her husband, possibly slow initially to read the severity of her symtoms or to comprehend the depth of the problems within their marriage, was deeply concerned for her.

Katharine was readmitted to the Edward VII Hospital, and this time there was little attempt to disguise the magnitude of her collapse. Officially, she was suffering 'nervous strain', but it was abundantly clear that she had suffered a major nervous breakdown, triggered by the death of her child but born in part from stress accumulated over the years.

Long ago, instinct had told her that she was ill-suited to the rigours of royal life; its formalities, its disappointments, its politics and, above all, its demand that – come heartbreak or despair – the mask could not slip nor the performance falter. Katharine had given this existence her bravest shot. In the face of her own despair, and the chilliness of others, she had courageously worked on.

Now, in a hospital bedroom, she faced the end of the road. Except that, as she knew, there could be no conclusion. However long the intermission, her sense of duty and her religious convictions decreed that the show would have to go on. The Duke's spokesman, Commander Richard Buckley, advised that recovery would be slow. 'It will be weeks rather than days. There is no time fixed for her coming out,' he said.

Ill as she was, the Duchess refused to give in, escaping briefly to rehearse with the Bach Choir and, a few nights later, to perform with them in the London première of David Fanshawe's 'African Sanctus' before she retreated once more to her hospital bed. Seven weeks passed before she emerged, frail and leaning on her huband's arm. 'I am still a little jaded,' she told reporters apologetically. 'I'm afraid I can't stand for long.'

If the Duchess of Kent's turmoil, and the public focus on her problems, was a new and disturbing phenomenon for the royal family, it was also being rocked by other unprecedented forces. Princess Margaret, whose wedding to the Earl of Snowdon had forced the Kents to wait their turn in the marriage queue, announced that she was to divorce, among stories about her friendship with Roddy Llewellyn, a landscape gardener eighteen years her junior.

But the cataclysmic blow to the Windsors came in the August after the Duchess had been released from hospital.

On the day that fifteen British soldiers were killed in an explosion at Warrenpoint, County Down, the IRA blew a twenty-nine-foot fishing boat out of the water at Mullaghmore, County Sligo. Earl Mountbatten of Burma, seventy-nine-year-old cousin of the Queen and *de facto* paterfamilias of the royal family, was killed instantly, along with his fourteen-year-old grandson and a local boy.

Though the Duchess was not particularly close to Mountbatten, his death sealed an era of horror and bereavement. The depth of her outrage was demonstrated in the work she would do, in later years, as patron of the Royal Ulster Constabulary Benevolent Fund in Northern Ireland. Now, though still ill and in the grip of depression, she insisted on going to his funeral and the reception at Broadlands, Mountbatten's home.

There she spoke to his former private secretary, John Barratt. Not much was said, but the brief conversation demonstrated two things. The first was that the Duchess had already selected God as the prime solution to a seemingly endless tide of grief. The second is the incomprehension, bordering on contempt, that even those on the outer fringes of royalty bestow on those who fail to conform to the accepted standards of chilly stoicism.

'At one time I was buttonholed by the Duchess of Kent, who is a very sweet, kind lady,' Barratt wrote scathingly in his memoir. 'She gave me an interminable lecture about how I should not feel sad, because Lord Mountbatten's spirit was still alive and looking over me.

'I am afraid I was not in the right mood to appreciate it: I was more worried about whether there was enough tea in the teapot.'

CHAPTER THIRTEEN

A Retrievable Breakdown?

THE ALMOST MYSTICAL tranquillity with which the
Duchess of Kent learned to counter suffering was a
product of her deepening faith. That spirituality in turn
flowed from the traumas that afflicted her in the years
following the death of her father. Bereavement, and in
particular the loss of her stillborn son, has always been
regarded as the catalyst for the Duchess's nervous breakdown. In fact, Patrick's death was only one element in a
wider pattern of family misery. By the mid-seventies, the
marriage of the Duke and Duchess of Kent was on the point
of collapse.

Edward, schooled to rate public duty above private
happiness, was resigned to a miserable relationship. According to one of his closest confidants, it was Katharine –
lonely, disappointed and disillusioned – who contemplated
seeking a separation or even a divorce. This resolution would
have been deemed almost unthinkable by the Queen, who
was fully involved in the problems facing the Kents. The
Duke, as he later told his friend, discussed his future with
the Queen once it became apparent that his marriage was
breaking apart. The Queen, in turn, gave him her view. The

Duke of Kent's subsequent 'pact' (his friend's word), made with Her Majesty's full knowledge, decreed that the marriage must survive. That personal pledge, fulfilled to this day, cemented a relationship unique even by the troubled standards of royal partnerships. Ostensibly the Kents' marriage remained one of the utmost stability. Another two decades were to pass before any rumours of a rift emerged. In fact, says the Duke's friend: 'The Duke and Duchess have spent years locked in a nightmare.'

The most obvious question is what say Katharine had in this compact. By the late seventies – when her wish to escape from her marriage was at its strongest – she had been weakened, emotionally and physically, by an abortion, the death of her baby and by nervous breakdown and depression. Vulnerable, ill and at her wits' end, she was hardly in a position to manipulate events or to forge a new life for herself. In addition, she would have been loath to offend the Queen, let alone to unleash a scandal of major magnitude. More than that, as a devout woman and a leading proponent of family values, she would instinctively have been averse to declaring her marriage over. That it ever reached breaking point is a measure of the distress and pressure afflicting Katharine.

Nor is it difficult to imagine why, whatever her private sympathy with the Duchess's unhappiness, a break-up would have been anathema to the Queen. The separation of her sister, Margaret, and the Earl of Snowdon, announced in March 1976, marked the onset of the scandals that would bedevil the House of Windsor for the remainder of the century. For months previously, the precarious state of Margaret's marriage and her friendship with the twenty-seven-year-old landscape gardener Roddy Llewellyn had fed tabloid speculation. There were stories of Margaret's possessiveness, of Snowdon's chafing against the constraint of royal duty and of fierce rows, both in public and in private.

Perhaps if Margaret had been permitted to marry her great love, the divorced Group-Captain Peter Townsend, she would have lived happily. Maybe that was in the mind of the Queen, said to have handled the Snowdon marriage collapse with tact and sensitivity. Nevertheless, this episode was a huge blow. A break-up so close to the throne would have been unthinkable in a previous reign. Even in the mid-1970s, the only precedent for divorce in the royal family was that of the Queen's cousin, the Earl of Harewood, in 1967.

The ending of Margaret's marriage failed to mar the Queen's silver jubilee year, which began a few months later. Through two triumphal tours she basked in the goodwill of millions – in Fiji, in New Zealand, in Papua New Guinea, even in Australia, where the seeds of republicanism were already growing. A hundred thousand congratulations cards poured into Buckingham Palace. On Jubilee Day, the Queen lit a bonfire at Windsor – the first of a chain of beacons stretching from Land's End to the Shetlands. Towns and villages throughout the realm held street parties in a carnival atmosphere not seen since 1945. From Cornwall to the Caribbean, Her Majesty was fêted and admired. What the royal family least needed at this juncture was another separation or divorce.

In the aftermath of the jubilee celebrations, the Duchess of Kent remained so distraught at the loss of her son that she would chat about him as if he still lived. Patrick thinks that, she would tell friends, even many years later, or Patrick did that. Some judged her sorrow to be immoderate, but that was to misunderstand. Her pregnancy was not only the final attempt to have the large family she had always longed for. She hoped also – like many unhappy women pregnant with a last, late baby – that a child might somehow resurrect a marriage that appeared beyond salvation. According to a close associate of the Kents: 'This was her attempt to rescue the marriage or to keep her footing in the royal family if it [the marriage] failed. She feared she would be cast aside.'

Both in the excitement leading up to his birth and the devastation afterwards, Katharine must have asked herself constantly: Where did that marriage go wrong? From the outset, the signals had been ominous. Her parents, and in particular her mother, had been over-eager to encourage their daughter's glorious match. Marina's warnings to Edward had not been heeded. Nor had Katharine listened to her own private doubts at being pitched – just as Diana would later be – into a world she understood only enough to fear that she, emotionally needy, would be starved by its coldness. For Katharine, as for Diana, there was no induction course. 'She was given a limousine and a lady-in-waiting and told to get on with it,' says a friend of the Kents.

Although the child of a Lord Lieutenant, Katharine was also a village girl, accustomed to walking down to the village shop in jeans and wellingtons, trailing a dog on a lead. Nothing in the life of a minor public schoolgirl, an affluent débutante or a squire's daughter versed in good works had equipped her for the life to come. With the exception of her musical talent, she, possessed of only a basic education, had few resources to sustain her in an inimical environment. Practically and emotionally, Katharine was spectacularly ill-equipped for life as a royal duchess. Like Diana, she adored charity work – the only medium in which her qualities of warmth and compassion could be deployed – and her children, whom Katharine smothered with love, probably beyond a point that was good for them and for her. In any case, charity and children were not enough to sustain her.

In order to have a chance of success in her new role, Katharine needed the love, understanding, warmth and support of an emotionally literate husband. Like Charles after him, Edward was simply unable to supply this survival package. According to one of the Duke's friends, Katharine increasingly found her husband 'dull and tedious'. Certainly, as a source of consolation and empathy, Edward was severely flawed. Deprived of his own father and brought up to repress his feelings, he could not conceivably have become the sort of husband Katharine required.

But his faultline, as perceived by his wife, ran deeper than that. Put simply, he was not her father. According to one of the Duke's friends, Katharine, doted on by Sir William Worsley, expected the same undivided attention from the Duke. Edward, by training, by nature and perhaps by inclination, could not deliver that degree of nurture. As a leading clergyman and great friend of the Kents says: 'She found that he wasn't the person she wanted him to be. He didn't fulfil her expectations of a husband. He wasn't attentive enough or interested enough in what she was doing. Most of the royals don't speak to each other about anything but horses. They keep it all to themselves. But she had been daddy's darling little girl. Her father was fascinated in anything that happened to her – from a new pair of shoes to where she'd been riding. Sir William's death absolutely shattered her. His death has been one of the major influences in her life. She was his life. And when he died, and that went, Eddie didn't fill the gap. Eddie was Eddie.'

Being Eddie was not necessarily a character indictment. The Duke's friends cite a charming man beyond the austere and effete public persona. Well-read, clever and cultured, Edward Kent is regarded both by his inner circle and by the organizations for which he works as a staunch crusader for Britain's crown and for its industry. But, although brought up in a household dominated by women, the Duke remained a man's man – clubbable, a former Army officer and the centre of a small coterie of male friends. Royal to the core, he retained the emotional distance common to men of his age, class and breed. Nothing had equipped him to help dissipate the terrible problems of a wife in the throes of a nervous breakdown and mourning two lost children.

No doubt Edward also mourned them. But the differences in the way the Kents expressed their emotions meant that grieving could not be a shared experience or a catharsis through which they might have been drawn closer together. A shortfall of human response on the part of the Duke would have exacerbated Katharine's sorrow and sense of loneliness. It would also have underlined the lack of emotional succour that had affected her so deeply in the more recent years of her marriage. But that shortfall, in itself, was not sufficient to prompt the Duchess of Kent, a devout Christian and loyal member of the establishment, to contemplate the scandal of a royal separation or divorce. There was another factor.

Although the fidelity of the Duke of Kent has never been questioned, a leading clergyman and one of Edward's close friends says that the Duke reverted – prior to the near-collapse of his marriage – to the flirtatious behaviour of his bachelor days. According to his friend, that fondness for attractive women was (hardly surprisingly) an element in Katharine's dissatisfaction. In the words of the Duke's confidant: 'Eddie had a roving eye. And she found that very difficult. The marriage was under considerable strain. She was absolutely determined to have a fourth child, and when she lost that child it somehow seemed to tip the balance of her reason. One has also to understand [in Edward's case] the extraordinary pressures that members of the royal family are subjected to. They are always meeting people who are very attractive, very come hither and only too willing to have a dalliance if they can. People are very flattered by the royals and very flattering to them. This has a very beguiling effect which is not good for their spiritual health.'

Whatever the scope of the Duke's 'roving eye', it is unclear whether his flirtatiousness was an initial contributor to the marital breakdown or whether Edward looked outside his marriage for some solace and companionship after he and his wife drifted apart. Either way, first impressions suggest that the Duke of Kent was a gravely flawed husband. But that, according to those who know him well, is not a wholly fair picture.

Edward, in his friends' version a more charismatic and impressive man than public opinion has allowed of, also found himself in a situation he could not cope with. He was no better trained to deal with Katharine's maelstrom of emotions than she was for a life of royal duty. The checklist of requirements – that he be charming, attentive, funny, convivial and uniquely devoted to his wife – might have been a *sine qua non* in some marriages. Royal marriages, however, rarely approached such an ideal. Short of a personality transplant, the Duke of Kent never could have lived up to such expectations.

By the mid-seventies, there were divisions in almost every area of the Kents' lives. Katharine adored her sons and daughter with a love bordering on possessiveness. Edward, though a devoted father who has remained close to all three of his children, hesitated on the sidelines, fearful, according to friends, of pushing himself forward and so interfering in his wife's domain. Katharine would have fits of what became known in royal circles as 'the vapours' – Windsorese for depression or unhappiness – under which she would plead a headache and say that she must stay in bed. Edward would have to coax and cajole her to carry on – not skills that came naturally to a man of uncertain temper.

Although there was no question of mental or physical abuse, one friend of the Duke admits: 'I think she could construe some of his tantrums into that. He could shout. But I think he found it a tremendous strain always having to make excuses for the Duchess. It takes two to tango. There were, still are, infuriating aspects to the Duke's personality – his ability to shout; his impatience. When someone's having the vapours, you need a great deal of patience. His weaknesses were not always geared to her needs, and that did not help matters. But equally, the way she behaved was not geared to his needs. Both sides tried to keep the façade going, and in some ways that weakened the interior structure. The Duchess would be absolutely flawless in public and collapse as soon as she got home.'

If there were outward signs of the strain afflicting the Kents' marriage, they were so oblique as to be unreadable. When, in 1977, the pregnant Duchess made her anti-abortion speech to the 21st Congress of Obstetricians and Gynaecologists, her paean to the sacred nature of 'Christian family life' contained a sad undertow of irony. As she knew, her vision of that idealized model had parted company with the reality of her own existence. With other partners, she and Edward might have achieved happiness. Together they seemed capable only of increasing one another's misery. Inevitably, their closest friends held partisan views on who was to blame: Katharine – ill, unhappy and therefore demanding – or Eddie, bleeding away her self-esteem by his failure to understand her and offer her some nurture. Wherever the blame lay, the root of the problem was incontestable. The Duke and Duchess, whatever their respective merits, were so ill-matched as a couple that they had never stood a chance of even tolerable contentment. Instead they were beginning to tear one another apart.

From the sidelines, the royal family watched. Charles, unwittingly witnessing the future template of his own marriage, took little interest. Anne, according to one friend, 'was much more understanding of the Duchess, but with an attitude of jollying along'. Philip, in the same friend's version, took the unequivocal view that the Duchess was a 'silly woman', consumed by the vapours. And the Queen, while opposed to a separation, did her best to help. 'She was very concerned in the nicest way – wanting not to be judgemental or dictatorial but to offer what support she could to both,' says one of her advisers of the time. 'The difficulty was that the Queen was the last person who could help the Duchess. She is completely unemotional in that sense – someone who has been in the rudest health all her life and has no idea what mental illness means.' Despite other suggestions that the Queen has herself suffered from depression – and was therefore not operating from a standpoint of incomprehension – there is no doubt that she was not unwilling to help the Duchess. Rather she was powerless to understand a woman whose personality and nature was so at variance with her own uncompromising toughness.

In any case, the Queen had an agenda beyond the dispensation of comfort and solace. If she hoped – and she certainly did – that the Kent marriage should not totally collapse, then what might have been best for Katharine was a subsidiary consideration. Sensitive as she was, the Duchess would have been mindful that she was, in one sense, a pawn in the royal gameplan. Her reaction to the scrutiny applied to her problems by her royal in-laws seems to have divided into two parts: fear and resentment. The deference she has always shown the Queen has been tempered by a nervousness of her; hardly surprising, given the influence a monarch exerts over the lives and livelihoods of lesser royals. Katharine's resentment, though never articulated, emerged obliquely and much later in complaints to friends about financial strictures imposed on her by the palace. At the time of her first marriage crisis, Katharine, weakened by all that had happened to her, was poorly placed to challenge the might and the mood of the royal family. For much of her life she had deferred to imperious women; first her mother and then Marina. In a time of great personal turmoil, it was always improbable that the Duchess of Kent would defy the wish of the Queen.

But, even in depression and despair, Katharine Kent was not a compliant cipher, happy to capitulate to the royal consensus that she should abandon her escape plan. Faced with an impasse, the Duke of Kent turned outside his family for advice on how to salvage his marriage. If the answers could not be found at home, he must look to the royal family's second line of recourse: the Church. The man from whom he sought counsel was a shrewd, wise and trusted adviser – a graduate of Sandhurst and Harvard and the newly appointed Dean of Windsor and domestic chaplain to the Queen.

The Right Reverend Michael Mann took up his post at Windsor in 1976. The Duke of Kent approached him shortly afterwards. 'The marriage problems were synonymous with just after the Silver Jubilee. That's when they were going very strong. Certainly there were difficulties. One did what one could to help. Any feelings for a separation or a divorce would have come from the Duchess. Eddie would have plugged on, come what may. The royal family live in an era which is long since past. I remember very senior members of the family saying: "Why can't the Duke of Kent just take a mistress?"'

What passed between Mann and the Duke is a private matter, but there is little doubt that the former Dean of Windsor played a crucial role in saving the marriage. Spiritual and highly educated, Mann was also a pragmatic churchman, able to bring a clear-eyed impartiality to a problem he could see from every aspect. An admirer of Katharine's brilliance, compassion and charm, he was also aware of her private gloom, the strain her problems placed on Edward and her rejection of him as an imperfect failure, judged against the model of her father. Equally, Mann was aware of Eddie's good qualities – loyalty, a fierce devotion to public duty, love of his children – as well as his shortcomings: fits of bad temper, an inclination to flirtatiousness and a lack of patience. Although deeply fond of the Duke, Mann is unlikely to have addressed Eddie's problems with the deference of a courtier eager to massage the ego of royalty.

It is more probable that where Mann saw flaws, temporal or spiritual, in the Duke of Kent, he would have had little compunction in pointing them out. At issue was the salvation of a marriage and – given the proximity of Margaret's divorce – the continuing reputation of the House of Windsor as an upholder of Christian tradition. These were high stakes; a fact that no one knew better than the Duke of Kent. According to his close confidant, he had resolved that the marriage would endure and promised the Queen that this would be so. As for Katharine, whatever wish she had for a release was, in the face of concerted opposition and her own beliefs, a forlorn mission. Whether it would have been kinder to both the Duke and the Duchess for the marriage to end is a purely rhetorical concept.

The Queen, the Church, the reputation of the royal family and the climate of the times all decreed continuity. There were, however, no guarantees of fairytale endings. The survival of the marriage, let alone any prospect of contentment, would demand huge personal sacrifices from Edward and even greater ones from Katharine, still facing a long battle against depression.

The course on which the Kents were embarked was less an odyssey of reconciliation than the acknowledgement of a life sentence. Whether they, and in particular Katharine, would emerge from it undamaged was still unsure.

CHAPTER FOURTEEN

Depression, Drugs and the Chemical Cosh

❖

THE DUKE AND Duchess of Kent's agreement that their
marriage would survive offered predictably few instant
solutions. Depression, which continued to haunt Katharine,
had inevitable repercussions on her family. The natural
consequence of her continuing grief for her dead baby was
its effect on her living children.

Least affected of the three was Lady Helen Windsor,
aged fifteen and away at boarding school when her mother
came out of hospital in 1979. Family problems notwithstanding, Helen remained an extrovert teenager; although,
like her mother, not academic, she was talented at art and
generally regarded as gregarious, attractive and well-equipped
to deal with the schizophrenic lifestyle foisted upon minor
royals of her generation. On the one hand, they were
accustomed to fuss, protocol and holidays with the Queen.
On the other, they were expected to be normal adolescents,
destined always to be on the outside of the glass showcase.
For Katharine's children, her illness added one more dimension of difficulty. While neither of her sons, both intelligent,
provided much in the way of lurid headlines, nor were their
lives developing as planned.

George, the Earl of St Andrews, was still at Eton. After one of Katharine's stays in hospital, her first solo engagement was a visit to the school's Fourth of June celebrations, attended by most of the parents of the 1,000 pupils. 'She is very much better, and she greatly enjoyed her outing to Eton,' said a friend. But George, a shy and reticent character, was not doing well there. Instead, the fears exhibited by the Duchess when she first visited the school as a new and hyper-anxious parent had been more than confirmed. Though a King's Scholar and thus exceptionally bright, George had wholly omitted to fulfil his early promise.

'He didn't do anything wicked,' says one of his masters. 'But he had a very difficult Eton career. Not in any immoral sense; he was just completely individualistic; did his own thing all the time and refused to conform or do the things he was required to do. He did an enormous amount of reading, and he was very knowledgeable and scholarly in a way. But I think he decided the ordinary schoolwork he was meant to be doing was a bit boring and beneath him. That did produce difficulties and problems. He was one of the best people in College – and they're all very clever – and still he managed to fail the exams. No Colleger had ever done it before. He simply hadn't done the work, and he became quite a problem. It was very serious. Passing into College is a very high standard. Most people couldn't do it, and George had genuine scholarly instincts. So perhaps there was some failure on Eton's part. And maybe there was also some failure on the parents' part.'

The Duke of Kent ('not a deep thinker, although his brain is in perfect working order,' says one close friend) was simply baffled by his son's lack of progress. 'I can't under-stand it,' he told a friend after a visit to Eton. 'George can do *The Times* crossword perfectly well, but he won't do maths.' Whether or not the Duke chose to be aware of it, some of the reasons for his son's problems were obvious. George had a streak of stubbornness, and perhaps arrogance, which contributed to his unwillingness to study properly. He was also no doubt affected by his upbringing.

Katharine, worshipped by her own father, had regarded their mutually loving relationship as ideal. It was natural that she should try to replicate that bond with her children and, most of all, with her elder son. But the circumstances were different now. Much as he had favoured his daughter as the most important person in his life, Sir William Worsley had not had a bad marriage; particularly by the standards of the estranged Kents. The fact that Katharine had little bond with the Duke meant that she invested even more love and care in her children than she might otherwise have done. Although she would have drawn no distinction between the three, Katharine – who had not had a close relationship with her own mother – focused the brunt of her attention and her anxiety on her sons' progress. The counterpoint of her love and pride was that she had high, perhaps unduly high, expectations of them. Those hopes, combined with her extreme protectiveness, meant that there was, on her part, some unconscious element of control. She, as the perfect mother, no doubt expected perfect children in return.

That is not to blame or judge Katharine as a parent. She gave her family all that she could at a time when frailty and depression were making it almost impossible for her to behave and work normally. The fact that her children were her last bulwark against loneliness and therefore even more vital to her than they had been in her happier days resulted, however, in a closeness that risked becoming almost suffocating to adolescents needing to assert their independence and separateness. If the Duke of Kent had any awareness

that this was so, then he – not an expert in family psychology
– is unlikely to have intervened.

George's failure to pass his Eton exams, in the year that
Katharine had her nervous collapse, must have been the
bitterest disappointment to her. According to Kent family
friends, the expected glorious school career ended in complete ignominy. As punishment for doing so badly, George
was instructed to spend his last day at Eton french-polishing
a table, while his parents sought advice from friends about a
suitable cramming college where he might redeem himself.

After resits at the chosen crammer, he succeeded in
getting top-grade History and French A levels and went on
to read History at Downing College, Cambridge. Though
one major anxiety was over, his difficulties were not entirely
resolved. The far graver problems of Nicholas, his younger
brother, were just beginning.

'It's a sort of double tragedy,' says Lord Coggan, Nicholas's godfather, talking about the Duchess's sons. 'There's
nought for her comfort there; nought.' That is not meant as
any criticism of George or Nicholas – neither of them
unaffectionate or particularly rebellious. It is simply an
acknowledgement that, in different ways and for an assortment of reasons – from their quasi-royal status to the
difficulties inevitably resulting from a family led by a father
who was often absent and a mother who was frequently ill –
both boys faced unexpected difficulties.

Katharine's attitude to her boys seems to have been
subtly different. She was ambitious for George, the older
and cleverer and the one in whom great hopes were invested.
Nicholas was a comfort, the child who would be with her –
more than his siblings – during her years of depression and
who would brighten dark days. When Coggan retired as
Archbishop of Canterbury in 1980, she rang him – full of

the laughter and good humour so rare in the bleak times – to tell him how his godson had greeted the news. 'Nicholas said: "Mummy, I haven't got an Archbishop for a godfather any more. He's retarded."'

For now there were no suggestions that Nicholas would ever cease to be the sunny child on whom his mother relied as her chronicle of ill-health continued. That is not to suggest that Katharine was a full-time invalid. Her indomitable nature, her wish not to falter or fail in her royal role and, most of all, her desire not to disappoint those who counted on her attendance, drove her to fulfil as many duties as she could. Engagements for the hospice movement, Macmillan Cancer Relief and Leeds University were all patched into a diary still dominated by episodes of illness.

'She is still playing herself back in,' said a York House source in 1980. 'Most members of the royal family are doing three, four and five public engagements a week – some more – while the Duchess is perhaps doing two or three.' Katharine's determination not to lag too far behind in this quota system may have perpetuated the array of problems she was now suffering.

In July 1981 she attended Wimbledon with her neck in a surgical collar to correct a misplaced disc. A few months later, she appeared so tense and pale at the British American Ball at the Grosvenor Park Hotel that it seemed as if she had scarcely progressed in the past two years. 'I cannot say that she is enjoying perfect health,' said her spokesman afterwards. 'But the Duchess has not cancelled one single engagement in over a year.'

By April 1982 she was back in hospital – this time with abdominal pains, diagnosed as a benign obstruction of a bile duct which required surgery. Exactly a year later, she returned for another operation to remove an ovarian cyst.

This time she cancelled all her official engagements for two months, on the order of her doctors, and the tenor of the official statement was less upbeat. 'A longer period for recuperation than was at first expected is necessary so that her royal highness can regain her weight and strength following her operation.'

The Duchess of Kent was fifty. She had not expected her life as a royal to prove smooth or easy. But nor had she expected that the life she embarked on with great foreboding and some hope would have proved so personally ruinous. She had tried with every means at her disposal to give some perspective to her own plight – working with the Samaritans and speaking to the suicidal and desperate; turning increasingly to religion and spending time at the 'English Lourdes', the Anglican shrine of Our Lady of Walsingham in Norfolk.

Her son George, who accompanied her on one such pilgrimage, said at around the same time how glad he was 'that I am never going to have to carry out official engagements like my parents'. It was a doleful epitaph to a family that risked being torn further apart by the clash of public duty and personal misery.

The Duke made no secret of the fact that he continued to be worried about George's diffidence and patchy levels of achievement. As for Katharine, her problems were never discussed within the royal family – whether through tactfulness, reticence or a dearth of any constructive input. Nonetheless, there was much quiet sympathy for Eddie. He – in the approving eyes of his family and friends – was doing the best he could to smooth over difficulties at home and preserve a public façade of normality.

That front was about to crack. In June 1983 it was first rumoured that the official line that the Duchess was still recuperating from her operation was intended to mask her 'secret battle against depression', for which she was still receiving hospital treatment. Still she refused to give in.

On George's twenty-first birthday she was at church in Norfolk with her family, assuring reporters: 'I am very well, thank you. I am feeling much better.' But at Wimbledon the Duke was alone, returning with a bunch of yellow roses offered by Martina Navratilova, who had ridden her new bike to a nearby florist's to buy the present for her absent friend and patron.

'I am sure she will greatly appreciate them,' said the Duke, but, by then, tokens of esteem or love may have meant little to Katharine. Five days afterwards, William Hickey, in the *Daily Express*, broke the story that the Duchess was to receive more hospital treatment for depression. 'I understand this treatment may include electro-convulsive therapy, a controversial method of tackling extreme depression which can affect the memory.'

The origin of this revelation – a source from inside the Edward VII hospital – was thought by the Hickey team and the *Express* to be impeccable enough to justify running such a sensational item. It was instantly and furiously denied by the Duchess's office as 'unkind' and 'a total fabrication'.

In fact ECT, or electric shock treatment, was regularly used in the early eighties in the treatment of severely depressed patients. It was, however, a deeply controversial therapy. The medical profession could not explain how it worked, other than saying that the induction of a state similar to an epileptic fit sometimes helped to reconstruct a disordered mind. In addition, the prognosis for patients was very uncertain, and a recent report by the Royal College of Psychiatrists had highlighted major shortcomings in the way the treatment was given.

Quite aside from the risks and variables, great stigma attached to the notion of being considered for such radical intervention. Given that the royal family was at a loss to understand the nature of mental illness, let alone countenance electro-convulsive therapy, the Duchess would have been deeply upset by the rumour. One measure of her hurt is the fact that her daughter, Lady Helen, then nineteen, publicly intervened for the first time to protect her mother. The stories that she was depressed were 'nonsense', she told reporters. 'My mother is absolutely fine. She is just feeling a little bit tired.'

The *Express*'s staunch defence of its story ('We stand by every word') was of course no guarantee of its veracity. But neither, naturally enough, did the official denial or Helen's comments allow of the extent and nature of the Duchess's difficulties.

Post-natal depression after the death of her baby, family tragedy, marital breakdown and now the menopause had combined to make Katharine's life almost unbearable. Those problems were exacerbated by a further dimension, one that has never previously been disclosed. According to a leading confidante of the Duchess, the problems of the late seventies and early eighties stemmed not only from depression but also from a secret battle against dependency on the drugs used to treat her condition.

'There was a great deal more to her breakdown than was put about,' says the Duchess's friend. 'She was put on very, very heavy medication – what many would now regard as an irresponsible amount of drugs. Her difficulty was the physical problems of weaning herself off them, and she needed help. Influential and wealthy people are frequently over-prescribed – and that creates a much, much bigger problem.

'It wasn't just one drug; it was at least two she was heavily dependent on. Psychiatry in those days was the chemical cosh. And if you are prescribed heavy amounts of drugs, you don't question it, do you? You just take what you're given. The package was anti-depressants and tranquillizers – a very powerful cocktail. There was no realization then of the dangers. The Duchess eventually realized the problem herself. She stopped taking certain things of her own accord. Others were more difficult.'

Katharine's loss of her baby and her slide into depression coincided with the introduction of a new family of tranquillizing wonder-drugs. Benzodiazepines were the Prozac of the seventies – a replacement for the barbiturates so popular in the fifties and lavishly prescribed by GPs everywhere.

The dangerous side-effects of barbiturates were well-chronicled. Moderate doses led to clumsiness, extreme emotional reaction and mental confusion. Physical dependence was common and the withdrawal effects severe and unpleasant. Accidentally to take an overdose was easy and often fatal.

Benzodiazepines, such as Valium and temazepam, were erroneously seen, by contrast, as safe and effective passports to tranquillity. Bottles of pills – 'mother's little helpers' – were handed out, Smartie-like, to depressed and unhappy women across the social spectrum, from miserable mothers living on bleak council estates to royal duchessses. Even now, they remain the most commonly prescribed drugs in Britain, taken by two in every ten British women on a long-term basis.

What was not understood, in the seventies and early eighties, was the ease and speed with which users became dependent on ever higher doses, or the effects of withdrawal

– including insomnia, anxiety, nausea and sometimes convulsions and mental confusion. Many patients experience emotional numbing – an awareness of dreadful events coupled with an incapacity to deal with them. 'The withdrawal symptoms are awful. Some patients can go psychotic,' says one leading psychiatrist. At the least, long-term users often become psychologically dependent, unable to face the prospect of life without drugs. Those who do break the habit frequently have such a legacy of insomnia that they never sleep properly again.

Cutting-edge research done by Dr Peter White, of St Bartholomew's Hospital in London – unpublished at the time of writing – has established the first link between benzodiazepine dependency and ME. The women he studied had all managed to break their tranquillizer habit but found that their sleep patterns never reverted to normal. In middle age a range of causes – from infections to broken bones – triggered fibromyalgia, a type of chronic fatigue syndrome.

Long before this connection was shown, the more obvious dangers of benzodiazepines were well rehearsed. They were discovered to be so addictive that some patients became hooked in as little as six weeks.

The Duchess's problem, as described by her friend, was far from unique. Indeed, by an ironic coincidence, Andrew Burnaby-Atkins, the former boyfriend who never lost his attachment to her, endured a cycle of depression and drug dependency in the same period of his life. But though many men, and far more women, risked falling into the tranquillizer trap in the seventies and eighties, Katharine was particularly vulnerable. There had been huge pressures on her to get better; many of them emanating from her. Much as depression failed to register on the royal list of approved complaints, no one in the family articulated to her any impatience they might have felt. Even so, she would have known very well that, in a royal family where doing the job was the first imperative, her frailty would have been viewed as evidence of failure. The Duchess, a perfectionist and harshly self-critical, increased the pressure on herself; anxious that she, as a public figure, was letting down those who depended on her.

While the medical profession was then far less aware of the problems of drug dependency, the suggestion that Katharine was subjected to 'irresponsible amounts' of medication and 'a chemical cosh' in turn implies more than an eagerness to cure her condition. Implicit pressure from the royal family, as well as the high standards she set for herself, meant that too much was invested in public appearances and too little in what would be best for Katharine. The objective seems to have been normality at any price.

Whatever the extent of Katharine's supposed problem, its root was more than physical. The strain of a lonely life and the pressure of having always to measure up to her own standards of perfection, in addition to her dread of public performance, all decreed that it may have been exceptionally hard for her to escape from a vicious circle in which the stimulating or calming effect of drugs served only to increase a depression and a sense of hopelessness. Privately, courtiers suggested that prescription medicines were largely responsible for what they called the Duchess's 'bad behaviour'; the mood swings that meant she could be charming and gracious at Wimbledon one day and, on the next, petulant, difficult and inclined to throw backstage tantrums because she felt she was not being sufficiently fêted. Few of those around her recognized the terrible pressures underlying this superfically doubtful conduct. Katharine's salvation lay in the fact that she was strong enough to realize that she must, alone and with little support, fight to overcome her problem. The fact that she did not succumb, gradually emerging instead from her blackest years, suggests an extraordinary fortitude and courage. So does the fact that, even in her most miserable times, she was forced always to conceal her problems from the outside world.

For all the press reporting of her illnesses, for all the public *frisson* at every ostensible weakness, few outside her immediate family knew how deeply she had suffered or what a toll depression and medication had exacted from her. Those were private sorrows, to be borne in secret. It is hardly surprising that the woman who began to emerge from the hardest years of her life was altered beyond measure. Home, family and royal duty had been the central planks of her existence. None had brought her contentment or peace of mind. Increasingly she broadened her search for solace.

Religion, always vital to her, began to play a more significant role in her life, and her visits to the Walsingham shrine became more frequent. On her many visits to Leeds, she continued to discuss with Gordon Wheeler, the city's Catholic bishop and her early mentor, the possibility of one day converting to Catholicism. Linked with her growing spirituality was a more holistic approach to her mental and physical wellbeing. She spent some time at a health farm, Forest Mere, strolling round its grounds in tracksuit and bare feet, and she started to investigate more enlightened forms of psychotherapy.

Although he has never admitted treating Katherine, the doctor credited with helping her escape from her downward spiral of misery is Maurice Lipsedge, of Guy's Hospital, in London, regarded by his peers as pre-eminent in his field. 'He's a bloody good doctor – the one I'd go to,' says one of Britain's leading psychiatrists. 'A mainstream, orthodox psychiatrist with a very, very good reputation.' Within the royal family, Lipsedge's stock was equally high. Years later he was said to have treated Diana for her eating disorders and other mental problems induced by her failed marriage.

There was nothing magical about Katharine's treatment. The basic management of depression, unchanged in thirty years, is a three-pronged system of therapy. First the physical element: drugs, and for very severely affected or delusional patients, electro-convulsive therapy. Then the psychological dimension: cognitive therapy or counselling. And finally an investigation of the social contributors, such as work and marriage.

For possibly the first time, Katharine may have been forced to confront catalysts other than the death of her baby. The insecurity she felt as a public performer, the fact that the Duke – even though he made continuing efforts to relate to her problems – was on a quite different emotional wavelength. All of this she had to come to terms with.

It was obvious that she was making headway and that her family were doing their utmost to help her. Helen became a temporary lady-in-waiting as the Duchess returned to public life, and Nicholas, by then thirteen, flew with her to Toronto in August 1983 for a two-week holiday at Stockingtop, the ranch owned by her brother, John.

Still worn, thin and pale, Katharine smiled seraphically for the airport photographers and cheerfully fielded questions about her health. 'I'm feeling just fine,' she said. 'Nicholas and I are going away – just the two of us – away from it all.' But release was not to be so simple.

Alhough her current cycle of ill-health was almost at an end – she returned to hospital the following year for one last operation, this time for a hernia – other problems loomed. Nicholas, a small, placid-faced boy standing at his mother's side, in a neat tweed jacket and collar and tie, had been her great source of consolation and encouragement through her time of depression. If she had known how their roles would one day be reversed, and how her son would, in his turn, suffer, that knowledge would have caused the Duchess to despair once more.

But for the moment it seemed that the hardest days were over. Throughout her illness, the Duke had accompanied her on the sunshine holidays she loves – once to Greece and frequently to Mustique, Princess Margaret's favourite haunt. Following her hernia surgery, the Duke and Duchess flew out to the Caribbean island.

If scarcely a second honeymoon, their break had all the hallmarks of a fresh start in life. The Duchess paused on her return to convey some of her new *joie de vivre* to reporters monitoring, as ever, her state of health. 'We had mixed weather, but we still had time to build a few sandcastles,' she said. 'We had a marvellous holiday and, despite the weather, I still managed to get a nice tan.' Even her outfit suggested a woman revitalized and reborn, no longer an invalid and once again the fashion icon of old, elegant in tight black leather trousers and a check shirt. She clutched a bouquet of flowers from a wellwisher, and her smile was radiant.

Beside her the Duke, not known for even tepid displays of public emotion, grinned too, possibly with the relief of a man who believed that, after all the gloom and anxiety, his wife had been restored to him. She looked as she used to look, smiled as she always had. But the Duchess of Kent had no wish to recapture the insouciance of long ago. She was emerging from her travails as a woman with a fresh purpose and a new mission.

CHAPTER FIFTEEN

Only Queens Wear Crowns

❦

As KATHARINE SLOWLY returned to health, she began to pick up the threads of her charity work. Though always an interested and a compassionate patron, her efforts now had an almost evangelistic fervour, coupled with a high public profile she would once have shrunk from.

In 1983 David Nicholas, the then editor of ITN, held a dinner party at the television company's headquarters for the Duke and Duchess of Kent. On the guest list was the reporter Martyn Lewis, a proponent of relaying 'good news', who had just completed a film about hospices for the dying with the help of the Duchess of Norfolk, founder of a new charity to support the movement.

Despite Lewis's personal crusade – his mother-in-law had been cared for in a hospice before she died – Nicholas was sceptical about the news value of his project. 'It will never get on the bulletin,' he said. Lewis's film would, nonetheless, no doubt provide some opportunity for polite small talk over dinner, since Katharine Kent, patron of Macmillan Cancer Relief, also had an interest in the hospice movement. The ITN hosts had underestimated the Duchess's passion. Enraptured by finding someone in the media whose concerns tallied with her own, she began to pour out to Lewis her experiences of hospices in general and, in particular, Helen House, near Oxford – the world's first hospice for children. Once or twice a week, she said, she would drive over, put on a volunteer's uniform and help look after the dying children under the care of Mother Frances Domenica, an Anglo-Catholic nun. She sought no publicity, she said. She merely loved the place and wanted to do what she could to assist.

For an hour the Duchess spoke to Lewis, almost oblivious to the other guests. By the end of the dinner it was obvious that his prospects of publicizing the hospice movement on prime-time television were not so bleak after all. Tentatively, Lewis asked whether Katharine might allow herself to be filmed with the children. 'Only if it will help Helen House,' she said, but she was clearly eager to go ahead, explaining that the hospice movement had a bad image and that people should know far more about the work. 'Then they would see that it's not all about death and dying.'

The hospice itself was happy to participate. Only the private office of the Duke and Duchess seemed hesitant. The implication was that senior courtiers retained private doubts about Katharine, fragile and not noted for her stability, taking on such a high public profile. Nevertheless it was agreed that the filming would go ahead, on the agreement – a condition stipulated by the Duchess – that the material would only ever be shown once, in order to avoid any possibility that parents of dying children might feel themselves exploited.

Katharine, always a star performer in front of the camera, agreed that she would become the first member of the royal family to wear a radio microphone – slipped into a pocket of her green smock and able to pick up every word she said. The camera was not only kept at a distance but also introduced the day before, so that the children could play with it and become used to its presence before the filming started. The result, a startling departure from any previous royal publicity campaign – was mandated to run at an unprecedented eight and a quarter minutes on *News at Ten*.

The exercise was successful. Viewers, touched by the children's plight and Katharine's genuine and immense empathy for them, wrote 200 letters a day to York House, enclosing donations ranging from children's fifty-pence pieces to cheques for £500. More than £10,000 was raised in the forty-eight hours after transmission, and by the following year the gifts totalled £100,000 – a testament not only to the courage of the dying but also to that of the woman who had overcome so much to help them and who clearly still suffered private anguish.

Though designed to be an altruistic exercise, the film was also a remarkable self-portrait of Katharine. She was not, it was clear from the footage, a volunteer like any other. Certainly she was warm and compassionate, but the regal presence was unmistakable. Swapping earrings with a little girl called Susan, treated with morphine and dying of an inoperable brain tumour, Katharine reminded her of how she had previously asked to borrow her 'duchess earrings' and how she had asked, on an earlier visit, whether she wore a crown. 'Darling, I told you: Only queens wear crowns.'

'Do you live with the Queen?' Susan asked. 'No, although I do live nearby. I couldn't live with her. I'd get in her way. She's so busy,' the Duchess said charmingly. Only those closest to her might have picked up the irony of the fact that the Queen may indeed have regarded Katharine's past troubles as an obstacle to the smooth running of the royal family.

There was a cuddle for one child, a piano lesson for a second and for a third, twelve-year-old Nicola White – destined, like her four-year-old sister, Kerina, to die of a congenital wasting disease – the gift of a doll and a promise that the Duchess would borrow a swimsuit and splash with her in the jacuzzi. Pale, beautiful and serene, Katharine seemed to be possessed of a mystical quality. As she admitted in an interview at the end of the piece, the compact with Helen House had much to offer her. 'I feel privileged and humble, drained sometimes, terribly drained, because you give an awful lot. I have never felt sad. After I had been here four or five times, it suddenly dawned on me how tears and smiles walk side by side. It is extraordinary . . . Bereavement and happiness walk side by side so often.'

The subtext of what she said could not have been clearer. She who had suffered loss and bereavement could learn from the children's example of hope in the face of death. She could sublimate her own misery in the contribution she was able to make to the ebbing hours and weeks of their lives. By sharing in their courage, she was able to rationalize her own unhappiness and assuage the guilt imposed by her sense of failure. The further sadness, unspoken of course, was that the Duchess of Kent was able to find, among the dying, a tranquillity that always eluded her at home.

There was another unarticulated message. The Helen House documentary signalled the new role she wished to forge for herself and marked a revolution in her relationship with the royal family. 'Only queens wear crowns.' It was more than a casual remark to a dying child.

Only the month before, Katharine had represented the

Queen in the Channel Islands, reading her message of reconciliation to a congregation of 3,000 islanders celebrating, with prayers and champagne, the fortieth anniversary of their liberation from German occupation. She fulfilled her quota of royal engagements and continued to travel abroad with her husband. It was clear, nonetheless, that much had changed. Katharine, her friends believed, was developing an increasingly ambivalent attitude to a royal family that had viewed her illness less as an almost inevitable consequence of tragedy and strain than as proof of her unreliability.

Though Katharine remained immensely respectful of, and over-awed by the Queen, her relationship with Philip, if ever warm, could not have remained so after his dismissive attitude to her depression. Charles she liked, albeit with reservations. 'She sometimes found him difficult,' says one friend. 'She found him hard to deal with on occasions and didn't know where he was coming from. In general, she feels, and has always felt, that she is a bit of an outsider.' But whatever Katharine's view of the personalities within the family, it was obvious that she was being marginalized principally by simple demographics.

The Queen's children were growing up into their natural role as ambassadors for the Crown. In addition, a new star was now centre stage. Even before her wedding in 1981, Diana and the Duchess of Kent had struck up a friendship based on their uncanny similarities. Both had held deep reservations about marrying into the royal family – Katharine because she was unsure that her affection for the Duke would provide sufficient counterweight for the trials of royal duty, and Diana because she already suspected that Charles's love for Camilla Parker Bowles would not be discarded at the altar.

Katharine saw herself as a sort of big sister to Diana –

someone who could teach the newcomer the rules of the game, in much the same way as Marina had instructed her. Diana's problems, manifested by bulimia even before her marriage, developed earlier than Katharine's, but both suffered the same dangerous lowering of self-esteem and the incomprehension directed at them by a family out of tune with mental anguish.

'I understood Diana very well, for obvious reasons,' Katharine said in an interview with the *Daily Telegraph* after her death. 'I understood the difficulties as well as the advantages, and we kept in touch through thick and thin. That is what friendship means.' In the revised version of Andrew Morton's biography, based on taped conversations with the Princess, Diana is quoted as saying: 'Feel sorry for her [the Duchess of Kent]. Would look after her if I had to.' That comment goes to the paradox in the notion that Katharine – so damaged during her life as a royal – should appoint herself protector-general of the young Diana's interests. If there was a route to security and happiness for an imported spouse, then Katharine had neither been shown it nor discovered it for herself.

By the time of the Helen House film, the two women were corresponding regularly. Though worried about the developing problems in Diana's marriage, Katharine was also struck by her success outside it. Again, there was a similarity in their situation. Just as Diana garnered all the adulation that Charles felt was his due, Katharine, charming and beautiful, eclipsed the saturnine public front of the Duke. Both had a genuine sympathy with the old and with children, a warmth enhanced by private suffering. Both played well to the camera – Diana with a more manufactured star presence, Katharine with effortless spontaneity.

Some have suggested that Katharine grew to resent the

younger woman's stardom and was particularly distressed that, after all her tireless and mainly unsung work for the hospice movement, its high profile was actually delivered by Diana's headline-grabbing visit in which she held the hands of an AIDS patient. But Katharine was not jealous. Rather, the impact Diana was having gave her a further clue as to what her survival strategy should be. Effortlessly, Diana was upstaging a royal family made to look dull and anachronistic in comparison to her more luminous presence. If warmth and human kindness were the new currency, then few could deploy them as successfully as Katharine Kent.

Uncalculating as she was, the irony implicit in the shifting of power cannot have passed her by. Just as she emerged from her suffering and just as she foresaw that she would inevitably be shuffled towards the margins of the family, here was an opportunity to do work she loved while becoming a serious and a leading player in her own right. Katharine saw her opportunity less as a chance to score points off the royal family – although that may have occurred to her – than as a chance to distance herself from a clan from whose damaging thrall she had been unable so far to escape. After all the wilderness years, the Duchess of Kent was finding her public role at last.

Even on low-profile occasions, Katharine's charity work had a dramatic quality. Some time after the Helen House film, Martyn Lewis followed her round another hospice, this time in the Midlands. 'Her staff despaired,' says one observer. 'The visit overran by hours. She sat for ages on patients' beds, and, when she moved on, her lady-in-waiting handed the dying person a china angel. Those people were utterly transformed. When she goes round a hospice, there is a religious feel about it which one cannot put into words.'

Increasingly, the Duchess trained a spotlight on her

work. Not every week, nor even every year, for much of what she did was clouded in obscurity. She was, however, happy to move out of the purdah of minor royal duty when the opportunity arose. Left to her own devices, she might have moved much further. Throughout the eighties she continued to tell close friends that, if she had the opportunity, she would prefer to leave her marriage and start afresh. Courtiers, aware of her wishes, believed that she did not have the gumption to go. But courage was not the issue. The cage that contained Katharine was a multi-barred one, constructed of her beliefs, her sense of duty, her love of her children and – at some level – her undoubted fondness for royal privileges.

And still she clung to dreams of freedom, unable wholly to draw a distinction between fantasy and practicality. Widely travelled and an accomplished public performer, Katharine, even in her fifties, had only an imperfect knowledge of real life and the real world. For most of her years she had lived a secluded and privileged existence; first as someone's daughter and then as someone's wife. Of course she had learned some of the tricks of self-survival. If not, she could never have pulled herself out of the darkest periods of her illness. Even so, the capacity for true independence was not in her repertoire. Practical as she was, she had never lived alone, forged a career, paid a gas bill or completed a tax return. The theatre of royal life offered, to women of Katharine's generation, no door marked Emergency Exit. As she must have known, she was, despite all her chafing, almost compelled to remain. All she could hope for then was a taste of independence and a modicum of freedom. Those, at least, were within her grasp.

Three years after her Helen House success, Katharine was back in front of the television cameras. Lewis, whom she trusted and who had orchestrated her first major foray in broadcasting, had now joined the BBC, and she agreed to do a piece for the *Nine O'Clock News*. This time the beneficiary was Age Concern, one of her favourite charities, which was launching a campaign, known as 'Breaking the Ice', to persuade people to become good neighbours to one million British pensioners living below the poverty line.

Katharine had been horrified the previous year when a hospital she was visiting laid on a reception deemed appropriate to royalty. Outside, elderly patients were lined up on park benches, wrapped in blankets to protect them from the freezing wind. By the time she arrived, they were shuddering with cold and barely able to mutter a rehearsed welcome. 'That's it,' she told her staff. 'I shall not let another winter go by without moving the situation on a bit.'

As usual, her contribution was hands-on. Wearing a dogtooth suit and yellow cashmere scarf, her hair pulled back into a ponytail, Katharine was filmed rushing up and down basement steps, pouring tea from a Thermos flask and playing darts at a club for the elderly. 'Keep well out of the way, won't you?' she warned as she aimed for the board.

In a dank flat with paper peeling from the ceiling, Lily Pibbins, in her eighties, explained that she always slept in her armchair because she could not move to her bedroom or manoeuvre her wheelchair to the bathroom. 'We must help you. I promise we shall see that a lot is done,' said Katharine, washing up her coffee cup with a rag in the sink. As many of her charities have found, occasionally to their anxiety, part of her strategy is never to opt for cosmetic reassurance when concrete action is required. Told by one pensioner that Age Concern used to send her a home help, Katharine said firmly: 'They will carry on doing that.'

If, at Helen House, she had been a royal presence, this time there was a grittier side to her contribution. Whether she was expressing horror that an old woman could only wash herself in her steel kitchen sink or explaining to another that she too suffered from bad circulation, the unspoken suggestion was that she was one of them. The pensioners she met treated her as such. Most addressed her as 'dear'. One old man reminded her: 'I had the pleaure of driving you in my taxi once. I had a chat with you about your wedding. You have been in taxis, haven't you?'

'Oh, often,' said the Duchess. The following week she was back in her official car, travelling to a community care centre in Lambeth, South London. This time there was no audience to play to, but her manner was entirely unaltered. An old woman called Lilian wept at her arrival, convinced that any unknown visitor heralded an attempt to take her away from her son and put her into a home. 'Who is it?' she said suspiciously. 'The Duchess of Kent. Don't know her. Never heard of her.'

Katharine crouched beside her, hugging her and pulling out her own handkerchief to dry her tears. From her bouquet she plucked one peach rose, pinning it to Lilian's mauve cardigan. 'You needn't be frightened,' she said. 'I promise you no one will ever take you away from your son. This flower is to promise you that.' Katharine, of course, had no way of knowing that this pledge could be honoured. No doubt she believed, probably rightly, that the most important thing she could do was to offer some reassurance to a confused old woman. Some years later, during her visit to India, aid workers would be exasperated by a promise made by the Duchess to an elderly petitioner of some assistance that could not be delivered. But, if her own belief – battered but intact – in happy endings occasionally drove Katharine to offer too much, she also had a genuine understanding of how people lived and how they might best be helped.

During her visit to the Lambeth centre – one of thousands of similar engagements – her manner switched easily from that of compassionate comforter to brisk home help. 'Now, you've got arthritis in your hands,' she said to one man. 'How do you manage to get the tops off jam jars? And what have you had for lunch?'

'Mince,' he said. 'Spaghetti bolognese,' a helper corrected him. 'Oh yes,' said Katharine, laughing at this echo of enforced politesse woven through her other existence. 'You must always make sure you use the posh words.'

Though increasingly known for a public and highly gracious endorsement of worthy causes, Katharine was also happy to puncture the stuffiness attaching to royalty. In 1987 it was revealed that a small money-making scheme of the Queen's – allowing holidaymakers to pick their own fruit on the Sandringham estate – had attracted the custom of the Duchess of Kent. Dressed in jeans and a jumper, Katharine toiled away in the royal blackberry patch along with other visitors until she had gathered 30lb of blackberries at 35 pence a pound. Having handed over her £10.50, the Duchess departed to do some preserving or jam-making. 'It's perfectly reasonable for the Duchess to go blackberrying at Sandringham,' said her spokesman, adding, no doubt tongue-in-cheek: 'After all, she has a very small garden herself in Norfolk – it's only about ten acres.'

But implicit in her expedition were two messages. The first was how much she relished occasionally shaking off the shackles of royalty and the second a small pointer to the fact that she was not, in her view, terribly wealthy or over-privileged. Friends believed that the fruit-picking – like her habit of hailing a black cab to go clothes-shopping – was not only a matter of practicality. It was also a gesture of defiance against the more irksome aspects of a royal existence.

On more serious matters, Katharine was increasingly establishing herself as her own woman. For years one of her favourite causes had been the Samaritans and its international arm, Befrienders International. Though she remains patron of both organizations, her great burst of activity followed her own breakdown; evidence, some thought, that she herself had recourse to the Samaritans' helplines in the darkest times. Whether or not that is true, she began to make herself regularly available to listen to the outpourings of the suicidal and the despairing.

In June 1987 it was revealed that she had temporarily stopped, after news of her involvement raised fears that lines would be blocked by the curious wishing to speak to her. 'Calls of that kind could cost lives,' said Simon Armson, the Samaritans' assistant general secretary. 'We have not said at which of our 101 branches Her Royal Highness has been working. In any case, she is not taking calls at the moment.'

Rather than waiting for the fuss quietly to die down, Katharine decided that, now her cover was blown, she would best serve the Samaritans by going public on the extent of her involvement. In an interview with the magazine *Royal Monthly*, she talked about those who had sought solace from her.

'Often a child will ring up pretending to be an adult,' she said. 'They use their parents' situation to describe their own problems. It's very common for young people to ring up, lose their courage and put the receiver down. Some ring again; others freeze in an anguished silence. We sometimes hold the line for two or three hours, saying occasionally: I'm still here if you want me. You simply try to put yourself in their position. I don't believe there's anyone in the world who has not suffered something. All of us have had some cross to bear, and it's through these experiences that one learns empathy and compassion.' Despair, she added, was not confined to a domestic setting. 'We go to pop festivals where you can find misery and isolation as well as more specific problems, such as drug addiction.'

If this was an oblique reference to her own experience of tranquillizers, then the wider message again linked back to her worst days. 'All of us have some cross to bear . . .' The entirety of her message echoed what she had to say at Helen House; that, in her view, an alchemy existed to forge hope from the most desperate of circumstances and that her role was to highlight that process.

The messianic edge to Katharine's work did not last. A decade later, she gave an interview in which she appeared to revise not only the wisdom of publicizing the plight of the dying but also her more private intervention. By then she believed that it was possibly wrong and disrespectful for someone in her position to push herself into someone's life at a time when they and their families were having to come to terms with a life-threatening illness. Care and visiting of the sick should, she said, be left to trained staff or to close family members.

This represented a total volte-face from the public carer and the distributor of china angels; a very honest acknowledgement, perhaps, that she – so newly recovered from breakdown – might have appeared to have an almost morbid preoccupation with the suffering of others. If so, she was judging herself harshly. Certainly Katharine's great involvement, in the eighties, with the dying and the despairing followed directly on from her own experiences of bereavement and heartbreak. Although she did not sever any of her patronages, she was never again to play such a high-profile role in the Samaritans or the hospice movement. But the Duchess's decision to distance herself from the dying does not imply any previous exploitation of their suffering to defuse her own. Rather, it suggests some acknowledgement that the role of deathbed comforter was a dangerous compact for her. In giving so much genuine compassion, Katharine invariably left herself exhausted and emotionally burned out, compounding the difficulties in her own family life.

In the last few minutes of her Helen House film, Katharine herself alluded to the uneasy balance between her role as public carer and that of royal spouse. Katharine spoke of the final hours of a dying child she had seen shortly before she was due to leave for a tour of Australia with the Duke of Kent. As she told viewers, she had promised Gavan Byrne a last visit. 'I had been seeing a child who came here last April. I had a feeling that I must see him before I went,' she said. 'My husband said I would never get back to catch the flight [to Australia].

'I went to Great Ormond Street Hospital at 6.30a.m. and talked to Gavan. I asked him, did he remember that I was going to Australia? He remembered and reminded me that he had asked me to bring him back a koala bear. So I gave him mine. I told him to keep it in case I didn't have time to go shopping, because sometimes I am very busy. He said: "Thank you very much, Your Royal Highness." Just as I was getting on to the plane to go to Australia, I heard that he had died that morning. He had said to me beforehand: "I know that I am going to die. I'm not afraid. I only hope I'm not around when it actually happens." He died a happy little child.'

Her account, moving as it was, also contained an insight into her domestic life. Although she certainly did not hint at tension, the scenario she painted contrasted a Duchess visited with a premonition that she must make one last dawn visit to a child's sickbed with a Duke preoccupied only with the mechanics of setting off on a major royal tour.

Some husbands, in these circumstances, might have reassured their wives that there would be plenty of time and that a mission to console the dying must of course take precedence. The Duke, in his wife's account, said simply: 'You'll miss the flight.'

Taken in isolation, that small remark meant nothing. It was, however, the first time that Katharine had hinted obliquely at the differences in the marriage. What sort of a man, the subtext suggested, would treat a matter of life and death with such apparent carelessness? Almost in the manner of a prisoner tapping out morse signals, Katharine appeared to be sending out a codified message that her serene existence was not as it seemed.

CHAPTER SIXTEEN

Two Funerals and a Wedding

THE DUKE AND Duchess of Kent celebrated their silver
wedding at St James's Palace and in a style reminiscent
of its early Hanoverian occupants. Crimson, cream and
golden staterooms were filled with flowers and silver birches.
The after-dinner concert programme, decorated with a silver
tassel, specified Julian Bream, the guitarist, playing Bach and
Granados, Sir Yehudi Menuhin performing, with children
from his school, part of Brahms's sextet in G major, and
Dame Janet Baker, who sang five songs.

Although the Kents, then receiving around £130,000
from the Civil List, did not – as they frequently let it be
known – consider themselves by any means affluent, this
was not an occasion for economy. Underlying the lavishness
of the party was the signal that their marriage, twenty-five
years old, constituted a success and a cause for celebration.

Calibrated on the measure of the modern royal marriage,
their union was indeed something of a public triumph.
Princess Margaret and Lord Snowdon had already parted, in
the vanguard of a spate of divorces that would afflict the
next Windsor generation. As one leading churchman put it:
'I have never heard a whiff of scandal about the Kents.'

Katharine and Edward remained united, if only by a mutual determination that the façade of their marriage should remain, in so far as possible, publicly intact. Increasingly, they were pursuing separate lives. Their interests, music apart, had always been divergent. Edward, a soldier and an outdoor man, was an expert skier. Katharine, nervous and accident-prone, was better known for the bruises and breaks she incurred. She was a devout Anglo-Catholic, he the chief Freemason. She adored the world of academia; he was at his most relaxed in male dining clubs.

Even those close to the Duchess and who understood the tensions underlying the obvious differences between the Kents were – and remain – loath to attribute blame. As Lord Coggan, the Duchess's friend, says: 'I don't know what their relationship is. But put yourself in Katharine's shoes. You go to a cancer ward or something, you give yourself totally, and you are adored by everyone there. Then you get into this glorious car, drained, and you go back home and depression comes. It's pretty tough on both partners, isn't it?'

Although that balanced view is perfectly sustainable, there is no evidence that the Duke had managed to transform himself into a paradigm of gentle understanding. Others point to quasi-public slights delivered by Edward. The society photographer Brodrick Haldane once told of how he overheard Katharine, at a function for children, bewailing the fact that she had left her teddy bear in the official car. 'Shut up,' said the Duke, sharply.

At the Kents' silver wedding party, no tension was on display. Furthermore, it would be wrong to suggest that they had failed to achieve some sort of *rapprochement*. In public, they still appeared frequently together. In private, they continued – when their schedules allowed – to meet up over an omelette or a scrambled egg lunch at their apartment.

Indeed, despite the intensity that drove her charity work, Katharine appeared by the late eighties to have recaptured her *joie de vivre* and interest in frivolity. A guest who attended one the Kents' dinner parties remembers it as a relaxed occasion, though segregated on the gender lines, according to the strict conventions of the aristocracy. When the women retired, the Duchess – content at being removed from more formal debate – steered the rest of the evening's conversation towards shopping and, in particular, duvets. 'It was when we were all deciding whether we should swap our blankets and sheets for continental quilts,' said her guest. 'The Duchess was all for duvets.'

Shopping remained a passion for Katharine. In particular she enjoyed commissioning the clothes necessary to her new, high-profile lifestyle. In her book *Fighting Fashion*, Helen Storey, the former British designer of the year, recalls the Duchess's almost childish delight at a trip to Belville Sassoon, where Storey, then a relatively junior employee, was involved in dressing the Duchess – whom she nicknamed, after her favourite colour and to protect her identity, Yellow Ma'am.

'I sat drawing at my table . . . I felt an itch at my feet but, alone in the room, couldn't place the irritation. I bent down, my cheek squashed on the table-top, my arm reaching to scratch. My hand came across another one, of a much softer texture. Fingers were rippling, childlike, on the arch of my foot. I jumped back and met Yellow Ma'am's soft, powdered face on the opposite side of the desk – a dismembered, yet happy vision. "Hello, Helen," she said cheerfully.'

While no one could imagine the Queen playing a similar prank at Norman Hartnell, the Duchess's fondness for jokes never eclipsed the minutiae of dressing as protocol demanded. On one occasion, Storey was asked to stand by as three chairs were lined up in a row to simulate a car. David Sassoon, the designer, sat in the front seat as 'driver', with the Duchess behind him – opening an imaginary door and beckoning Storey into a crouching position.

'Can you see anything as I do this?' she asked.

'No, Ma'am.'

'Good,' said the Duchess, finishing her cup of tea and preparing to leave for her next appointment, as a seamstress explained to the perplexed Storey what the car charade signified. 'Fanny check,' she said.

Although constrained by the sartorial restrictions – modesty, conservatism and practicality – of royal dressing, Katharine was peculiarly fascinated by matters of style. 'She milked every glamorous opportunity she could, and she was always very up on what was happening in fashion,' says Storey. 'She was quite clear on her own style. Long skirts and tailored jackets just above the knee; those proportions suited her body very well. Occasionally she would see something she liked in the main collection, but on the whole her itinerary was so specific that one would design for the occasion.'

After Sassoon had ordered fabrics and colours specified by the Duchess, she would ring in advance, so that the studio could be cleared before she arrived with her detective. Storey would sketch designs as Katharine looked over her shoulder. 'She used to ask for my drawings so that she could take them home with her. Sometimes she'd bring them back with a line on here and there. She loved drawings, in the same way other people like photographs.'

The result, ten outfits a year, formed the backbone of Katharine's official wardrobe. Like Diana, who also patronized Belville Sassoon, she would buy from the Emanuels, designers of the Princess of Wales's wedding dress. In addition, Katharine shopped at Zandra Rhodes and at Caroline Charles – later a favourite of Cherie Blair. Underwear, in a rare concession to budgetary constraints, came from Marks & Spencer.

The assumption (not necessarily correct according to courtiers who later viewed the Duchess's dress bills as evidence of borderline shopaholism) was that Katharine had an 'arrangement' with her favourite designers, under which a couture outfit would be sold for far less than the retail price. But, whatever the outlay, Katharine's view remained that beautiful clothes were vital to the job. So was elegantly coiffed hair, styled in a formal chignon or a ponytail, depending on her mood. Twice a week, Katharine visited David, of David and Josef, a small salon in Berkeley Square also patronized by Princess Margaret, for a shampoo and blow-dry behind screens pulled round her to shield her from the rest of the clients.

On her way home, she might window-shop for cosmetics – beguiled, as she has always been, by the latest shade of lipstick or a new wonder brand of face cream. Or she might wander into Russell & Bromley for shoes, undeterred by once having had her handbag snatched by a teenage couple in a Mayfair branch of the store.

For such an other-worldly woman, Katharine has always had a strong streak of vanity, reinforced in part by her interest in style and in part by the fact that, even in those times when she could do nothing about inner turmoil, she could compensate by ensuring that her appearance was never less than perfect. According to Princess Margaret, not a competitor in the fashion stakes, she has always been one of the best-dressed royals; perfectly styled whatever the occasion.

On 19 June 1986, a week after her silver wedding

celebrations, the Duchess wore black silk. The razzmatazz of the previous days was forgotten as 100 mourners gathered at the church of St Nicholas, in Kelvedon Hatch, Essex, for the funeral of Olivia Channon. Olivia, a brilliant Oxford undergraduate killed by a drugs overdose, was not only the daughter of one of the Duke's most trusted confidants, Paul Channon, the Conservative Secretary of State for Trade and Industry. She was also a friend to the young Kents, another silver-spoon child raised in the best educational establishments and the smartest social circles. Lady Helen Windsor, a confidante of Olivia's and a former schoolmate, walked from the church with tears on her face.

Deeply as Katharine grieved for the Channons, she must also have felt a *frisson* of fear for her own children. Helen had already provoked a stream of lurid headlines, stemming from a set of topless photos taken on a Corfu beach. 'Melons', as she was thereafter known – much to her disgust – also smoked Marlboro, changed boyfriends frequently and lived on the margins of a coterie of rich young socialites, described by the Duke of Kent as 'louche'.

Both Kents were said to be worried over Helen's presence at parties where LSD and heroin were taken freely; though never by her. Katharine's Samaritan experience and her knowledge of the effects of drugs made her, it was also claimed, so anxious for her daughter that their relationship began to freeze.

Olivia Channon's fate shocked Helen terribly. So did the death soon afterwards of another close acquaintance, Henry Tennant – a companion from family holidays on Mustique and the first of her friends to die of AIDS. But even before these tragedies, the indications were that Helen was actually destined to be the least problematic of the Kents' children.

By her early twenties, she was settled into what she

described as a 'serious career' at the Karsten Schubert art gallery and living in an Ebury Street flat she rented with an old schoolfriend, after confessing to another acquaintance, in a tactful understatement: 'It's been a bit of a strain being at home all the time.' Unlike her brothers, she had no academic pretensions, leaving Gordonstoun with one A-level in art and adding a second, in history of art, after a year at a crammer.

Intellectually, and in appearance, Helen was her mother's daughter. Like her, she devoted some of her youth simply to having fun. Like her, she developed a rigid sense of propriety and duty. Aside from a few minor and early indiscretions, she emerged as the star in a generally murky constellation of younger royals. The Duke, who had always adored her and had relied heavily on her assistance when Katharine was at her most troubled, called her 'my perfect daughter'. The Duchess, also indebted to the strength she had shown throughout her breakdown and aware that any disputes over conduct were over, loved to have Helen drop in for breakfast or lunch at home. Out together, at Katharine's charity functions, they would stroll arm-in-arm, their closeness a proof that the Duchess, despite – or, more probably, because of – devoting less anxious attention to Helen than to her sons, had contrived to build a less troubled relationship.

Helen was not at her mother's side for the second funeral of 1986. On a bright spring day, senior royal mourners, led by the Queen, watched Wallis, Duchess of Windsor, laid to rest at her husband's side under a plane tree overhanging the royal burial ground at Frogmore. After half a century of exile, Wallis Simpson was home, in the adopted country that had spurned the woman who had lured away their King. Fourteen years had passed since David died, leaving

Wallis to a desolate widowhood shared, in her final, infirm years only with a few devoted household staff.

Her will left only two bequests for the royal family: a piece of jewellery each for the Duchess of Kent and Princess Alexandra, in a last acknowledgement by David that, despite the estrangement caused by his marriage to Wallis, George – the father of Alexandra and Edward – had been the brother he loved the best.

The funeral merited no pomp, no ceremony and no tears. It was, instead, the final epitaph to a marriage whose seismic consequences to the monarchy flowed from the disastrous history of the bride: an American and a divorcée.

Although much had changed in the intervening years, and although George St Andrews, elder son of the Duke of Kent, was only seventeenth in line to the throne, his announcement – some months after Wallis's funeral – that he wished to marry also caused disquiet within the royal family. Sylvana Tomaselli, to whom he got engaged in 1987, was Canadian, Catholic, divorced and, at twenty-nine, five years older than her future husband.

Unlike Helen's, George's life had not moved smoothly. By now, his reputation as royal intellectual – dented by his disastrous Eton career – had been further eroded. At Downing College, Cambridge, the pattern of under-achievement had repeated itself, and George had failed his second-year history exams. The college policy was not to demand a resit but to decide, on the basis of a candidate's merit, as assessed by the Master and Fellows, whether he or she should be allowed to continue with the course. It decided, after some debate and a suggestion of unrest among less fortunate failures, that the Earl of St Andrews should proceed.

His final degree, a lower second, was unimpressive, given his talents, but still just high enough to allow him to continue in higher education, this time on a Master of Philosophy Course. By then he and Sylvana, a brilliant student and a research fellow at the all-women Newnham College, had set up home together in George's £70,000 terraced house in the centre of Cambridge.

George was a gauche and diffident young man whose stammer had further undermined his social confidence. Though he worked successfully to overcome it, shyness continued to haunt him. 'A charming man but, even now, too nervous to look you in the eye,' says a close friend of his father. Among the Duke's friends, the consensus – even now – was that Katharine remained almost too devoted to her son to allow him the best chance of developing into an independent and successful man. That opinion must, of course, be tempered by the formality and ostensible loveless-ness with which royal fathers treated their sons. If the Duke of Kent exhibited little obvious warmth and fondness towards his firstborn, theirs was, however, to be an endur-ingly amicable relationship, based, according to the Duke's friends, on 'mutual respect'.

An outsider to the family might have considered that marriage to Sylvana, a serious intellectual who had published a number of academic papers on the social sciences, might be the ideal boost for George's self-esteem and happiness. This was not Katharine's view. From the outset, she regarded her prospective daughter-in-law warily. The Duchess – and no doubt the Duke – was perturbed on a number of counts. Sylvana was not only a divorcée. She was also a woman whose nationality, education and style meant that she had nothing obvious in common with the Kent parents. More practically, George had not yet demonstrated any aptitude for earning a living.

Furthermore Katharine, always at pains not to do anything that might embarrass the Queen, would have looked bleakly forwards to the stories of rifts and divisions that would inevitably follow a controversial engagement. It was not long before it was reported that the fact of Sylvana's divorce and the Cambridge *ménage a deux* had provoked a 'total freeze-out' by the Queen; which, in turn, had led to a widening split with the Kents, who felt they must be loyal to their son. The truth was that Katharine had other reservations. She found it difficult to welcome her future daughter-in-law; not principally because Sylvana was divorced or a Catholic or an older woman, but because, as one friend puts it, 'no one would be quite good enough for her darling George'.

If Katharine was confused and unhappy about the impending wedding, that is not surprising. She, pushed by her mother into the best possible marriage, had been deeply unhappy. Would her son, intent on choosing a seemingly less suitable partner, have any better chance of contentment? For all of George's life Katharine had striven – albeit with no great success – to ensure that he should be happy, blessed, successful; all the things she was not. Now, when he claimed to have found, in Sylvana, the catalyst for a fulfilled life, she balked – frightened that he was making a mistake and fearful that she was losing him. These were not sufficient obstacles. Nor was Sylvana, even by royal standards, an unsuitable bride.

By then Prince Michael of Kent had married, naturally with the Queen's permission, a Catholic whose previous union had been annulled. In addition, Her Majesty had acquired as a daughter-in-law the Duchess of York. While it was not yet apparent what the Fergie factor would do for the uxorious reputation of the House of Windsor, it is fair to assume that the Queen was rapidly undergoing a crash course in pragmatism. As for the Kents, they were aware that a Marina-style edict demanding an enforced wait would have no effect on George's newly discovered implacability. Much as Katharine might have wished to cast herself in the Marina role, there was no option but to accede to his wishes.

The Queen gave her consent under the Royal Marriages Act of 1772. In an announcement from Buckingham Palace, it was further spelled out that by marrying a Roman Catholic, albeit a lapsed one, George would be excluded from the succession, as stipulated in the Act of Settlement of 1701. This would hardly have troubled George, whose stated ambition was to be as anonymous as circumstances allowed.

Unenthusiastic as Katharine was about Sylvana, she went out of her way to be publicly charming, arranging a family lunch and photocall to mark the engagement and, in defiance of royal formality, holding a New Year barbecue round a bonfire at the Queen's log cabin at Sandringham to welcome her future daughter-in-law into the family.

Even so, the Duchess was fiercely upbraided by the press on the day after the wedding, held in Leith town hall in Edinburgh to circumvent the Royal Marriages Act provision that a previous divorce precluded remarriage in a church or register office in England and Wales. How outrageous, said critics, that the Duchess of Kent should turn up in her old clothes – the scarlet, Cossack-style outfit she had worn on Christmas Day at Windsor. Sylvana was rumoured to be 'heartbroken' after this 'massive snub' from a mother-in-law who – as one newspaper recalled – had herself been married in a rose-filled York Minster, watched by every leading British royal and scion of the European houses. However overblown the reports, the truth was that Katharine had not relished either her own grand ceremony or her son's, the first, though certainly not the last, royal wedding in a United Kingdom register office.

Katharine's intention was not to embarrass George, who is unlikely to have minded or much noticed what his mother was wearing. Her old outfit may have simply been an acknowledgement that a register office wedding with twenty-two guests and overheads totalling £24 (£22 for the registrar and £2 for the certificate) demanded a low-key approach. Nor was her attitude, cheerful and upbeat, designed to cast any shadow on the day. In the town hall, Katharine smiled beatifically for the wedding photographs; an expression that belied her non-existent relationship with her new daughter-in-law.

From the start, Sylvana had not stood a chance of acceptance by the Duchess. On one level, Katharine's reservations about George's marriage were understandable. At every previous juncture of his life, she had prayed for him to shine and watched him fail; first at school and later at university. That track record, in Katharine's mind, did not augur well for the success of a marriage.

But beyond that, she had other, less rational worries – that her beloved son was being taken away from her. If Katharine had been less unhappy herself, she would have realized that, in opposing his hopes and failing to form a relationship with Sylvana, she was effectively forcing him away. One of Katharine's great tragedies is that she – so good at forging bonds of intense warmth with total strangers – has been far less successful at cementing relationships in the private domain. The scars of her failed marriage, coupled with the acute loneliness of depression, made it hard for her to create durable bonds. Unhappiness made her inconsistent; sometimes charming, sometimes glacial. Over the years, friends, ladies-in-waiting, even her charities, have either basked in the warmth of Katharine's approval or found themselves, temporarily or permanently, out of favour. That mercurial attitude flows not only from depression but from the fact that Katharine, often hurt and frequently disappointed, found it difficult fully to trust people. Inevitably, in most of the episodes of rejection, she was the most badly hurt.

As a newcomer to the family, Sylvana could only partially have comprehended the unhappiness that shaped Katharine's attitude to her or understood that her mother-in-law's reservations were not aimed specifically at her. Almost anyone planning to be George's wife might have expected a similar coolness. Nevertheless, the differences between the two women did not help.

Katharine and Sylvana were polar opposites. Sylvana was highly educated, where Katharine, to her chagrin, had never had, or seized, the chance to maximize her potential. Katharine's strengths – compassion and warmth in public duty – had little tie-in to the esoteric world of a junior don. Katharine liked beautiful clothes, expensive make-up and historical novels. Sylvana lived simply and had just completed a scholarly tome on rape.

Not only because of their differences but also because she knew herself to be disapproved of, Sylvana's manner with the Duchess was awkward. She had two styles of striking up contact. The first was to adopt an ironic, academic tone unfamiliar to Katharine. The second was to discuss small and banal matters of domestic life and house-keeping, which the Duchess may have thought patronizing. The response to both gambits was a cold hauteur.

Whether Katharine wanted to be imperious and distant is dubious. No doubt some part of her longed to welcome her new daughter-in-law and treat her not as a rival but as a welcome addition to a family in need of an injection of happiness. The fact that she was unable to do so says more about Katharine's own pain than any wish to inflict suffering on someone else. As so often, there was no one around to help the Duchess come to terms with the estrangement she felt from Sylvana. The Duke's tactic, since he was unable or unwilling to connive at any reconciliation, was to adopt a stance of studied and formal impartiality. Over the years, Sylvana would phone him to complain about some real or perceived slight by the Duchess. 'I am sorry,' the Duke would tell her. 'I cannot intervene between you and my wife.' Occasionally Sylvana would extend her quest for help outside the family, phoning one of the Duke's best friends in tears to discuss a row or difference with Katharine. Unsurprisingly, Edward's allies came to regard Katharine as a mother-in-law from hell, while admiring Sylvana as a model of stoicism and good sense.

Katharine's behaviour, in one naturally so kind, is explainable only in the context of deep depression. In Katharine's mind, she was always losing – losing her father, her babies and now her son. Everything dear to her was being swept away, and – in that perceived process of demolition – Sylvana must have seemed, however illogically, like one more architect of unhappiness. If George had married later, when Katharine had fought her way through the aftermath of her tragedies, then she might have been able from the start to love her daughter-in-law. As it was, the differences between the two women were too deep ever to be fully eradicated.

But Katharine's pessimism about her son's decision was misplaced. George, in opposing his mother and asserting his independence, had made the right decision. This Kent marriage was to be a success. George and Sylvana set off, shortly after the wedding, in his Ford Escort, to Hungary, where he was to take up a six-month posting as Third Secretary in the Budapest Embassy; a two-way trial to establish whether he wished to embark on a career in the diplomatic service and whether they wanted him. Sylvana, using her break from university to work on a book about the Enlightenment, had also decided that this would be an ideal opportunity to have a child. Lord Downpatrick, eighteenth in line to the throne, was born in early December, just less than a year after his parents' marriage, in the private Lindo wing of St Mary's Hospital, London. Sir George Pinker, who had looked after the Duchess in her last, tragic pregnancy, was in attendance.

Despite their joy at the new baby, the St Andrews family faced a new difficulty. George, who had spent hours swotting in their Cambridge home, had nonetheless failed his Foreign Office exams. Sylvana, as a new mother, was now also the family's only breadwinner. Concerned as Katharine must have been over her son's fresh setback and dubious as she had been over his choice of bride, she now had the consolation of a grandson. But Katharine's life had not schooled her to be a naturally ecstatic grandmother. Almost inevitably, the birth of her son's child reawakened in her all the sorrow she had endured.

No doubt she told herself rationally that the loss of

Patrick, her last son, was far in the past – a fading scar, if not a healed one. But grief does not bend to time or to logic.

For Katharine, who has never ceased to mourn her child, to hold this new baby in her arms must have been, at some level, a reminder of a pain still scarcely dimmed; one more signal of a loss she would never erase.

CHAPTER SEVENTEEN

Other People's Children

O N AN AUTUMN day in 1984 the Duchess of Kent arrived in Jordan for her first solo overseas tour in more than a decade. This was a private visit at the invitation of King Hussein and Queen Noor, who had suggested combining a brief holiday at their palace with a trip to inspect centres for deprived and handicapped children.

As a co-patron, with the King's sister, Princess Basma, of the charity involved, Katharine was happy to accept. It was arranged that she should take half a day out of her schedule to inspect a children's project run by another organization, one that would play a huge and redeeming role in her future life. In the early seventies, Unicef, the United Nations' children's fund – casting around for a royal patron – had asked Katharine if she would take on the job. Her acceptance coincided with the onset of her years of tragedy and depression; factors that initially precluded her from offering any more than a minimal input and a name for the headed notepaper.

Her troubles nothwithstanding, Katharine had a deep interest in work that resonated with her love for children and consciousness of their fragility. Occasionally, on an overseas tour with the Duke, she would ask for Unicef to arrange for her to see how they were helping the impoverished and the dying. On the afternoon carved out of her Jordan programme, she was taken to a hospital where new oral rehydration techniques were being used, in place of intravenous drips, to save the sick. There, chatting to volunteers and marvelling at their success, she revealed that another of her children had almost died.

'She said that one of her sons had become severely dehydrated in Hong Kong, through diarrhoea or dysentery, and had to be rushed into hospital,' said one of the aides accompanying her. 'It was obvious from what she said that it was really serious; a real threat to his survival.'

Once again, anguish gleaned from personal experience linked into Katharine's work for others. Looking at infants rescued from the brink of death, she was reminded of a child of her own; in this case probably George, who had spent his infancy in Hong Kong.

But Katharine's love of children, and her increasing wish to focus her work on them, went beyond a natural empathy and an ability both to comfort and to draw comfort from the very young. In Unicef, she saw a task more fulfilling even than her contributions to palliative care and charities for the elderly – and certainly more rewarding than the routine tasks open to a minor royal.

Over the next years she would regard Unicef as her career; a job with a large charitable function, certainly, but also one that contained a diplomatic dimension and, in her view, an opportunity to bring her skills and influence to bear at the highest levels. Increasingly it was becoming clear to her that neither her skill as a comforter or her reputation as one of the most telegenic royals was sufficient fulfilment.

Katharine, in short, wanted a proper job. If the Queen,

as her cousin, Lady Elizabeth Anson, has said, is a housewife *manquée*, then the Duchess of Kent was a putative careerist. Her father, recognizing many years before that her happiness and, possibly, her survival hinged upon her having a meaningful and serious role of her own, had been instrumental in securing for her, at an extraordinarily young age, the Chancellorship of Leeds University. Just as Unicef was, in a different sphere, an ideal niche for her, so the university was an inspired choice, providing her with a serious function while feeding two great passions: her love for Yorkshire and her interest in academia.

The Duchess, fashion-conscious, occasionally frivolous and devoid of any serious educational qualification, is always viewed as the queen of compassion rather than a doyenne of higher education. That is both to under-estimate and to misunderstand her. Despite having no further education of her own, beyond a splash of finishing-school veneer, Katharine did not intend to be a Chancellor useful only for distributing garlands. From the first, she made it clear that she wanted to play a wider role in university life. On one of her early visits to Leeds, she was introduced to a new history professor, David Dilks – the youngest don in the university to hold a chair and someone whose name had already been mentioned to her by the royal biographer, Kenneth Rose. Like Rose, Dilks had written a biography of Lord Curzon, the former Viceroy of India and Foreign Secretary. The Duchess, then barely thirty, was familiar with both works.

Though also a devotee of authors more in tune with her lifestyle, such as Catherine Cookson (northern heroine makes splendid marriage) and, later, Joanna Trollope ('Aga sagas' featuring the affluent and a glimpse of how a county set existence might have been), Katharine was assiduous at background research. And so, when Dilks was introduced, she– perhaps recognizing a young and kindred spirit among the ranks of the distinguished and venerable – said graciously, 'Oh, I have heard all about your work from Kenneth. You and your wife must come and see me when you are in London.' Even before the formal invitations duly followed, Dilks was impressed. 'Considering all else she had to concern herself with, that was an example of her taking trouble with someone of no public importance at all. As one of four history professors, I was certainly not that.' In the years before he left Leeds, to become Vice-Chancellor of the University of Hull, Dilks continued to be impressed not only by her devotion to higher education but by her polish and dedication.

'She wants to do everything she takes on as well as she is capable of doing it. It's not a question of her demonstrating her excellence. It's a matter of living up to other people's expectations. She looks well, talks well, delivers a good speech. That is out of her desire to do the best by people.'

For days on end, Katharine handed out degrees, spending all day on the platform, offering a charming word to each graduate and retaining enough sense of humour to upbraid the presenters – of whom Dilks was one – if any hiccups occurred.

'On one occasion I said, reading from the marked-up programme: "Your Royal Highness and Chancellor, I present to you for the degree of Bachelor of Arts in the second class Fiona Arabella Stuart" – or some such name – and a man with an enormous beard sprang up the steps. The Duchess was very funny about this afterwards and refused to let me forget it. 'David, I should have thought you could have seen this wasn't Miss Stuart.'

The Leeds University of the sixties provided an interesting social and political education for the sheltered Katharine.

Student activists floated the black and red banners of the Sorbonne activists over the commuter traffic of Woodhouse Lane and conducted sit-ins in protest at alleged 'secret files' kept on them by the authorities.

Older dons regarded both the demonstrations, in support of the Paris student rioters, and the conspiracy theory with carefully suppressed scepticism bordering on derision. The students, a member of the university senate said, 'simply want to make a lot of noise', while Emeritus Professor Maurice Beresford, a noted historian, commented recently on an episode of perceived espionage.

'Students complained about rebels being spied on by two men in raincoats under a tree. They turned out to be from the council, checking that buses were keeping to time.'

Katharine did not engage with the rival factions. Instead she made a point of being charming both to the university authorities and to the president of the student union. Jack Straw, later to be Home Secretary, was already making a name for himself, in the fractious days of the sixties, as an organizer who could marshal his volatile troops into order. As for his social graces, he was pictured – a rather gauche young man with ill-disciplined hair and Buddy Holly glasses – waltzing at a university function with the Duchess of Kent, who wore sequins and full-length white gloves and gazed serenely at some point just beyond Straw's right shoulder.

If theirs was not entirely a meeting of minds, then the Duchess would have to put up with far less gracious protesters during her long tenure as Chancellor. Twenty years later, in the closing stages of the Cold War, Caspar Weinberger, the American Foreign Secretary, was invited to deliver a lecture on international relations and to receive, from Katharine, an honorary degree. Outside, a large and chanting crowd gathered to protest about 'US murderers' and nuclear weapons. Invitees to the degree ceremony were jostled and harangued, and Weinberger spoke against the baying from outside the hall. Katharine was mortified; horrified and ashamed that a guest who had crossed the Atlantic purely for this occasion should be subjected to such treatment.

Even so, her first thought was for the eight-year-old boy deputed to be her page for the evening. 'Are you frightened?' she whispered, bending down so that she could be heard. 'I am, a bit,' he said nervously. 'So am I,' said Katharine. Throughout the official dinner, she continued to apologize as the racket continued, insisting, when it was all over, that she must leave, publicly and by the front entrance, with Weinberger at her side.

Greatly to her pique, she was overruled by the head of security and smuggled, with the chief constable, out of a back door. 'There are a great many people, ma'am,' he warned her. 'You would be very wise to do as I say.' Only Weinberger, ushered through the protesters and into the back of a car, was sanguine. 'I've always found that if they shout, they don't shoot,' he said, gazing back at the receding mob.

In addition to her public functions – degree days and dinners – Katharine has also worked, over the years, on projects that attracted no outside notice. After Edward Boyle, the Leeds Vice-Chancellor, died in 1981, following a two-year struggle against cancer, she agreed immediately to be patron of his memorial fund.

When Boyle was appointed in 1970, she had not even liked him, finding his reticence and inability to relate to women difficult to deal with. Gradually she warmed to him, and, on his death, consented to head a fund designed to sponsor music and the arts. In the normal run of events, this would have been an obvious function for a Chancellor, but Katharine – still frail and suffering the after-effects of her breakdown – was poorly placed to oversee a mammoth whip-round for a man in his lifetime too quiet and unfashionable to have sponsors reaching without question for their chequebooks.

Immediately she offered to hold an evening function at St James's Palace, inviting 400 people, including every surviving British prime minister, bar Margaret Thatcher, who was with the Queen. A concert with the Birmingham Symphony Orchestra raised £30,000, and the final total for the fund reached £400,000. David Dilks, a trustee of the appeal, was impressed by her dedication. 'She was helpful far above the ordinary call of duty.'

Leeds University was not the only institution to benefit from Katharine's interest in higher education and the arts. She was devoted to the Royal Northern College of Music in Manchester and to the prestigious Leeds International Piano Competition, organized from scratch and on a budget of nothing by Fanny Waterman, a renowned international music adjudicator and wife of a Yorkshire GP. From its inception, Katharine insisted on being there – on one occasion missing a nephew's wedding because she felt it would be wrong to renege on her commitment. Like all functions in Yorkshire, the piano festival brought out the informal side of Katharine. When a Canadian winner, Jon Parker, kissed Mrs Waterman after accepting his cheque for £3,500, Katharine called after him: 'Do you think I could have one too?'

'So I kissed her twice on the cheek,' said Parker. 'It was the greatest moment of my life.' An admirer of high achievers, Katharine also defended the rights of all youngsters from all walks of life to fulfil their potential. Though she did not discuss politics with the Leeds University authorities, it seemed clear that she regarded higher education as a birthright, rather than a privilege.

Many years later, she was bold enough to say so. In 1996 she opened a new building at Hull University – another Yorkshire institution she admired and supported so wholeheartedly that she insisted on fulfilling her engagement, even though she had been diagnosed, a few weeks before, with Epstein-Barr Virus and was feeling deathly.

She did not, she explained, feel well enough to offer a speech. 'I think it's as much as I can do to carry on,' she said. Even so, on the day, she arrived with a few typed paragraphs and asked whether, after all, she might say a few words. She took as her text the 'rights' of students to higher education and, subsequently, to employment.

It was an unusually firm declaration from a member of the royal family, and one that indicated that – ill as Katharine was – she had no intention of being a token grandee, useful chiefly for cutting ribbons. Shortly afterwards, maintenance grants would be axed by the Blair government, making university less attainable for poorer students.

'I think she would have had grave reservations about that,' says one don who knows her well. 'I think she would have a strong current of concern that the people who most needed help would be deterred. Her argument on degree days was that standards should always be upheld and that, wherever the money comes from, there should be no question of driving standards and prices down.'

University funding, one of the political hot potatoes of the nineties, was not the natural debating ground of a lightly educated royal duchess. Her outspokenness demonstrated that she wished to be seen as more than a kindly figurehead, universally charming to students and their parents. Certainly she was adept in that role. As one professor says: 'She has a genius for making every graduate feel that it is his or her day. It is more than a knack to find the right thing to say to hundreds of them, crossing the stage at ten-second intervals.'

But at Leeds – the place she had called 'my university' in her first speech there – at Hull, or at the many foreign universities she visited, Katharine made it plain, through every address, that she took higher education, and her role within it, with the utmost seriousness.

The hybrid of the radical, politicized Duchess – a woman of strong views and careerist intincts – and the compassionate carer more familiar to the British public coalesced in her job for Unicef. At first the work she did for the charity was minimal. Gradually, as her depression receded, she began to take on more work, Even so, in the eighties, she remained more a royal figurehead than the activist of later years.

In 1986, the year of Unicef's fortieth anniversary, she was present for the first time at the British committee's annual general meeting. Two years later, she attended a charity showing of *Miss Saigon*. Shortly after that, she danced with young barristers at a ball held in conjunction with the legal profession.

Her enthusiasm was obvious. When 100 stars gave up their Sunday evenings to give a concert at the Dominion Theatre, she broke her rule of never delivering an unscripted speech and jumped to her feet to deliver a few impromptu words from the auditorium. Speaking without a microphone, she called out: 'I can't sing, dance or act like the rest of you, but thank you for saving thousands of children's lives tonight. It's been a wonderful show.'

Another star-studded bash in 1990. Another effort to save children's lives. This time the event was at the Barbican, with Audrey Hepburn in the audience to watch *The Diary of Anne Frank* with the London Symphony Orchestra. By now Katharine was entirely at ease at Unicef functions, just as she was relaxed in Leeds.

Never an inscrutable royal, Katharine – so attuned to the emotions of others – has always been honest enough to reveal her feelings; but only on territory she regards as her own.

So, on the night she chatted to Audrey Hepburn and applauded a fund-raising initiative designed to save the poorest children in the world, it was clear to a few of those who surrounded her that Katharine had another child on her mind – Nicholas, her youngest son. As the curtain fell for the interval, the Duchess asked if she might borrow a private office to make a telephone call too urgent to wait until the end of the show. 'I must phone Nicky,' she said. 'I am so worried about him.'

CHAPTER EIGHTEEN

Like Mother, Like Son

J UST BEFORE CHRISTMAS 1988, Lord Nicholas Windsor,
  seventeeth in line to the throne, was cautioned at Bow
  Street police station for having a small amount of cannabis. He had, reportedly, been seen by officers sharing a joint
with a friend in St James's Park. After ninety minutes of
questioning he was freed without charge. There was no
question, in the Kent household, of minimizing the domestic
fallout from this relatively minor scandal. The episode,
according to one of Katharine's friends, constituted 'a great
crisis'. The Duke was furious, the Duchess distraught and
Nicholas himself deeply ashamed.

Although anxious that nothing she or her family did
should ever embarrass the Queen, Katharine's worry had less
to do with the ground-rules of royal behaviour than with
the problems – far graver than a few drags at an illicit joint
– now afflicting her eighteen-year-old son. As the youngest
child, Nicholas had been her particular solace and comforter
in the aftermath of her breakdown. Shortly after the *Daily
Express* ran their story, vehemently denied, that she might
have to undergo electro-convulsive therapy, it was announced
that the Duke and Duchess had, in an unprecedented break

with royal tradition, rejected Eton for their younger son and opted instead for Westminster School.

Quite apart from the fact that Eton had failed with George, Katharine had good reasons for her decision. Nicholas, like his older brother, was a shy and retiring boy whose personality was unlikely to be any better suited to boarding school life. In addition, he was used to being at his mother's side on both formal and informal occasions. Sometimes, when she gave out degrees at Leeds, he would travel with her to act as her pageboy. When she went on holiday to Canada in 1983, still convalescing after surgery and depression, Nicholas was her chosen companion. 'Just the two of us,' she said. Even if Katharine had been fully well, it would have been a great wrench for any mother as family-minded as she to see her last child leave home to spend eight months a year at boarding school.

Westminster, therefore, seemed the perfect choice. It had no royal links or any particular social cachet. It did, however, have a fine academic tradition and a track record of producing high-flyers across a range of disciplines. Its mixed bag of alumni included, as Katharine found out, six prime ministers, fourteen archbishops, Tony Benn and Peter Ustinov.

As a day boy, Nicholas – Snoopy as his mother fondly nicknamed him – would have only a ten-minute walk across St James's Park from his front door at York House to his classroom. Katharine herself would be able to oversee his life, finding games kit, packing snacks and lunches and frequently being there to welcome him home in the evening and supervise as he did his homework at the kitchen table.

That scenario, at least, was the public version of events. The truth was rather different. After the Duke and Duchess vetoed Eton, as a result of George's unhappy time there, they decided to approach Michael Mann – the former Dean of Windsor, spiritual adviser to the Queen and the man who had counselled the Duke when his marriage was at breaking point. As chairman of the governors of Harrow School, Mann was ideally qualified to suggest the most suitable school for Nicholas.

Visit Radley, Wellington and Harrow, he told the Kents. All were within easy reach of London, and at least one should be ideal for their son. The Duke and Duchess settled for Harrow, and Nicholas was duly accepted. Almost as he was due to leave, the Duke visited Mann again. This time he appeared anxious, perplexed and apologetic. He was terribly sorry, he said, but Nicholas could not be sent away after all. Katharine's psychiatrist had told him: 'If your son leaves home, then I cannot be answerable for the Duchess's health.' As the Duke explained, he could not conceivably ignore such a warning. The Kents had decided that Nicholas must go to Westminster instead.

Privately the Duke remained anxious that his son, living at home and often cared for by a nanny, would become susceptible to what he viewed as the temptations of London life. His fears had already been borne out when he returned, shortly after Nicholas's O levels, for further counsel from Michael Mann. The Kents had decided, he said, that their son, now displaying rebellious behaviour, should no longer stay at Westminster. Would Harrow take him after all?

Despite grave doubts on Harrow's part about admitting a boy nearing the end of his school career and with even a very minor history of being troublesome, a place was found for Nicholas. Although he passed his A levels, the move was not a success. By the time he left, he was showing signs of becoming a drifter, a boy with the potential to mix with those his parents saw as the wrong crowd. 'The whole thing was very unsatisfactory – a very unhappy business,' says a friend of the Kents.

For Katharine, emerging from years of depression and despair, the transformation in her son must have been particularly distressing. Nicholas had been a sweet and untroubled little boy. Those who met him later, both as a teenager and a young man, remarked always on his kindness and his politeness. In a portrait taken by Lord Snowdon, shortly before he took up his place at Westminster, he smiled for the camera – a chubby schoolboy wearing a casual shirt and trainers, his hands stuffed into the pockets of his jeans.

Even a generation on, Diana's choice of similarly informal clothes for her sons, William and Harry, provoked a mild tremor among a royal family which preferred even the youngest members of the male line kitted out in lounge suits and ties like miniature city lawyers. Katharine, in so many respects Diana's precursor, also appeared to want for her son a natural, normal childhood uncluttered by the stuffy constraints of royalty.

Despite his charm and some academic talent, it was clear, by the end of his schooldays, that Nicholas's future was far from assured. Though his father was said to harbour a vague hope that his younger son might eventually train at Sandhurst, as he had done, and follow a military career, it was clear that Nicholas was entirely unsuited to the rigours of life in the armed forces. Eventually he decided that he would have a gap year before taking up a university place. In the summer after his final exams he moved home. Late in December the Duke and Duchess learned that he was with the police, being questioned over cannabis possession.

The Kents were on the point of leaving for Anmer Hall – the grace-and-favour home on loan to them from the Queen and their Sandringham base for the festive season. It was almost certainly the least joyous Christmas the family had spent at Anmer. It was also close to the last. The following year, the Duke and Duchess announced that they were leaving Norfolk to live closer to London.

Their choice, bought for a reported £2 million – actually far less – was a spacious former vicarage near Henley-on-Thames. Although the given reason for the move was that the commute to Norfolk – a county that Katharine had grown to love – had become too arduous, the location of the new house may also have been connected with Nicholas's whereabouts. Once the renovations were finished and once he had taken up a place at Oxford University, Katharine – whether in London or Henley – would never be more than a short drive away. The Duke of Kent was enormously saddened by the move. To him, Anmer had been more than a home. It was also his passcard to the nucleus of the royal family; a place that gave him his only chance to meet the Queen on an informal basis during her time at Sandringham. But, whatever his private regrets, Edward consented to the move.

However ideal the geography, Crocker End House had considerable drawbacks. Planning permission had to be sought for a staff cottage, a swimming pool installed and renovations carried out to the house, formerly the home of the Earl of Arran. Eighteen months after completion of the purchase, Katharine prepared finally to move out of Anmer. As a gesture of her fondness for Norfolk, she held a charity auction of all her unwanted possessions, including her bicycle, which fetched £50, and a Victorian dinner gong, knocked down for £80. The takings, a total of several hundred pounds, were spread between local good causes before the removal vans arrived.

Though Crocker End House was still not quite finished, a more radical problem had emerged. The local police force, Thames Valley, was disturbed by the security implications of an isolated house whose grounds were skirted by a public footpath. Despite the installation of an alarm system linked directly to Henley police station, concerns remained about the safety of the Duke and Duchess and their personal property.

Katharine, however, was – at least at first – determinedly enchanted with her new home. Still a fanatical gardener, she decided totally to redesign her two acres. Having tried – and failed – to grow the rhododendrons she had loved in Norfolk but which drooped and died in Oxfordshire soil, she evolved a new plan, drawing on the advice of, among others, the society landscape designer David Hicks. The Duke, clearly anxious that this move should be a success, evinced a close interest in the project. One consultant designer, visiting the property, was hastily summoned back just as she was leaving to be reminded by him that the Duchess had stipulated an avenue of lime trees running through the gardens.

The limes, along with the extensive rebuilding, suggested that Katharine regarded Crocker End as a project for the long term if not a home for life. In fact the Kents were not destined to be particularly happy there or to stay for more than a few years.

For now, however, Katharine was as content as her health and imperfect marriage allowed. She was also, as she had hoped, just down the road from Nicholas, who had taken up his place at Oxford to read philosophy. Manchester College was not one of the great seats of learning attended by his brother or by his Worsley uncles. Indeed, when he began his studies, Manchester was not part of the university at all, although it was annexed soon afterwards, renamed Harris Manchester and designated a centre for mature students.

At the beginning of Nicholas Windsor's course, it was merely an independent college, offering external London University degrees. If not a showcase of academia, Manchester had other attributes which the Kents hoped might benefit their son. Billed as 'a small and friendly community', its historic old houses accommodate only fifty students. It was hoped that, in this quiet and cloistered atmosphere, Nicholas might thrive. Instead he completed only a year of his philosophy course before announcing that he wished to take a sabbatical. After spending his twenty-first birthday in Borneo, on a Royal Geographical Society expedition to promote saving the rain forest, he told his college – which had agreed to hold open his place – that he would not be returning until the following year and intended instead to travel to the Far East.

On finally returning to Oxford, he decided to switch courses, this time opting for an Oxford University joint honours degree in philosophy and theology. By now Nicholas's particular spheres of interest closely mirrored Katharine's. His travels had instilled in him her fascination with third world relief projects, and his theology course – based round the Christian doctrines and their ethical implications – suggested that he, far more than his siblings, shared his mother's fascination for religion.

But Nicholas was not best known by the media for his penchant for good works. Occasional newspaper diary items began to wonder what Lord Nicholas Windsor was up to, alluding – rather scornfully – to his 'artistic temperament' and comparing him, unfavourably of course, to the suave and dynamic contemporary art dealer Tim Taylor, to whom his sister Helen had recently become engaged. Why did Nicholas appear so restless and indecisive, a gossip columnist wondered? Was he fitting himself for the mantle of 'royal wastrel'?

These were questions that also preoccupied those who were extremely close to Katharine and to Nicholas. His godfather, Lord Coggan, tried strenuously to keep in touch, attempting to look up his godson when he was preaching at Oxford and inviting him to lunch at his club. Like all who realized that Nicholas's life was not going smoothly, Coggan half expected him, whenever they met, to have been tranformed into a spoiled and strident rebel. Instead, he found a sweet, polite, beautifully mannered and rather innocent young man; an image vastly at variance with the unkind wastrel tag.

The truth, as few outside the Kent family knew, was that Nicholas – the child who had been a prop to his mother during her years of depression – was now also suffering grave problems. Katharine never dwelt in detail on his breakdowns and his long spells of treatment, except to say sometimes to friends: 'Nicky is in hospital again. I am so worried about him.'

His life is not the concern of this book, except in so far as it illuminates Katharine's. Few of those who watched her emerge from her years of personal sorrow, as a woman who had not only rebuilt her own life but had managed to enhance, through her compassion and courage, those of many others, knew that, throughout her ordeal, she had to bear an additional burden of private sorrow and guilt.

As Nicholas's condition worsened, Katharine decided that he – the child who most resembled her – might be helped by joining in the sort of work that always offered her joy and inspiration. In 1993 an obvious opportunity arose. Unicef had set up, at her request, the first of several major foreign tours she would undertake on their behalf. For Katharine this was a major stride into an arena she would come to see as her career, a world far removed from the glad-handing engagements on offer to minor royals. The trip had been lavishly arranged. The Queen had loaned a plane of the Royal Flight, enabling Katharine and her party to make short-haul flights to various capital cities along the way. At most stop-off points there would be private meetings with important diplomatic and political connotations for Unicef. On the way out, Katharine would fly via Rome to Cairo, where she was scheduled privately to meet the wife of the Egyptian president, Hosni Mubarak, to discuss the World Summit for Children.

On the way home, she was to meet the Jordanian Cabinet. In Tanzania itself, every leading member of government planned to welcome her at an open-air dinner and discuss her input into humanitarian projects. In short, this was exactly the sort of major trip that preoccupies Katharine for weeks beforehand, as she pores over statistics and facts and, self-doubting, tortures herself over whether she will be up to the job.

This time, as the very last programme details were being put together, she had another question. 'May I bring Nicholas with me?' she asked the organizers, hopeful that the trip would jolt him out of his lethargy and unhappiness. Although this unusual request caused a tremor of surprise, naturally no objections were raised. The greater amazement to those who met Katharine during her visit was how overtly normal and charming her supposedly problematic son was.

'He was an extremely bright and intelligent young man,'

says one observer. 'He fitted in very well, and he seemed an extremely good companion; not at his mother's elbow all the time. He was interested in everything, took some extremely good photographs and appeared to get on very well with the organizers.'

Katharine, a great success in her own right throughout the tour, was cheered by the impression her son was making. One dignitary who met her and had heard previously that Nicholas had 'problems' decided on first meeting that these could not have been so great. 'I thought any problems might lie in his own psychological approach to life. He wanted to be more of a chap. He didn't want to be involved in the world of royalty. That's the impression he gave. His mother saw the visit as a sort of therapy – a way of putting him into a world he considered to be a hostile place and one he couldn't cope with. I'm sure she thought it would be a good experience for him, and it seemed that she was right.'

Katharine actually had more ambitious hopes. Nicholas, so much his mother's son and – like her – so interested in the third world and humanitarian programmes, had already visited Tanzania during his years out of university and had evinced great interest in the country. Perhaps this second visit would spur him on to find himself a job with another voluntary organization engaged in local field work. In other words, maybe this expedition would be the catalyst to inspire Nicholas and to transform his life. But, on the plane home, the Duchess – already fearful that her strategy had not worked – seemed fretful and anxious, eager to be reassured by Nicholas that he would not have another of 'his attacks'.

His relapses continued. Three years later Katharine, by then ill again herself, told a friend that Nicholas was back in hospital, receiving yet more treatment. Long before that, he had begun to lose weight. Only a handful of confidants of the Kents learned of the seriousness of his condition. Nicholas, they were told, was suffering from an eating disorder.

A tentative phone call was made by a Kent aide to a close friend of the royal family, herself a recovered anorexic. Would she be prepared to visit the Duke and Duchess to discuss the illness? That call was never followed up, suggesting that Katharine had found counsel elsewhere. Certainly, even within the family, there was no shortage of knowledge on eating disorders. Diana, by then a close friend of the Duchess, had had bulimia. Both Diana's sister Sarah and her sister-in-law, Victoria, were former anorexics. Katharine herself, though never formally acknowledged to be suffering from an eating problem, was prone to faddish diets and periods of what some around her described as near-starvation. According to one close acquaintance, she spent two years having only chicken in public. At home, she would often raid the fridge and eat whatever came to hand.

Nicholas's eating disorder, although unusual, was by no means exceptional. The majority of British anorexics are young women – currently 70,000 of them aged between fifteen and twenty-nine. But the disease spans most ages, from eight-year-olds to the elderly, and runs through all strata of society. Although the incidence of anorexia has not altered in 200 years – unlike bulimia, which has increased exponentially – it has become less gender-specific. Currently 10 per cent of sufferers are young men. Despite a greater understanding of the disease, outcomes remain worrying, particularly for male patients. One in ten sufferers dies prematurely, either from the effects of starvation or by committing suicide.

The roots of Nicholas's problems are likely to have been both biological and developmental. Children of the depressed are genetically predisposed to inherit mental problems of some description. The more severe the parent's condition, the stronger the genetic link. It is possible, therefore, that Nicholas's difficulties were inherited from his mother.

But the pattern of his behaviour suggests other factors. Adored and highly protected by Katharine, he had been expected – however tacitly – to conform, perhaps to her wishes and certainly to the patterns of behaviour demanded from young members of the royal family. The rebelliousness he showed at school and the cannabis episode represented a classic pattern displayed by a child wanting to establish his own independence and identity in the face of perceived constraints.

At the heart of any eating disorder is a heightened struggle for control. While girl victims are more prone to low self-esteem and influenced by fashion industry stereotypes of the perfect body, boys – less worried by self-image – develop a subconscious need to assert their ability to exert leverage over their family and their lives. The illness becomes a powerful weapon, invoked by sufferers desperate to reclaim their independence and to become the focus of their parents' attention.

Any family therapist speaking to the Kents – or any of the many families in their position – would have looked at the relationship between father, mother and son to see whether that triad represented a balance in which a child could be both sufficiently protected and independent. Although good parenting from both a father and mother is desirable in achieving that balance, it is not a prerequisite for a child's successful development.

In the Kent family, the Duke – often working away from home and bred to be distant even when in residence – had deferred to Katharine on child-rearing, her particular province. Much as he loved his children, the Duke, by contemporary standards, was far from being a hands-on father, involved in every stage of their upbringing. Katharine, by contrast, was an adoring and protective mother, desperate to create the perfect family as measured against the inclusive bond she had had with her father. In this mission, almost everything was stacked against her. Her own marriage was largely devoid of affection, and she had lost two children; circumstances which left a vacuum in her life. Inevitably she sought to fill that void with a close relationship with her two sons, recipients of all the love she had to offer. In that sense, the Kent sons were the last keepers of their mother's forlorn dream of contentment, the object of all her hopes and ambitions. They were also – as minor royals – expected to measure up to the public demands of the monarchy and to emerge as emblems of perfect family life; a rigorous demand since the Kents were, by any standards, a dysfunctional family. That is not to judge or to blame Katharine.

For most of her life, she had been controlled – by her parents and by a royal family who intervened in most aspects of her existence, from her workload to the future of her marriage. Personal tragedy had triggered a loneliness and depression that blighted an already imperfect existence. Even leaving her own illness aside, to bring her children up in textbook fashion, within the constraints imposed on her, would have demanded more than psychological robustness. It would have required a woman who was emotionally super-fit. If Katharine, so often manipulated herself, sought to exercise too great a level of control on her sons' lives, she had no malign motive.

Undoubtedly she loved them. Perhaps if she had loved them a little less, or retreated from their lives a little more, they might have developed differently, but that is academic. In a sense it is almost a miracle that the Duchess of Kent – often operating virtually as a single mother in the emotionally sterile confines of the royal family – had succeeded as well as she did. George, her older son, was happily married. Helen was a model daughter.

It was, perhaps, inevitable that Nicholas would have the most difficult life. He was the one who had witnessed his mother's unhappiness. He had watched her attention to diet and picky eating habits – a possible trigger in the development of an eating disorder in a child. He may also have perceived his older siblings as more successful than he was and worried that he could not match his brother's academic potential – again a factor predisposing children who feel themselves inadequate to eating disorders.

If ever Katharine needed help, it was in ensuring that the problems she had faced did not also overwhelm her son. There was no sign that she received much support or guidance. Concerned as the Duke was over Nicholas, he involved himself in practical remedies, first choosing schools and later asking aides to track down the best doctors. Although he undoubtedly considered his son's personal happiness, the Duke of Kent was probably no more adept at dealing with psychological problems than he had been at the height of Katharine's depression.

As for Katharine, she – faced with the evidence of Nicholas's illness – almost certainly perceived herself as having failed. All the vulnerability and frailty she had fought to overcome was now being played out once again in her son's young life. Her sense of failure in turn reinforced her own lack of self-esteem and self-worth. In this vicious cycle of family suffering, she had no option but to carry on with hope and courage. Even with her closest friends, Katharine did not discuss the seriousness of Nicholas's eating disorder or his treatment, beyond mentioning, at intervals, that he was being reviewed in hospital for some aspect of his ongoing problems. Other women as frail and overworked as she might have inclined more towards bitterness at the cruelty of fate or circumstance. Katharine did not.

In private she must sometimes have despaired. Of her two brilliant sons – the focus and the purpose of her life – the older had to submit to constant failure and disappointment in an effort to gain qualifications that fell easily into the hands of less talented men. Nicholas remained ill and without any prospect of a job.

Whatever the forces that had undermined her attempts to create an untroubled family, Katharine must have partly blamed the corrosive forces of a royal lifestyle. True, it had given her enormous privileges. But she had repaid that debt in the unstinting work she had offered over the years. Even in the worst times, she had attempted to carry on with the job, ignoring her own suffering in a way that she could not now ignore her son's plight. Once again, it seemed that her efforts were rewarded only with failure.

On a practical level, she could find doctors for Nicholas. But where could she find healing? The answer was not yet available. But, with every new crisis and disappointment, Katharine was moving closer to the Catholic Church.

Those who have watched Katharine work – at Helen House, at Wimbledon, at a Cup Final – have caught occasional glimpses of a woman struggling against great anguish. Few realized that she frequently carried a double burden of pain, of which her doubtful health was the minor part. Like any loving and anxious mother – and Katharine was certainly both – she found her child's illness infinitely harder to bear than her own.

CHAPTER NINETEEN

Rebranding Romance

❀

T HE IRONY OF Katharine's distress over Nicholas was that she appeared to the outside world – which knew nothing of his problems – as a blessed and fortunate mother. The most visible testament to her success was her daughter, Helen.

Having once detected the trappings of a vestigial royal rebel – topless sunbathing, Marlboro cigarettes and fast-living friends – the press had been forced to abandon this line of inquiry. In fact Helen had never provided much fertile ground for scandal, beyond the unshocking rumour that she had once smuggled a boyfriend into her parents' apartment. In her early twenties, she appeared to be emerging as a prototype Sloane Ranger, beautifully groomed and mildly educated. After St Mary's, Wantage – a school more noted for its élite register than its academic results – and A levels at Gordonstoun and a London crammer, she moved on to a £60-a-week job as a receptionist at Christie's, a traditional staging post for well-bred girls seeking a hiatus between school and marriage.

Although closer to her father, who – perhaps because Katharine's attention was particularly focused on her sons –

detected a gap in which he could deploy some parental involvement, she was almost a mirror image of the younger Katharine, both physically and in terms of scholastic achievement. But the blend of adventure holidays and selfless good works that Katharine had chosen at the same age seemed slightly anachronistic even in the Duchess's generation.

Helen, both through inclination and financial necessity, took a different tack from her mother. After rising through the lower ranks at Christie's and earning herself a temporary posting in Manhattan, she moved on to the London modern art gallery Karsten Schubert, rapidly becoming a director on the strength of her knowledge and professionalism. Rumoured to be slightly 'dull' – possibly a virtue rather than a fault in a generation of junior royals where staidness was in short supply – she jettisoned her long-term boyfriend, David Flint Wood, an estate agent and reputedly 'desperately dull', and, in 1989, began a relationship with a fellow art dealer.

Tim Taylor, level-headed and hard-working, had started out in the art world sweeping floors at a Mayfair gallery before progressing to Leslie Waddington, an establishment selling modern works. In addition to having an identical career path to Helen's, he – said by the press to resemble the film star, Rob Lowe – was almost as photogenic as she. Both Katharine and Edward would have acknowledged Taylor as an entirely suitable son-in-law, and, after a Christmas of celebrations, the engagement was announced. Despite the fact that Helen lived in a flat in Earls Court and that neither she nor her future husband had great pretensions to grandeur, the wedding was trailed in the manner befitting a woman twenty-first in line to the throne: 'It is with the greatest pleasure that the Duke and Duchess of Kent announce the betrothal of their daughter, Lady Helen Windsor, to Mr Timothy Verner Taylor, eldest son of Commander Michael Taylor, Royal Navy, of Stoke St Gregory, Taunton, and Mrs Colin Walkinshaw, of Compton, Guildford, to which union the Queen has gladly given her consent.'

The Queen must actually have had rather mixed feelings, since even her most uncynical subjects had come to regard royal weddings as merely a prelude to disaster and to scandal. In 1989 the *Sun* newspaper was handed, by an unidentified man, a package of four stolen letters sent to the Princess Royal by the Queen's equerry, Commander Timothy Laurence.

Their contents were said to be 'tender and affectionate' and Laurence 'furious and humiliated' on learning of their theft. Though the bundle was passed straight on to police, friends of the princess revealed that the naval officer was 'besotted' by her and spoke of trysts at a country house. The marriage between Anne and Captain Mark Phillips staggered on for another four months before the couple ended the pretence and announced their formal separation.

In the same year, Katharine's niece, Marina Ogilvy, made the first attempt to patch up a bitter public row with her mother, Princess Alexandra. Having announced that she was pregnant by her photographer boyfriend, Paul Mowatt, but had no plans to marry him, she gave a newspaper interview suggesting that her family was more concerned about its image than about her wishes. Finally she reneged; saying she would after all get married (the couple were later acrimoniously divorced), and Alexandra and her husband, Angus Ogilvy, issued a statement saying that they loved their daughter and would welcome her home.

Far more than Anne's marriage break-up, the Ogilvys' plight would have touched the Kents deeply. Katharine had briefly been very close to Alexandra, in the days when Marina, the Duke's mother, was seeking to delay her wedding. Then her future sister-in-law acted as go-between for her and Edward. Now Alexandra was far more allied to her brother, who – highly protective of his own daughter – would have been horrified by Marina's rebellion.

That episode was, however, a minor drama in comparison with the growing rumours that the Prince and Princess of Wales's marriage was tearing itself apart. Katharine, who had corresponded with Diana since William and Harry were born, would certainly have some inside knowledge of the Princess's misery and sense of betrayal, but even she would have been shocked by the scope of the scandal about to break.

In the month before Helen Windsor married, the royal reporter Andrew Morton published his book *Diana: Her True Story*, in which he revealed that she had tried five times to commit suicide in desperation over Charles's uncaring attitude. Morton's biography, the strongest evidence that the Wales's marriage was a sham, was condemned as an unforgivable intrusion into the lives of the royal family. It was not known until after Diana's death in 1997 that the source material came not from her trusted friends but from tape recordings made and supplied by her. Given that the Duchess of York's marriage was also in the process of collapse – a particularly messy break-up soon to be followed by the publication of toe-kissing pictures taken during a holiday with her 'financial adviser', John Bryan – one more disastrously failed royal marriage would start to look careless.

It was the unhappiest of ironies that the Duke and Duchess of Kent, locked in a miserable sham of a marriage, were designated impresarios of an occasion designed to resurrect royal romance. As for Helen, she had seen from the example of her parents' frosty and loveless relationship the corrupting effect of a dreadful marriage. Now the restitution of the battered royal image rested on her. It says a great deal about her strength and placidity that she coped not only with the burden of being deputed to spearhead the Windsors' fightback but with the knowledge that royal marriages, in her first-hand experience, can be the most frigid of institutions and the most empty of charades.

Newspapers, knowing nothing of this turmoil, classified her as the model royal bride and embarked on a forensic scrutiny of every detail of the forthcoming wedding. Just as Katharine's wish-list of gifts had been published thirty years previously, Helen's too was leaked. Although the original source was not discovered, Brian Sewell, art critic of the London *Evening Standard* and a most implausible source of royal gossip, admitted that the list had fallen into his hands and he had shown it to his newspaper, on the grounds that he thought it was 'terribly funny'.

Certainly it provided a kaleidoscopic portrait of a life-style, plus a fund of intimate detail. Lady Helen and her future husband would, newspaper readers learned, sleep under a Blue Pyramid king-size duvet cover (£77) and eat boiled eggs with horn-handled spoons (£3.82) off a break-fast-in-bed tray (£24.50). From the expensive (video camcorder, £599) to the personal (chrome bath rack with two soap dishes, £92.50) to the sternly utilitarian (steel dustbin, £15.98), no detail was missing from the £20,000 starter pack for a well-heeled marriage.

The Wedding List Company, holders of the masterlist, were said to be deeply embarrassed. Katharine and her daughter, both practical women and ardent shoppers who would have enjoyed putting the dossier together, were more probably amused. Bitter as her own memories were,

Katharine seems to have revelled in the early preparations for her daughter's wedding. *Vogue*, where Katharine had close friends, was allowed to run the engagement 'kiss' pictures, taken by the French photographer Michel Comte, and Catherine Walker – Diana's favourite designer – was chosen to design the bride's and the bridesmaids' dresses.

Always a fan of Giorgio Armani, Katharine decided that she and her daughter should be kitted out not at the firm's London branch but at its Milan headquarters. Helen chose one suit and Katharine – dithering over what might look best on the day – picked two, one in cream and one in pale blue. Each had a price tag of £1,400. If clothes were a barometer of Katharine's mood, then this outlay suggested that Helen's wedding carried a higher approval rating higher than George's marriage, for which Katharine – unhappy with his choice of bride – had worn old clothes. A more general extravagance reflected the fact that the Kents were responsible for the public relaunch of royal romance.

The four-tier cake, weighing 80lb, was baked, at Katharine's request, by the Army Catering Corps, of which she was Colonel-in-Chief, and the flowers were ordered from the Flower Van in Fulham. 'Country flowers since we are country people,' the Duchess stipulated. However ostensibly simple the tone, this was never designed to be a cut-price wedding.

It would, according to the pundits' best estimate, cost the Kents – often to be heard pleading impecuniousness – in the region of £85,000. Though many scoffed at the notion that Edward and Katharine were poor relations – they did, after all, receive £130,000 a year from the Queen – this was not the view of those closest to them. Edward had sold off the remains of the family silver to buy Crocker End House, and most of the money bequeathed to Katharine by her mother's side of the family, the well-to-do Brunner industrialists, is thought to have been spent. Certainly Katharine's later lifestyle – complete with borrowed country cottages and complaints that she had to economize on clothes – was not that of a rich heiress. Sir William Worsley had left only the relatively small sum of £100,351, the bulk of which was split between Katharine and her brothers, with Hovingham Hall and its estate the automatic bequest to Marcus, the eldest son.

In the year of Helen's wedding, news emerged that the Duchess had been a major loser in one of the Lloyd's syndicates – once an easy and virtually automatic form of enrichment to affluent 'Names' but now, in some cases, close to collapse. She, one of the most famous victims, was linked with syndicates run by Richard Beckett Underwriting Agencies, facing losses caused by the deterioration of the American liability business. Initial reports suggested that Katharine – along with co-investors including Adnan Khashoggi, the billionaire arms magnate and one of the world's richest men – stood to lose £100,000. It is likely that the actual figure was far lower; possibly less than £500, according to a market guide which claimed that Katharine had taken out insurance cover to cap her losses.

At any rate, the Lloyd's episode did nothing to cramp the style of Helen's wedding, once no more than a royal sideshow but now the vehicle which would demonstrate that, for all the recent turmoil, royalty still retained some vestige of romantic mystique. Since few genuine happy families of the royal blood existed, they would have to be faked for the occasion. Charles and Diana – now upgraded from the 'Glums', a nickname earned on a South Korean tour distinguished only by their palpable misery, to the 'Warring Waleses' – were expected to be together and to look pleasant. Andrew and Fergie would also reportedly be side by side, as would Princess Margaret and her former husband, Lord Snowdon.

This cast list, and others, were assumed to be the co-opted players in a PR crusade designed by the Queen to display her tarnished family in the most flattering light possible. In fact, the Queen operates in a far more subtle and osmotic manner. Far from laying down rules, she expects those around her to absorb her thoughts on a given subject and behave accordingly. The appropriate reaction in this case was undoubtedly to lay on a show of unity, a tableau designed to demonstrate that discord was giving way to dignified resolutions.

In the circumstances, Katharine might have felt that her daughter's big day had been hijacked to a hollow charade; one in which she and her husband were, unknown to the world, the leading players. On the day, she was palpably nervous – a state attributed by royal-watchers to her sensitive nature and innate frailty. In fact, Helen's wedding evoked not only her terror as she walked down the aisle at York Minster but all the unhappiness she had endured in the last thirty years. Now it was her daughter's turn. Neither Helen's even temperament, nor the fact that she was clearly in love with a man different in every way from a Duke of the royal blood, could quite have assuaged Katharine's dread.

Besides, royal weddings, however diverting in the planning, are formidable occasions. Whatever Helen's and Katharine's personal preferences – and they are likely to have been for a more simple setting – the chosen venue for the service was St George's Chapel, Windsor, where Helen's great-great-grandparents, the future Edward VII and his bride, Alexandra, had been married in 1863. Here, in the burial place of ten sovereigns, Tim Taylor, a minor public schoolboy and picture salesman, would wait at the altar for his twenty-eight-year-old bride.

He might have been expected to be nervous. As the time of the wedding approached – 3p.m. on Saturday, 18 July, it became increasingly clear that the person most consumed with nerves was his future mother-in-law. Allocated inter-connecting guest suites at Windsor Castle, Helen, her mother and the bridesmaids were attended by hairdressers and make-up artists from the Duchess's favourite salon, MichaelJohn, while Catherine Walker hung out the bride's gown – a simple column of white silk with a six-foot train. While Helen dressed, Katharine dithered over the three possible outfits she had finally shortlisted.

At the ceremony itself, she looked – even by the standards of a bride's mother – deeply uneasy and anxious, consumed not only by her own unhappy memories but by the unease always awakened in her by large and formal gatherings of royalty. Through no fault of Katharine's, the royal line-up looked slightly less glossy than the Buckingham Palace fourteen-page press dossier issued to mark the occasion. The Duchess of York did not in the end turn up, remaining closeted at home, first with her self-styled 'financial adviser', John Bryan, and later with the comedian Billy Connolly and his wife, Pamela Stephenson. Charles, who had sparked off speculation that he too would be absent by departing to Cardiff to present an honorary degree to Neil Kinnock, returned in time but barely spoke to Diana.

As for Katharine, she was aware throughout the service that the most taxing part of the day lay ahead. She had wanted her wedding reception at Hovingham, and it was decided that Helen's party should also be at home. A neighbour's field had been set aside as a car park for the 500 guests converging on Crocker End House, and Lady

Elizabeth Anson, the Queen's cousin and royal caterer, had prepared canapés for the early evening reception, held in a marquee on the lawn.

There was no grand sit-down dinner, or any dancing, but clearly holding a vast party for such a heterogeneous collection of guests was a major undertaking for the Kents. The tensions were barely perceptible, except possibly to Lady Elizabeth, a veteran of large royal parties. 'What a difficult day that was,' she was heard to remark afterwards. For Katharine, watching her daughter leave for her honeymoon in Mauritius, the aftermath of the wedding must have instilled in her a mixture of emotions. A release of tensions, certainly, but also a great sadness for what might have been, coupled, perhaps, with a touch of smugness. After all the rifts in the royal family, about whom the Duchess felt an enduring ambivalence, it had taken a child of the Kents to remind the nation that royal dignity, charm, romance and charisma were not entirely spent commodities.

Any mother in Katharine's position would also have felt some sense of loneliness and anti-climax. By this point in their marriage, the Kents – different people pursuing different lives – were beginning, in private though not in public, to present a more fractured front. 'I used to notice how, at Crocker End, they would drift glacially past each other in the corridors, neither turning their head,' says one frequent visitor.

It would have been quite possible for Katharine, recovering from the drama of the wedding, to sink back into the shadow of her old depression. On the contrary, she seemed to have gained not only a new verve and radiance but also a wish to expand her horizons. In the lead-up to the ceremony she had enjoyed, at second hand, some of the glamour attaching to her beautiful daughter. She was, as she had realized, by no means too old or too staid to capture a little of that fun for herself.

Even before the wedding, Katharine had subtly reminded the public that matronly, mother-of-the-bride status was not for her. Her last portrait, painted in 1989 by the artist Leonard Boden and hung in London's Glaziers' Hall, depicted an ethereally lovely middle-aged woman with upswept hair and wearing a puff-sleeved satin gown designed in a style appropriate to young milkmaids and dowager royals. In March 1992, just after the publication of Helen's romantic set of engagement pictures, taken by Michel Comte for *Vogue*, Katharine achieved covergirl status in *Tatler*, the rival glossy monthly.

Possibly Katharine had been encouraged by Diana. Certainly she chose the Princess's favourite fashion photographer, Patrick Demarchelier, whose catchphrase, 'Smile and be sexy', had helped him to produce glowing portraits of Madonna, Kim Basinger and Lauren Bacall, as well as the Princess of Wales. The stylist for the shoot was Anna Harvey, later deputy editor of *Vogue*, who was a close friend of Katharine and Diana's confidante and fashion guru.

After the Princess's death, Harvey wrote in *Vogue* of how she helped the younger woman evolve her style. 'Diana has been called a fashion icon, but at the start she was incredibly unsophisticated. Her taste was typical of her background; upper class English girls weren't as knowing as they are now – there were no It girls then . . . One birthday I gave her a pair of Pucci leggings with some Gap teeshirts, and she was delighted that I thought she might wear something so zany.'

While Katharine was not necessarily opposed to the zany – she was once seen shopping at Kookai, a high-street store geared to fashion-conscious girls – she undoubtedly lacked It girl pretensions. However, in choosing Demarchelier –

'incredibly flirtatious and not remotely deferential', Harvey wrote of his sessions with Diana – she was obviously seeking an image divergent from that of a grandmother approaching her sixtieth birthday.

Four pictures were eventually published. In one Katharine wore pink sequins by Anouska Hempel and drop earrings, in another pearls and an Armani wrap dress. A third showed her in a long skirt and moccasins, but it was the final picture that defined her as a covergirl. Her hair was shorn and swept back, her legs casually crossed as she sat on the ground. The outfit was a navy crêpe Armani trouser suit worn with a white silk top and mannish flat shoes, and the impression was that of a carefree fortysomething career woman.

According to Jane Procter, the editor of *Tatler*, the Duchess was not seeking to redefine herself in the public eye. Instead, Procter says, the magazine spreads were purely an afterthought. 'Demarchelier took the pictures entirely for the Duchess's own personal use. I'm not sure why she wanted them – Christmas cards or whatever – plus, I think she needed a new set of official pictures. I've seen two of them many times since in programmes; although not the one we ran on the cover.

'When the pictures had been taken, the Duchess was so thrilled with them that Anna Harvey said: "Would you like me to show them to Jane and see if she'd like to run them?" The Duchess said: "Yes, I would," and of course I said that they were wonderful pictures and I should love to use them. That's the true story.'

Even if she was an accidental covergirl, there is no doubt either that Katharine was thrilled with her new image or that she wanted the world to see it, not in a fit of look-at-me exhibitionism but, no doubt, with some sense of defiance. The old tags – sad, depressed, frail and unwell – still haunted her. Here was a chance to display herself as she wished to be seen. As Katharine knew, however, from long experience, no story about the Duchess of Kent, however upbeat, was ever entirely free of medical connotation. On this occasion those who marvelled at her vitality and apparent youthfulness decided that some of the credit must certainly go to hormone replacement therapy. Others close to the Duchess believed that she – like several others in the royal family – had had a facelift.

The hormone replacement story was backed up by John Studd, a leading gynaecologist, who told a newspaper that the Duchess was certainly taking HRT; a view he has not altered. 'I said then that she's an intelligent woman and that of course she would be taking it. I would guess that she's on the lowest dose of Premarin – a low dose, almost a homoeopathic dose of oestrogens.'

Studd, although he has never treated the Duchess, is respected as an expert in his field by his colleagues and peers. He is also a flamboyant figure – he drives a car with the personalized registration HRT 1 – and a controversial one. In September 1997 he was condemned by a medical tribunal for removing a patient's ovaries without her consent but told that his actions would not affect his ability to practise and that he could continue his career. Throughout that career, Studd has taken a great interest in Katharine Kent. Some years after he first pronounced her an HRT user, he would consider writing to her to say that he believed his research could help her in her subsequent fight against ME. But, for now, that was all in the future.

In 1992 Katharine was clearly transformed from the unhappy figure of the eighties. Her daughter was due to be married. George, who had spent some time as a house-husband after his son's birth, and his wife, Sylvana, were expecting their second child, a daughter. Although there was little *rapprochement* between Katharine and Sylvana, she could hardly have failed to be pleased at the success of George's marriage.

The Duchess had just passed a milestone of her own: her thirtieth wedding anniversary, an occasion noted in the *Tatler* spread. The pictures were displayed at the editor's discretion – 'She trusted us implicitly,' says Procter – but the brief text accompanying them was personally checked and approved by Katharine. It is therefore fair to assume that she believed it fairly summarized her life thus far.

'When the young Duke of Kent fell in love with Katharine Worsley, the consensus was that he was displaying characteristic good taste ... Two years the Duke's senior, she was not only beautiful; she was also intelligent, talented and gentle. Last year the Duke and Duchess of Kent celebrated their 30th wedding anniversary. Katharine, not as robust as she first appeared, has survived the anxieties and crises of normal private life and the pressures of an abnormal public one; still beautiful, still gentle.

'She started as an army wife and has shouldered her share of royal obligations. An accomplished pianist and a member of the Bach Choir, her real passion is music; the happiest of her many responsibilities are as president of the Royal Northern College of Music, Patron of the Leeds International Pianoforte Competition and the Yehudi Menuhin School. She remains Yorkshire practical and tough-minded.'

If Katharine had not cared for the slightly barbed suggestion that her public role was 'abnormal' and the strong implication that the royal round was a burdensome one, in comparison with music, her 'passion' and source of greatest happiness, she could presumably have said so. If she had wanted to pay tribute to her husband of thirty years, rather than citing only the 'anxieties and crises of normal private life', she could have done so.

Above the few paragraphs of text, the magazine published, nonetheless, a small snapshot picture of the Duke – a weary-looking man in an open-necked shirt, whose juxtaposition with his covergirl wife suggested, more powerfully than words, that Katharine now intended to project her own image rather than operate as an adjunct to a husband she did not love.

She, stepping out of the shadows, was praised for an 'elegance and beauty' which, as the magazine noted, 'make her the best-kept royal fashion secret'. By then Katharine was harbouring another well-kept secret. If her vivacity and charm could not be attributed to an idyllic marriage, nor were her daughter's wedding or a rumoured facelift or a 'homoeopathic' dose of HRT or her passion for music the driving influences behind her newfound vivacity and youthfulness.

Far away from the world of glossy magazines and tarnished marriages, Katharine Kent had discovered for herself a new vision.

CHAPTER TWENTY

On the Road to Rome

❖

O N 14 JANUARY 1994 the Duchess of Kent was received
into the Roman Catholic Church. It was the end of a
long spiritual odyssey. Although Katharine suggested later
that she had undertaken her conversion almost on a whim,
her dalliance with Catholicism had begun almost thirty years
before and soon after her marriage.

Gordon Wheeler, the former Catholic Bishop of Leeds
and a shaper of her early fascination with his Church, was
reported as saying, at the time of her conversion, that Katharine had approached him 'ten or twelve years ago. She was
very interested, but she didn't feel that she could do it then.
If you are part of the Royal Family, it is always difficult. She
thought it would upset them very grievously. But she was very
interested in the Church of Rome because, like Our Lord, it
speaks with authority on questions of faith and morals.'

Wheeler's time frame left out their meetings in Yorkshire,
many years before. From their first encounters, Katharine –
attempting then to adjust to the strictures of royal marriage
– was impressed by a warmth and lack of stuffiness that
marked him out from the normal run of churchmen and
dignitaries she met in her capacity as the Lord Lieutenant's

daughter and the Chancellor of Leeds University. A conservative churchman but an ebullient character, a piano-playing bishop who invited the homeless to his Christmas lunch, he possessed interests and priorities that chimed with hers. But, according to his friends, it was not until the mid-seventies that Wheeler mentioned to them her serious longing to become a Catholic.

In other words, her real fascination began at precisely the time that her marriage first foundered; a time when the only moral guidance forthcoming from the House of Windsor, ineluctably linked with the Established Church, was that the Kents, however deep their differences, must soldier on. Condemned, as she was, to an unhappy personal life, it is hardly surprising that Katharine sought solace elsewhere. Even among other priests and fellow-Franciscans, Wheeler was cautious about revealing much of his conversations with the Duchess, whom he described as 'a very, very intensely spiritual lady'. Those in whom he confided were left in no doubt that the Duchess had always found irksome the formality and ceremony enshrined in the culture of the Church of England and bestowed, sometimes in obsequious measure, on the royal family.

'Every time she showed up at church, she would have been fêted and greeted at the door and all that stuff,' says one Westminster priest. 'Here we wouldn't bother. Had she never married the Duke of Kent, she might still have been an intensely spiritual lady, but the likelihood is that she would not have become a Roman Catholic.'

That is undoubtedly true; although Katharine's reasons went far deeper than a distate for irksome ceremonial. It is probable that she was seeking not only an avenue to a new spirituality and simplicity but also, and perhaps subconsciously, something more temporal. The leading priests she began to meet were not only men of God; they were also thoughtful, kind, charismatic and engaging – qualities she found entirely lacking in the Duke of Kent.

Gordon Wheeler not only inspired her. He also amused her. As Chancellor of the University of Leeds, she bestowed an honorary doctorate on him. Later, in December 1988 and at Westminster, she unveiled a plaque to him, in honour of his founding an order of Franciscan Friars. 'I want very much to thank the Duchess of York,' said Wheeler, inadvertently mixing up Katharine's home city with Fergie's title. 'Sorry about that,' he added. 'I didn't even deserve to get an honorary O level from you.' The Duchess, unoffended, laughed at his error.

But for suffering a heart attack, Wheeler would probably have become Archbishop of Westminster and therefore the man who formally brought Katharine into the Catholic Church. Instead the post went to the former Abbot of Ampleforth, Basil Hume – the man who had driven Wheeler from London to his first northern posting and a close confidant.

Priests at Westminster believe that Wheeler effectively delivered Katharine into his spiritual care. 'Bishop Wheeler made certain that the Duchess established a very good friendship with the Abbot,' says one. 'There would have been no desire on the part of either man to go out and convert the Duchess, but the friendship and the Yorkshire connection was very strong.'

But in 1976, when Hume was consecrated Archbishop of Westminster and Katharine was struggling through her marriage crisis – miserable and determined still to conceive one last child – there was no question of conversion. The Northern Ireland troubles – Catholics at bitter war with Protestants – would have made the timing impolitic. More relevantly, there was still no obvious fracture line between the royal family and the Established Church. The spate of royal divorces was still to come, and the Windsor edict remained, as Katharine knew better than anyone, that marriage was sacrosanct and break-ups to be avoided if at all possible.

Although Katharine's reception into the Catholic Church posed no constitutional difficulty, any talk of a conversion at that stage would have displeased the Queen. Determined to be loyal and fearing becoming further ostracized, the Duchess of Kent would have known that she had no option but to bide her time. In the interim, Katharine had no obvious quarrel with the Church of England. Rather, she had great respect for many of its luminaries. The Revd John Andrew, a former chaplain to Donald Coggan during his time as Archbishop of Canterbury, has been credited with helping her after her miscarriage and influencing her in the years she considered conversion. While the Kents stayed in his New York flat, decorated with pictures of them, after he moved to be rector of St Thomas's Church on Fifth Avenue, it is unlikely that an Anglican priest allied to both the Duke and the Duchess had a seminal influence on her.

The Anglican priest most involved with her life was Andrew's boss, Lord Coggan, who – in his role as Nicholas's godfather and Katharine's friend – used to drop in for an informal cup of tea in the Duchess's kitchen in York House and catch up with her news. Though he has never said so publicly, he was wholly supportive of her decision to become a Catholic, recognizing, like most liberally minded churchmen, that Christians are entitled to find the key to their own spirituality in whatever manner they choose. 'I think [critics] were making a mountain out of a molehill. There was a girl floundering, with appalling problems in her life, awful tensions. It was: let's get our feet on a rock; let's get the pieces sorted out. I think what she wanted was a sort of anchor she didn't find in Anglicanism. I don't feel she worries about points of doctrine and the Pope. I think she simply felt secure in Catholicism.

'And, of course, the Roman communion and the Anglican communion are more and more understanding of one another. That's all going ahead at grass roots level.' In an age of ecumenism, in which leading churchmen made clear their respect for other denominations, it was – in the years before her conversion – quite permissible for Katharine to forge links with Catholicism. In 1980, along with Coggan's successor, Robert Runcie, she made an historic pilgrimage to the shrine of Our Lady at Walsingham. Runcie was the first Archbishop of Canterbury and Katharine the first member of the royal family to undertake such an expedition since the Reformation.

While protesters, horrified by this apparently papist taste for Mariolatry among leading Anglicans, waved posters reading 'Pray to Christ and not to Mary', the Duchess slipped unnoticed through a side door, sat with other pilgrims and queued to receive communion. As an Anglo-Catholic – a position barely different in spiritual terms from that of a Roman Catholic – she continued to work with those whose views meshed with hers.

At Helen House, the children's hospice near Oxford, she became close to Mother Frances Domenica, the hospice's director and an Anglo-Catholic nun. At the Passage, Westminster Cathedral's centre for the homeless, she worked with the Catholic organizer, Sister Bridie, and with other volunteers and patrons from diverse backgrounds and denominations. Frank Field, the Labour MP and a High Anglican, was frequently seen there, as was the mother of Harriet Harman, Field's one-time boss at the Department of Social Security.

As sources at Westminster said later, the Duchess had for years been a Catholic in all but name. Over those years, the relationship between the royal family and the Church of England had altered, at first imperceptibly, then seismically. The distaste felt, though not always expressed, by the clergy over the flood of royal divorces culminated in the tense relationship between the Established Church and the man expected, one day, to be its titular head.

Prince Charles, whose marriage had fallen apart in the most tawdry and tragic of circumstances, was exposed as a man presiding over what his wife later described as a 'crowded marriage': a triangle containing both Diana and his long-time mistress, Camilla Parker Bowles. Speculation about whether it might ever be proper for Charles to remarry consumed Church leaders, anxious about how they would accommodate such a union. To worsen matters, in the eyes of many in the Church of England, Charles appeared to regard the position of Defender of the Faith as an anachronistic position, not entirely appropriate to a multi-cultural Britain.

Increasingly, he evinced a great interest in Islam and announced that he would prefer to see the Church of England brief widened to that of 'defender of faiths'. Although the saga of the difficulty between Church and monarchy had not fully unravelled before the Duchess's conversion, the Church was also being torn apart from within.

The rift caused by the sanctioning of women priests threw the Church of England into turmoil. Those who deplored the move believed, far beyond any anti-feminist tendency, that the Church had sold out on a vital strand of orthodoxy and betrayed its historical tradition. Barring an allegiance to Mary and to the Pope, there are no great doctrinal differences between Catholicism and Anglicanism. The issue was the integrity of the institution created at the Reformation. High-profile protesters who felt those values betrayed began to defect to the Church of Rome.

At the same time, the Duchess of Kent realized that the Queen would place no obstacle in her way. No approach, formal or informal, was initially made. Instead, under the osmotic system of communications operating in the House of Windsor, Katharine absorbed the growing sense of unease in the royal family over developments in the Church of England. A word, a gesture, a disinclination on the part of the Queen to attend a Church function; any one of these would have sufficed to make clear to the Duchess that when she did seek sanction for her move, no objection would be raised.

The timing – at the height of the row over women priests – led to a spate of speculation that Katharine was allying herself to the anti-ordination bandwagon and planned to convert for that reason. In fact, the issue did not interest her at all. Nor did she have the slightest intellectual preoccupation with moral theology or the more complex smallprint of the faith which she was to embrace.

As Coggan was wise enough to realize, hers was a move based in large part on a yearning for security and on emotion. The 'smells and bells' dimension of Catholicism – traditionally sniffed at among the royal family – was a magnet. She loved lighting candles, she loved simplicity, and she craved human warmth. As one of the Cardinal's priests puts it: 'At its best, the Catholic Church is a family.' For

Katharine, whose marriage had proved so empty, that clannishness represented perhaps the greatest charm.

The qualities she had failed to find in her own husband – wisdom, kindess and understanding – were available to her from another source: the Roman Catholic Church and, specifically, its leader. In Katharine's life, there had been only one authentic icon and hero: her father. She had longed to find his strengths in her husband and could not. Now, at last, she could again be guided by someone she admired and revered.

After her conversion, she explained that it had nothing to do with reading the Bible. Instead she had been influenced by the people she met, in particular Cardinal Hume. She paid tribute to his gentleness, humility and affectionate nature, explaining also that she referred to him as 'The Boss'. Katharine also said, in an interview with the *Daily Telegraph*: 'I do love guidelines, and the Catholic Church offers you guidelines. I have always wanted that in my life: I like to know what is expected of me. I like being told: "You shall go to church on Sunday and, if not, you're in for it."'

Her interpretation of the lure of Catholicism is revealing. Katharine, dominated all her life by what her parents wanted and by the demands of royal life, was not, in her conversion, seeking a liberal regime, offering absolute individual choice and freedom of expression. As Coggan guessed, and she confirmed, she wanted a new rulebook for her future. In a sense, Katharine was seeking an alternative form of control, one exerted by papal edict and interpreted by a man who, however gentle and humble and kind, she regarded as 'The Boss'.

In the Catholic Church, Katharine was seeking an influence that could both reshape her life and turn, through an alchemy of faith, her perceived failures into successes. She felt sorrow over her son, Nicholas, and his illness. The Church would absolve her of all guilt and self-blame. She had not been happy in her marriage. The Church, in outlawing divorce, would tell her that she had been right not to press for a separation and that she had acted in accord with God's will. For Katharine, who had toyed with the idea of ending the marriage for so long, that approval would bring a sort of peace.

The personality of Hume was, as she said, important to her. Powerful men – 'boss' figures – had always been a fixture in Katharine's life. In the main she had been at their mercy. She, brought up to be a compliant daughter, seems to have had less difficulty with male hegemony than with the manner of its expression. In her temporal life she had had to submit to a bad-tempered Duke, shouting at her to pull herself together, or an array of machiavellian courtiers noting, silently and with disapproval, the awkward ways of the Duchess of Kent. Now, in her spiritual life, she could welcome Hume's power; a controlling influence delinked from harshness or coercion.

Cardinal Hume officially began to prepare the Duchess for her reception into the Catholic Church in 1993, the year before her conversion. Even prior to that, she was known as a dropper-in to Cathedral House, visiting the Cardinal after he was recuperating from a hip operation. In the main, prominent converts – John Gummer, the former Agriculture Minister, and the Conservative Health minister Ann Widdecombe – along with possible converts, such as Alan Clark MP, are seen by Father Michael Seed, a young and brilliant

Franciscan, accustomed to debating with high-fliers and, occasionally, managing their expectations.

As another priest points out: 'Some converts want their absolutes, and half the job is bringing that down to reality. It's not a draconian church but one of faithful dissent; a dissenting church, not a robotic one. We don't want fascists, *Brave New World* and *Logan's Run*.'

Katharine, in terms of papal orthodoxy, was a dissenter herself – a frequent and interested visitor to contraceptive advice centres in the third world. She certainly needed no lectures on fundamentalism from the two men who would prepare her to be received into the Church. The Cardinal decided that the more formal instruction, including details of the reception service, would be given by Father Daniel Cronin, his Master of Ceremonies.

The Cardinal would do the rest himself. Though Hume is a Benedictine monk, there is nothing austere about him or his surroundings. The office where he and Katharine met is a large space with vivid yellow walls and bright curtains. On the mantelpiece sits a teddy bear in the strip of Newcastle United – his favourite football team – with his red Cardinal's hat propped next to it. In the armchairs next to his desk, he and Katharine would sit and discuss their faith.

'She was familiar with Catholic practice and belief,' says a friend of Hume. 'Their conversations were not rudimentary or basic in any way. There was a lot of personal stuff; simply because you have to know the human condition before you can guide someone.' In other words, Katharine would have been able – for the first time – fully to unburden herself of the miseries she had endured; not to a sombre priest but to a man full of jollity and as playful and almost childlike as she herself could be in happier moments.

'He is a very charming man, and his manner would be immensely attractive to someone like the Duchess,' says the Cardinal's friend. 'He doesn't tell anyone what to do. He just listens. He's the most wonderful listener. They struck up quite an intensely spiritual friendship, with the highest amount of respect on both sides. It was like a mutual admiration society. The Cardinal would have looked at this person who had made herself so vulnerable because of her own personal problems and her great struggles in life and regard it as a great honour to listen to someone loved by the nation for her humility and gentleness and beauty.'

While the frequent meetings with Hume bore some of the atmosphere of the confessional, the Duchess's appointments with Father Cronin were more functionary. He saw, again in 1993, to the signing of the necessary documents and instructed her formally in the rudiments of Catholicism, the seven sacraments, the Pope, Mary and the Saints. The date for the admission ceremony – the term conversion strictly applies only to the non-baptized – was set for January 1994.

Even in the more liberal climate of the nineties, Katharine's decision was an unprecedented step. The Queen, who had attended the first Catholic Mass of her life the previous year, at the funeral of King Baudouin of Belgium, made it clear that, having given her formal consent, she proposed to distance herself from something she regarded as being purely a matter for the Duchess's conscience.

As for the Duke of Kent, his stance was suitably gracious but remote. He let it be known only that he regarded his wife's decision as a question of personal faith. His constitutional standing, eighteenth in line to the throne, was of course unaffected by her move, but, as Grand Master of Britain's Freemasons, he was put in a slightly odd position.

Despite the Duke's influence as a liberal and a modern-izer – at least by the organization's previously arcane stan-dards – Freemasonry and Roman Catholicism were seen as mutually exclusive. Technically this was not so. The Catholic Church's rather vague updated guidance was that if a Catholic found it within his conscience to become a Mason, and if he had discussed the matter with his bishop or priest and family, the Church would offer no objection. Nonethe-less, a number of British newspapers ran stories alleging that the Duke of Kent might have to stand down as Grand Master as a result of his wife's impending conversion.

Accepting as he was of Katharine's decision, this charge enraged the Duke. A senior Freemason, acting on his behalf, was instructed to write to the newspapers rebutting the allegation. When his refutation failed to appear, Edward telephoned the organization's headquarters in Great Queen Street, demanding that every editor who had published the initial story should be phoned and told of the Duke's annoyance and his wish that his version of events should be printed.

Given their other differences, the trumped-up divisions between Catholicism and Freemasonry caused little problem between the Duke and Duchess. She was almost wholly uninvolved in his Masonic work, barring a visit or two to homes run by the Masons' Benevolent Society. Even when the Masons held a party for 12,500 people at Earl's Court to celebrate the Duke's twenty-fifth anniversary as Grand Master, Katharine missed the early part of the proceedings. On this occasion, however, there was no suggestion of a snub. Katharine, who had recently broken her ankle, turned up for the dinner, belatedly and in a golf cart; circulating round a drinks reception and remaining with the Duke for his formal dinner.

On the day of her conversion to Roman Catholicism, he was at her side, along with George and Sylvana, Helen Taylor and her husband Tim, and Nicholas. Three hundred reporters and cameramen waited as Katharine, in a dark green velvet jacket and black skirt, walked through the side entrance of Cathedral Clergy House.

She had made this small pilgrimage many times before. Up two flights of red-carpeted stairs, past the pale green door of the Cardinal's private office, where they had spoken for so many hours, and into the private chapel where he rises to pray every day at 6a.m. The room, untouched for a century, is simple and wood-panelled, hung with the Stations of the Cross and fitted with a dozen simple wooden pews.

Katharine knelt, as she had been instructed, on the worn green velvet cushion of the first pew on the right, beneath a statue of the Virgin Mary and in front of the green and cream marbled altar with its crucifix and six silver candlesticks. Above it hung mosaic panels and, to the right, a sanctuary lamp. The service was as simple as the setting. Katharine spoke only once, to say, as she had been taught: 'I believe and profess all that the Holy Catholic Church believes, teaches and proclaims to be revealed by God.' Cardinal Hume placed his hand on her forehead and made the sign of the cross in holy oil. At that moment the Duchess of Kent was officially admitted to the world she had wished for; the first royal to abandon protestantism since James II's deathbed conversion in 1685.

There was no great fuss to mark the occasion; only tea and sandwiches set out on the table by the window of the Cardinal's reception room. The salon, due for a repaint, was simply furnished with old brocade sofas, burning logs in the grate and an oil portrait of a past cardinal on the wall.

Katharine, according to Hume, seemed 'very peaceful and at ease'.

Still in a reverie, she walked back down the steps and into her car, pausing only to tell reporters: 'This has been a very big day for me.' That was an understatement. The realization of Katharine's dream had been a long journey and often a solitary one. Even those she liked the most and respected the best had not been privy to her feelings.

A few days after her conversion Lord Coggan opened, in his flat in Winchester, an envelope delivered in the morning post and containing a handwritten note from Katharine, explaining her decision to one of the most eminent Anglican churchmen of his age and a man who had counselled her through the worst times of her life.

She hoped that Coggan understood and that he 'didn't mind'. He was instead overjoyed for her, hopeful only that her transition might mark, at last, a more peaceful chapter in a troubled life. But Katharine's omission was telling. It seems extraordinary that she should have failed to tell such an old and influential friend of her decision or discuss her plans with him. There are two possible reasons for her oversight. The first is that she feared opposition. Other Anglican clergy speak of how Katharine distanced herself from them prior to her conversion, as if she – so used to coldness and criticism at home – could not believe that they would be happy on her behalf.

But Katharine knew that Coggan, of all men, would not have opposed her. Yet she, who had sought his counsel at every juncture of her life, chose not to speak to him, possibly for the very reason that they had been so close. He had sat at her bedside after her baby died. He had also been a spiritual adviser at the time of her abortion; a decision which has, as he acknowledges, 'troubled her all her life'.

In turning to Catholicism, Katharine was also turning away from an Established Church that had been involved in the darkest areas of her life. The Anglican Church had married her and, through Michael Mann, the Windsor Dean, intervened to save her marriage. This time she wanted no guidance, even from Lord Coggan, as she attempted to cast off all the ghosts of a damaged past. The road to conversion was, in her eyes, a route to a more enlightened future. She chose to walk it alone.

CHAPTER TWENTY-ONE

A Field of Battle, Not a
Bed of Roses

Marriage is like life in this – that it is a field of battle,
and not a bed of roses.
        Robert Louis Stevenson, *Virginibus Puerisque*

I F LEADING CLERGY of both the Established and the
Catholic Church both supported and understood the
Duchess's new allegiance with Rome, the same could not be
said for all the members of her own household. On learning
that Katharine was to convert, a very junior member of staff
said, uncomprehendingly and dismissively: 'What for? She
never even goes to church.' Though substantively untrue –
Katharine has always been a devout woman – this throwaway
remark illustrated a tension at York House that extended far
beyond the Duchess's churchgoing habits.

For close to twenty years, the Duke and Duchess of Kent
had been living out a hollow marriage while presenting, in
public and in private, a façade of togetherness decreed by
the exigencies of royal duty. At first a separation had been
ruled impossible; in part because of the scandal it would
bring. Even now, as royal marriages imploded on a regular
basis, the news of one more doomed union – particularly

one of such long standing – would have been deeply damaging to the Windsors. There was, in any case, no question of a split.

In converting to Catholicism the Duchess had put herself beyond the reach of divorce. As for the Duke, the idea remained unthinkable. Long ago he, a man possessed of an unshakeable sense of duty, had determined that there would be no split and told the Queen of his decision. From that moment on, there was no possibility that he would consider reneging on his word. Despite the Duchess's agreement to keep the marriage going, the Kents had achieved little tranquillity. Unlike some couples, able to sustain a loveless but an entirely amicable marriage of convenience, the passing of time had not smoothed over their differences.

In almost every way, the situation was less bitter for Edward. As a royal Duke, aware that, over the centuries, miserable royal marriages outweighed the tolerable variety, he would press on, in the dignified manner befitting his birth and his obligation to the Crown. Although Katharine had been infinitely more damaged, the compact they had chosen had not been easy for either of the Kents. While Crocker End House accorded some space and freedom, when in London the Duke and Duchess lived cheek-by-jowl in York House. There was no garden, little privacy and a warren of small rooms with two larger salons for their receptions and their dinner parties. While scarcely cramped by council flat standards, neither their tall, narrow living quarters nor their public role allowed much opportunity for entirely separate lives. Like it or not, the Kents remained very much a couple.

Coupledom, in their case, included a joint staff with offices on the premises, jurisdiction over their diaries and insights into almost every area of their existence. Under this structure, it was inevitable that Katharine would be the loser. Though great deference was paid her to her face, the Duchess was said to be 'difficult': mercurial in character and prone to lightning switches of mood.

Despite her emergence from breakdown and grave depression, Katharine was not cured. Even in the early nineties, some of those around her suspected that she was taking a variety of medication – from unspecified 'pills' to large doses of cold cures – to see her through bad days. In addition, she slept badly. Sometimes a diary meeting, arranged with her staff to plan and list future engagements, would run on for most of a day as Katharine, exhausted and unable to concentrate, attempted to sort out what she would most like to do.

Even after schedules were prepared with her agreement, she – tired and irritable – would complain at the last minute about the fixtures for the day. Courtiers' tactics varied. One would assure the Duchess that, if she did not wish to fulfil an engagement, it could easily be cancelled; whereupon she would go. Others tried gentle encouragement. One maid, particularly expert at cajoling Katharine, was designated persuader-in-chief by more senior staff.

Some of those around her believed that her worries about her weight contributed to her lassitude and occasional crank-iness. Always diet-conscious, Katharine would sometimes starve herself and sometimes resort to binge-eating, alarming those close to her. Often, she would appear self-abnegating, mocking herself for precisely the qualities the British public adored her for. Sometimes, according to one aide, she would throw a temper tantrum at Wimbledon if she did not think herself sufficiently in the spotlight.

In 1993 millions of television viewers watched across the world as Katharine consoled Jana Novotna, the tennis player who had victory at Wimbledon snatched from her grasp. The twenty-four-year-old Czech had been leading Steffi Graf 6–7, 6–1, 4–1, 40–30 when her game, and her dreams of the championship, collapsed. Afterwards, Katharine offered one kind thought before Novotna broke down, literally weeping on the Duchess's shoulder as Katharine embraced her, murmuring words of comfort. The image – still remembered as one of the most telling cameos of the Duchess's great talent for warmth and empathy – endeared Katharine more than ever to the British people and consoled Novotna herself long afterwards. Weeks after the episode she told an interviewer: 'The Duchess wouldn't let go of me. She wanted to calm me down. That was so nice, wasn't it?'

But the following day, back at York House, Katharine was reported to have said, crossly and self-mockingly: 'Oh, that was just me doing my caring bit again.' Those who heard her, and who sided with the Duke, took this as evidence of cynicism on her part. Far more probably, it was a sign of Katharine's lack of belief in herself and her capacity for self-destruction.

The pressures on the Duchess continued to be enormous. On the public stage, she, a genuine carer, was never less than perfect, for she demanded, as she always had, fearsomely high standards of herself. Never a performance and always a genuine display of empathy, every appearance exacted from her reserves of energy that, on the worst days, she simply did not possess. In private she was surrounded by courtiers who, in many cases, failed or did not wish to understand her loneliness and fear of failure; preferring to interpret any difficult behaviour as wilful awkwardness. The result was that Katharine came home to an unwelcoming milieu.

Any public evidence of her troubles remained slight. But

in the week before Novotna's Wimbledon defeat and the Duchess's bravura display of consolation, a small item appeared in the press, claiming that the Duke and Duchess had arrived separately at the tournament because she was late in her preparations. The Duke was said to have warned her: 'Be ready in five minutes, or I go without you.' Having missed the deadline, she had to order a black cab and settle the £14 fare, finally arriving half an hour after her husband, the President of the All England Lawn Tennis Club.

Though regarded as an amusing anecdote, this story has curious undertones. How natural to complain about a partner's lateness; and how odd actually to depart without waiting for them. This sort of event had occurred before. Katharine herself, in her Helen House film in aid of the children's hospice, had made a point of saying that her husband had grumbled about her visiting a dying child in case she missed a flight.

Both episodes, minor as they were, suggested that – even in the most trivial matters of timetabling – the Duke and Duchess could not achieve unison. But the discontent went far deeper. According to one former member of the Kents' staff, 'he was pretty bloody' to her. Even friends of the Duke say that he would, on occasion, shout at Katharine so loudly from his bedroom that servants working in the kitchen would quake at the cries of rage.

That is not to argue that the Duke of Kent was a stereotype of Victorian melodrama, a villain and oppressor. Charitable character references for the Duke of Kent are not difficult to acquire. Eminent and thoughtful men – fewer women, for the Duke surrounds himself with male friends – point to his kindness, his intelligence, his good relationship with his children and his sense of fun; a set of qualifications entirely at variance with his public profile as a dull and a saturnine figure. Although one would expect his liegemen to hold this view, the Duke of Kent's professed admirers come from too varied and independent a background to suggest that their praise is purely deferential.

Nor is it surprising that fewer people attest to Katharine's fine qualities. Although she is admired, liked and sometimes revered by those, relatively few, people with whom she has maintained unbroken contact through the years, Katharine is a lonely person. As her friend the Marchioness of Lothian says, depression is, in itself, a great excluder; a condition that makes it hard for a sufferer to maintain a normal rapport even with those they love best. Perhaps inevitably, for every Tony Lothian there are many others whose friendships with Katharine have proved less enduring. And yet she can be a wonderful ally and comforter; an assiduous letter-writer and someone who will use the worst of her own experience as a means to reach out for others. Close acquaintances of the Duchess who have lost a parent or a baby always receive a note offering her sympathy and explaining that she understands how dreadful they must feel. But Katharine's warmth is tempered also by reserve. Brought up by her father to be trustful, life has taught her to exercise care over deciding in whom she can place reliance. Some, particularly new friends she has met through the Catholic Church, see Katharine's carefree side and her sense of fun and irreverence. Others incorrectly interpret a shortness induced by the fact that she is feeling ill as deliberate coldness. Yet others, often allies of the Duke, bewail her swings from charm to iciness.

It is probable that Katharine decided long ago not to expend much effort on those she perceived as acting against her interests. In a failed relationship between a royal Duke and a commoner, it is not difficult to imagine which partner

will garner the most support. Increasingly the Kents' problems inspired a 'camp' mentality – his friends and hers.
Supporters of the Duke found it easy to find fault with
Katharine. She could be 'provoking' or 'awkward'. At a time
when the Kents professed themselves in severe financial
difficulties, she could also be extravagant, particularly in her
clothes purchases.

On one occasion the Queen's private secretary, personally vetting the expenses of both the Waleses and the Kents,
is said to have professed himself (and therefore the Queen
herself) displeased with the wardrobe bill of both the Princess of Wales and the Duchess of Kent. Katharine's spending
was on a far more minor scale than that of Diana. Nonetheless, a clampdown was ordered – one so stringent that a
senior member of the Kent staff appointed himself wardrobe
consultant, setting limits for the Duchess's spending, cross-
matching her engagements with the sort of clothes she would
need and even dealing directly with her designers in a bid to
curb her expenditure. In the new climate of restraint and
accountability, unsolicited gifts to Katharine – such as tennis
shoes and clothes – were, without any consultation with her,
returned immediately, tissue paper unruffled and carrier bags
unopened.

The counterpoint between a Duchess of simple standards, engaged in unsung work for the poor, and the heroic
and profligate shopper has always been an interesting one.
Katharine herself confesses to an acquisitive nature and a
love of clothes, and there is no doubt that she, however
admiring of simple values, also likes – on one level – the
grandeur and the perks that attach to royalty. Less consciously, she – so unsure of her own talent and her own
worth – relied on her glorious wardrobe as a prop, a concrete
affirmation that she was truly beautiful and royal and

admirable even at those frequent times when she felt herself to be worthless and beneath notice.

The royal family did not grasp such subtleties. Even within her own home, Katharine was regarded as being difficult and, on occasion, profligate. To be perceived as the less important partner and a blight on the Duke's happiness must have gravely damaged the self-esteem she had managed to claw back after her years of illness and which remained under constant assault. As she knew, every aspect of her life and her privacy was under constant review. It became the habit of York House staff, in the early nineties, to check the bedrooms of the Duke and Duchess for evidence that they ever slept together. They never did.

Although she had acquired some strength to fight back against coldness and intrusion, Katharine's marriage offered her less succour than ever. The sadness was that the bulk of claims by the Kents' respective friends was true. The Duchess was a charming ambassador, possessed of great warmth, immense spirituality and a vast capacity for doing good. To the dying, the dispossessed and the forgotten she offered a solace no other royal – with the single exception of Diana – could deploy. The Duke, for his part, is undoubtedly a more subtle and a kinder man than the received public wisdom allows. But, bar the odd glimpses of a genuine affection, the moments when the Duke would embrace his wife almost, according to one friend, 'as if he were her father', both were condemned to a life of spectacular loneliness.

Again, Katharine was the greater sufferer. The Duke had his three-day-a-week job as vice-chairman of the British Overseas Trade Board. He was an assiduous worker for the War Graves Commission and possessor of a vast portfolio of patronages. As someone with an almost photographic memory and a sharply honed sense of duty, he was always in public demand. Whether he always enjoyed the constant round of royal duty is highly debatable – but self-amusement was hardly the point. To relax he had his music, and particularly opera, on which he is more knowledgeable than anyone else in the royal family. Holidays would often involve a trip to Bayreuth with a small group of friends: usually Lord Kelvedon, formerly Paul Channon, his wife and Kenneth Rose, the royal biographer. Weekends might entail a trip to see his son, George, and his grandchildren, or to hew trees with his brother, Prince Michael, in Gloucestershire. An evening out might be spent at an all-male dining club with industrialists, policy-formers and other friends.

Katharine's work for Unicef and her other charities preoccupied her. Her social life was more difficult to organize, for the networks that embrace single-status Dukes have few equivalents for women in the same position. Shopping, work, the occasional lunch with a girlfriend at Le Caprice, her favourite restaurant; tea at home with old acquaintances or her daughter, Helen, who would drop in often – all of these featured in her calendar. She continued too to ski, loathing the downhill sport at which her husband excelled and preferring to escape for a Langlauf, or cross-country skiing, break.

Gradually the Kents had taken up entirely compartmentalized lives. Whatever the strain on the Duke, his training – duty before emotion – cushioned the impact. For Katharine, sensitive, emotional and vulnerable, the toll exacted was perhaps greater than any human being might be expected to pay. The problems of her later years – further illnesses were just around the corner – have always been thought to be rooted in chronic depression. The truth was far more complex.

For years, Katharine had struggled to be the epitome of

the perfect royal. In that, she had succeeded. But her life – one of loneliness, unhappiness, of lack of understanding by the royal family she served and unwelcome scrutiny by those who served her – would have driven a lesser woman past the brink of endurance. She, so quick to offer sympathy to others, received little herself.

In the cold goldfish bowl of royalty, emotional struggle is not viewed as a wholly valid form of pain. Courtiers, looking on, wondered whether the Duchess, like Diana, might have considered suicide. 'She wouldn't have had the courage,' says one. 'Do not believe that she is so fragile,' says another. 'The Duchess is tough; as tough as old boots.'

To survive unscathed not only her loveless marriage but the imposed lifestyle it entailed – the slurs and the slights – would have demanded a Herculean toughness. The Duchess, indeed a stronger woman than anyone imagines, could merely do her best and fight on against the pressures in her public and private life. A direct and straightforward person, imbued with the honesty of her Yorkshire roots, she had no choice but to maintain the charade.

At York House, the Kents' dinner parties were surprisingly successful. There would be no excessive grandeur, beyond staff to collect coats and caterers to cook food, but the Duke and Duchess were always punctilious in making sure that their guests – including friends from Katharine's university connections and actors such as Charles Dance and Jeremy Irons – felt at ease. 'Good-humoured, informal and gracious,' said one invitee. 'The Kents are always so good at introducing people, mentioning friends they might have in common and generally ensuring that everyone has a pleasurable evening.' And afterwards, the goodbyes said and the guests departed, the Duke and Duchess would retreat silently to their different rooms.

Whatever the debris of argument and disappointment along the way, it had long been clear to both that the root of their difficulties lay not merely in the burden of a royal life. Katharine, encouraged by ambitious parents to set her sights at a Duke, had taken too little account of the fact that the differences in their characters would be destructive rather than complementary. He, as a gauche young man, charmed by her sophistication and sense of fun, had not the subtlety to realize that, beneath the gloss, she was potentially a more complex and troubled personality, someone who would give everything and return home drained almost to the point of catatonia.

Put in its simplest terms, the Kents were polar opposites and their relationship seemingly irredeemable. At the point when they might have expected a closer life, now that their children were grown and their grandchildren arriving, there was no sign of *rapprochement*.

On 7 August 1994 Lady Helen Taylor gave birth to her first son and the Kents' third grandchild at the Portland Hospital, London. The Taylors called him Columbus, and the press sought in vain to find the source of this unusual name. In fact, the only known Columbus in the Kent clan was the Duke's old dog, a favourite during his courtship of Katharine and a companion on their Birkhall honeymoon. If there was any link between Columbus the dog and Columbus the baby, the choice of name offered a rare flashback to a happier era. Even in the presence of her grandchildren, Katharine was always reminded of her own stillborn son, whose death had extinguished any last hope of reviving her marriage.

Nevertheless, as royal marriages began to splinter and the Windsors' reputation to flake away in the last decade before the millennium, the Kents – in the public eye – remained emblematic of the stable values of traditional Britain. Here was a marriage that had lasted; evidence that royal coupledom could still offer an example to a nation that, however irrationally, expected the monarchy to offer an epitome of beautiful behaviour. To the outside world, the Kent union was a testament to enduring love. For the Duke and Duchess, the emphasis remained on endurance rather than on love.

CHAPTER TWENTY-TWO

Working a Miracle

THERE WAS NO fuss, no advance phone call, no detective at her side. From the time of the Duchess's conversion onwards, she would turn up unannounced at Westminster Cathedral each Sunday. Katharine rarely went to the Cardinal's sung services, complete with Gregorian chant, preferring what his priests called the 'hillbilly Masses', held at 5.30 and 7p.m. and attended mainly by young people.

Among them, Katharine was an inconspicuous figure, dishevelled almost and normally wearing jeans, a T-shirt and sneakers. The cathedral priests would notice her only when she trekked up to the altar, one of 500 people receiving communion. Afterwards she might linger to say goodnight to the celebrant. At other times she would just slip away into the evening, an anonymous parishioner.

After the formality of the Church of England, Katharine loved the obscurity on offer here and the chance to be, for an hour or two, a private citizen at prayer. But her contact with the cathedral was not limited to devotions or to her work at the Passage and her role as patron of the Cardinal's Night Shelter Appeal for the homeless. Often a priest walking through the corridors of Cathedral Clergy House would hear the bell ring and find the Duchess on the doorstep, waiting to be let in for a meeting or, later on, for a reunion of those who attended the Cardinal's pilgrimage to Lourdes.

Although they knew nothing of Katharine's domestic problems, the priests who worked closely with Hume understood something of the lure the cathedral held for Katharine. 'The Duchess became more and more rooted,' says one of them. 'She needed that because she has had such an unstable life.' Far beyond spiritual fulfilment, Katharine had found a camaraderie to dispel the loneliness in other areas of her life. Westminster was to become for her a rival social base and, in many ways, an alternative family.

So enthusiastic was she to join in with everything the cathedral had to offer that she had, on occasion, to be restrained. When a parishioner attempted to recruit her to the in-house folk group, which performed at a Sunday evening Mass, one of the Cardinal's staff discreetly intervened to block the plan, on the grounds that 'she was a little too old for a group that was supposed to be for young people. Besides, they did not rejoice in the most glorious of sounds; that is, they couldn't sing, and they couldn't play.'

But among parishioners and priests, Katharine found other interests and other friends – among them Father Vladimir Felzmann, the Cardinal's director of pilgrimages and his close confidant. Direct, straightforward, down-to-earth and charming, Father Vladimir had come late to the priesthood after moving on from a career in engineering. One of the British leaders of Opus Dei, the fundamentalist wing of the Catholic Church, he later revised his allegiance to a sect dedicated to preserving Catholic orthodoxy against liberal encroachment. As such, Opus Dei was regarded with distaste by those within Catholicism who abhorred its secrecy, ultra-conservatism and anti-feminist stance, as defined in its maxim that 'women needn't be scholars; it is enough for them to be prudent'. Long before Father Vladimir met Katharine, he had renounced all links with Opus Dei, becoming instead one of the closest associates of Cardinal Hume, who admired his qualities of integrity and forthrightness. The Duchess of Kent was equally struck by Felzmann's charisma.

As she preferred, he forbore to treat her with the deference due to a Duchess, greeting her instead with a kiss on both cheeks. She, frequently starved of human warmth, reciprocated his friendliness. As one priest says: 'If she saw him, she would bound up the stairs or across the room to greet him, crying: "Vlad, Vlad." It was like a scene from *Romeo and Juliet*.' Katharine, an outgoing person, found in Felzmann and others of the Cardinal's lieutenants qualities of friendliness and openness that contrasted sharply with the *froideur* of the royal family.

Felzmann's other charm was that he refused to buy the line, constantly peddled by the press, that Katharine had turned to Rome less through conviction than through despair. 'People say she's a depressive and that she looked to the Church because she was suicidal. That's total crap. She's not like that at all when she's with us. She's great fun. The lack of formality is very good for her, and she's enormously good for people. She empathizes. That's her great strength. It's also why she suffers a lot. She empathizes so much with someone who is suffering that she almost takes on that suffering herself.'

Given her skills with the sick and her fondness for her new mentors, it was inevitable that Katharine longed to join the Westminster Diocese's annual pilgrimage to Lourdes, organized by Father Vladimir and attended by the Cardinal. In July 1995 she flew out on VIP status from Gatwick airport *en route* for the three-star Hotel Méditerranée. Despite its boasts of *'une ambiance chaleureuse'* and *'171 chambres spacieuses et silencieuses avec bain, douche et WC séparé'*, the Méditerranée was not a natural VIP destination. As Father Vladimir points out, the glowingly advertised bath was 'so small that you could wet either your top part or your bottom part. If you lay down, your feet were in the air. It's not plush. It's a pilgrim's hotel designed for pilgrims.' And the Duchess, despite her single luxury of being accompanied by her hairdresser, Sarah McCormick – who was interested in any case in the Lourdes work – was a moderately ordinary pilgrim.

Her room cost £32 a night and had no phone or television. Breakfast was a croissant and a cup of coffee and dinner a modest meal of meat or eggs and vegetables, eaten when the shift system allowed. Often Katharine rose at dawn to start work at 6a.m., getting the pilgrims – some wheelchair-bound, some incontinent and some dying – dressed and ready for the day. On other days, she would work late into the evening, settling the sick down for the night.

Lourdes *accueils*, or hospices, designed for the very sick, have no indigenous staff, bar two nuns in charge of administration. Otherwise, the entire staff is an imported crew of voluntary helpers, made up, in the case of the Westminster party, of 'red caps' – fit young helpers acting as *'brancardiers'* (stretcher-bearers) and marked out by their Diocese of Westminster baseball caps. One of a group of 'handmaids', Katharine was assigned lighter duties. As she said at the beginning of her visit: 'I am here to help in any way I can. I am not a trained nurse, but I will be cleaning the wards, cleaning the toilets and washing floors. I've never done anything like that in my life before.'

As Father Vladimir confirms, Katharine did indeed take some part in the lavatory-cleaning rota for which her first Lourdes visit became famous, but the practical side of the job, though emphasized by Katharine, was a minor one. The more vital role was one she had trained herself for rigorously. All her past work for Age Concern, for the hospice movement and for Macmillan Cancer Relief, of which she is patron, had schooled her for the other aspects of Lourdes work: easing the progress both of those who yearned for recovery and those who wished only for a tranquil death.

The brochure Lourdes is a place of dreams and miracles, shrine to Bernardette Soubirous, a miller's daughter brought up in an abandoned jail after her father lost an eye and, with it, his job and the means to support his six children. On 11 February 1958, Our Lady, in the Catholic legend, appeared to Bernardette; the first of eighteen apparitions and the precursor to the miracles with which Lourdes has been credited ever since, shortly after Bernardette's vision, Catherine Lataple, a local woman, was cured of paralysis in two fingers.

On Katharine's first visit she was also, in the view of Father Vladimir, responsible for a miracle. The Westminster party included a pilgrim of long standing: a stroke patient named Francis, confined to a wheelchair and living in a North London hospice. Although a youngish man, in his late forties, Francis was withdrawn to the point of catatonia – unable to utter a word and barely capable of movement. Though he sat, day after day, immobile in his wheelchair, helpers saw the intelligence in his eyes and realized that he could understand, at least to some degree, what was going on around him. 'What food would you like, Francis?' they would ask, and he would occasionally point at his choice from the items on offer. When Katharine arrived, that was the sum of his contact with the outside world.

Assigned to help care for him, Katharine took a particular interest, spending hours not only looking after his physical wellbeing but talking to him constantly as he sat, immobile, in his wheelchair. After only a few days in her company, Francis began to emerge from his state of complete withdrawal, demonstrating first by the flicker of an eye and later by hand gestures that he had begun to return to the real world. 'What food would you like, Francis?' the helpers would ask, as usual, and he would this time gesture animatedly at his preferences from the dishes on the table.

His recovery ran entirely counter to the medical opinion spelt out to Father Vladimir by regular carers who had failed to pierce his withdrawal from the world. 'They said that he could not communicate. But, by the end of the Duchess's first pilgrimage, he was communicating. Then he began to speak; to come back to life. In fact, he was pulled back into life. He had something to live for and someone who cared.

'Those are the sort of miracles we talk of in Lourdes – not physical miracles, but God was in that event, and she was in part responsible. I wouldn't say she did it all, but she was certainly a part of it.'

Both on her first pilgrimage and on her second – two years later – Katharine helped not only those who could be coaxed back to life but those who wished to be helped towards death. One pilgrim, a mother of baby twins, accompanied by her two older sons, travelled back to England rapturous at the peace she had found. She died three weeks later. Another visitor, an elderly priest, had said he wanted to visit Lourdes one last time, either to die or to be cured. He died on the second day of the pilgrimage.

If there were pressures on Katharine – skilled at absorbing the suffering of others but exhausted by the depth of her own emotional response – they were not apparent. In the wards she was treated more or less as an equal by young helpers, who called her Lady Katharine or Lady Kay – the latter an echo of the pseudonym her mother-in-law, Marina, had used for her wartime work as a hospital auxiliary. As one young volunteer says: 'She would do all the normal wheeling and pushing jobs, just like everyone else. Certainly she wasn't a Lady Bountiful. She was very keen, very alert and very practical – the first person to scuttle off if something needed doing.'

When it rained, at the last Mass of one pilgrimage, the Duchess of Kent was the volunteer who elected to dash into the downpour, collecting wheelchairs and drying them, ready for the journey back to the hospice. At the end of each long day, she would sit and drink coffee and wine with her new friends, sparkling and cracking jokes. As Father Vladimir says: 'She enjoyed being there because she could be herself.'

But, although none of her fellow-pilgrims knew it, this was not quite the normal Katharine. At home in London, she would work equally hard and provide equal comfort to the suffering and the distressed. But afterwards, once her own front door closed, she would still frequently retreat to bed, pleading exhaustion and headache. The public and the private Duchess had always been two different women. At Lourdes they blended into one.

Of course, the ghosts of a royal existence did not leave her. Her first pilgrimage naturally attracted huge media interest; in particular from *Hello!* magazine and from British newspapers eager to see her at work, at prayer or sharing an outdoor picnic with the sick. For her second, less-reported, visit, Katharine relinquished all VIP status, asking instead whether the tour operator could send a car to pick her up from Toulouse airport.

The chosen vehicle was the battered old Mercedes, without air-conditioning, used by Father Vladimir to drive the sick. Katharine arrived at her hotel, on a baking day, soaked in perspiration and announcing that she must have a bath at once but delighted, it seemed, both to be back and by the complete lack of ceremony. Although there were many times in her life when she expected to be treated like a royal Duchess, there were others when the thought of any fuss genuinely horrified her. Her pact with the Catholic Church was predicated on equality and inclusivity. 'It gives me a sense of belonging,' she said.

It also offered her a passport to another world. Away from Lourdes, Katharine maintained the contacts she had made there; attending, whenever possible, Father Vladimir's reunions, held in the Westminster Cathedral crypt and an opportunity for her to exchange reminiscences with a new network of friends, a few of whom became important pinions in her life. In addition to the company of priests, Katharine loved the company of the young; in particular two boys whom she came to regard almost as adopted sons.

Vincent Anandraj and his older brother, Gerald – both in their early twenties – were altar-servers at the cathedral and already under the wing of the Cardinal and his priests. Their Singaporean father had died several years before Katharine's conversion and their mother, recovering from cancer, spent much of her time in Singapore. The Anandraj brothers were charming, uncomplicated and intelligent young men. Gerald, the more reserved, was an economics graduate and Vincent, outgoing and friendly, a student of English. Both planned a postgraduate course. Both were – unlike Katharine's own sons – apparently free of any personal problems, beyond angst over the loss of one parent and the illness of another. It was, perhaps, the bond of family suffering that first drew Katharine to them. It was also likely that she, perhaps subconsciously, was attempting to compensate for the difficulties and failures in her relationship with George and Nicholas.

According to other pilgrims, the friendship with Vincent – the brother who became her particular confidant – began slowly on her first Lourdes pilgrimage. He, while ignoring the fact that she was a Duchess, talked to her only on a cursory level; absorbed, as she was, in the daily workload and the problems of others. Nonetheless, he had admired the impact of her kindness, mirrored in the faces of the sick. She had liked his *joie de vivre* and the fact that he was unimpressed and undaunted by her status. By the time they had met up again in London at post-Lourdes fund-raising events – roadshows, piano recitals and garden parties – their friendship had been cemented.

It is doubtful that Katharine saw herself in any quasi-maternal role. Friends believe that instead she had found someone with whom she could relax, in whom she could confide how uneasy she often felt in large gatherings and in her public role and to whom she could simply gossip. If Katharine had discovered a book she loved – such as Nelson Mandela's autobiography, *The Long Road To Freedom*, which she read in a single sitting – she could discuss that. Mandela, one of her great heroes, was of huge importance to her, and she would sift through newspapers for stories about him, saving them up to discuss with Vincent.

While the bulk of the conversations between them

remain private, it is likely that he came to learn much about the Duchess: faith, hope, interests, fears, her good days and her bad. Certainly the constancy of Katharine's contact suggested a need for a confiding ear that she lacked in her family. When Vincent returned to Singapore to visit his mother, she would write him long letters. In London, she would phone him constantly. The habitat of the Anandraj brothers, a Westminster mansion flat piled high with young men's student paraphernalia – football videos, newspapers and books – was vastly different from Katharine's milieu. Despite, or because of this, the phone would ring 'two or three times a day' as the Duchess of Kent called for a chat.

Once more Katharine was proving that she could strike up, with a relative stranger, an uncomplicated camaraderie and warmth that failed to imbue her closer relationships; perhaps because, in the case of her sons, she invested too much in them and expected too much back. Her friendship with Vincent posed no demands on either of them, while offering Katharine a link with the real world and a contact with someone whom she could talk to almost on equal terms; a friend who would not patronize her or offer grovelling deference; someone who was on her spiritual wavelength and who would listen. Though this was one of her closer contacts, it was only one of the bonds she developed at Westminster – all of them a measure of how she was pushing out her social boundaries to compensate for the void in her home life.

While the royal family may not have registered how much the Catholic Church had offered the Duchess of Kent, providing her not only with a new religious affiliation but also with a new and less constrained life, any hint of opposition to her choice faded on 30 November 1995. Protesters jeered and chanted in the plaza outside Westminster Cathedral as the Queen arrived for vespers on St Andrew's Day, the service marking the end of the commemorations for the cathedral's centenary. She was the first reigning monarch to attend a Roman Catholic service in an official capacity for more than 400 years.

A congregation of 1,500 had gathered to watch the closing of a chapter begun with the Settlement of 1559, establishing the Protestant Church as the official Church of England and driving the Church of Rome underground. Four centuries on, the Queen was formally acknowledging that the millions of Catholics who had served their country and who had lived and died for it were indeed her loyal citizens.

She may also have been indicating a certain frostiness on her part towards the Church of England, riven by internal strife. Whether or not there was any hint of a snub on the Queen's part, protesters carrying a banner marked with the names of the Protestant martyrs – Cranmer, Latimer, Ridley and Rogers – could scarcely have been more outraged if their monarch had revealed herself as a closet Moonie.

To the peal of bells and to organ music, she was welcomed at the cathedral entrance by Cardinal Hume, who presented to her other Church leaders: the Archbishop of Canterbury, Dr George Carey; the Moderator of the General Assembly of the Church of Scotland, the Rt Revd James Harkess; and the Greek Orthodox Archbishop, Gregorios of Thyateira and Great Britain. The Queen, wearing a cerise suit and hat, walked up the cathedral nave to fierce applause, taking her seat as the Cardinal welcomed her publicly. 'It is a joy to have you with us,' he said.

During his homily, after the psalms, antiphons and canticles in Latin Gregorian chant, he reiterated his gratitude. 'Our friends from other churches, and, indeed, from the Jewish community as well, will readily understand this special joy that is ours, the Roman Catholic community, as we welcome you. The presence of your Majesty in this cathedral . . . is a further affirmation of the place that we Catholics have in the nation.' In contrast, the voices of the protesters sounded small and soured. Some claimed that the principles of the Reformation were being ripped asunder, others warned that the Queen's gesture was steering her country back into 'the dark ages of Roman Catholic superstition' and that her attendance constituted betrayal of her position as Supreme Governor of the Church of England.

Inconspicuous in the congregation, Katharine Kent watched. As she had wished, she – determined not to be seen to detract in any way from the Queen's central role – was a background figure. As prearranged, she had arrived five minutes before the star guest and joined the greeters at the door before being shown to her seat not by a priest but by a layman assigned by the Cardinal's staff.

But afterwards, at the reception following the service, the Westminster priests noted with satisfaction that the Queen and the Duchess – their Duchess – worked the room almost as a double act; arriving at the same moment, standing side by side to greet guests and leaving together for the drive home. On two counts, the Cardinal's priests felt quiet satisfaction. Not only had the Queen crossed a 400-year-old rubicon between Catholicism and the monarchy; she had also demonstrated, or so they felt, that the Duchess's conversion had her official sanction, her approval and her blessing.

There was undoubtedly a mood of solidarity between two women who had never fully come to understand one another. There was also, among those who knew them best, an unspoken acknowledgement that – while the schism between Rome and the throne of England might easily be breached – faultlines within the royal family were less easily bridged.

CHAPTER TWENTY-THREE

'The Royals are in a
Terrible Mess'

❖

IN A TROUBLED decade for the royal family, Princess Diana's interview for the BBC programme *Panorama* set a new high water mark of turmoil. Tremulous and pale, Diana had confided in millions of viewers that her marriage was 'rather crowded' – a reference to her husband's mistress, Camilla Parker Bowles. She also confessed to a previous affair with James Hewitt, a former Army Major, alluded to her misery and eating disorders and appeared to shed doubt on whether Charles would ever occupy the throne.

Shortly after the programme was broadcast, in November 1995, the Duchess of Kent phoned an old friend of the Duke's. 'The royal family is in a terrible mess,' she said. Many of her acquaintances believed that Katharine, a woman of strong discretion and even stronger religious convictions, had been appalled by the behaviour not only of Fergie but also of Diana. Where Katharine had concealed her personal misery, Diana had flaunted hers. The general presumption was that the Duchess would not approve.

The friend whom she called in the wake of the *Panorama* programme had no doubt where her sympathies lay. Although she did not directly criticize Charles, it was clear that she believed the 'mess' in which the royal family was embroiled was not the fault of Diana, with whom Katharine had the greatest sympathy.

Later Katharine would add that she understood Diana very well – 'for obvious reasons'; implying that she had first-hand experience of the more awful aspects of the Princess's life. They had kept in touch, she said, through thick and thin, and her loyalties had been torn during Charles and Diana's separation as she maintained her 'love' and friend-ship for both. Though, as she admitted, she had been entirely powerless to help, Katharine had understood both sides while acknowledging that, when something goes 'terri-bly wrong', the problem might be traced back to something that happened in childhood. There was no point, she added, in being judgemental about people.

This softened the fact that the Duchess's sympathy was less than bi-partisan. She had every reason to side with Diana. Katharine's own experience of how the royal family had treated her own complaints about an unhappy marriage – professed goodwill on the part of the Queen, coupled with a lack of ability to understand depression; lukewarm interest from Charles and exasperated incomprehension by the Duke of Edinburgh – was the template for the reaction Diana would receive when the Wales marriage began to disinte-grate. Watching Diana deliver her *Panorama* rebuke to a family that had failed fully to comprehend her unhappiness evoked in the Duchess not only understanding but also a touch of triumph or glee. Katharine would not have been dismayed to see the Windsor counselling service suddenly finding itself on the receiving end of advice that she, unlike Diana, could not publicly deliver.

While the Duke and Duchess of Kent remained ostensi-bly content and certainly untouched by scandal, Charles and

Diana had converted their affairs and their unhappiness into a national property. Charles had revealed the fact that he had a mistress to his biographer, Jonathan Dimbleby, on prime time television. Diana had reciprocated with her *Panorama* confessions. Amid what seemed to be a pitched battle between two toughened pugilists, the Duchess of Kent was perhaps the only member of the royal family fully to understand how much higher a price Diana was already paying and would continue to pay.

If Katharine feared for Diana, as she must have done, then she certainly did not pity her. Nor, as some of her friends suspected, did she resent her encroachment on her territory – hospice-visiting and Catholicism. When Diana took her sons to visit the homeless at the Passage Centre at Westminster, royal-watchers wondered whether this implied a signal that Diana, whose mother had already converted, was herself going to follow in Katharine's footsteps and become a Catholic. As both Katharine and the Westminster priests knew, she had no such plans. Even if Diana had planned a conversion, the Duchess would no doubt have been flattered rather than jealous.

Katharine admired Diana. When the Princess gave her a small silver rabbit, Katharine told a young Catholic friend that, rather than leave this special present on a mantelpiece or in a drawer, she had arranged to have it fitted to the bonnet of her private car. Whatever the significance of the rabbit – a frightened, hunted creature or simply a cute souvenir – it became, for Katharine, a private emblem of a relationship in which the early roles were being reversed. The mentor and pupil scenario once hinted at by Katharine no longer fitted. In publicly expressing a (mutual) dissatisfaction with royal life and royal marriage, Diana was leading the way.

By the time of the *Panorama* programme, the first public whispers of unrest in the Kent marriage were just beginning to surface. The move to Crocker End House, the home of Katharine's dreams, had – for all the refurbishment and the David Hicks garden – not been a success. The Duchess became increasingly reluctant to spend time there, claiming, according to friends of the Duke, that she 'felt overlooked'. Even though the grounds were adjoined by a public foot-path, that reason did not quite explain Katharine's restless-ness, since six-foot walls and two acres of landscaped gardens should have been sufficient cover for privacy. Nor had she developed a dislike for the area. A few years later she was to find herself another, much tinier, country retreat virtually down the road from Crocker End.

For the time being she began increasingly to return, alone, to Norfolk, the county she had regarded as home until her decision to leave Anmer Hall five years previously. This time she chose a simpler base: a cottage on the Earl of Leicester's estate, from which she could travel to Sunday Mass at Our Lady of St Edmund in Hunstanton or to its sister church, Saint Cecilia's, in Dersingham. Although her children had largely been brought up here, and although the Duchess was a popular local figure, Norfolk was a strange choice.

Far from holding universally happy memories, the Fens evoked some of the worst times of her life; not only her miserable schooldays at Runton Hill but also the time when, after the death of her son Patrick, she would collect birds' nests and bring them home, symbols of her own empty nest. Possibly Norfolk now accorded the Duchess a tranquillity she could not find elsewhere. As a Catholic friend was quoted as saying at the time: 'Her faith has made her realize how pretentious and shallow the high social life of the capital can be.'

This was not a fully plausible explanation, particularly given that Katharine had established in London a new circle of acquaintances, devout and unpretentious in the extreme. Nor did a parallel theory, that the Duke of Kent was having difficulty with the marriage because he could not comprehend the depth of his wife's devotion, tell more than a fragment of the story. Norfolk, for Katharine, was probably the most easily accessible bolthole.

The Duke and Duchess's miserable marriage had reached a new nadir. There would, however, have been not the slightest public hint of a rift but for the disaster of the Duke's sixtieth birthday party, thrown for him by the Queen in October 1995. The evening began with a concert given by the London Philharmonic Orchestra and the Hanover Band, of which he is patron, and ended with a dinner at St James's Palace for 250 guests, including Princess Margaret and the Duke's sister, Alexandra.

The Queen had spared no effort in acknowledging her fondness for – and indebtedness to – a cousin who had not only served her faithfully but who had elected to live out his existence as one half of a failed marriage, thus following the course she had hoped for. It was hardly surprising if the Duchess, whose own happiness had, in part, been mortgaged to the Duke's personal pledge, could summon up little enthusiasm for this glittering tribute to her husband.

When the concert began, she was not there. Friends who inquired as to her absence were told: 'She will be along later.' As the dinner began, the Duchess of Kent's seat remained vacant. The word, whispered around the table, was that she had been seen earlier, wearing evening dress. The empty place stayed laid, the chair unmoved, just in case she should arrive, late and apologetic. The dinner over, Paul Channon, the Duke's great friend, rose from his chair, next to Katharine's empty seat, and made his speech of tribute to the Duke of Kent. The party went on into the night. The Duchess did not appear.

The mood, among the Duke's friends, was one of barely suppressed fury. In their view he had been humiliated, in front of his own closest circle of friends and the establishment at large. 'People were horror-struck – gritting their teeth in anger,' says one dinner guest. Their anger was made worse by a whisper that Nicholas had been summoned from the dinner table to sit with his mother at York House.

An official explanation quickly emerged. Katharine had flu. An alternative suggestion, barely plausible, was that she had not felt her presence to be absolutely necessary, since Eddie's actual birthday had been three days previously. Both explanations were greeted with scepticism by guests, particularly since the Duchess, before and after the party, had appeared to be in the soundest of health. She had spent the two preceding days in Cumbria, at one stage donning yellow oilskins to make a brief journey out to sea in a lifeboat, and, on the morning after the party, she was fit enough to read the lesson during Mass at Westminster Cathedral. The chosen text was Leviticus, Chapter 19, and included the words: 'Thou shalt not hate thy brother in thine heart.'

As news of the supposed slight leaked out, the relationship between Duke, Duchess and the palace was being scrutinized, for the first time, by those in royal circles who had previously believed that any problems between the Kents were a small and a manageable matter. 'The royal family are very family-minded,' says one. 'The fact that she did not appear at the party, even though she had been seen in evening dress, would be taken as a major, awful thing for Eddie. They would think: "How could she do that? And why?"'

One answer is that Katharine had planned a devastating and premeditated snub, directed not only at her husband but at the Queen and at the Windsors in general. Given her devotion to duty and the respect, bordering on fear, in which she held the Queen, such a move would have been so fantastically out of character as to defy comprehension. The simpler explanation is that the Duchess was indeed unwell. She had just returned from a two-day excursion of the kind that always left her drained and lethargic, except when she was at her fittest. Even so, those closest to the Kents – and in particular to Edward – placed only one construction on the débâcle of the birthday dinner: the Kents were now officially at war.

Whatever the truth of that presumption, Katharine was indeed not well; nor had she been for some time. As long as three years before the ill-fated birthday party, she had sensed that she was now battling with a new problem. Others detected a revival of old problems. Those close to the Duke claimed that her frequent exhaustion was attributable to binge-and-starve eating problems and mood-altering pills. Katharine thought otherwise. As she brooded over possible causes for her lassitude, one possible explanation suggested itself very close to home. An aide to the Duke and Duchess had been ill for some time when she was diagnosed with myalgic encephalomyelitis. The causes of ME, or chronic fatigue syndrome, remain an enigma even now, but, in the early nineties, the disease was so under-researched and misunderstood that it was rebranded under the derogatory and inaccurate label, 'yuppie flu'. Later Katharine was to learn a great deal more about ME. In December 1996 she was officially announced to be a sufferer who would have to cut back greatly on her public duties.

In the three years before that announcement, she had

become interested in the illness and the debate surrounding it. More than that, the symptoms shown by a member of her own staff seemed so much to mirror her own that she inclined increasingly to the belief that she too was a sufferer. Although this notion was regarded with some scepticism by the Duke's friends – never sympathetic about Katharine's ill-health – Edward himself seems to have taken some considerable interest in his wife's suspicions, possibly because he would have been as delighted as she to isolate a physical cause for her problems.

At least two years before her diagnosis, not only the Duchess but also the Duke read a moving text about ME. Michael Mayne, the Dean Emeritus of Westminster, was the vicar of Great St Mary's, the university church in Cambridge, when he was first stricken by the illness. *A Year Lost And Found*, his personal memoir of ME, begins on the day of the Heysel Stadium football disaster, in May 1985. Mayne, driving home from a private retreat and listening to the horror unfolding over the car radio, began to feel ill: 'strangely inert, with swollen glands, discomfort in the neck and shoulders and mild pains in the chest'. Over the next months, he was brought to the point of collapse with crippling chest pains, aching limbs, lack of concentration and complete weakness. Mayne, a dynamic priest, an eminent Anglican churchman and the former head of religious programmes for BBC Radio, was reduced to a state where the only exertion he could tolerate was a daily lap of his garden. After a string of mistaken diagnoses, ranging from toxoplasmosis to pleurisy, he was finally confirmed to have ME. Despite uncertainties about his recovery, he was offered the Deanery of Westminster. Justifying the faith of those who appointed him, he was sufficiently well to take up his new posting.

Despite the successful outcome, Mayne's book is more than a cheering tome about decline and recovery, concentrating rather on a meditation on suffering, redemption, hope, love and spirituality – all interlaced with practical insights and common sense. Though never a depressive man, Mayne believes (a view not universally supported by psychiatrists and others in the medical profession) that a factor in ME is the build-up of pressures on those required to present an impeccable public front.

'You are, consciously or unconsciously, trying to live up to people's expectations, and that is where the pressure starts,' he says. 'Every day is different, if you are a member of the clergy – or, no doubt, of the royal family. In part you are responding to people's needs. So you are out to prove you are doing a proper job, and that can lead to internal pressures. Your outer and your inner self are conflicting.'

That theory, elaborated on in Mayne's book, must have struck an immediate chord with the Duchess of Kent, who was impressed and moved by his account. Though friends say she spoke to him only briefly about his book and his illness, she may well have felt that much of what Mayne had written could both explain her suffering and offer it a new legitimacy. Mayne was not only an object lesson in successful recovery. He was also a respected and charming churchman who, perhaps sensing some shared experience, was a great admirer of the Duchess. Although the Dean of Westminster has no pastoral responsibility for the royal family, who worship elsewhere – in the Queen's case at Windsor – Westminster Abbey is of course the venue for special occasions, royal weddings included.

The Queen would visit perhaps five times a year and the Duchess of Kent slightly less frequently than that, even before her conversion. But, whenever she was there, Mayne would be hugely impressed by what she had to offer. 'At the Children of Courage service in December, she would be brilliant; absolutely brilliant. She has a marvellous rapport with children.' Others who presided at the service included Margaret Thatcher and Princess Diana. 'I have seen a number of people do it, and she [the Duchess] was far and away the best,' says Mayne. 'She has this very remarkable empathy with the young, some of whom have suffered very deeply, with cancer or other illnesses.'

Mayne looked forward to this annual engagement, welcoming her at the door, introducing her to parents after the service and pleased to be in her company. 'She was someone I enjoyed relating to right from the start. She has a good, easy manner; and I felt that she understood suffering from the point of view of someone who had actually been through it. There is a certain quality about people who have battled with something painful. Suffering can embitter or suffering can enhance and deepen. There are people who use suffering positively and those who let suffering use them negatively. I think there is a kind of compassion that grows in people if they have been in the shadowlands; if they have seen the darker side of things.'

Beyond admiration for her, the Duchess of Kent might have sensed in Mayne, and would certainly have gained from his book, a view that had remarkably little currency in royal circles: a staunch belief that suffering was not always a destructive force but a catalyst for good, for empowerment and for redemption. She would carry on wondering, for some time to come, whether or not she had ME. But, long before her formal diagnosis, she was certainly seeking to put a name to her problems, to overcome them and to move on, beyond her recurring troubles and beyond the shadowlands.

CHAPTER TWENTY-FOUR

Suffering in Silence

✦

KATHARINE HAD SPENT less and less time at Crocker End House. The catalyst to sell the house which she had earmarked as perfect five years previously and to move on came at 5a.m. on Monday, 29 January 1995, when burglars broke into the empty property. The Duke was on a skiing holiday, the Duchess in London, and the house was supervised only by a housekeeper living in the grounds. Under the elaborate security system devised when the Kents had moved in, five years previously, an alarm apparently sounded at Henley police station. According to the family's private secretary, officers were on the scene 'within two or three minutes'. Despite this excellent response time, the intruders – who entered through a ground floor window – had fled, taking with them antiques and silver worth £55,000.

This was not the first time the Kents had been burgled. In September 1973 personal possessions valued at £500 disappeared from their rooms in York House. A painter and decorator was later charged with the thefts. The Crocker End House heist was a far more skilful job.

Despite the speed of the raid, the intruders appeared to

know exactly what they were looking for in the fourteen-room house. The twenty-two missing pieces, mainly silver-ware and porcelain, were described as 'items of great historical and sentimental value, some with family connections'. Among them were a gold Fabergé photograph frame, set with jade stones and holding a portrait of Queen Mary, a George II silver chalice, a George III dessert knife and a pair of Derby glazed sweetmeat dishes. Other stolen items included six snuff-boxes and a pair of Chinese figures of pheasants with plumage in rose enamels from the Qianlong period of 1736–95.

To the Duke, in particular, the loss would have been devastating. His family antiques had been whittled down over the years, sold off by his mother, Marina, to raise funds when times seemed hard. The residue, the stolen pieces included, had mainly been acquired by his father, George – a great collector of *objets d'art*. Although the Kents offered a 'substantial reward', there seemed little hope that the arte-facts would surface on the market for several years, if at all. In the event the publicity attached to the case brought results within a few days. A Brighton antiques dealer called police after seeing, in the *Daily Mail*, a picture of the glazed sweetmeat dishes which he had bought and sold in good faith, and the Chinese pheasants, again sold on in Sussex, were recovered from Sotheby's.

Despite the return of some of the property and an initial comment from the Kents' private secretary that both the Duke and Duchess were extremely fond of Crocker End House and had no plans to move, the break-in proved the final straw. In April, four months after the burglary, con-tracts were exchanged with an unnamed buyer, offering in the region of £1 million. As the private secretary explained: 'The children are all grown up, and it's a bit large for just the two of them. They would like to save money on running costs.' In other words, the Kents had decided that, for the first time in their marriage, they would forgo a property of their own, basing themselves solely at their grace-and-favour apartment in York House.

Although money was certainly a factor in their decision, there were other determinants. Increasingly the Kents spent their weekends apart, so lessening the need for a family retreat. In addition the Duchess was probably feeling too unwell to supervise another programme of renovations, even if she had wished to do so. Not that there was any public signal of her frailty. On the contrary, at the time of the burglary, Katharine was putting the finishing touches to one of her most ambitious and potentially taxing overseas tours.

Ever since her successful visit to Tanzania three years previously, she had wished to head another Unicef field visit, designed to raise the profile of third world poverty and the agency's role in its eradication. This time the destination was India. The small blue booklet detailing the Duchess's itinerary represented months of planning. Her route, from Delhi in the north to Madras in the south, had been carefully reconnoitred. As on the previous African trip, a plane of the Queen's Flight had been borrowed to ferry Katharine and her party around the sub-continent; partly because this was still a normal facility extended to someone of her status and partly because scheduled internal flights were not deemed to meet the safety standards required for a royal passenger. Katharine's party, including her secretary and a handful of journalists, were to travel out – in short-hop stages allowing for refuelling – on the royal jet. She, along with leading Unicef representatives, plus her lady-in-waiting, hairdresser, maid and detective, was booked on a British Airways scheduled flight to Delhi to begin a tour scheduled to last from Wednesday, 7 February 1996, to Friday, 16 February. Unicef workers, British diplomats and Indian government ministers were all involved in a pro- gramme intricately designed to avoid the smallest hiccup.

The first engagement of the ten-day visit was a dinner party at Bungalow Three of the British High Commission in Delhi. The invitation list included two Indian ministers of state, various local dignitaries, and the author Mark Tully, whose coverage of India for the BBC had enchanted Kathar- ine for years. She had particularly asked that Tully should be invited to her introductory dinner, designed to set the tone of a major tour. Some time before the dinner com- menced, the Duchess sent her apologies. She was too ill to be there.

Katharine's non-attendance was successfully explained away to the small group of journalists and aid workers selected to travel round India with her as the result of over- tiredness following a long flight. In fact she had been told, almost on the eve of her departure, that she was suffering from an illness called Epstein-Barr Virus, the cause of her recurring bouts of exhaustion. This was devastating news to Katharine who – the luxury of the Queen's jet notwithstand- ing – would have to spend many hours travelling by dusty station-wagon while presenting an impeccable front to the volunteers and communities preparing to welcome her. It was also a very unusual diagnosis.

Epstein-Barr Virus (EBV) is a trigger for glandular fever, whose symptoms include swollen neck glands, a fever, sore throat and loss of appetite. Usually the illness passes in a matter of weeks, but it can linger, causing aches, tiredness and lack of energy. The virus, a member of the herpes family, is also one of the few established precursors of ME. That link had been established by Peter White, a leading pyschiatrist based at Bart's Hospital in London, who had found that 10 per cent of EBV sufferers went on to develop full-blown ME. The average age of his study group was twenty-one and the oldest forty – an age selection based on the fact that EBV, a common and non-recurring virus, mainly affects the very young. By the age of thirty, nine out of ten British people will have caught the illness and be immune to it. At sixty, the immunity rate is 98 per cent. The Duchess of Kent was sixty-three.

Like other forms of glandular fever, EBV is a 'kissing disease' spread by close contact with other people. Had the Duchess been without boyfriends prior to her marriage, she would have been slightly more likely not to have caught the illness. In fact she, popular and sociable as a young unmarried woman, had no shortage of admirers. Virological tests, repeated after a month, would have established beyond doubt whether she had EBV. If not, then an ordinary blood test might have shown up some other, similar virus. The third possibility could have been that she had an entirely different problem. But, at least for now, medical dictionary definitions were not at the top of the agenda. The Duchess of Kent was in India, and she was ill.

At morning briefings she appeared faintly stressed and distracted and unusually pale. When she spoke, her mouth was dry. Sometimes she would be unable to talk for more than a few minutes without swallowing a saliva tablet passed to her by her lady-in-waiting. Physical symptoms notwith-standing, no one around her guessed that the Duchess of Kent was seriously unwell; a measure of her courage and of the tact shown by the very few people who knew of her problems. This small group had been instructed, prior to departure and by her private office, on how she must be treated.

The Duchess, it was stipulated, could undertake no evening engagements. She disliked addressing public meetings, especially when she was ill, and would certainly not make any impromptu remarks at any time during her Indian tour. While acknowledging that her frailty demanded some concessions, some of those who know her best wondered whether Katharine, on the instructions of the London office she shared with the Duke, was also being excessively protected, almost to the detriment of her own freedom and self-esteem.

As one friend says: 'Most people in public life do not mind if, for instance, they are ushered into a room, presented with an article of cut glass and expected to make a few off-the-cuff remarks. Unicef was told no. That she really could not do that. The truth is that she is perfectly capable of doing that sort of thing and is very good at it.'

Whatever Katharine's skills, close tabs were kept on her public pronouncements in India from York House. Comments suggesting that impoverished Indians were, in some ways, more blessed than the affluent of the west because of their adherence to family values and a simpler way of life were widely reported in British newspapers and duly faxed back to the Duchess's lady-in-waiting for observations and comments on the accuracy (impeccable, as it transpired) of the reporting. This watchfulness did not appear to disturb Katharine. On the contrary, even allowing for her illness and exhaustion, she appeared to be enthralled, far beyond mere politeness, in what she saw.

On the morning after the cancelled dinner with Mark Tully she was up early for a morning briefing, followed by a midday flight to Varanasi in Uttar Pradesh for an inspection of a service dedicated to nutrition and pre-school education. The following day began with a three-hour drive over rough roads to Mirzapur, a centre of the carpet industry, and a visit to a school espousing 'Joyful Learning' – an initiative under which songs and games are used as educational aids. Katharine sat on dusty classroom floors and joined in with the music before the long drive back.

Only those who knew of her illness sensed the tension underlying the public warmth and prayed, as Katharine retreated early to her hotel room for a light snack and an hour of watching cable television before bed, that she would be able to sustain the pace of the tour. The next day, a Sunday, was a quiet one, set aside only for the long flight south to Madras. By the time she boarded her plane, still pale and tired but marginally more relaxed, it was clear, to those who watched most closely, that the Duchess of Kent had no intention of caving in.

By then, both the vastness of the problems she saw and the romantic splendour of the country were beginning to overshadow her own problems. 'Africaaa, Indiaaa . . . they are such wonderful words, aren't they?' she said, drawing out the last syllables in an imitation of Meryl Streep, in the film *Out of Africa*. But Katharine, who had, as always, done her homework, was also aware of horrific undercurrents to the glories of India.

At the time of her visit, 40 to 50 million girls were 'missing' from the Indian population, aborted by parents attuned to seeing a daughter as another family's wealth; a child who, notwithstanding legislation brought in to ban dowries, must be married off with a large lump sum in a transaction guaranteed to impoverish the affluent and bring ruin to the poor. A son, by contrast, was viewed as a blessing – a helpmate who would ease his parents' lot in their lifetime and light their funeral pyre after death. A study carried out by the Indian government at around the time of the Duchess's visit showed that, of 8,000 abortions carried out in Bombay following amniocentesis tests – ostensibly to check for genetic defects – 7,999 of the foetuses were female.

To Katharine, not only a newly converted Catholic but someone preoccupied since the loss of her stillborn son with abortion and infant mortality, this cull must have seemed particularly horrific. Even so, her tone was practical rather than moralizing. At clinics she was interested in contraception programmes and fascinated by the status of women in general. 'Tell me, how is the barren lady treated here?' she asked one helper. 'Is it still bad for her? Does she lack respect?' The questions echoed her own struggles to conceive a last, healthy child, and the lack of understanding she had received.

She was also well-briefed enough to be sceptical; publicly polite when told officially that infanticide of girl babies was really not a problem and privately scathing. 'They are lying to us, you know,' she said, after one such disclaimer, knowing that the truth was bleaker. 'There is no doubt that one way of killing their children is to feed them water instead of milk. There is no doubt that does happen.'

If some examples of brutality were shadowy and denied, others were on public display. Katharine's motorcade drove past children aged four or five, mortgaged into work akin to slave labour to pay off the loans raised by their families merely to stay alive. The bonded labour children she was introduced to worked in the 'beedi' industry, rolling cigarettes and cigars on twelve-hour shifts for a pay rate of 30 rupees or about 60 pence per thousand.

She also met those working on the ground to help mothers extricate their children from subservience and found hope in their initiatives. But Katharine did not view the problems she encountered with quite the view of a normal royal patron. There was much in the life of the poorer Indian citizen to enrage or horrify her. There was also, as she had said at the outset of her tour, something that she envied.

'How courteous they are,' she said after one visit. 'They know something called respect, something called courteousness, something called gentleness. There's no guile in their eyes. None of the shifty looks you would find if you were doing the same thing in the slums of Liverpool.' Snippets of this attitude – an anachronistic viewpoint evoking Jean Jacques Rousseau and the sanctification of the noble savage – continued to provoke a minor flurry of shock when fed back to Britain. The press remained quick to point out that such a view sounded rather hollow when articulated by a Duchess ferried around by royal plane and ensconced, between her forays into the field, in India's five-star hotels.

But Katharine was not speaking in a spirit of *noblesse oblige*. Her admiration, however naïvely or sentimentally expressed, of the spirit displayed by the Indian people she met was an accurate reflection of the loathing she had come to feel for a secular Britain moving, in her view, towards a culture of materialism, selfishness, waste and violence; a disaffection quite possibly sharpened by the wretchedness of feeling ill.

Paradoxically, her own illness seemed to dissipate as the tour wore on, while those around her began to flag. One Indian official was rushed to hospital suffering from asthma. Several of her party, aid workers included, succumbed to stomach complaints. Her lady-in-waiting, Lucy Tomkins, had been prescribed medication to ward off such ailments, and it is likely that Katharine herself had taken preventive measures against any new disease.

She found – in the children and the elderly of India – a

source of inspiration and strength. In schoolrooms, she continued to huddle on grubby floors with children on her lap. In Kerala, her next stop after Madras, she inspected mushroom-growing and coir-making projects, run by women and intended to help the poorest sector of the population. At every stage, she listened politely to addresses made by local dignitaries and prefaced with glowing references to a dignitary of whom, unsurprisingly, they had never heard. 'Welcome to the Respectable Madam, the Honourable Lady of Kent,' one such speaker began.

Only once, at a feeding centre, the tables were unwittingly turned. In a country village, many miles from Madras, a makeshift stage had been built, and the entire population gathered expectantly, hoping that – prior instructions from Unicef notwithstanding – the Duchess might consent to say a few words. There was a brief pause before Lord Bridges, the agency's chairman, climbed the steps to address an audience as easily as if making a prepared speech from the cross-benches of the House of Lords. Katharine followed him, offering one brief sentence of support.

The whole episode had been so tactfully conducted that none of the listeners, most of the Duchess's party included, detected any hitch. Only she was mortified, horrified that she had felt unable to speak when asked to and convinced that she had appeared a failure. Her composure survived until she reached the privacy of her car, bewailing her incompetence until her lady-in-waiting finally managed to calm her down and reassure her that no one had minded or indeed noticed her lapse.

That small sign of strain apart, her public performances were flawless. She was kind, generous, warm, consoling and – on her final engagement – possessed of such stamina that those around her wondered how she could survive. In ninety degrees of heat, she lit candles at a Buddhist temple before leaving for a mile-long walk through the slums of Bombay, barely able to move and engulfed in the crowd that had turned out for her. Chalky pale but determined to go on, she moved from classroom to classroom at a city school, sipping fruit squash from a cardboard carton when her voice began to fail. Her detective and her lady-in-waiting hovered in the background, knowing better than to rush her. This was not a perfunctory gesture of goodwill by a gracious visitor. The Duchess's engagements never were.

There was, of course, another side to the charm and the warmth. In public, Katharine was entranced by all she saw, insisting on taking pictures with her own camera. 'I'm going to photograph it all myself,' she would say. 'The colour is so wonderful.' In private she remained a distant and occasion- ally a chilly figure. Those who met her in India nicknamed her the Maharani – the Queen – and her private demeanour reflected that title. Though universally polite, she struck up no cosy relationship with the handful of journalists or more junior aid workers travelling with her. During flights she would remain, surrounded by her closest entourage, in a curtained-off front portion of the royal plane, receiving briefings or throwing out the few speeches she was scheduled to give and dictating revised versions to a secretary with a laptop computer. Her wardrobe, a fabulous collection of pastel suits and long silk skirts, was as suitable for Wimble- don as for poverty-stricken India. While Princess Anne opted for stout shoes and headscarves and even Diana wore jeans for working in the field, Katharine's dress code never slipped below Sloane Square standards. On one occasion a new outfit was produced mid-flight, presumably on the grounds that the Duchess could not appear – even at a rehydration centre in a far-flung village – with a drop of coffee or a spot of grime on her official outfit.

Katharine drove herself fiercely, and, like all ferocious workers, expected impeccable support in return. In addition to a maid, a secretary, a hairdresser and a detective, she had at her disposal the luxuries of the royal plane – well-stocked with delicately-cut sandwiches, scones and strawberry jam for afternoon tea and crewed by a staff attentive to the Duchess's comfort and safety. At every stop, the fridge containing litres of type-matched royal blood was removed from the plane and transported by taxi to her hotel.

This was not a concession to Katharine's state of health; merely a routine precaution invoked on any similar trip in case an emergency transfusion should be necessary. Despite such attention to every possible eventuality, the refrigerator batteries failed on the last, long taxi journey from Bombay airport to the Taj Mahal Hotel, where the blood fridge finally arrived with the inbuilt warning alarm wailing.

By then the tour was almost over. Katharine had one last speech to give at a dinner hosted by Unicef in the hotel's Crystal Room. In the afternoon before that engagement, her staff were excused to visit the nearby shops and buy a few souvenirs before the flight back to London. Sarah McCormick, her hairdresser, had been absent for only a few minutes before a messenger was sent out to recall her, explaining that Katharine had decided to have her hair done at once. 'Bloody Duchess,' Miss McCormick was overheard to say, resignedly. 'The dinner doesn't start for hours.'

The remark was indicative of Katharine's fretful and nervous state of mind whenever she felt under pressure. The evening's public speaking engagement would, as always, have daunted her. It was, however, the last hurdle in what had been an impeccable tour. Despite her ill-health and her fear of collapse, coupled with the suffocating heat and hours of travel, she had maintained an immaculate public front. Now that it was almost over, she could at last begin to relax – to congratulate herself on a job well done and to look forward to the conclusion.

She was going home; a prospect that should have enchanted the Duchess of Kent. Instead the notion appalled her.

CHAPTER TWENTY-FIVE

Search for a Destiny

O N THE LAST afternoon of her visit to India, the Duchess of Kent sat in her suite at the Taj Mahal Hotel, reflecting on the past ten days. Her speech for the evening was written. Her suitcases were packed, apart from the three last outfits she would need: one formal dress, one beige Armani trouser suit for the drive to the airport and the jumper and leggings she would wear for the British Airways flight to London.

Her presents were wrapped and ready to distribute. She had ordered, for each member of her party, a gold and green enamelled box decorated with a map of India, marked with every stop on her tour. Inside the white porcelain was stamped with a message in her handwriting. 'With my thanks, Katharine. India 1996.' Away from the cameras at last, Katharine, in a linen skirt and jacket and straw sandals, could relax with her lady-in-waiting, Lucy Tomkins, a woman she referred to affectionately as 'my mate'. Another tour was almost finished, but the tensions remained.

The Duchess of Kent has always been a woman of contrasts – compassionate, vibrant and professional in public and, in private, frequently drained, exhausted and subject to self-doubt. That is a side of Katharine that no one, beyond her closest family, staff and confidants, ever sees. But, on the last afternoon and with the experiences of India churning in her mind, she chose to lower the barrier between public warmth and private unhappiness.

For an hour or so she talked to me in a rare interview for *YOU* magazine both of hope and disappointment. 'I do know that when I get back to England, I feel very lonely to start with. And you do feel a sense of hopelessness. It's very difficult to make people in Britain aware of what goes on here. I'm not even inspired to make people in Britain understand. I can't talk to the Rotary Club in Bradford and say: "Will you help us at Unicef with landmines in Egypt?" It's too distant.'

She brushed aside the notion that she was seen as taking on the mantle of a saintly woman. 'I don't see myself as anything, quite honestly. But this work is very humble-making – an intense privilege and part of the learning process of life. But you go back home a zombie. I did after Tanzania. I couldn't get my sense of values right for three or four weeks.'

It was clear that she looked back on her experiences as a spiritual, almost a mystical interlude. It was obvious too that she had strengthened her view that the poor of the third world had much to teach the decadent west. 'Yes, oh yes. What I find here in these dark, dark eyes is an acceptance of life's destiny. We are never satisfied. We are always looking for our destiny, aren't we? They accept theirs, and it is more peaceful in a way.

'I just love people. I value them. What's the world about? Not possessions but people caring for one another. I think it's important for people to keep a sense of wonder. These people have it; we are beginning to lose it. But it's not difficult to have that sense of wonder. The miracle of a birth or, when we get back, the bluebells coming out and the bracken starting to unfurl. Those are the things I wanted my own children to see, and I think they have retained a bit of that sense of wonder.

'It's a matter of allowing children to remain children. They are all trying to grow up at sixteen, and that's so bad. You see a child's body acting as an adult's, and they don't mix. They are unhappy.'

Intellectually, Katharine's argument was – as the press had already pointed out – subject to question. The thought, however distasteful, of a British sixteen-year-old having sex is surely not to be seen as more heinous than the plight of a six-year-old rolling cigarettes by the roadside for a starvation wage. But she did not intend, as she talked on in her luxury hotel room, such a stark comparison. Rather, she appeared as a woman haunted by three things. The first was the awfulness of the problems she had seen. The second was the romantic beauty of the country. 'The memories are so vivid. People bathing in the Ganges – those biblical scenes out of a picture book. The colour, the lovely, graceful ladies with flowers in their hair. If you don't think of the problems, it's the experience of a lifetime.' The third ghost, and perhaps the most powerful, was a disillusion with British life, heightened by what she had seen in India.

'AIDS is starting here, prostitution is rife; spread by the lorry drivers. It's so terribly different from our problems. The lesson we in Britain have to learn – but it's too late – is family values. To give you an example: Philip Lawrence wouldn't have been murdered in London if the boys who attacked him had family values. They've gone, and I don't see how we are going to reinstate them.'

The murder of Philip Lawrence was to continue to

preoccupy her. A headmaster and a father of four, he was knifed by a teenager in December 1995 as he tried to protect a pupil from a gang of youths outside his Catholic comprehensive, St George's in Maida Vale, London. Katharine, impressed by the courage of his widow, Frances, stayed in close touch. Several months after her India visit, she would support Frances Lawrence and her youngest child, Lucien, at her husband's memorial service.

In Katharine's eyes, Lawrence's murder epitomized the evils that follow when family values fail. The irony was apparent only to those who knew her best. Much as she lauded the concept of close-knit and loving families, its alchemy had eluded her. Beyond India, the familiar patterns waited: a loveless marriage and all the fallout of personal unhappiness that flows from a failed relationship. For the first time Katharine spoke openly of her loneliness. Asked if she was happy, she said not. 'No, I'm a very up and down person. Very up and downy, but I put a brave face on it. I feel sick and tired and unhappy, just like anyone else. I was very very tired yesterday. I didn't feel at all well, and I had to drive myself. In the evenings, when I've had a bite to eat and washed my hair, I just watch a bit of television to force myself back into reality for the next day. Here I watch cable. At home it's *EastEnders*.'

It was clear that the prospect of home did not fill her with rapture. There was no sense that she would rejoice in a job well done and a reunion with those she loved. As she admitted, it was more probable that she would retire to a corner and weep. 'Oh, good heavens yes. I shall go into a corner and think I have let everyone down. Why? Because that's me. I'm dreading the day I get back – of thinking of all the things I could have said and done.

'Getting back is very, very difficult. The first few days are particularly tough. I'm sad, disoriented and muddled. I might talk about it with a few friends, but friends who will understand what I am trying to say. Luckily you do eventually work out of it, and you have to believe you will, even when you think it won't happen. And you are the better person. A few weeks later, you think: "Oh God, I am lucky. Heavens, I'm lucky."'

There was, tellingly, no mention of her husband. She described her struggle to change misery to contentment as a purely personal battle against a disillusion that broadened out from the private to the public domain. If the return to York House held little allure, then so, it seemed, did British life in general.

'Oh, I love London,' she said. 'I'm intensely proud of it, and I'm very happy there. I have to love it, because I live there all the time. I have nowhere else. At the moment, though, I'm simply hating the climate of cutting and chipping at something to be proud of. I'll give you a tiny example. It's cheaper to maintain a fence than a beech hedge. In Green Park, they've just ripped out the most beautiful copper beech hedge. I know we're all – we are ALL – under financial constraints, but sometimes we forget our priorities. People all over the world think we in Britain know the answers, and we jolly well don't.'

If her purpose had been only to carp about the shortfalls of British life and the evils of a society that had turned its face against fundamentalist family values, then she might have sounded sour. But much of her criticism was directed against herself. She got so muddled, she said, on a tour where she had to absorb vast quantities of detail. Speeches she had prepared in Britain had sounded wrong, and she –

always the perfectionist – had made herself write something better. She admitted that she found it impossible to relax, even though her serene image had rarely slipped.

The beautiful wardrobe, a curious contrast to the poverty of the places she had visited, she regarded as a necessity and a courtesy. If she was regarded as a Maharani – a Queen – then it was her duty to present herself as such. 'I sort of think it matters. I am a great one for respecting people's cultures and traditions. If I was here on holiday, I would be wearing shorts. But, because I am the Maharani, it's my duty to appear reasonable; not elegant, but tidy. The people I meet make the effort. So should I. I've ruined so many clothes though. You should see the bills I get for dry-cleaning and the worn-out shoes.

'But I do try, although there is no need to be extravagant. It is not over the top budgetwise – that would be unnecessary. People often say that what you wear does not matter; not exactly true. It's usually a man who says that. It boosts your morale as well and gives you a bit of confidence. So I am all for it.'

In dress code and in manner, the Duchess of Kent at times appears more regal and more distant than those born to a royal life. Even so, she retains the outsiderish dimension of the streetwise commoner who once settled her own dry-cleaning bills and who still replaces her worn-out shoes at high street shops. Beyond the formality, there remains a sense of mischief and an ability to laugh at her own extravagances. But, of course, Katharine's perspective was also skewed by the life she was leading. Her wardrobe was not that of a careful spender who wanted to put on the best appearance she could on a rigid budget. It was, instead, that of a grand Duchess on a royal tour – more elegant and probably more costly than anything the Queen might wear on a Commonwealth visit.

Katharine was honest enough to be aware of the anomaly. Asked whether staring real poverty in the face always made her vow to cut back on material things, she said: 'I do try, but then I slip back into my old English ways all too quickly. It's human nature. I'm as grabbing as anyone else. Oh, if I can get anything free, then I will.' She was partly joking. She was also being honest, happy to admit that she was easily seduced by the latest wonder face cream, designer bargain, newest shade of lipstick, must-have dress in a shop window. Naturally, she did not say that material pleasures were the antidote to a frequently bleak existence, although that is undoubtedly true. She did, however, paint the picture of a woman sustained by the frivolous as well as by the spiritual. At first she made light of her spirituality.

'Spirituality is a word I cannot pronounce. Like diarrhoeal. But if spirituality means gaining from other people, then yes, I am. I've got great faith in human beings. You can see the faith in the people here. There's a spirituality in their faces. And the children . . . you just fall in love when you see them. I'm always falling in love – about fifty-five times a day – not just with children or with old people, but with everybody.'

There was a terrible poignancy in her enthusiasm – the verve of a woman who could fall passionately in love with strangers but who found, in her own marriage, only coldness. A woman who so adored children that her whole life had been shadowed by the loss of her own youngest son. If the Duchess of Kent was aware of the irony, she gave no signal of the fact that her own life had long ago transposed the normal routines of existence. Love belonged to the public part of her life, formal arrangements to the private.

For the past ten days, she had witnessed squalor and heartbreak. She had also seen hope; not only in Unicef's projects but in the wisdom of some of India's officials. Encouraged by her, businessmen had pledged money towards schemes to get more children into school. In terms of raising both money and consciousness, she had been an unqualified success. But India had also offered her a great deal. This, she clearly felt, was a place where she belonged. Now it was over, and she was going home to an existence which offered no such inclusiveness. She would be miserable. She would be lonely. Katharine had perhaps not meant to paint so bleak a picture, but her words bore no other interpretation.

At the evening reception in the Crystal Room, she mingled politely with local dignitaries. As always, she spoke well, giving no sign of how such occasions alarmed her. Outside her car waited to take her to the airport. Most of her party would travel back on the royal flight, a longer journey involving a refuelling halt in Egypt. The Duchess would be whisked through the VIP lounge and on to BA flight 138. She was booked on the list of first class passengers as Mrs Mills – the name chosen to protect her anonymity.

By then she looked an unremarkable figure. Her Armani suit had been packed away after she changed in the first class washroom into the jumper and leggings in which she could sleep. Whether or not she was able to rest on the overnight flight from Bombay to Heathrow, the images of India crowded in. Earlier that day she had spoken of her sense of impotence at the trust people vested in her.

'The awful thing is that some of those people – the most innocent – really do think you can work a miracle. I don't mean a miraculous happening from above, but something that would instantly alter their lives. And you feel so awful that you can't. I remember these things for weeks afterwards – seeing again the face of the old lady who really believed that you could do something for her.'

Human lives, as the Duchess of Kent knew to her own cost, are never so easily rearranged. She, diagnosed as suffering from Epstein-Barr Virus, was ill again. She was exhausted. She was contemplating her return home, to a soulless marriage and a crowded diary, with dread. As always, on such tours, Katharine had been allowed the freedom to strip the best elements from all the different compartments of her life. As at Lourdes, she could be regal, she could be feted, she could reach out towards simpler values, she could offer and receive compassion; all in the absence of the coldness and scrutiny she was used to at home. This cocktail offered her a rare fix of happiness. The withdrawal symptoms, compounded by exhaustion and the dismal prospect of a return to reality, had kicked in even before she settled into her first class seat.

But, much as she hated the thought of going home, Katharine was not despairing. For some time, she had been eager to broaden her career to a wider stage. The means, she believed, were now within her grasp.

CHAPTER TWENTY-SIX

Trials of a 'Sparkly'

✦

DESPITE HER ILLNESS, the Duchess of Kent did not
return from India with any intention of telescoping
her charity work. Rather, she hoped to expand it. As she had
made plain in Bombay, she wished to relay what she had
learned directly to the Unicef board in New York, combining her visit with a planned spring concert by the Bach
Choir. 'I sing with a choir that is going to New York,' she
had explained. 'And I'll be able to report to New York
headquarters. By then I shall have some ideas in my mind.'

The subtext to Katharine's statement was obvious. Compassion, her great strength, was no longer enough to satisfy
her. She also now saw herself as a player in elevated political
and diplomatic circles, in which she hoped to deploy her
wider skills and air her first-hand experience. The American
trip, however, was two months away.

In the short term, her return to London, on a February
morning, was as dismal as she had foretold. As she explained
later, she found her cosseted existence so hard to cope with
that she was upset even by the sight of bottled water on a
dinner table, regarding such luxuries as a reminder of the
suffering she had witnessed. Unhappy and, as she had

predicted, disoriented, she caught a plane to Norway for a cross-country skiing holiday, buttonholing uncomprehending Norwegian skiers and pouring out to them the misery she had seen in India. She saw this as useful therapy; a means to defuse the images that continued to haunt her. Katharine's choice of confidants – strangers selected at random and unable to understand a word of what she said – was also indicative of how few real friends she had in whom she could confide her troubled emotional state.

On 10 March the story broke that the Duchess of Kent had Epstein-Barr Virus. The news, picked up by most of the British media, attracted interest and concern not only from the press but also from organizations associated with ME or myalgic encephalomyelitis. Although there was, at this stage, no suggestion that Katharine had full-blown ME, the link between the two illnesses implied the possibility of such an outcome.

Charitable organizations working in the field of ME had long felt themselves under pressure. The dismissal of the disease as 'yuppie flu' – a title suggestive of little more than a phobia for overworked neurotics – had been dispatched as ignorant and misguided. Even so, controversy about an illness without specific cause or cure continued to heighten. Organizations dealing with sufferers had felt themselves marginalized by psychiatrists who believed that, in some cases, ME was merely depression under a more socially acceptable name. At the time of Katharine's EBV diagnosis, a joint working group of the Royal Colleges of Physicians, Psychiatrists and General Practitioners was preparing what promised to be the most definitive – and possibly the most controversial – report so far on chronic fatigue syndrome (the preferred medical term for ME).

In this climate of uncertainty, charities working in the

field were eager to inform, and no doubt to enlist the help of, a potential high-profile victim. Brown envelopes stuffed with information packs began to arrive at York House. One of the first charities to contact her was the ME Association, whose patrons include Sir Harry Secombe and whose most prominent medical figure is Charles Shepherd, a former GP and a recovered ME patient himself. Mavis Moore, the organization's administrator, confirms: 'We wrote to the Duchess when it was first confirmed that she had Epstein-Barr Virus, saying how sorry we were she was not well and including information about ME. As far as we were concerned, it was a gesture on our part. No doubt a great many other organizations also wrote to her.'

For several years, Katharine had been interested in ME and suspicious that the illness might explain her symptoms and problems. It is likely that the material she was now receiving bolstered that view – particularly since she had shown no signs of complete recovery since she returned from India. On the contrary, those who knew her well saw in her a continued tiredness, air of distraction and lack of concentration; none of which prevented her from working as hard as she had always done.

The renewed worry over her health coincided with a visit to Hull; long-planned and with a dual purpose. Katharine had strong links with Hull University, whose Vice-Chancellor, David Dilks, had got to know her well on her frequent visits to Leeds University, where he was previously a distinguished professor of history. She had agreed to open Hull's new Ferens Building, dedicated to the teaching of modern languages and industrial chemistry, before opening a centre for the city's children.

Just prior to her visit, Katharine said that she would be flying, as planned, to Humberside Airport and would be delighted to meet the students. 'But I can't speak. I really can't,' she said. Having been assured that would present no problem and that the speeches would, in any case, be kept as brief as possible, she changed her mind as she arrived at the new building. 'I want to speak after all,' she said. 'I know I said I wouldn't, but I felt I wanted to say something, so I wrote a little speech last night. Can you find an opportunity?'

The university was naturally delighted to accommodate a rare royal visitor. Since the Duke and Duchess of York opened its main building in 1928, there had been only one other major royal occasion – the Queen Mother's inauguration of the new library in 1960, at which she was introduced to Philip Larkin, the university librarian. Some of Mr Larkin's verse may not have been entirely to the Queen Mother's taste – his most remembered first line remains: 'They fuck you up, your mum and dad' – but Her Majesty was impressed by the symmetry of his portfolio. 'Poet librarian?' she said. 'That is the perfect combination of roles.'

Katharine's task involved a side of the university far removed from Larkin's traditional library. As well as opening the new building, she inaugurated information technology links between the main university and its halls of residence, three miles away, in which 2,000 study bedrooms were linked up to the Internet and the campus computer system; an innovation which put Hull at the leading edge of university technology.

Her speech, unusually written without a first draft or, at the least, a list of suggestions being supplied by the university, returned to a theme she had first broached in India – the financial constraints bedevilling Britain. Two years later, higher education would become a major political battleground, as both maintenance grants and tuition fees were eroded by the Blair government amid protests that poorer students would be disadvantaged. The Duchess of Kent showed herself to be radical and opinionated on a subject that would have inspired caution in other members of the royal family, wary of any charge that they might be straying into politics. Katharine, less interested in royal caution than in how real people live, spoke directly. 'The Ferens Building has been constructed in spite of the prevailing climate of financial constraints on universities – and on students,' she said. '. . . Many people in Britain are unaware of the quite extraordinary facilities offered to students. Facilities which are the right of the student. They merit this "right". We must hope that, eventually, the education they gain here gives them the "right" – and I use the word again – of secure employment.'

Having devoted the greater part of her brief, impromptu address to a foray into students' rights and the right to work, the Duchess reverted to the more typical pattern of a royal visitor for the rest of her stay. Fascinated by the building project and charming to the students who waited to meet her, she had to be coerced by her hosts into sitting down for two minutes to eat a sandwich. Only those who knew her realized how much she had altered. 'She was manifestly not well, and we had to be solicitous of her health,' says Professor Dilks. 'But she is so diligent and so interested that it was hard to persuade her to have anything to eat or drink.'

Outsiders who watched her would not have registered Katharine's appearance as anything other than normal. When two- and three-year-old children from the university nursery rushed out to greet her – an unscheduled reception committee – she paused in the wind and rain to talk to them and to receive flowers and pictures they had drawn for her. As usual her morning engagement overran. As always, she planned to cut no corners in the second part of her programme – opening a multi-use centre for emotionally, physically and educationally disadvantaged children. Among all the projects Katharine saw, she was particularly enthralled by a session held by a child psychologist for the siblings of children who were severely disabled. The purpose was to deal with the mixed feelings of love and resentment and to explore the emotions of children who had lost a brother or a sister.

Katharine watched through a one-way mirror as a little girl of ten or eleven wept from the stress and sorrow of thinking of a brother who had died eighteen months previously. Afterwards she sat with a group of ten children, aged between seven and thirteen, talking to them about their bereavements. 'What do you remember most about your brother?' she asked the child who had cried earlier. 'The way my mum used to make chocolate cakes for him,' she replied.

Those who watched were surprised at Katharine's empathy, given how wretched she obviously felt. 'People who didn't know her thought she was lovely and radiant,' says one observer. 'I felt she was much less naturally at ease than usual. She was having to try very hard to concentrate, and she was obviously having to force herself to take things in.

'Even so, the children opened up to her. She obviously feels very strongly about children and is concerned, in particular, about their difficulties and vulnerabilities.' This concern, extended to other people's children, also focused on her own. It is one of the many ironies of Katharine's life that she, so adept at comforting and understanding strangers, had never managed to ensure, for her own two sons, a wholly happy existence. On a bleak March day in Hull, the bereaved and unhappy children she had met reminded her once again of the death of her own baby, a memory reinforced when, during her visit, a child handed her a storybook entitled *Patrick*. She was also preoccupied once again by the troubled life of her younger son.

As she left the children's centre, she said, almost in passing to a friend and loud enough to be overheard, 'Nicholas is in hospital again. I am so worried about him.' She left, shortly afterwards, for London, conscious that all her problems seemed to be coming to a head. She was ill. Her son was undergoing further treatment.

Katharine's own health seemed more fragile than ever. Certainly, in the months after the Hull trip, her impression deepened that she was suffering from ME. Comforting as it may have been to put a name to her illness, this tentative diagnosis offered more problems than solutions. Some private practices, even in Harley Street, contain dubious practitioners, eager to part rich hypochondriacs from their money in return for implausible and unsuccessful courses of treatment. The nature of the illness – cause still unspecified – and the lack of any reliable prognosis or successful therapy, beyond a managed programme of exercise, has inevitably led to a combustible mix of desperate patients and unscrupulous or foolish practitioners. The Duchess of Kent was soon to learn of the vagaries that exist.

She did not, however, propose to take to her bed – languishing, in the Victorian style of an Elizabeth Barrett Browning or a Florence Nightingale. Both were sufferers from the then-fashionable complaint of neurasthenia – an ailment seen by some doctors as having strong parallels with ME. Both were described, in the diagnosis of the time, as 'being off their feet' and condemned to a sofa existence. The Duchess had no wish to follow their example. Rather – and despite the raft of problems now facing her – she planned to carry out the plan she had outlined in India: to visit the headquarters of Unicef and to sing in New York with the Bach Choir.

This combination encompassed two of the most satisfying elements in her life. She had joined the choir in 1978, undergoing the same rigorous auditioning procedure as all other candidates. Having demonstrated, by singing scales and arpeggios, that her voice had suffecent quality and range and after satisfying the examiners on breath control, intonation and aural perception and singing, she – one of few applicants to succeed – was enlisted as a second soprano. Thereafter she was reassessed every three years, like all other members, to ensure that she was still meeting the demanding standards. Throughout her nervous breakdown she continued, when possible, to perform, finding, in her music, a rare release from personal anguish.

As Sir David Willcocks, the choir's former musical director, puts it: 'I like to think that it has been for her a pleasant and satisfying relaxation from her onerous royal duties . . . The therapeutic effect of choral singing has been widely recognized. It can be especially helpful for those who are constantly giving of themselves to others through public service and private charitable activity.'

In 1994 Katharine joined the choir in New Zealand for performances of Britten's *War Requiem* in Wellington Town Hall and a cathedral concert forming part of the city's arts festival. Her New York trip, in 1996, included Bach's *Magnificat* and Handel's *Coronation Anthems* in the Lincoln Center and motets by Gabrieli, Mendelssohn and Bruckner at Somerville College, New Jersey. When not performing, she had other work to do.

Invited to sit in on the Unicef board meeting, the Duchess of Kent, royal patron of the UK committee, was introduced by Carol Bellamy, the agency's executive director. Katharine greatly admired Bellamy – a woman regarded with respect and some fear within Unicef. A former Wall Street lawyer and financier and the first woman president of the New York City Council, she was known as a formidable operator. In her days with the American Peace Corps, of which she became director, she once sawed the head off a dog that had bitten her in order that it could be sent for analysis to see whether it was rabid. It was.

A personal friend of Hillary Clinton, Bellamy was so admired by the President that she was his personal choice of candidate for the directorship of Unicef. A hands-on manager, she combined a restructuring programme for the agency with a gruelling programme of overseas visits. She had been in the post for only a few months when Katharine arrived in New York. 'I introduced her from the podium and attended a luncheon that the UK people held for her,' Bellamy says. 'Each of the [Unicef] committees has a patron. It might be a first lady, or a member of a royal family. There are also showbusiness people involved. They all give publicity to the organization, and they are a variety of what I call sparklies.'

However Katharine regarded herself, it was certainly not as a sparkly. Thrilled by her début on to a new and high-powered stage, she suggested to the British wing of Unicef that she wished to return to New York the following year, this time to address the board meeting. It was explained to the Duchess that this would not be possible. For a start, Britain was not at the time even a board member; temporarily relegated, under a rotating system, to observer status.

In addition, it was gently pointed out, the sort of humanitarian speech at which Katharine excelled was simply not appropriate to a forum occupied with technical, intellectual and diplomatic business. Furthermore, the meeting was basically made up of government representatives, and the Duchess of Kent was not acting on behalf of the British government. Last of all, the UK committee played a relatively modest role in a vast organization. While it had succeeded, as a one-off special venture, in fixing her attendance at the board, it would not be possible to repeat – let alone to extend – the arrangement.

The facts were explained tactfully to Katharine, and the obstacles spelled out. In a year when the debate would revolve around the fantastically complex task of reshaping the United Nations, a podium speech from the Duchess of Kent – royal patron of a committee that currently lacked delegate status – was simply not an option. Faced with this explanation, Katharine – so humble during her charity work in the field – did not withdraw her request gracefully. On the contrary, she was reported to be livid, railing against her own office staff and senior representatives of the charity for their perceived failure in not securing the invitation she wanted.

'She was very disappointed that the idea was not possible,' a friend says tactfully. 'She very much wants to play a part in the board. I think she felt, temporarily, that Unicef was not quite proving the vehicle she had hoped for her.' That was undoubtedly shorthand for a row of major proportions.

Although Katharine finally had to accept that her plan must be shelved, it is certain that no one involved was left in any doubt as to the extent of her fury; a rage wholly at odds with the image of a humble volunteer and helper, a woman who was happy to scrub lavatory floors and who demanded that no deference be paid to her royal status. The autocracy that Katharine showed over the Unicef episode was not, however, simply a fit of pique displayed by a disappointed prima donna. Rather, it reflected how weary she was becoming of her public image as a gracious and saintly dispenser of care and concern. Those qualities may have been her strongest suit. They were also, as she realized, a limiting factor on the independence she was now seeking. Increasingly, the stereotype of the compassionate Duchess played to the charge often made in royal circles: that the Duchess of Kent was the intellectual inferior of the Duke and that the status and the nature of her work reflected it. If Katharine was to counter such slights, she could not rely on her academic track record as proof of superiority. Instead, she would have to find a role in which she could demonstrate her cleverness and grasp of a difficult portfolio. Having found an opportunity to shine, she was furious that her advancement was being blocked. The slights delivered to her in royal circles had become a fact of her life, hurtful and confidence-sapping but unavoidable. To appear marginalized at home was the norm. To be so in her own sphere of excellence seemed an unbearable snub to Katharine.

That is not to say that she was driven principally by personal ambition or ego. Despite her anger, she did not distance herself from Unicef. Soon her thoughts would instead be turning to another major overseas tour. But the board meeting row emphasized that Katharine, in public so gentle, was perfectly prepared to fight her corner in private. The episode also underlined her frustrations.

A serious career working with people she liked and admired would not only be a balm to her personal unhappiness and a means of confounding all the snipers who chose to question her abilities. In addition, a wider stage would distance her from the more stultifying aspects of royal duty.

Wimbledon, 1994. Comfort for the vanquished Jana Novotna. *PA News*

Left: The strains of their marriage reflected in the faces of the Duke and Duchess of Kent.
Universal Pictorial Press & Agency

Below: With her dogs in the West End. The Duchess has always enjoyed good clothes.
All Action

Awarded her honorary degree from the University of Hull in 1996.
Yorkshire Post

The Duchess pictured at home in Wren House. *Camera Press*

. . . and at work. *Camera Press*

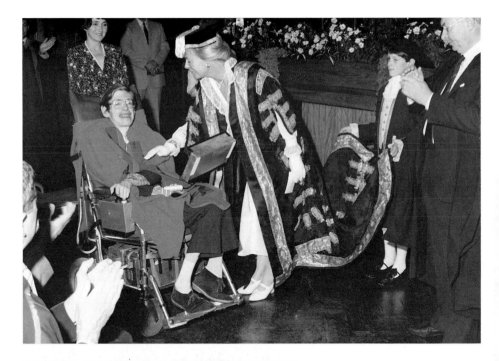

Above: The university
Chancellor . . . Katharine
talks to the theoretical
physicist Stephen Hawking.
*Winpenny Photography
of Otley*

Left: Tryst with a hero.
Meeting Nelson Mandela
in Africa. *PA News*

A simpler world. The Duchess, on tour for Unicef,
greets the old in India . . . *PA News*

. . . and the young in Africa.
PA News

Royal status, on the other hand, remained her passport to public recognition while imposing obvious limits on what she could do. Trapped in a vicious circle, Katharine seemed no closer to shedding the 'sparkly' tag still attached to her. She also remained haunted by the continuing problem of ill-health.

Although she had appeared healthy and effervescent during her Unicef board visit to New York in April, the remainder of 1996 passed quietly. As always, she was at the Wimbledon tennis championships and, in July, attended the Royal Tournament. After the summer she was hardly seen in public. In November she emerged from her growing purdah, regal and dressed in black, to hand out awards at a Unicef reception held at St James's Palace. On 5 December she was scheduled to attend the annual awards ceremony of Childline, the children's charity organized by Esther Rantzen.

Instead her office issued a brief statement. The Duchess of Kent had ME and had cancelled all her official engagements. Her spokesman told the media: 'She made it known earlier this year, at the time of her visit to India, that she was suffering from a virus with symptoms similar to ME. She was later diagnosed with ME. It is nothing too serious,' the spokesman added. 'She is just rather tired in general terms. She has been advised to take it easy. Rather than let people down, she felt it better not to accept engagements in the first place.'

There was no link, he stressed, between her current illness and any previous episode of depression. Even so, and quite naturally, the press rehearsed once again what it knew about the sad history of her earlier life. It also pointed out the bitter controversy over whether chronic fatigue syndrome stemmed primarily from organic or from psychological causes. Whatever the debate over the causes of the illness afflicting Katharine, no margin for doubt was left as to its nature. As the spokesman had made plain, the diagnosis was absolutely clear-cut. The Duchess of Kent had ME.

CHAPTER TWENTY-SEVEN

The ME Mystery

THREE DAYS AFTER the announcement that she had ME and would be relinquishing all her engagements, the Duchess of Kent appeared publicly to commemorate the first anniversary of the death of Philip Lawrence, the murdered London headmaster. Sombre in her black coat, she held the hand of Lucien, Lawrence's nine-year-old son, and helped him climb on to a wooden box to draw back the curtain from the plaque dedicated to his father's life.

Lucien said, steadily: 'Now I shall unveil the memorial to my daddy,' and quietly read the inscription. 'Philip Lawrence, head teacher of St George's School, gave his life 8.12.1995 in defence of a pupil. Love does not come to an end.' Then he stepped down into the Duchess's embrace. However ill Katharine felt, she would have been loath to miss this occasion.

In India, two months after Lawrence's murder, she had spoken of how deeply his stabbing by a teenage boy had affected her. The brutal attack on a devout and courageous man, a beloved husband and a father of four, epitomized to her a wider corrupting force. The abandonment of family values, which she held responsible for the killer's action, affected – in her view – not only the Lawrence family but British society at large. 'May we all try to live up to the shining example of Philip Lawrence,' she told guests at a service held at his school and presided over by Cardinal Hume. The ceremony finished, Katharine returned to the shadows, universally praised for her courage in attending the Lawrence service. Although no one remarked on it, her presence was also curious, given the gravity of a newly announced illness whose symptoms included chest and back pain, aching muscles, dizziness, nausea and extreme weakness.

The causes of ME remained obscure. Three months before the public announcement of Katharine's illness, the Royal Colleges had published their exhaustive study of chronic fatigue syndrome. An arduous researcher, Katharine would certainly have read the working party's findings. These had in part mollified patient groups – notably the ME Association and Action for ME – by acknowledging that the illness was a seriously debilitating condition, frequently poorly managed and badly understood by doctors. Conversely, the groups believed that the report's findings were loaded towards psychiatric rather than physical factors. In other words they refuted the working party's suggestion of a large overlap between chronic fatigue syndrome and depression.

Despite some *rapprochement* between leading psychiatrists and patient support groups, the basic uncertainties remained. ME was an enigma – cause unknown, cure uncertain and treatable, in the view of mainstream experts, only by 'cognitive therapy', encouraging sufferers to take up a managed exercise programme rather than simply resting. Beyond that, ME represented a minefield of conflicting views. It afflicted burnt-out high achievers; too unselfish to slow down, said patients' champions. Rubbish, countered leading psychiatrists. The million British people who claimed to have the disease were no more driven or successful than anyone else – and there was no magic cure. Not true, said a number of therapists and 'experts' offering a raft of treatments including 'anti-allergy' injections at around £2,000 per course.

Like other new and rich sufferers, the Duchess of Kent dabbled in what Harley Street had to offer. Or, as one friend puts it: 'She did the rounds.' Dispirited and confused, she was finally put in touch with someone able to offer helpful counsel. Clare Francis, best-selling author and round-the-world yachtswoman, had contracted ME in 1986 and later became founding president of Action for ME, a leading support organization for patients and their families. Lady Elizabeth Anson, the Queen's cousin, party-caterer-in-chief to the royal family and another sufferer, later took over the presidency.

But, although Lady Elizabeth had organized the wedding reception for Helen, Katharine's daughter, the Duchess preferred to confide in a less familiar figure. Francis, intelligent and an over-achiever, had a clear view on the likely profile of an ME victim. 'People who have a lot of commitments and are very dedicated often ignore what their body is telling them,' she says. 'So high achievers or people who lead busy lives can be prone to get it more seriously. These people know something is wrong, but they plough on, hiding from the world and themselves just how bad they are feeling.'

In Francis, Katharine found not only a source of sage advice but a confidante. It is likely that their long conversations ranged wider than illness; into the rough terrain of Katharine's troubled marriage. She also found echoes in

Francis, who had encountered the same lack of help, of the bafflement that she was experiencing. As Francis says: 'There aren't many ME doctors around who take on patients with any real understanding. Patients need to talk to someone who will reassure them. These patients are very demanding. Not many doctors take it on. Most of the private doctors in Harley Street are embedded in other philosophies about the illness. It has to be a virus. Or it has to be bacterial. So there aren't many who offer that much understanding.'

Having learned something about the unsympathetic and the unconventional, Katharine was finally told of two doctors offering sympathy and held in high regard by ME suffers. Dr David Dowson, based mainly in Bath, was seen as sympathetic, effective and offering a holistic package including nutritional advice and magnesium injections – expensive but justified in his *Lancet* paper claiming that a factor in ME could be low red cell magnesium. Some leading psychiatrists, however, remained unconvinced, claiming that no one had been able to replicate his findings.

The second man was Charles Shepherd, former ME victim, a GP and leading light of the ME Association. Although neither doctor has confirmed that he was involved in Katharine's treatment, Shepherd, certainly, scored a singular coup.

At exactly the time that the Duchess's illness was revealed from York House – in December 1996 – the Duke of Kent was signed up as royal patron of Shepherd's association. Its administrator, Mavis Moore, confirms: 'There had been various conversations between Dr Shepherd and the Duke's private office. We did have confirmation that he would be patron prior to the announcement that the Duchess had ME, but we did not announce it until afterwards. It was all confirmed in November.'

On this timescale, and given the slowness of securing such a major patronage, it seems certain the Duchess was convinced for many months before the official announcement that she had ME. The more curious element is the Duke of Kent's willingness to take on a task far outside his normal portfolio. His decision ran against the grain not only of royal family tradition – uncomprehending of any illness with a possible psychiatric dimension – but also of his public image of a cold and uncaring husband. The fact that the Duke, by then living a life largely detached from his wife's, undertook this commitment suggests one of two scenarios. The first is that he was acting principally at her behest. The second, and more probable, is that he was enthusiastic at the idea that Katharine's history of illness might be laid at the door of a disease which, however imprecise, at least bore a name.

In 1997 the Duke wrote a touching personal message in the association's twenty-first anniversary magazine. 'I have seen through experience with my own family the debilitating effect which ME has on those suffering from it, and the difficulties found by those who care for them ... I look forward to a close and positive involvement with the Association in the future ... I extend to all those affected with ME my deep understanding, and my hope for their future recovery.' For the first time, the Duke was acknowledging the gravity of Katharine's condition and, obliquely, suggesting a strain in the marriage caused by its impact on those around her. ME patients (and sufferers from depression) are prone to be tearful, low, miserable, difficult and irritable. With an unusual openness for a male member of the royal family, the Duke was spelling out the Kent family problems; difficulties to which ME, grave as it was, offered a number of solutions.

Publicly to be able to lay the blame for strained relations and marital unhappiness at the door of a physical illness must, in some ways, have offered comfort to the Duke and the Duchess, who had struggled and failed to instil much happiness into their marriage. Hence Edward's emphasis on the linked problems of sufferers and carers. Quite who 'those who cared' for Katharine were remained unclear. There was no suggestion that the Duke himself ever took on an overtly nurturing role. Nonetheless he was, inevitably, affected by Katharine's illness. His message offered a signal that he recognized its gravity and was, in public at least, doing whatever he could to help.

More widely, his words were welcomed as a positive intervention in an illness bedevilled by stigma. Although the 'yuppie flu' tag had long since been dropped, the inference remained that many sufferers might be depressives dressing up their illness as a purely physical affliction. In this climate, high-profile figures – like Clare Francis or the TV presenter Esther Rantzen, whose teenage daughter, Emily, had ME – were looked to as potential ambassadors, willing to speak out on behalf of less famous patients.

It was obvious from the outset that Katharine had no wish to be a crusader. She did not speak in public of her illness. In a rare television interview, any questions alluding to ME or her state of health were excised from a submitted list. But behind the scenes, in medical consulting-rooms all over the country, her case aroused great interest.

Even those doctors who had never treated her were eager to judge how her illness might mesh with their own research projects. John Studd, the gynaecologist who had said four years previously that he was certain Katharine was taking HRT, was particularly fascinated. Studd claimed to have established a link between ME, pre-menstrual syndrome and post-natal depression. Such patients, in his thesis, frequently had low-value oestrogen levels, often allied to low bone density, a condition leading to early osteoporosis. The majority, he submitted, could be cured of ME by high-dose oestrogens administered through patches or implants.

The Duchess of Kent, Studd believed, had the classic profile of such a patient. 'I see patients like the Duchess who say that the last time they felt well was when they were pregnant. I have this quartet of symptoms that tell me whether a patient ... with depression will do well on oestrogens. A history of being well during pregnancy, a history of post-natal depression, pre-menstrual depression and menstrual migraine.'

Other doctors saw some merit in this thesis. Professor Leslie Findley, a neurologist at the National ME Support Centre and consultant to Esther Rantzen's daughter, refers some patients to Studd. 'There is no reason to suppose that oestrogen deficiency is the cause of chronic fatigue syndrome; but neither is there any doubt that, for some people, oestrogens do improve the symptoms. It's one factor.'

Since Katharine knows Rantzen, she would be aware of Findley's work and, possibly, that of Studd. She would not have been aware of leading edge research, unpublished at the time of writing, by Dr Peter White – a member of the Royal Colleges working party and a senior lecturer in psychiatry at Bart's Hospital – which might also have had some conceivable bearing on her case. The Duchess was previously thought to have been prescribed heavy doses of drugs to counter her depression. White, for the first time, had established a link between over-use of benzodiazopenes – such as Valium and Mogadon – and contracting ME in later life.

In addition to pioneering research by the leading doctors mentioned here, ME also continues to attract the attentions of the crankish and the incompetent. As Leslie Findley says: 'There are more fanatics in this branch of medicine than any other.' But, beyond the wealth of reputable investigation and half-baked theory, one very simple question preoccupied experts from the day of the announcement of the Duchess of Kent's latest illness. Did she have ME at all?

According to Professor Simon Wessely, a member of the Royal Colleges team and one of the country's foremost experts on chronic fatigue syndrome, there is a vast overlap between ME and depression. 'There is no hard and fast distinction between the two. Both have fatigue as a principal complaint. Both include poor concentration and disturbance of weight, appetite and sleep. Cardinal symptoms of both are mood disorder, loss of pleasure, not enjoying things any more. People try and pretend there is a clear distinction between the two. There isn't.

'If people have a history of very severe depression, we would refuse to diagnose chronic fatigue syndrome, because we would think the depression trumps the CFS. It would be unlikely that God would be malicious and give you two completely separate illnesses which happen to overlap quite a lot. It would be much more likely that the two are related.'

Wessely's research does, however, show some clear distinctions between patients suffering solely from depression and CFS victims who, in 50 per cent of cases, are also depressed. Depressives were more guilty and more likely to harm themselves or commit suicide. ME patients blamed the virus, not themselves, and were less prone to suicide. 'Blaming a virus is better than thinking you are a wicked person who has wrecked your life and your marriage. The

ME attribution protects patients. It makes them feel less guilty and vulnerable. All the rows and passions over ME boil down to guilt, responsibility and blame. As soon as you introduce any psychological dimension, it is viewed as an attack on the sufferer's legitimacy.'

In 1997 there was no publicly aired question as to Katharine's legitimacy. She had been diagnosed as suffering from ME. Her office had formally confirmed it. Her husband had written, in his message to the ME Association, of seeing at first hand the devastating effect the illness has both on patients and on their families.

There is no reason to suppose that Katharine's symptoms differed in any way from those of other sufferers. She was, however, recovering faster than medical experts might have supposed. The prognosis for ME is not particularly cheerful. According to the ME Association, 35 per cent of patients improve slowly over several years. About half of this group go on to make a fully recovery. The majority, about four in ten patients, never recover fully and are prone to severe relapses. Between 15 and 20 per cent remain severely disabled and make little or no progress, while a very small number – 5 to 10 per cent – deteriorate steadily, becoming chair- or bed-bound for most of the time. The Duchess of Kent did not obviously fit into any of these groupings.

By April 1997 she was sufficiently recovered to undertake a seven-day tour of South Africa – once again on behalf of Unicef. A spokeswoman from her office was quoted as saying that the Duchess, now sixty-four years old, was coping well with ME and that it was hoped the physical and mental exertion of the trip would not make the condition worse. In fact, although the press pointed to 'gruelling conditions' and noted that Katharine had put her own health priorities on the back burner for the sake of children, great care had naturally been taken to ensure that the programme was as light and undemanding as possible.

Even so, it presented – like all such field trips – a reasonably rigorous schedule and a wide-ranging itinerary, beginning in Johannesburg, including a visit to the province of KwaZulu Natal and ending in Durban. Katharine's transport was more basic than on her visit to India the year before. A Mercedes car and helicopters were supplied by the South African government, and she was booked, for the journey from Durban to Cape Town on flight SA 647, a scheduled South African Airways flight. This time there was no question of a plane of the Queen's Flight being put at the disposal of the Duchess of Kent and her party. A new climate of economy prevailed – soon to be heightened after the death of Princess Diana – and luxurious transport for minor royals, even those in flagging health, was not to be countenanced.

Despite anxieties before her departure, the Duchess's state of health gave rise to very little concern. She began her tour spending a rare private weekend abroad with her husband, who had coincidentally been in Africa, working. When Katharine first stepped from her helicopter, stumbling slightly, some of those waiting to greet her remarked on how tired she looked. Those who had seen her working in India saw, conversely, how much she appeared to have improved. The fussy gestures, as she nervously adjusted her clothes, had disappeared. So had the blank expression – once semi-permanent except for those times when she was either absorbed in talking to the people she had come to see or when she was forced to perform for the cameras.

'In India, she walked gingerly, like a little old lady,' said someone who had seen her on both tours. 'Sometimes she could be great and smiley. But if the cameras were off her, she would just stare into space, as if there was something on her mind.' In South Africa, she appeared rejuvenated; smiling as she was introduced for the umpteenth time as 'the lady who brings happiness to so many people at Wimbledon' and running joyfully to meet crowds of children at the schools she visited. 'Guess what his name is?' she called out, holding a two-year-old boy in her arms. 'Information. Isn't that a wonderful name?'

Her senior personal staff – detective, lady-in-waiting and hairdresser – were the same team which had accompanied her to India. Her wardrobe was as splendid and her public manner was warm. But, even more than on her previous trip, the Duchess made it plain that she was a career woman engaged in important business. At one point she asked her detective to fetch her a dictaphone, so that she could personally record an official's statement. She would, she said, again be compiling a report of her visit – a document presumably intended for Carol Bellamy, the executive director in New York.

The storm over Katharine's unsuccessful bid to address the board had been smoothed over – by diplomatic staff at Unicef and by her own realization that it had been impossible to accede to her wish. Her more traditional strengths were on display as the tour progressed. She was as compassionate as always – but, as ever, she appeared to play down her genius for dealing with people as a belittling of her abilities. A list of questions submitted for one media interview was rejected instantly, on the grounds that the chosen areas were too trivial and the Duchess wanted a more rigorous interrogation.

Assuming that the central purpose of her visit was to open doors and raise consciousness in a tribal country which lauds the ceremonial role, Katharine was faultless. The King of KwaZulu Natal came personally to meet her by the roadside – a signal honour – and sat next to her later at a party, clearly enthralled by her company.

But Katharine's greatest ambition was to meet another leader. Nelson Mandela, a man she hero-worshipped, had not been able to confirm prior to her departure that he could definitely see her. A few weeks previously he had met Princess Diana, who had called on him during a private visit to her brother, Earl Spencer, to discuss South Africa's AIDS epidemic. Katharine would no doubt have been mortified if the same courtesy had not been extended to her.

In the end, there was no hitch. Unicef staff had been told that Mandela would not be on the pavement personally to greet her, but – as the Duchess's car drew up outside the presidential offices – he appeared to offer his welcome. Arm in arm they walked up the steps towards his study – 'like two old dears leaning on each other for support', as one spectator said – and sat, side by side, on his sofa for a meeting to which he had allocated ten minutes.

Their agenda was simple. Katharine made it clear how much she admired him. They discussed the children of South Africa. He presented her with a traditional painting, and she gave him a personal cheque made out to his charity, the Mandela Children's Fund. The ten minutes spun on to fifteen or twenty, until Mandela gently told the Duchess that they must leave. People were waiting outside to see her. The press had been told that while Mandela might agree to answer a few questions, the Duchess of Kent must be asked nothing.

In the end he casually threw the press conference over to her, inviting her to talk while he stayed silent. Even before

ME, impromptu speaking had been Katharine's *bête noire*. This time she talked charmingly and graciously for a few moments, totally in control and showing no sign of strain, emboldened by her audience with one of her greatest heroes. Like Cardinal Hume, her other inspiration, Mandela was powerful, kind, humble and a great force for good. Undoubtedly such men stirred memories of her father, whose influence she had never managed to replicate elsewhere. Certainly they were the antithesis to those who influenced other areas of her life: courtiers, Establishment figures and, of course, her husband.

On her South African tour, Katharine – careful, this time, not to let her guard slip – omitted to mention the feelings of despair and loneliness that would overtake her on her return home. There was no reason to suppose that the prospect of her reunion with the Duke of Kent filled her with any greater joy than on previous occasions, but she naturally had no intention of discussing that.

Nor, as she made plain, did she wish herself to be portrayed as a working woman who, through courage and determination, had overcome the spectre of ME in order to lend assistance to the children of South Africa. Any mention of her illness was deemed to be strictly off-limits.

It was clear, nonetheless, to those who travelled with her that Katharine, hardly surprisingly, was under some stress. Though her programme was undemanding and she was able, on most evenings, to go back and rest at the British diplomatic residences where she stayed, she drove herself as hard as ever. A keynote speech, to be delivered on her last night, was endlessly rewritten, and there were traces of imperiousness in her demands on staff; less evidence of autocracy than a symptom of strain. To some who watched her, she appeared oddly vulnerable – a woman made distant by the demands of a royal role but with no adviser to smooth her way and shape her strategy.

In front of the camera she – charming, compassionate and wonderfully photogenic – needed no help. Away from it, there was a sense, although Katharine never said so herself, that she was striving furiously to be treated more seriously and accorded a respect beyond the deference accorded to royalty. Like many perfectionists, low on self-regard, she seemed to belittle her own great skills of communication – aspiring, always, to a more meaningful role.

Whatever her insecurities, she had done an impressive job, and she was conscious of it. On the flight back to London, before settling down to sleep, she walked down the aisle of her British Airways flight, from first class to economy, to see the journalists and aid workers who had accompanied her. Beaming and enthusiastic, she told them she thought the tour had been wonderful. Where should they go next year, she wondered. South America? Brazil?

Vibrant and entertaining, Katharine gave no hint that she was a sick woman, an ME sufferer, returning to a long and uncertain convalescence. In the ensuing months, ME was mentioned less and less. It was, by then, abundantly clear that she had no intention of becoming a patients' crusader. Though Katharine's wish not to get involved disappointed some campaigners, that decision was entirely her prerogative. More puzzling was the pattern of her illness. She remained unwell, complaining frequently that she had 'bad days and good days' – a pattern familiar to ME sufferers. But outwardly she was stoical – partly though bravery and partly because she was irked by her current illness invariably being linked by the press to her past mental illness. ME was turning out to be a double curse to the

Duchess of Kent; on the one hand a crippling illness and, on the other, a reason to label Katharine a frail depressive; the very definition that she had hoped and expected to ditch by letting it be known that she was suffering from an illness she – and a number of practitioners – regarded as being wholly physical in origin.

Through all this time, the Duke of Kent had carried out not a single engagement for the ME Association. Every invitation submitted by the association was politely turned down by his office, on the grounds that no slot could be found in the Duke's busy engagement diary. Valid as the excuses may have been, it was most unlike Edward to be a sleeping royal patron. Known for his hard work, he was determined on finding time for all the organizations to which he lent his name. In addition, the ME Association was not just any other patronage. Its work involved an illness affecting his wife, her family and the Duke himself.

All of this he had acknowledged, movingly for such a strait-laced man, in the message he had offered about the Kents' troubles and the large role he hoped to play in the work of the ME Association. At the time of writing, he had not once found the time to combine those words of encouragement with any positive action. Other factors may have weighed on the Duke. From the moment that Katharine had started to voice her suspicions that she had ME, some courtiers wondered whether she had been subconsciously influenced by watching an aide who suffered from chronic fatigue syndrome and discovering that they had some symptoms in common. The Duke had no doubt discounted this theory, hopeful that Katharine's illness was not merely another form of depression but a disease that might be amenable to treatment.

Edward's back-tracking from any active involvement in

the ME Association raises the question of whether he had now changed his mind, inclining to the view, held by some courtiers and interested psychiatrists, that the Duchess's illness – for all the formal declarations and public concern – was actually a condition whose symptoms may have replicated those of chronic fatigue syndrome but which was not the real thing.

That is not to belittle Katharine's suffering. Depression, with its attendant misery and loneliness, is a grave and debilitating condition and a ruiner of lives. It is not, however, ME. The possibility remained that Katharine – justifiably confused by the unquantifiable overlap between depression and chronic fatigue syndrome – had been misdiagnosed. She, who had always refused to discuss her condition, never said so.

But, eight months after she returned from South Africa, she sought, in an interview in the *Daily Telegraph*, to scotch the enduring notion that she was a fragile creature. 'If I were to climb Mount Everest . . . they would invariably say that it was "despite the fact that she suffered from acute depression and permanent ill-health".' On the contrary, she suggested, she was a robust figure – perfectly capable of working in India, in Africa and at Lourdes.

More surprisingly, Katharine explained that doctors had now isolated what was wrong with her. She had, she said, been diagnosed earlier in the year as 'possibly' having coeliac disease – an illness that interferes with the absorption of food – and put on a gluten-free diet. 'It means that I may not have been absorbing food properly for fifteen or twenty years. That could account for my sudden exhaustion [before India].'

In other words, she appeared to be revising the initial diagnosis of Epstein-Barr Virus, a precursor of ME. That, in turn, seemed to cast a doubt on the later annoucement that she was suffering from ME. Whatever was wrong with the Duchess, it taxes credulity that a glandular fever-type virus could have been mistaken for a food allergy.

It is, however, undoubtedly true that Katharine had, for many years, been an exceptionally fussy eater. Early in her marriage, she had adored sticky puddings; in particular mounds of peppermint ice cream with bitter chocolate melted over the top and allowed to set. In later years she became more and more cautious about food. On one occasion, according to a close friend, she sent back every dish presented to her at a Windsor gathering, entirely untouched. At another country house dinner, she ate only apples and Cheddar cheese. At a third get-together – a meal cooked by a friend's resident chef – she declined the prepared offerings and said that she had brought her own soup to be warmed up.

Though always slim, attractive and radiant, Katharine worried increasingly about her diet, to the point where some of her friends considered that her weaknesses could be attributable simply to eating hardly anything for days before embarking on one big meal. Loss of appetite, of course, is associated with chronic fatigue syndrome; one of a raft of symptoms from which Katharine appeared to suffer.

By now the word was spreading among the Kents' friends that Katharine did not have chronic fatigue syndrome after all. If, as seems possible, the whole ME episode had been a mistake from beginning to end, that does not suggest that she was in the grip of hypochondria or self-delusion. What-ever the label attached to her illness, the symptoms had undoubtedly been genuine.

The causes were harder to isolate. Katharine, determined to slough off the notion that she was a perpetual invalid, chose to cite a food allergy – a relatively straightforward and controllable condition. If only, she must have told herself in her bleaker moments, every problem in her life were so amenable to treatment.

CHAPTER TWENTY-EIGHT

Separate Lives

❖

O N 22 JUNE 1997, the *Sunday Mirror* claimed in a
front-page story that the Duchess of Kent's marriage
was 'over'. The Duke and the Duchess, the article alleged,
were 'living under the same roof but leading separate lives'.
Theirs, in the words of a 'royal insider', was a sham marriage,
and the Queen was aware of the problems. The report was
denied by Buckingham Palace in unusually strong terms as
'hogwash'. Although inaccurate in some details, its content
was broadly correct. It was also twenty years late.

The relationship of the Duke and the Duchess was not,
as the report said, 'the latest royal marriage to fall apart'. It
had collapsed in the mid-seventies, around the time that the
Duchess lost her stillborn son, Patrick. The ingredients of
the 'sham marriage', as the *Sunday Mirror* labelled it, had
altered little over the years. The root of the Kents' problems
remained a total mismatch of character, interests and background. The Duke was bred to royal life, the Duchess
temperamentally unsuited to its formality and rigours. She
was vulnerable and in need of infinite patience; he was a
man of quick temper. She was overtly emotional; he had
been trained to repress outward displays of feelings. He was

a sportsman, an Army officer and a denizen of a male world; she – the daughter of an adoring father – expected to be at the centre of her husband's universe.

Other factors have been cited here as contributors to the initial troubles: the Duke's alleged 'roving eye' in one stage of his marriage; the Duchess's tendency to what royal-watchers called 'the vapours' and the supposed difficulties her lassitude and misery caused Eddie. But, for all their differences, some threads had bound them together over the years – their three children, their sense of duty to the Queen and their shared allegiance to the notion of family. According to one of the Duke's closest confidants, he had promised the Queen that his marriage would not break apart. That pledge, once given, was non-negotiable.

Katharine, for her part, was not by instinct a 'bolter'. Religion, duty and the fact that she was the child of an enduring marriage all militated towards her staying. So did her romanticized notion – never fulfilled – of perfect family life and the fact she, frail and resourceless, was effectively a prisoner of the royal machine. If she had been able to walk away from her marriage many years before, then she might have increased her chances of a happy life. But that was hypothetical.

Two decades previously, the Kents had embarked on the quest to save their marriage. It was a shaky endeavour, made more difficult by the fact that Katharine had been driven, by an assortment of sorrows, to depression and a succession of illnesses that would have tested the most robust of relationships, let alone a marriage that appeared to be at the end of the road.

The fact that Katharine and Eddie – once viewed as the most charming couple of their day – were together at all at the time of the *Sunday Mirror* story demonstrates an exceptional tenacity and obligation to duty on the part of both. In an age when the major players on the royal stage had become such a model for venal values that the institution of monarchy was threatened, the Duchess and the Duke remained exemplars of irreproachable public conduct. The Prince and the Princess of Wales appeared on prime-time television to reveal their respective affairs – Charles with Camilla Parker Bowles and Diana with James Hewitt. Prince Andrew's marriage collapsed, freeing the Duchess of York to pursue a freelance career driven by debt and defined by vulgarity. Through the storms of the late eighties and the nineties, the Kents side-slipped most rumour and all scandal to offer a contrasting picture of unstinting and unsullied public service. Having chosen their route, they did not deviate from it. It had been a lonely and a difficult odyssey with, at least for Katharine, no prospect of a happy resolution. Throughout the eighties she is said to have told close friends that she still toyed constantly with the idea of leaving. By then she knew, as the friends in whom she confided knew, that there was no way out.

By 1997 the Kents were living in a pretty, cottage-style residence in the grounds of Kensington Palace. The Duchess had been eager to move from their previous grace-and-favour apartment at York House to a leafier setting, and Wren House fitted her specification perfectly. Traditionally the house had been the residence of the private secretary of the Prince of Wales. As such, it had been occupied by Commander Richard Aylard, formerly secretary to both Charles and Diana. When the Waleses separated, Diana was said to be irked that a man so closely involved with her husband's life, and therefore someone she viewed as potentially acting against her interests, should be living virtually opposite her apartment at Kensington Palace. When Aylard left his post, it was decided that Wren House should cease to be the private secretary's home, and – as an indirect result of the intervention of her friend, Diana – Katharine was offered a house she loved. Although grand, charming and idyllically situated, Wren House is not particularly spacious. Aside from two reception rooms and a dining-room, there are only three bedrooms, and the low ceilings give it the air of a rural cottage.

The Kents had no other home, except for a cottage on the Stonor estate of Lord Camoys, the Lord Chancellor. This weekend retreat, not far from the Kents' old home, near Henley, was primarily a bolthole for the Duchess and a substitute for the borrowed cottage in Norfolk to which she had escaped in previous years. The Stonor house was so small that a friend invited to see it wondered how the Duke, a rangy man, could telescope himself into such a tiny space. As she said: 'When you consider how tall the Duke is, you wonder how he could possibly lie down in the bedroom.' The Duke, in fact, did not often have to tackle this logistical problem. In the main, Katharine spent her weekends alone.

Although hardly under-housed by normal British standards, the square-footage of the homes at the Kents' disposal meant that, judged in royal terms, theirs was a cheek-by-jowl existence. It was also, despite their enforced proximity, an almost entirely separate one. Any excerpt taken at random from the engagements diary of the Duke and Duchess in 1997 demonstrates the disparity in their public duties.

In the period beginning Thursday, 12 June, the Duke, as Chancellor of the University of Surrey, conferred degrees at Guildford Cathedral. On Friday, 13 June, the Duchess carried out an engagement on behalf of Macmillan Cancer Relief, of which she is president. And so it continues.

'Saturday, 14 June: The Duke of Kent, Colonel, Scots

Greys, will lunch with officers attending the Queen's Birthday Parade, at Wellington Barracks, London SW1.'

'Sunday, 15 June: The Duchess of Kent, Patron, the Yorkshire County Cricket Club, will attend the Surrey versus Yorkshire cricket match, the Oval, Kennington, London SE11.'

'Tuesday, 17 June: The Duchess of Kent, Patron, the Arthritis and Rheumatism Council, will open the new Kennedy Institute Building, Charing Cross Westminster Medical School, the Sunley Building, Aspenlea Road, London W6.'

'Wednesday, 18 June: The Duke of Kent, President, will chair/preside at the quarterly meeting of the Commonwealth War Graves Commission, Marlow Road, Maidenhead, Berkshire. His Royal Highness, Royal Fellow, will attend the Royal Society's New Frontiers in Science Exhibition, Carlton House Terrace, London SW1.'

'Thursday, 19 June: The Duke of Kent will visit the Regular Commissions Board, Westbury; will open the Bradford-on-Avon Youth and Community Centre, Frome Road, Bradford-on-Avon and will visit Clouds House, East Knoyle, Wiltshire.'

A few days later, Saturday, 5, and Sunday, 6 July – the ladies' and men's finals of the Wimbledon tennis championships – the rare listing TRH, or Their Royal Highnesses, appears on the schedule of forthcoming engagements. With the exception of the FA Cup Final, those were their only formal joint appearances in the calendar.

Tim O'Donovan, who compiles the royal family's annual workload in a yearly letter for *The Times*, assessed the Kents' output for 1997 as follows. The Duke carried out a total of 168 engagements in the UK and 66 on official overseas tours. In the same categories, the Duchess's scores were 47 and 11 respectively – figures that give some measure of how little opportunity they had to spend time together, given the totally different nature of their work portfolios. Even when they were free simultaneously, their lives – with the exception of occasional dinner parties at Wren House – continued on different orbits.

Edward liked to lunch at Boodle's – the most conservative of London clubs – sometimes with a friend and sometimes alone, in which case he spoke to no one until his solitary lunch was over. Katharine preferred Le Caprice, a fashionable London restaurant popular in media, political and showbusiness circles. At weekends, Edward might spend time with his brother Michael at his Gloucestershire manor house, Nether Lypiatt, or visit his older son, George, his wife Sylvana and their children. The relationship between Sylvana and Katharine remained uneasy, and the Duke retained by far the closer links with his son's family. Where Katharine had, before his marriage, demonstrated her adoration of her eldest child, the more durable relationship between father and son followed the formal royal model, non-effusive but, in this case, secure.

Katharine's weekends were chiefly spent at the Stonor cottage, where villagers knew her as someone so unpretentious that she offered to babysit for the children of a local farmer's son who occasionally helped her with the chores. On weekday evenings, Edward would sometimes eat at an all-male dining club. Katharine would often have a snack at home, where the couple had no staff, bar a cleaner and a soldier valet to look after the Duke's uniforms. Their official offices, and their joint private secretary, remained at York House.

By the early nineties, with their children grown up, the Kents had separate work agendas, separate leisure activities, separate friends and a marriage largely defined by sacrifice, loneliness and work. Among other things, British industry and British Freemasonry preoccupied the Duke. As his friend Kenneth Rose wrote in *Kings, Queens and Courtiers*: 'He visits British companies to see their problems for himself, from shop-floor to boardroom. He addresses conferences on the strategy and tactics of exporting. And he makes regular tours abroad, sometimes with teams of businessmen, to fly the flag and bring home orders. Other members of the royal family also make spasmodic incursions into the industrial scene. Unlike the Duke of Kent, however, they do not always manage to avoid the pitfalls of such a vocation: the misplaced pleasantry that rankles, the facile denigration of Britain's methods and achievements.'

In his role as the Grand Master of British Freemasonry, Edward is said, according to one insider of what remains a secret society, to be 'a great force for good'. When, in 1985, a book called *The Brotherhood* by Stephen Knight portrayed Freemasonry as a sinister society with possible links to the KGB, the Duke – not a natural modernizer – played a leading role in promoting a new climate of relative openness. According to John Hamill, the curator of the Grand Lodge of England: 'He said it was time we changed some of our old policies. He wasn't advocating public relations or a recruiting campaign, but he thought we should educate the general public to change the perception that people like Knight were trying to give them.'

After the publication of *The Brotherhood*, the Duke agreed to open an exhibition organized by Freemasons – but only on condition that the guest list included not only Masonic VIPs but guests from all strands of public life. Challenged by a journalist from Radio Four's *Today* programme, who was attending the launch, to 'put his money where his mouth was' and do an interview for *Today*, the Duke agreed to give his view from a radio car parked outside York House. Although some within the organization took a dim view of the Duke of Kent's stance, Edward was determined both that Freemasonry must open its doors and that the most atavistic practices should be abolished. He abhorred, for instance, the notion of physical penalties, under which Masons faced having their tongues cut out and their throats slit if they broke their oaths. The Duke's view was that such references contributed to the society's reputation for secrecy and idolatry, and the penalties were duly abolished in 1986.

Considering that the Duke had been in his post as Grand Master for twenty years, this move had not been particularly speedily executed. Nor was his genuine desire for greater openness by any means an absolute measure. In February 1998 the House of Commons Home Affairs select committee, chaired by Chris Mullin MP, demanded the names of police officers belonging to the Freemasons and who had been involved in the investigation of the Birmingham pub bombings in 1974 and in the Stalker inquiry in Northern Ireland in the mid-eighties. Prior to Labour's general election victory, the then chairman, Sir Ivan Lawrence, had required only an assessment of numbers of Freemasons involved. Mullin's demand for names infuriated the Duke, who was, according to one of his closest friends, 'hopping mad' at this supposed intrusion.

Senior Freemasons – not the Duke – were summoned to appear before the committee and told that their refusal to supply the names would leave them in contempt of the House and liable to be summoned to the Bar of the House to explain themselves. After taking legal advice, it was decided that Freemasonry should not put itself in contempt of parliament, and the names were finally given, with the agreement that they would not be disclosed to any other source.

That was not the end of the matter. Jack Straw, the Home Secretary (and the student leader who had once danced with the Duchess of Kent at Leeds University) wanted all those Freemasons applying to be a judge, a magistrate, a police, probation officer or prison officer, plus anyone working for the Crown Prosecution Service, to declare their membership. The society was obdurately set against any voluntary register or any suggestion that they would supply a list of names. If the Home Secretary wanted to pursue his plan, he would have to legislate.

At the time of writing, the issue remains unresolved. It is certain, however, that the Duke of Kent remained wholly opposed to the government's wishes. As John Hamill says: 'He has been extremely supportive. We see registration of people simply because they are Freemasons as being an attack on the individual's right to privacy and an attack on the individual's right to join a lawful association.'

That hardline stance is most unlikely to strike any chord outside Freemasonry, but then the Duke has rarely been accused of populism. Vitriolic in his denunciation of intrusive newspaper reporters, Edward Kent, a rather shadowy figure, could not fairly be represented as a 'people's duke'. But according to his friends he is a likeable man, so modest that he was reluctant to accept his promotion to Field Marshal in 1993, following a spontaneous recommendation by the Queen to the Army Board, complying only when told to obey orders. There is something rather poignant, even childish, about Edward's supposed gratitude and humility at a paper promotion he had never been allowed to pursue in his truncated career as an active soldier. Katharine, certainly, was not impressed by his promotion. To the intense fury of the Duke's circle, she apparently received the news without joy or congratulation.

If, in private, the relationship between the Duke and Duchess had degenerated far beyond the stage of even forced politeness, Katharine never allowed that coldness to impact on her public life. In the public arena, the Duchess of Kent has always displayed a dimension her husband has been unable to offer: a star quality that means she is instantly recognizable on the most far-flung of stages. In India and Africa, those bereft of television set or the faintest interest in the royal family are able to pick her out as 'the lady from Wimbledon'. And, even when they cannot, they recognize in her – the commoner who found royal ritual suffocating and cloying – a regal quality that many of those born into royalty have failed to replicate.

Beyond stage presence and innate compassion, Katharine – though frail and vulnerable – possesses indomitable determination. To be charming, natural, well-briefed and amusing goes with the territory. To be so when one is miserable and ill is harder. To fulfil difficult engagements despite utter weariness, frayed nerves and shattered concentration demands a rare sort of tenacity. Down the years, the Duchess of Kent has consistently overcome such obstacles, offering performances so seamless that only those who knew her best understood what she had to endure. Hers has not been a light or an undemanding schedule. Her major undertakings – patron of Unicef, president of Macmillan Cancer Relief, Age Concern, the Samaritans, Leeds University and the Royal Northern College of Music – are only some of the planks in a raft of other patronages.

Her secret is to make the art of performance secondary. As she has said, she adores both children and the elderly and 'falls in love about fifty times a day'. Never manufactured, her empathy is marked out by an authenticity that has overridden both illness and despair. If personal suffering can be transmuted into a force for good and for understanding the sadness of others, then few have achieved that alchemy more successfully than the Duchess.

The irony is that their different skills and psychological make-up should have rendered the Duke and Duchess the perfect team. Her charm, warmth and charisma could have been the perfect foil to his cleverness and allegiance to duty. Like Charles and Diana, the sum of their skills might have added up to more than the individual components. Like Charles and Diana, the combination of their personalities, potentially a force for mutual enhancement, was a mixture that proved both combustible and ultimately corrosive.

Any marriage is in the end a private compact, the full scope of its virtues and its flaws known only to the principals involved. The relationship of the Duke and Duchess of Kent was inevitably less private than most. Although the public knew next to nothing of their difficulties, the problems were apparent both to their joint staff and their separate groups of friends; all of whom made their own judgements. Since the Duke was the more influential and the Duchess the lonelier and more friendless, the bulk of partisan approval inevitably devolved upon him.

As one friend says, with some accuracy and some hyperbole: 'It is a real tragedy. He is good-looking, highly intelligent and hard-working. He could have had the pick of any girl. It has turned out to be a disaster.' In the eyes of Edward's circle, Katharine was awkward and unpredictable. Sometimes she would pick up the telephone at home and be charming to an old friend of her husband. 'Hello, I'm the switchboard operator today,' she would say. At other times she would be distant and withdrawn. When it was wrongly rumoured that Edward found his wife's passion for Catholicism difficult to cope with, his associates countered with the opinion that she (hardly surprisingly) preferred to go to Mass alone, informing her husband on one occasion that he could not accompany her because there was no space in the pew.

Certainly Katharine's almost mystical attachment to religion was beyond the grasp of her practically minded husband – and, occasionally, beyond the grasp of others who met her. Charles Ritchie, a former Canadian High Commissioner in London, included the following comment in his diary: 'In the afternoon to St Paul's Cathedral. The Duchess of Kent says it would be impossible to be inside the cathedral without believing in God. I feel exactly the opposite – as if I were in a magnificent, poorly filled opera house.'

In accentuating the Duke's undoubted virtues, his friends naturally tended to overlook his less good qualities, character traits that had certainly damaged Katharine over the years. His capacity for screaming rows, conducted in earshot of office or domestic staff, remained a constant throughout the marriage. Perhaps the Duchess could be provoking. Given her problems, it would have been remarkable if she were not. She had not, however, been brought up in an atmosphere where she was ever once shouted at. Nor is verbal abuse, regarded with apparent tolerance by some of the Duke's friends, deemed acceptable in any normal modern marriage.

But this, of course, was not a normal marriage. Lonely as the Duke undoubtedly was, and great as the demands made of him had been, he retained the bulk of whatever semblance of normality and contentment was on offer. The royal family, the Queen included, regarded him with distant fondness as one of their own – albeit not quite of the inner circle – and his group of close friends was both loyal and admiring. His workload, though always taxing and often dull, played to his skills and interests. The Duke, in short, remained the insider, while Katharine was merely the incomer who had never quite made the royal grade.

Bitterly resentful as she was of a system, a royal family and a succession of courtiers who had colluded in her unhappiness, Katharine had created her own hinterland – principally the Bach Choir and Westminster Cathedral, the latter a hub for a new network of acquaintances and friends. Elsewhere, her contacts had dwindled. Depression, mood swings and her natural solitariness had meant that some friends and ladies-in-waiting had either been rejected or felt themselves spurned. A few, like Tony Lothian (an Italian socialist who prefers not to use her Marchioness title) and her daughter, Lady Cecil Cameron, had remained close. The actor Charles Dance and his wife were privy, particularly in the eighties, to Katharine's worries and fears.

Her contacts with her family and with Hovingham – her childhood home and the centrepiece of her life for so long afterwards – had all but lapsed. After the death of her parents, she visited rarely and had no obvious fondness for the Hall's incumbent, her eldest brother, Marcus. Locked into a schedule of royal duty, she had also drifted away from her two other brothers. John, in any case, lived in Canada. Oliver, the third brother and now a retired businessman and art dealer, was flying home from a visit there when, in 1996, he was told that his Army officer son, Richard, had been killed in a road accident. A car driven by a friend had skidded on ice and crashed into a tree as the two young officers headed for an assignment at Fallingbostel, the Duke of Kent's former base in Germany.

Despite that bond of family tragedy, Katharine remained in general distanced from her brothers, who regarded her behaviour – according to a close friend of the Duke – as 'high-hatty'. Like all descriptions of Katharine's attitude, that supposed grandeur must be seen in the context of depression; a distorting prism that alters the capacity for normal relationships. No one who has watched her work could doubt Katharine's warmth. The lack of it in so many dimensions of her private life only increased the loneliness that had become a constant in her marriage, by now a testament to frozen emotions.

With the single exception of the period in the mid-seventies when Eddie was deemed to have 'a roving eye', not a breath of scandal touched the Kents' marriage. Katharine, by far the more charismatic of the two, made friends easily. Any men she particularly warmed to would be drawn into the family circle and invited to parties she and the Duke gave together. In a scrupulously honourable private life, the few pieces of gossip that ever existed were as malicious as they were untrue. An unauthorized biography of Tony O'Reilly, the newspaper proprietor and leading Irish businessman, written by Tom Rubython, floated the following passage: 'Rumours would later circulate about O'Reilly's relationship with the Duchess of Kent . . . There was never anything to these rumours, which were just that. Actually it was highly unlikely that they ever met. But the rumours were to persist and circulate for two decades. [They] were tittle tattle put around by O'Reilly detractors.'

Although manifestly untrue – the Duchess of Kent was not even in Ireland when the meetings with O'Reilly were supposed to have taken place and, as Rubython admits, had most probably never even been introduced to him – the repetition of this rumour illustrates one point. Any whisper of any indiscretion with any third party would immediately have been whipped up into a storm. Since no such indiscretions existed, those disposed to brief against Katharine devised another whisper – equally unkind and again wholly untrue. The Duchess's links with Martina Navratilova and her Centre Court embrace of Jana Novotna, both of whom are lesbian, suggested, her opponents claimed, that Katharine also had lesbian tendencies. If the Duchess was even aware of this falsehood, she would no doubt have regarded with puzzlement the fact that she, always so honest, could be the subject of blatant untruths.

In part, any rumours were born of incomprehension. In pre-millennial Britain, there are few parallels to the Kent marriage. For a modern couple to live out most of their lives without love, without a physical relationship (if the York House bedroom snoopers are to be believed), without friendship and without the remotest interest or delight in one another's company is almost beyond credence. In an age of choice, of counselling and of an increasing divorce rate, this sort of enforced penance evokes horror rather than admiration. Even within the royal family – on the one hand cryogenically preserved in its Victorian notions of enduring relationships and, on the other, the new epitome of the disposable marriage – the Kents' life sentence of a partnership was unique in its awfulness.

It is hardly surprising that even the participants had to devise for themselves some sort of rationale for its continuance. For the Duke, the solution was easy. He was bound by his pledge that the marriage would last. Katharine had found, in Catholicism, a diktat decreeing that marital vows were sacrosanct. That decree released her from the torment of alternately wishing and fearing to leave. At least one close family friend believes there are reasons more practical than promises or faith for continuation.

'You couldn't have yet another divorce,' he says. 'One reason is the scandal. But another is the financial settlement. The Duke does not have much money.' As this friend points out, only one of the Kents' three children – Helen – was wholly financially independent. George's part-time consultancy at Christie's, plus Sylvana's wage as a junior Cambridge don, meant that, even in 1997, they were far from wealthy. Nicky's psychiatric condition had meant that he must be cared for and his hospital bills met. The Duchess's high public profile and love of shopping ensured that her clothes bills were high. Given his outgoings, the view of the Duke's friends was that a divorce, even if it had been deemed desirable, would not have been affordable.

To most of the population, this might seem very hard to credit. The Kents had a grace-and-favour residence, their expenses were met by the Queen – who paid their annual £260,000 from the Civil List – and the Duke drew expenses from the Overseas Trade Board. In addition, Katharine's mother had been wealthy in her own right. But, whether they were spent or salted away, there was nothing in Katharine's lifestyle to suggest that she had any Brunner riches at her disposal.

Compared with Prince Michael of Kent, the Duke's younger brother, and his wife, Princess Michael, the senior Kents lived modestly. In April 1997 the *Observer* ran a story claiming that Prince Michael, the Queen's cousin, was earning as much as £500,000 a year by hiring himself and thus his royal connections out to businessmen. The article quoted a memo from the political lobbyist Derek Laud, said to have met the Prince earlier in the year on behalf of an engineering firm. 'Prince Michael would prefer to be retained on a yearly retainer of about £60,000, payable quarterly, or half-yearly, in advance,' the memo was quoted as saying. This article represented nothing new or startling. Instead it was merely the latest in a dossier of stories relating to the lifestyle of the 'Rent-a-Kents' and, in particular, Princess Michael.

The former Marie-Christine von Reibnitz, otherwise known as Princess Pushy, had been ritually lambasted for her grand ways, her embarrassing *faux pas* (she once claimed that the Queen had called her 'the most royal of England's princesses') and her forthright attitude to money. Although she and her family have a grace-and-favour home at Kensington Palace – which she once likened to living in a high-rise flat – their main residence, Nether Lypiatt Manor, was magnificent enough to prompt continued wonderment at how Prince Michael's directorships, thought to be worth about £50,000 a year, and the Princess's income as an author could begin to meet such a grandiose lifestyle.

To make up the shortfall, Prince Michael had taken on other work, explaining, in a *Daily Telegraph* interview: 'I have to make a living like everybody else, and I'm rather sad that trying to do that has been misrepresented and turned into something wrong. I feel I can help companies. I can do certain things for them that perhaps others can't, so I'm very able and willing to talk to those organizations with that in mind.'

In addition to his business portfolio, Prince Michael became a television presenter. Heavy-browed and bewhiskered, Michael evoked a hybrid of his grandfather, George V, and his Russian cousin, the assassinated Tsar Nicholas II.

This polyglot image of royalty made him an ideal presenter for a two-part television documentary, *Nicholas and Alexandra*. Having suggested himself for this job, he was subsequently asked to present a further series, *Victoria and Albert*.

The Duke of Kent was fond of his younger brother. He certainly did not chafe against his entrepreneurial spirit, perhaps recognizing that Michael had found an ideal niche. 'Michael is a most charming man but not awfully clever,' says one friend of the Duke. 'If he had stayed in the Army [he retired in 1981], he would probably never have been promoted beyond the rank of Major.' Although the Duke was not irked by his brother's glamorous lifestyle, he certainly did not wish to emulate it.

Always conscious of his role as the head of the family, he preferred a more austere existence, in keeping with his position. The price was an impecunious existence, in royal terms, although certainly not by any normal standards. Having lived mainly in accommodation provided by the Queen, the Kents appear not to have been greatly enriched after the purchase and sale of their own home, near Henley. Quantities of family treasures had been sold to meet bills. Although scarcely impoverished, the senior Kents certainly had no access to fabulous wealth.

Occasionally the Duke would tell a friend, rather wistfully, that what he most longed for was a house big enough to have all his family to stay. By the mid-nineties, the clan comprised George, Sylvana and their two children; Nicholas, and Helen and Tim, who by then had two sons, Columbus and Cassius. Not a vast gathering but over-large for the three-bedroomed Wren House. It would, of course, have been an easy matter for the Queen to put a more spacious property at the Duke's disposal, but he would never have dreamed of requesting such a favour. As a friend says: 'He would never ask, and she would never think.'

While money is unlikely to have smoothed the difficulties in the Kents' marriage, the (very relative) lack of it certainly did not make matters easier – particularly for the Duchess. Not only is she the most beautifully dressed of all the royals. She is also someone who justified her extravagances by claiming that respect for others decreed that she should look as wonderfully turned out as possible – a difficult feat to achieve on what she has sometimes painted as a chainstore budget. Once she grumbled, over lunch and to a journalist friend, that she might have to turn down a major overseas engagement unless her wardrobe bills were met by the Queen. During one period of enforced frugality, her spending was strictly monitored by her own household.

No doubt those holding the purse strings saw themselves as simply obeying orders, but it is easy to imagine that the Duchess herself would have been deeply upset by such interference in a life which – ever since her wedding day – had never belonged wholly to her. The artificiality of being permanently on display and the constraints implicit in royal life dictate that a happy private life is essential to a tolerable existence. The corollary is that royal marriages are infrequently havens of contentment.

By 1997 the Duke and Duchess of Kent had long ago abandoned such ideals. Occasionally a member of staff would see some hint of a rapport – a quick embrace or a word of comfort from the Duke. Such moments were rare. The Duke and Duchess had decided long ago how their marriage must evolve. However hollow, the façade must remain as neat as possible. There would be no public tantrums, no undignified recriminations and no scandal. As one of the Duchess's confidantes says: 'In most respects, the marriage was identical to Charles and Diana's. The only thing missing was a Camilla.'

CHAPTER TWENTY-NINE

The Diana Inheritance

I N THE EARLY hours of Sunday, 31 August 1997 the Mercedes saloon car carrying Princess Diana and her boyfriend, Dodi Fayed, crashed into a concrete pillar in a tunnel at the Pont d'Alma in Paris. Fayed was killed instantly. The driver, Henri Paul, died seconds after the collision. Trevor Rees-Jones, the front seat passenger and the Princess's bodyguard, was gravely injured. Diana, according to the first news reports, had escaped with superficial injuries, including cuts to her legs. Her death was announced several hours later.

Freed from the wreckage, she had been taken by ambulance to the Pitié Salpetrière Hospital, where doctors massaged her heart by hand in a last attempt to resuscitate her, before abandoning, at 4 a.m., their three-hour struggle to save her life. The most famous, most photographed and most idolized woman on Earth died in a French operating theatre, far from family, friends and her two teenage sons. She was thirty-six.

The news, filtering into the public consciousness on a sleepy Sunday morning, stunned Britain and the world in a manner unseen since the assassination of President Kennedy.

In a sense the death of Diana was the greater shock to a country that had long ago promoted her to the status of a living legend. The misery she had endured in her desperately unhappy marriage had struck a chord with all those who had suffered and who saw her – a woman defined by glamour and good works – as a role model of survival.

All summer long, the British people had been presented with images of a changed Diana – contented, carefree and possibly in love. The backdrop was the glamour of the French Riviera and the opulence of *Jonikal*, the lavish yacht provided by Mohamed Al Fayed, the owner of Harrods, as a retreat where the Princess could relax in the company of his son and heir. Dodi Fayed was both a curious and an obvious choice of companion for Diana. A forty-two-year-old playboy, more famous by association to his colourful father than through any personal achievement, he was ideally qualified to offer some of the fun so lacking in her life.

The Princess was probably, as her closest associates claimed, merely embarked on a diverting holiday romance. Mohamed Al Fayed's counter-assertion was that this was a great love affair, in which she had consented, just before her death, to marry Dodi and set up home in the Paris villa once occupied by the Duke and Duchess of Windsor. The only certainty is that whatever vestiges of peace Diana had found in the last weeks of her life were not to last beyond the grave.

Her blood family, the Spencers; her family by marriage, the Windsors; and Al Fayed – mourning a daughter-in-law that never was – were all to contribute to the cataclysmic consequences of her death. The fall-out from the tragedy of the Princess of Wales affected, in one way or other, almost every inhabitant of Britain. Some would grieve her like a lost relative. Others would recoil from the mood of near-hysteria unleashed by her death. Yet others would be affected by the knock-on effect of a nation's emotion. The Duke and Duchess of Kent were among the latter group.

Katharine, according to one of her closest friends, took the news of the Princess's death 'quite badly. She was very, very moved by the national reaction. She said that initially she was simply shocked, like everyone else. That gave way to disbelief, and then the disbelief to utter sadness.' In that reaction, the Duchess of Kent was no different to any other British citizen. But she had also regarded Diana as a close friend; someone she understood for 'obvious' reasons.

The Duchess did not elaborate on these reasons, but they are clear enough. The histories of Katharine and Diana are almost eerily similar. Both were well-connected, beautiful and parachuted into a gilded world, quickly transmuted into hostile terrain. Both had married men who failed to live up to their expectations and to make them happy. Both had been driven close to despair. The chief difference between them – aside from the fact that the Duke of Kent did not have a mistress – was the manner in which they chose to deal with their sorrows.

Diana, child of a media age, was not prepared – beyond a certain point – to suffer humiliation and misery in silence. Her bulimia, her suicide attempts, her 'overcrowded' marriage – all of those were made public property. It is not certain that airing her sadnesses in the public confessional resolved her grief. At the time of her death, she was adored for the daring and the honesty she had displayed in her public fightback against the House of Windsor. Even so, and for all her courage and cleverness, it was far from certain that she had yet secured any chance of personal tranquillity.

Katharine had chosen a quieter way of coping with sorrow. Brought up in the decorum of an earlier generation, her instinct was to suppress problems rather than publicly to air them. Many of the symptoms of her unhappiness were similar to Diana's but more quietly expressed. She was never disclosed to have any kind of eating disorder; but, even at official functions, plates of food were frequently pushed aside, untouched. Despite her fascination with the Samaritans, there is no suggestion that she ever contemplated suicide. 'She didn't have the guts,' says a royal source, in a remark that speaks volumes about the hostility bordering on contempt that the Duchess sometimes had to endure in machiavellian court circles.

Both women suffered pain. Both developed different strategies for dealing with it. Where Katharine's last refuge was the Church, Diana's was *Panorama*. That counterpoint between spiritual and temporal encouraged many royal-watchers to suppose that the Duchess – a model of unimpeachable behaviour – would have disapproved greatly of the Princess's tactics; not least her decision to admit adultery with the former Army Major, James Hewitt, and to question, before millions of viewers, whether Charles would ever be King. On the contrary, the Duchess was admiring of Diana's bravery.

Whatever their private similarities and allegiances, the public ones were obvious. When Diana, at the height of her marriage problems, dropped a large tranche of her charity portfolio, it was suggested that 'Caring Kate' – the only member of the royal family able to demonstrate real empathy and compassion – should take on some of the workload. Katharine never wished to appear to move in on Diana's orbit, partly because she had a multitude of good causes of her own and partly because she had a genuine respect for her charisma and her drive.

The Princess's landmines crusade, undertaken in the last

year of her life, had particularly impressed Katharine. Although she envied Diana little, she too had longed to take on a major project with humanitarian and quasi-political dimensions. By the end of her life, Diana had moved far beyond displays of empathy into an area of more focused compassion. That also was Katharine's ambition.

Whether Diana was a bosom friend remains doubtful. Although neighbours at Kensington Palace, there is no suggestion that the two women spent vast amounts of time in one another's company. Perhaps they were too similar in personality to forge the closest of bonds. Certainly their roles had been rather reversed over the years, as Katharine's guidance to the *ingénue* royal bride gave way to Diana's sympathy for a woman clearly in need of care and nurturing.

But neither was as fragile as the public image sometimes suggests. If Diana was a fighter, adamant that she would not be ground down by a loveless marriage and the machine of royalty, then Katharine was, in her different way, equally tenacious. In the months after Diana's death, she was to put into practice some of the lessons she had learned from the younger woman's life as she began to forge a new role and future for herself.

In the immediate aftermath, there was only grief. As the royal family gathered outside Buckingham Palace to watch the funeral cortège move past, the Duke and Duchess of Kent forbore to be together. Edward exchanged a few words with his sister, Alexandra. Katharine positioned herself at the opposite side of the royal group. The Duke and Duchess of Kent, married for thirty-six years, stood as joint witnesses to a tragedy that would shake the House of Windsor to its foundations. To the outside observer, it was as if they had never met.

Both individually, and as a couple, the Kents were to be

affected by the aftershock of Diana's death. The first tremors began even before the funeral. Tony Blair, the Prime Minister and a man of sure populist touch, had identified Diana's appeal in the tribute he gave immediately after her death, describing her as the 'People's Princess'. If the mood of the people, and the strength of their feeling, surprised Downing Street and newspaper proprietors, it appeared wholly to baffle the royal family. As the flower-stall bouquets spread in front of Kensington Palace and those who mourned the Princess queued for up to twelve hours to sign the inadequate number of books of condolence laid out at St James's Palace, the royal family remained silent at Balmoral.

Within hours of learning of their mother's death, her sons, William and Harry, had been pictured on the road to Crathie church, where the morning service was conducted without any reference to Diana's death. The fact that the Princes had been encouraged to follow the routine of a normal Sunday, in the first wave of shock and grief, struck many as evidence of callousness at the heart of the royal family. As the days wore on, and the Queen stayed silent, the unrest grew.

By Thursday, 4 September, a mood of outrage was increasing, promulgated by the press but driven by the people. The *Sun* demanded on its front page: 'Where is our Queen? Where is her flag?' The *Independent*, not normally a vehicle for hysterical royal coverage, also ran a page one picture of Buckingham Palace. The accompanying headline read: 'No Flag Flying, a Family far away, and the people feel uneasy.'

The reason why a Union flag was not raised at half-mast – observance of the protocol that it must fly only when the Queen is in residence – was a measure of how greatly the royal family had misgauged the national mood. Charles, whose first priority was to comfort his bereaved sons, was accepted to be in an impossible position. The Queen, a figurehead able, many thought bounden, to offer solace to her people in their grief, appeared – by her continued muteness – to be incapable of understanding or sharing an unprecedented wave of national sorrow.

A statement by a palace spokesman – 'Grieving is a private process and people should be allowed to do it in their own way' – served only to inflame resentment. In a rare step, Downing Street intervened, letting it be known that Mr Blair had had a fifteen-minute phone call with the Prince of Wales, in which the Prime Minister offered his full support. His office at Number Ten warned the press that they could not expect the royal family 'to jump in and be extras at a media event'.

But already the mood at Balmoral was altering, less as a result of press clamour than because it was by then obvious that the media was only a mouthpiece for public opinion. The Queen, Philip and Charles made their first gesture of *rapprochement* by appearing, with the two young Princes, at the gates of Balmoral to inspect the wreaths laid there in the Princess's memory and to read the messages. Shortly afterwards, they left for London. In a touching scene at Kensington Palace, Charles and his two sons – two little boys compelled to be heroes in their own tragedy – talked to public mourners weeping on their behalf and pressing flowers into their hands.

At Buckingham Palace, the Queen – so unskilled at the effortless emotion her daughter-in-law had offered in her lifetime – appeared slightly stiff, doubtless grief-stricken and almost humbled by the magnitude of the public wake. 'Are these for me?' she asked quietly, as someone pressed a bouquet into her gloved hand. As Big Ben struck 6p.m. on

5 September, the Queen – seated in the Chinese Room on the first floor of Buckingham Palace – finally spoke the words her subjects had waited to hear. Though her manner was as formal as ever, she was deemed to have offered a message from the heart.

'I want to pay tribute to Diana myself. She was an exceptional and gifted human being. In good times and bad, she never lost her capacity to smile and laugh, nor to inspire others with her warmth and kindness. I admired and respected her – for her energy and commitment to others, and especially for her devotion to her two boys. This week at Balmoral, we have been trying to help William and Harry come to terms with the loss they have suffered. No one who knew Diana will ever forget her.'

This bizarre chapter in the life of the royal family had a particular resonance for Katharine Kent. Beyond her personal shock and sorrow over Diana's death, she must also have felt amazement – and perhaps even some gratification – that the cold heart of the monarchy was finally being exposed to and judged by a furious populace. For years, Katharine had experienced this chill at first hand. Far away from the public gaze, her personal tragedies had been treated clumsily and insensitively by the royal family and the Queen, a monarch who professed to want to help but found herself at a loss to know how best to intervene. But that failure, in Katharine's case, had another, less altruistic dimension. The Duchess of Kent had never been purely a woman who was suffering. She also, through her frailty and unhappiness, posed a threat to the supposedly stable foundations of the royal family.

Similarly, in the aftermath of Diana's death, the wrong moves made by the Windsors were not only the product of a failure properly to respond to the public mood. At heart, the Queen loathed and mistrusted the national fuss – evidence of the dangerous adulation of a daughter-in-law who, whatever Her Majesty personally thought of her, had sought, in her lifetime, to undermine the House of Windsor and who continued to do so in her death.

The Queen's grief, though no doubt genuine, was therefore ambivalent, just as her concern over the problems of the Duchess of Kent had been tempered by self-interest. Although the death of a Princess and the failed marriage of a Duchess are not to be compared, the bungled reaction of the royal family in the time after Diana's death must have struck a particular chord with Katharine.

The Windsors were being revealed, on a public stage, for all she had known them to be. It would be surprising if Katharine did not share, to some degree, the public's revised and jaundiced view of their royal family. Of course, the monarchy could hardly be blamed for the Princess's demise. But the apparent chilliness of the royal family in the days after her death had damaged them in the eyes of a public minded increasingly to view them as over-blown, anachronistic and, in the absence of their best-loved performer, more lacklustre than ever. This unpopularity was to have further ramifications for both the Duke and Duchess of Kent. Although any real mood for republicanism was to be short-lived, the death of Diana sharpened the focus on the overblown nature of a suddenly unpopular royal family.

Long before the night of the Paris car crash, the Queen and Charles had been aware of the need to modernize, but the process of change, under the aegis of an internal committee entitled the Way Ahead Group, was ponderous. The

Queen had begun to pay tax after the Windsor Castle fire prompted anger at the burden the ordinary taxpayer was expected to meet. There had been talk of minor economies.

Diana's death expedited the need for change. Objections to the size and the splendour of the royal machine had once been aired only by rabid republicans and part-time anti-monarchists patchily angered by examples of extravagance. By the end of 1997 the demand for a slimmed-down monarchy, pared of its minor figures – the Duke and Duchess of Kent included – was more universal and more specific than it had ever previously been.

The seeds of revolt were sown before Diana's funeral. The Queen, who could have been forgiven an ambivalent attitude towards her mercurial daughter-in-law, must have been horrified not only by the funeral oration given by the Princess's brother, Earl Spencer, but by the public acclaim it received. A television audience of 31.5 million people watched as the Earl offered his words of support for William and Harry directly to Diana. 'On behalf of your mother and sisters, I pledge that we, your blood family, will do all we can to continue the loving and imaginative way in which you were steering these two exceptional young men, so that their souls are not only immersed by duty and tradition but can sing openly, as you had planned.' The congregation in Westminster Abbey applauded him, first in a spatter of handclaps and then in a sustained ovation.

Cardinal Hume clapped, the young princes joined in, and Charles – his face masklike – tapped his hand nervously against his knee as the other senior members of his family sat in frozen silence. Although the constitutional historian Dr David Starkey said that the tirade 'seemed to be an act of such calculated vengeance', few others, on that day or later, opted to criticize the Earl for what amounted to a devastating attack on the royal family and, in particular, against Charles.

Whatever his flaws, the Prince of Wales was a loving father who had faced the bitterest task of any parent: to wake his children and to tell them that their mother was dead. In the days, and the months, that followed he strove to comfort them and to help them find some semblance of normality. If the influence of the Spencers – the 'blood family' – could ever have been a seminal one, that prospect was extinguished with the Earl's harsh words.

Beleaguered on all sides, the Queen had found a new ally in the struggle that faced her. The influence of Tony Blair, and his official spokesman, Alastair Campbell, will not fully be known for many years. It is, however, certain that Blair's impact on a royal family in turmoil, and frequently at loggerheads with one another on the correct reaction, was considerable. In-house squabbles, according to Penny Junor's biography of Prince Charles, included a debate over whether the Princess's body should be taken to a public mortuary and an alleged reluctance by the Queen to provide a plane until a courtier asked whether she would rather see Diana brought home 'in a Harrods van'. By the eve of the funeral, Blair was making clear that he was prepared to assist a beleaguered monarchy to reform. In a BBC interview with Sir David Frost, he said: 'I personally think the monarchy is an institution we want to keep. But the monarchy adapts and changes and will change and modernize with each generation . . .'

For now, the Duchess of Kent was untouched by the spirit of revolution. Consumed as she was by her personal grief for Diana, she had been deputed to assist at another funeral. Five days after Diana's death, Mother Teresa – the Albanian Catholic nun who had devoted her life to working in the slums of Calcutta – died of a heart attack at the age of eighty-seven. The Indian government announced that it would honour her in a state funeral, to be held exactly a week after Diana's burial. It was agreed that Katharine should attend on the Queen's behalf.

Diana had been Mother Teresa's friend and supporter. If she had lived, she would undoubtedly have been at her graveside. The Duchess, however, was an eminently suitable royal emissary. Her view of Catholic moral theology was less conservative than that of Mother Teresa, to whom contraception was anathema, but she would certainly have applauded the denunciation of abortion she delivered when she received, in 1979, the Nobel peace prize. Despite the sadness of the circumstances, Katharine welcomed a chance to revisit India, a country where she had found a rare spell of personal peace and a vision of a gentler life. Magnificently dressed in a long black suit, with a large crucifix strung round her neck and a lace mantilla draped over her head and shoulders, Katharine walked up to Mother Teresa's casket after the funeral mass to lay her white and green wreath.

Beside her sat the deputy prime minister, John Prescott, America's first lady, Hillary Clinton, Queen Noor of Jordan and the Indian Prime Minster, I. K. Gujral, who laid their wreaths beside Katharine's. Lepers and the poor mourned with them, running through the streets of Calcutta in the monsoon drizzle to watch the open casket, borne on the same gun carriage that had taken Mahatma Gandhi to his cremation half a century before.

Mother Teresa's successor as head of the Missionaries of Charity, Sister Nirmala, spoke of a life's work that Katharine, albeit on a minor scale and from a position of great privilege, had attempted to emulate. 'The hungry, the thirsty, the sick and the dying, the orphans, the leprosy sufferers, those of broken bodies and broken minds – these were the special objects of Mother's love.'

In life, Mother Teresa had embraced poverty. In death she was given a funeral not far removed in splendour from the wake for Diana. Hundreds of dignitaries from two dozen countries gathered to sing and to pray as millions more around the world watched on television. So much pomp and such an overload of grief might have been expected to swamp Katharine. In the space of a week she had been called upon first to mourn a woman she regarded as one of her dearest friends and then to fly half-way across the world to witness, on behalf of the Queen, the final honour paid to a figure she regarded both as icon and inspiration. Frailer women than the Duchess might have been reduced to utter sadness by two such poignant and draining reminders of mortality.

On the contrary, Katharine appears to have withstood her journey with aplomb. Afterwards, a newspaper diarist reported stories of her flight to Calcutta and back in the film star Tom Cruise's private jet and of how she had slept in his in-flight duvet. The plane had been chartered for other emissaries, who had offered the Duchess a lift, an experience that had clearly entranced her.

The sadness of the occasion had not diminished the excitement – an almost childlike wonderment – that India, or Africa, always instilled in the Duchess. She might have attributed that to many factors: different cultures, spiritual renewal, a chance for her to be of comfort or of value. Her buoyancy, so soon after Diana's death, may also have been due to the fact that the truth was being displayed. The royal family were being exposed for what they were: harsh and lacking in emotion to those who cried out for understanding.

There was another dimension to Katharine's apparent cheerfulness as she undertook her trip to India – a sense of being freed from the gilded cage of royal life. On this occasion her escape was brief. Within a couple of days she was cage-bound once again. By now the gilt was wearing very thin.

CHAPTER THIRTY

A Dying Breed

Two months after Diana's death, reports began to surface about the detail of the proposed slimming down of the royal family. This was presented less as a judicious pruning exercise than as a wholesale clearance operation in which a parasitical sideshoot would be lopped off and discarded. According to newspaper stories, the Queen planned to 'pension off' those members of the family living at Kensington Palace.

Princess Margaret was said to be in line for alternative accommodation at St James's Palace. Princess Alice, Duchess of Gloucester, then approaching her ninety-sixth birthday, would also be rehoused. The rest, including the Duke and Duchess of Kent, would be the subject of a genteel but non-negotiable eviction order, allowing Kensington Palace to be converted into a permanent memorial to Diana and a splendid new home for the 7,000 widely scattered pictures in the Royal Collection.

By opening the palace to the public in this way, it was argued, the £20 million cost of the Grant-In-Aid – the sum paid by the government for maintenance of the occupied royal palaces – would be cut. In addition, as the *Daily*

Telegraph noted, the Queen 'cannot go on paying for minor members of the Royal Family'. Under the terms of the Civil List, the Queen reimburses the Treasury for the allowances made to all its beneficiaries, bar the Queen Mother and Prince Philip. In 1997 Princess Margaret received an annuity of £219,000, the Duke and Duchess of Gloucester – known as assiduous workers – got £175,000, Princess Alexandra £225,000 and the Duke and Duchess of Kent £236,000. Prince and Princess Michael received no payment.

'We've just got to make some savings,' a royal source was quoted as saying. 'These people will still be part of the family and turn up at state occasions when appropriate, but the Queen cannot go on paying for them all. It will be done very sensitively.' Tactfully pensioning off superfluous relatives was, it was stressed, being carried out at the behest of Buckingham Palace, rather than the Prime Minister. The Prince of Wales was thought to be particularly keen on a more skeletal royal taskforce.

Both retirement packages for supposedly supernumerary minor royals and the conversion of Kensington Palace were said to be under examination by officials. Although the lifestyles of members of the royal family and the costs involved were not exactly a secret, the mood after Diana's death heralded a time of reckoning and an acknowledgement, even among the normally inert ranks of senior royals, that a move towards greater accountability was imperative. The arithmetic produced did not reflect much previous appetite for change. Despite talk of reducing the number of grace-and-favour homes, employees' residences and pensioners' apartments maintained out of the public purse, the total had remained at 285 since 1994. At the time of Diana's death, the family was receiving £7.9 million a year from the

Civil List – allocated to pay major royals and 296 staff – plus £20 million for the upkeep of the royal palaces.

To a country that believed the loss of Diana had decimated the appeal of royalty, the cost of an overblown clan looked increasingly intolerable. Other cutbacks were mooted or agreed. In November, as the royal yacht *Britannia* completed her farewell journey round British waters before being decommissioned, it was suggested that the royal train – in less frugal times a favourite form of transport for the Duchess of Kent – would be the next to go. It had cost taxpayers £12.3 million in five years, the equivalent of £67,000 for each of its 183 journeys.

Despite the recognized need for strictures, the initial notion that minor royals would shortly be forced to procure their own bed-and-breakfast deals was slowly tamped down. Speaking on *Panorama*, Simon Gimson – formerly the special adviser to Sir Robert Fellowes, the Queen's private secretary – acknowledged that the inevitability of a slimmed-down monarchy had been hastened by Diana's death. 'It's going to happen,' he said. 'The palace is looking at specific changes, at radical changes, at gentle changes.'

While the wildest speculation had suggested that the Queen would move out of Buckingham Palace, a palace spokeswoman made clear in December, a few weeks after the *Panorama* transmission, that even the rumours concerning the fate of minor royals were misconceived or premature. Minor royals were not to be evicted after all. As she said: 'No grace-and-favour accommodation has been granted since 1991, and as they [the current occupants] die, it will become vacant. We made it clear that there are no plans to move members of the family who are currently there out.'

It must have been scant consolation to the Duke and

Duchess of Kent to have it made publicly clear that they would not, whatever populist opinion might decree, be decanted unceremoniously on to the streets of London. The Duke was patron of 116 organizations, and the Duchess held 102 voluntary sector patronages; a far greater workload, in both cases, than any of the other lesser royals and several of the major ones. If Edward's or Katharine's *amour propre* was hurt by having their usefulness and relevance called into public question, neither said so. Katharine, always ambivalent about the royal family, may have regarded the latest crisis with some cynicism. Certainly she, as one of the most hard-working and charismatic members of the family, could not be held to blame for their evaporating popularity.

As for the Duke, it is likely that he regarded the mood of the time with anger. He had been trained from birth for royal duty. His Army career, which he loved, had been stifled because he was viewed as a security risk – a target less for murder than for kidnap. All of his life he had worked hard, knowing that his efforts had been largely unrecognized and entirely unsung. In the weeks when the British press adopted a Bastille-storming aversion to the minor royals, the Duke's name was mentioned frequently for the first time in years. There is no suggestion from Edward's friends that he allowed any disquiet or unhappiness to show. When he lunched at Boodle's, he did not chew his lower lip – a reliable sign that he was under stress – any more frequently than before. In a sense, the Duke of Kent was bred to be fatalistic. Certainly a man with so much Romanov blood could hardly think that the prospect of a respectable redundancy package constituted tragedy on the epic scale.

Katharine's attitude was different. Although the changes she set in motion were subtle, she was moving on – establishing the first foothold in a life she had renounced long ago but had never ceased to yearn for. Increasingly, the Duchess of Kent was embarking on a clever strategy. The discontent following Diana's death, though not personally aimed at her, offered her the chance of a freedom that had eluded her for the past twenty years. Just as she had waited patiently and seized the right moment for her conversion to Catholicism, she could now grasp, in a time of unparalleled royal stringency, her chance to become less of a minor royal and more of a private citizen.

Even so, the backlash from Diana's death must have seemed both an irony and an injustice to both the Kents. The Duke was viewed as superfluous to a role he saw as his unassailable birthright. The Duchess, by contrast, was being made aware that the job she had been forced into and had undertaken at great personal expense was viewed as unnecessary and dispensable.

The clamour against minor royals was not, however, entirely rooted in the discontent of the post-Diana months. The rot had started long before, and its origins lay not on the fringes of the royal family but at its heart. The mystique surrounding the House of Windsor was eroded gradually. Memories of the abdication crisis, which had shattered the notion that a monarch's duty to his or her country must come before all else, had been smoothed away by the reigns of George VI and Elizabeth. But neither the young Queen, nor her father before her, had any real concept of a *fin-de-siècle* Britain in which the institutions of Church and Crown would lose much of their sway and in which the public would turn an increasingly cynical eye on even an unimpeachable royal family, let alone one whose central players specialized in venality rather than virtue.

In an information age, Britain had the means and the right to know how its monarchy comported itself. The

Queen herself had vaguely realized years ago that an ivory tower monarchy headed by an autocratic ruler was an anachronism. When her children were small, she permitted cameras to film a Windsor family picnic. See, the subtext implied, we are just like you. That small hint of *rapprochement* would evolve into the soap opera of the nineties, in which every detail of royal behaviour would be scrutinized and judged. If the Windsors had been, at heart, like everyone else, then the demystification of royalty might merely have been a much-needed modernizing trend. Instead it proved to be more the unmasking of a collection of the damaged and the destructive.

The decade had begun smoothly. Margaret Thatcher, ejected from Downing Street, had concluded her tenure by boosting the Civil List from £5.09 million to £7.9 million – a move speeded through parliament without opposition from the Labour leader, Neil Kinnock, on the grounds that this increase would see the Windsors through to the millennium. But already the value of the monarchy, in terms of pay, cost, size and usefulness, was being brought into question.

At the same time, the troubles within the Queen's family were barely suppressed. The strain in the marriage of Charles and Diana was increasing, and the Duchess of York made no secret of the fact that she was bored with her naval officer husband, whose frequent absences were punctuated by home visits largely devoted to golf and videos. At Christmas at Sandringham in 1991, Andrew and Fergie told the Queen that they wished to separate.

Nothing could have prepared the Queen for the furore centred on her daughter-in-law, a woman in search of fun and gratification and heedless of the scandal she would attract. Photographs emerged first of her holiday with Steve Wyatt, a Texan oilman, and later with his replacement, John

Bryan. The *Daily Mirror* published the pictures of the Duchess, in a swimsuit and having her toes kissed by Bryan, her 'financial adviser' during a French vacation. Again, her daughters were staying in the same villa.

During the next few years, the Fergie scandals drifted on. Garrulous in her confidences, she discussed her sex life with the American media. Profligate in her spending habits, she ran up vast debts and settled them with a carpet-bagger's profits – the proceeds of an autobiography and a contract to promote a range of diet foods. But the image that lingered was that of the infamous 'toe-sucking' pictures of the louche, dishevelled Duchess – a new Rabelaisian, greedy and wanton in all her desires.

Like all parodies, that portrait was not entirely fair. If not especially clever and not wholly scrupulous in her attachments, Sarah Ferguson was at heart a kind woman; hopelessly insecure, a child of a troubled home and – like the Princess of Wales and the Duchess of Kent – a woman made miserable by her royal role. Where Fergie's response was simply to kick against perceived restraints, Katharine chose stoical endurance. Diana's strategy was a tactical war, designed to establish her own future while offering an exposé of how badly she had been treated.

When, in November 1992, the Waleses agreed that their marriage was finished, the Queen was furious, miserable and disappointed. She was also entirely wrong-footed. Whether the Windsors could ever have countermanded the power of Diana is debatable. Certainly the image of Charles, whose public lustre reached its nadir when, in the Camillagate tapes, he revealed to his mistress that he wished he was a Tampax, was not an obvious asset in a public relations battle.

As for the Queen, scarcely a proponent of breakneck

reform, she was facing a crisis beyond her family's behaviour. If she had pre-empted the public mood and reacted faster, she might have fared better. But, as in the days after Diana's death, the inertia ingrained in the Windsor credo was to prove deeply damaging.

On Friday, 22 November 1992, a pall of smoke rose from the Queen's private chapel at Windsor Castle. The fire, started by a restorer's lamp igniting drapery, swept through St George's Hall. At nightfall the blazing castle was silhouetted against the sky; a symbol of the destruction assailing the House of Windsor. Shortly afterwards the Heritage Secretary, Peter Brooke, offered £60 million of public money to cover the damage.

In a page one editorial, headed, 'Why The Queen Must Listen', the *Daily Mail* asked: 'Why should the populace, many of whom have had to make huge sacrifices during the bitter recession, have to pay the total bill for Windsor Castle, when the Queen, who pays no taxes, contributes next to nothing?' Six days after the fire, the Prime Minister, John Major, announced that the Queen and the Prince of Wales would pay tax on their private income. Rattled into bowing to pressure that she should have heeded years before, the Queen took the unusual step of appealing to the kindness of her subjects. In a speech to mark the fortieth anniversary of her accession, she talked of her 'annus horribilis'; a phrase interpreted by the *Sun* as 'One's Bum Year'.

The Queen's admission was a clever piece of phraseology on the part of her speechwriters – a subtle indication that royal marriage crises and charges of miserly conduct were part of a finite timespan. The implication was that a line had been drawn under one bad year in an otherwise impeccable reign. The events of 1992 had, on the contrary, merely been a prelude to nemesis. The sympathy and adulation extended to Diana at the time of her marriage break-up was only a foretaste of how she would be glorified, and the House of Windsor further demonized, immediately after her death.

On the question of money, the Queen's tax gesture was publicly deemed insufficient. The Prime Minister announced that the National Audit Office would be looking into public spending on the royal palaces, and the Lord Chamberlain promised better public access to the royal collections. The restoration of Windsor Castle would be completed without taxpayers' money.

Such initiatives were not sufficient to stem a rising tide of opinion that too many of the royals were under-productive and over-privileged. The Queen, advised by an old guard of courtiers, had erred for too long in favour of the status quo to countenance radical changes. In the lead-up to Diana's death, there was little evidence of change in the House of Windsor. In the direct aftermath, the Queen's withdrawal to Balmoral and the insistence that a Buckingham Palace flag could not be flown at half-mast for reasons of protocol demonstrated how badly the lessons of the 'annus horribilis' had been learned.

Once again, the royal family was jolted into delayed modernization; this time with the support of Tony Blair, whose front-of-house backing included an upbeat speech for the Queen's golden wedding anniversary and whose background advice clearly included changing etiolated courtiers for spin doctors able to reshape a post-millennial royal family.

A survey among focus groups commissioned by the palace concluded that the royals were out of touch and bad value for money – a result that briefly shocked even the Duke of Edinburgh into casting around for image-boosting ploys. Apparently with encouragement from the government, the Queen decided that an image-consultant with the title of Director of Communications should be appointed and report directly to her. After a five-month search, Simon Lewis, a high-flying public relations man, was seconded from Centrica, part of British Gas, at a salary of £230,000, of which the Queen was reported to be paying £90,000 and his old employer the remainder. Whether Lewis could repackage an ailing House of Windsor on the lines of Camelot plc remained to be seen, but his appointment marked a serious acknowledgement that the momentum for change must be stepped up. 'So much is altering,' a close friend mused to the Queen, two years before the end of the century. 'Will anything be the same, come the millennium?'

'Hmmph,' the Queen replied. 'Mummy will still be around.' As for the Queen herself, seemingly as durable as her ninety-seven-year-old mother, there was never any prospect of abdication. Told by a leading Church of England churchman that he had decided to retire, she forbore to offer either thanks or congratulations. 'You're retiring?' she said, grumpily. 'I can't.'

Whatever her appetite for revision, many of the Queen's problems remained resistant to change. Despite his excellence in caring for his sons, Charles's merits failed wholly to convince a sceptical public. The Duchess of York complained on American television that she had been 'excluded' from the Queen's golden wedding anniversary, blaming 'the courtiers, the grey men'. In a second interview, with Oprah Winfrey, Fergie went on to explain the sleeping arrangements at Sunninghill, the Berkshire home where she and Andrew lived independent lives. 'When Papa brings home company for the weekend, the girls and I step down to my father's house. If I want to have boyfriends, then I do it out of the country house, because it's easier.'

In 1998 the monarchy remained in limbo – haunted by echoes of old scandals, battered by the backlash from Diana's death and in the process of a modernization programme that remained unclear, unspecified, largely unarticulated and broadly unconvincing to a British people seeking a more convincing revolution. In this climate of national auditry, the Duke and Duchess of Kent contemplated their future.

Both had worked hard and behaved impeccably. The Duchess, in particular, had demonstrated the human touch that the public now demanded of the monarchy at large. Even Edward, though scarcely blessed with populist flair, had hardly done worse than first-rank royals. While Charles hunted or played polo, the Kents, always together at the FA Cup Final, were given the task of supporting the people's sport. On the one occasion when Charles – seeking to redeem his image – took over the job, he was so uninterested in the game that he attempted to present the trophy to the losers.

Despite the merits of the Kents, the question – as applied to all minor royals – remained: What are they for? In a leader column published at the height of the demand for a slimmed-down monarchy, the *Daily Telegraph* lamented the possible loss of those deputed to 'stage events to give pleasure to children, open new libraries and schools and to celebrate countless small landmarks in human progress. "Minor royals" have given – and continue to give – in abundance. The Duke of Kent, for example, is patron of 116 organizations in the voluntary sector. The Duchess of Kent does outstanding work for children, and in Northern Ireland.'

Around the same time, and in its news pages, the

Telegraph reported the view that, where patrons were required, Richard Branson or Sir Cliff Richard might do just as well in an egalitarian age where the public image of a charity was more important than the royal patronage on the headed notepaper. Meanwhile Buckingham Palace continued to play down the notion that lesser royals were to be put out to grass, inisting, once again, that 'members of the royal family will continue to carry out charitable and other engagements for as long as they and their organizations wish. The intention is that members of the royal family who live at Kensington Palace should continue to do so.'

Given the Queen's fondness for playing a long game, it is unthinkable that she would willingly have countenanced any precipitate solution. Nonetheless, the writing was on the wall. Whether or not the British public had any taste for an over-large and excessively grand royal family – which they did not – minor royals were a dying breed. Although some of their children and grandchildren retained titles, there had never been any prospect of them embarking on a life of royal duty.

Nevertheless, there was an inherent irony in the fact that those who had worked hard and provided no scandal – notably the senior Kents and the Gloucesters – were being castigated for the failings at the core of a family in which the inner sanctum had little truck with the outer fringes. That is not to say that the Queen was not very fond of her cousin, Eddie; simply that the delineation between major and minor royals was clearly defined. A clergyman who worked closely with the Queen and her family refers to the two groupings as 'the chalk and the cheese'.

'It's been terribly difficult for the chalk. They have none of the resources the inner family has, and almost everything they do have is on charity from the Queen. So it's been very hard for them; and particularly for Eddie.'

To some extent, the 'chalk' had been gradually marginalized. The fact that the Duke and Duchess of Kent, by then middle-aged, worked so furiously hard at the beginning of the nineties stemmed more from their own desire to look useful and important rather than from any impetus from the 'cheese'. The nucleus of the royal family, and Charles in particular, would have been happy for the Kents to drift quietly away from the limelight long before the post-Diana calls for a slimmed-down monarchy began.

This wish had not been formally articulated. Rather, it was conveyed in the vague and osmotic manner peculiar to royal communications. Even the nucleus of the House of Windsor does not specialize in family small talk. Where outsiders are concerned, the Windsors are so notoriously reticent that incoming Deans of Windsor – Her Majesty's personal spiritual advisers – were traditionally given two pieces of advice by their predecessors. The first was that one must never believe anything the Queen was alleged to have said unless the message was delivered by her. The second was that she would not speak a word to a new Dean for the first four years of his incumbency. Even with closest family members, horses remain the chief conversational currency. As Prince Philip is alleged once to have said, when someone suggested that the Queen should visit a leading-edge scientific project: 'If it doesn't eat grass or fart, then she isn't interested.'

Post-Diana, the frail bonds between the chalk and the cheese looked more overstretched than ever. The debate on the future of the monarchy went much wider than the public denigration of its minor players as expensive fête-opening fodder. Under the government's constitutional reforms, it sought a swift fulfilment of its manifesto pledge to abolish the right of hereditary peers to sit and vote in the House of Lords. Reform of the Lords called into question the future role of the Prince of Wales and the three Dukes of Blood Royal – the Dukes of York, Gloucester and Kent; a matter referred to the Palace for discussion.

It is hard to argue any case for the retention of an over-large and extravagant royal family – expensive, anachronistic, aloof and, in some cases, unloved. Equally it is difficult not to have some sympathy with the Duke of Kent. To be middle-aged, to seem unwanted, unthanked and redundant, must be a fate as bitter to a royal Duke as to a superannuated executive. Not that the Duke ever gave any hint of such feelings. Nor was he likely to starve, or indeed, to be summarily sacked. According to friends, he regarded the question mark over the future of minor royals as an over-blown media fuss, directly at odds with the facts as spelled out by the Queen. Even so, he would have been less than human not to feel some distress.

In the service of the royal family, he had given up his career and taken on mundane tasks along with the presti-gious. He had also sacrificed, in the name of the royal family, any chance of a happy private life and a successful marriage, partly for fear of inviting the sort of scandal that turned out to be the Windsors' in-house speciality. For the Duchess, the blow must have been even more bitter. In the service of a monarchy deemed wanting by her and by the public, she had also endured a largely miserable life and a disastrous marriage in silence. Of those who came after her, and who broke out of the system, Fergie was hardly more than a figure of national derision. Diana, the incomer who most resembled her, was dead. The manner of her death must have seemed almost immaterial. Although the blame rested with a drunk driver, it was impossible entirely to separate the tragic circumstances of Diana's life with those of her life. While she would have expressed it more delicately, it is likely that Katharine would have echoed Diana's resentment, offered long ago: 'After all I've done for that fucking family.' Like Diana, she had known the claustrophobia of living in the shadow of courtiers watching her every move and deeming her neurotic, difficult and unstable.

The Duchess of Kent is not a saint. She is capable of being misguided, unrealistic and autocratic. She has also paid an inordinately high price for a life whose ostensible privilege masked a loneliness exacerbated by the coldness of the royal family and the unkindness of fate. Abortion, stillbirth, depression – the causes and the results of a grim marriage – might have wholly destroyed a less strong woman. But for that strength Katharine, at sixty-five, would have had little option but to maintain the public charade of the serene royal Duchess; another emblem of the House of Windsor's bogus perfection.

It was undoubtedly the catalyst of Diana's death that persuaded her there was another way. Always hollow, the role of minor royal now seemed devalued and largely without allure. Katharine broke out of the shackles quietly. Her escape was conducted in the same manner as her years of endurance. In silence.

CHAPTER THIRTY-ONE

Private Citizen

❖

T HE PARTY WAS an informal gathering at the home of
one of the Duchess of Kent's friends from television.
Like the other guests, Katharine was informally dressed for a
day in the garden. Above the low hubbub of chatter, her
voice was heard, raised in irritation or anger. 'Don't call me
Ma'am,' she was saying to the Queen's cousin, Lady Elizabeth Anson. 'And don't curtsey.'

Few people witnessed this small public demonstration of
short temper, later relayed to Prince Charles, who was said
to be appalled. Of those who did hear Katharine, fewer still
would have understood her shift in how she wished to be
perceived – less as a minor royal and more as a private
citizen. As the debate over the future of the House of
Windsor continued, Katharine – behind the scenes – was
seeking a less stultifying career.

By 1998 she had her own agents, Knight Ayton Management. From opposite sides of a table in a cluttered office in
London's Argyll Street, Sue Knight and Sue Ayton acted for
an impressive client list; among them Jon Snow, Michael
Buerk and Martin Bashir, who conducted the *Panorama*
interview with Princess Diana. In addition to the Duchess

of Kent, the women on their books included Anna Ford, Julia Somerville, Angela Rippon and a host of other correspondents, presenters and newscasters.

The Duchess of Kent had always regarded herself as a communicator. On her overseas trips, she would always have her own pocket camera and dictaphone to hand. Signing up with an agent was the first indicator that she now saw herself in a quasi-journalistic role – a woman committed to reportage and with a mission to explain. Her charities heard whispers of possible future projects, including – among more plausible rumours – a suggestion that it had been considered that she might stand in with Richard Madeley, substituting for his wife and co-presenter, Judy Finnegan, while she was off work having a hysterectomy. Another scheme floated involved the Duchess travelling to Bosnia under the auspices of the show to do a 'Richard and Judy' special on a children's charity.

Whether or not the Duchess ever seriously considered doing anything for *This Morning*, she was undoubtedly eager to polish her broadcasting skills. Generally, on an overseas charity tour, she had agreed to one setpiece television interview for broadcast at a later date. Questions were submitted in advance, and even then Katharine appeared to be nervous and hesitant – wholly different from the spontaneous performer whose television films for Age Concern and Helen House had shown her as natural and unforced.

Katharine was determined to improve her technique and recruit those who could best advise her on the direction of her work and on her self-projection. In addition to Knight Ayton, she also sought her own spin doctor; someone able to help her on both counts. Peter Cunard, a leading PR man, was first contacted by an intermediary eager to see whether he could offer Katharine some help. Cunard was an interesting choice. Formerly the chief executive of the Rowland Company UK, a Saatchi and Saatchi subsidiary, he later became an independent consultant to TV-am, the Victoria and Albert Museum and the Press Association and an expert on corporate strategies. He was also known as the man who gave Sarah Ferguson her first proper job, paying her £80 a week (later raised to £100) to handle accounts including Mumm champagne and Seagrams whisky for his then employer, Durden-Smith Communications.

Despite revealing that one of the main tasks of the future Duchess of York was 'talking to her friends on the telephone', Cunard remained in close contact with his former assistant, attending the Yorks' wedding and – after her separation from Andrew – praising her familiarity with the press. 'Without doubt, she knows how newspapers work,' he once said. 'She learned the important things, like deadlines and what makes a good news story.' Cunard has never revealed who introduced him to the Duchess of Kent or what projects he arranged for her – although his good press contacts make it likely that he had some involvement in the series of *Daily Telegraph* interviews, late in 1997, in which she set out her stall as a modern, independent woman, tired of being labelled as the frail and vulnerable member of the royal family and eager, equally, to gloss over the idea that she was – or indeed ever had been – crippled by ME.

Certainly Cunard was impressed with the informal Duchess of Kent he met at Wren House. 'Do you want coffee?' she asked him once, foraging in vain through her kitchen cupboards. 'I don't normally buy it because I can't drink it. But, if you would like, I could easily nip down to Marks and get some.' Armed with Cunard's advice, Katharine was ready, by 1998, to embark on other television projects. For years, she had regarded the best broadcasters as performing a role of almost mystical significance. In 1981, presenting an award to Jon Snow, she told him in her address: 'Jesus wished that all people should be true to one another and courageous for His sake; should care for the weak, the unwanted . . . In this context, the men and women of the media who speak for those who cannot speak for themselves, and who risk their lives and security to do so, are indeed dedicating themselves to something that transcends earthly science.'

Katharine, who had discarded some of her mysticism in favour of practical solutions, now shared an agent with Snow. She also wished to become, in her own right, a media communicator for the unheard. There was a second strand to her plan. In securing for herself agency representation, she was able to sever herself from the office she shared with her husband and whose staff, in years past, may have been deemed to have judged her harshly and poured cold water on some of her plans to extend the range of her work. Even on foreign charity trips she had, in the past, been watched and monitored, as her London office kept tabs, through faxes and phone calls, on how she was behaving and what she was saying.

Theoretically, the public life of the Duchess of Kent was still, in 1997, controlled from York House. In practice, as some of her leading charities confirmed, courtiers had an increasingly shaky grasp on what the Duchess was doing. Those seeking fuller information knew to ring her agent.

Although Katharine was seeking to loosen her royal ties, her strategy had a curious synergy with the royal family's own modernization programme. The Duchess had a spin doctor. So did the Queen. The Duchess opted for a more informal style. So did the Queen. But Her Majesty's forays into populism – such as autographing a Manchester United football for a young fan – tended to look clumsy and unwise. Katharine, a repressed and junior figure in the traditional royal family, was now leading the way in the field of modernization techniques.

As an early move, she chose to publicize one of the causes closest to her heart. In a contribution to a BBC 1 'Make Yourself Useful' week, designed to encourage viewers to volunteer some time to charity, she invited cameras into the Night Shelter in Westminster – a centre run under the patronage of Cardinal Hume and offering food and a bed to fifty homeless people. The Duchess, known to those who stay there simply as Katharine, has worked in the shelter, attached to the Passage Day Centre, for years, cooking and serving food, washing up and cleaning.

As she pointed out in the film, while stirring a pot of mashed potatoes, she did not have a cook herself and was therefore quite used to preparing a few meals. She also made clear that, as with all her charity work, she gained enormously from her input. 'I like to come here once a week. I am lucky I live in London. I have the time, and it's easy for me. I like getting to know the clients. We are all more like friends here – the volunteers too. I like being with them.

'They [the homeless] need respect and a roof over their heads, as we all do. They need feeding. They need warmth and companionship. They are very dignified, and we respect that. They didn't choose this way of life. In some ways, they had this forced upon them.' Katharine's text was a social message on the plight of the rootless, people trapped in a miserable existence whose rigours they had not elected. Her words, as she must have known, applied not only to homeless men but also to herself.

It was clear, from this short film, how much her television persona had altered. In her report for Age Concern, recorded some years earlier, she had retained the patina of an affluent do-gooder. This time she had discarded the elegant clothes and the pearls in favour of a cream sweater and a cropped, almost boyish haircut. No longer simply a performer, she spoke directly and confidently to camera. The impression, deliberate or not, was that of a would-be professional broadcaster, the Kate Adie of the soup kitchen.

But there was also a deliberate if subliminal poignancy in Katharine's short film; a sense – even beyond her own affirmation of how much she gained from her work – that she, a helpmate to the homeless and the lonely, was almost as rootless as they. She had, she said, only worked for one Christmas at the shelter, but on Christmas Day 1998 she planned to do so again. 'I think a lot of us have had our families by teatime on Christmas Day, and we're only too happy to come out and see some other people,' she said, no doubt aware that, while most mothers and grandmothers might confess to finding a family Christmas stressful, few would actually seek a reason, however altruistic, to escape from their loved ones. In her mind was her own recent experience. The Kents had spent the previous Christmas with old friends in Scotland. By then their relationship was so strained that other friends wondered whether the Duke and Duchess would be able to endure spending an entire festive season in one another's company.

Increasingly, Katharine's life was focused on a self-fulfilment outside the bounds of family and royal duty. In some ways, the timing of her new independence was dictated for her. As the focus on the £45 million annual cost of the royal family continued, the House of Windsor decided, in July 1998, to open its audited books in the interests of openness and accountability.

There was particular public interest in the travel section

of the balance sheet, which divulged that the cost of flying
Prince Charles to bring home his wife's body from Paris had
been reclaimed, for the public purse, from Diana's insurance.
But the major scrutiny concerned the costs of ferrying the
royal family to engagements. There was some evidence of a
new thriftiness. Of the £19.4 million allocated for travel,
only £17.3 million had been spent, and Prince Philip and
Princess Margaret had demonstrated their frugality by using
their OAP passes to buy cheap rail tickets. Other expeditions
demonstrated to the public just how costly a royal awayday
return can be. The Queen's visit to the Derby, involving a
short-haul royal train trip from Victoria to Tattenham
Corner – a journey that cost punters £4.10p – registered at
£11,843. Among all the vast bills of more senior royals, the
expenses of the Duchess of Kent came in for particular
mention by an unnamed Whitehall official who expressed
his anxiety that, in publishing their accounts, the royal
family could be 'setting itself up to be shot at'.

'The difficulty is that when one of the big names goes
anywhere, it seems that they can often pack in five or six
visits,' the official was quoted as saying. 'But when the
Duchess of Kent spends £3,000 travelling to a hospital in
Manchester, some people are going to ask: Why didn't she
just take the [normal] train?' It was a fair question, underlin-
ing a central paradox in Katharine's character. Emotionally
and spiritually short-changed by her contract with the House
of Windsor, she had no intention of missing out on the
material benefits.

Her clothes bills had been, at times, viewed by the palace
as preposterous. Her charity tours, designed to illustrate the
plight of the dying and starving, once required a plane of
the Royal Flight, a designer wardrobe and five-star accommodation; props which seemed almost vulgar, given the

nature of the job. Here was a woman who scrubbed lavatory floors at Lourdes but who took her personal hairdresser with her. Katharine was aware of the contradiction between the Lady Bountiful side of her character and the soup kitchen volunteer.

In the past she had rationalized her extravagances as a necessary part of the job; knowing, probably, that they represented more than that. The luxury of royal life had been one of the few paybacks for her unhappiness. They had also been invaluable for the times when she, hardly well enough to work, could face a trip by royal helicopter but not by British Rail. In addition, beautiful appearance offered her a mask – a camouflage to her perpetual state of turmoil. More simply, Katharine, indulged from childhood, loved luxury.

In 1997 her wish for a less royal life, coupled with the economy drive the public demanded of royalty, decreed a simpler existence. Scruffy clothes and informality had always appealed to Katharine, but only on a part-time basis. Discarding the trappings of grandeur was not easy for her.

The practical aspects were the easy ones. By 1998, Sarah McCormick, the hairdresser who accompanied her to Lourdes, had left to work in a salon in Surrey, offering no comment on her departure, and the Duchess had abandoned her formerly elaborate coiffure for a utilitarian style; the wash and go crop of the busy working woman.

But Katharine was not a natural career women. She was, instead, an inhabitant of a world insulated from ordinary people and everyday practicalities. At first, friends said, she had difficulties evolving her new plans. On the vision side, she never lacked drive or enthusiasm. On detail, she was hazy; encouraged to believe by some of her richer friends that, in straitened times, perhaps it would be possible to get corporate sponsorship for some of her charitable expeditions, now that royal transport was in such short supply. Gently, charity workers explained that sponsored duchesses would be unlikely to attract much backing.

There was, however, a genuinely practical side to Katharine – a woman who had heated her own precooked lasagne or Fray Bentos meat pies (a particular favourite of the Duke's) for supper and who was regularly seen shopping in a Kensington Marks & Spencer food hall.

Quickly she realized that the new deal involved economy-class travel, packing one's own hairdryer and a vastly reduced retinue. When she travelled to Macedonia, in the summer of 1998, on behalf of Voluntary Service Overseas, she dispensed even with her detective. Only Lucy Tomkins, the lady-in-waiting on whom she most relied, went with her. The Duchess's mission was to highlight the plight of children with learning disabilities – scores of abandoned infants and teenagers, shaven-headed, dressed in regulation orphanage garb of blue and white striped pyjamas and propped in nodding rows on the floor of Demir Kapija, an institution whose horrors had rarely been exposed to the outside world. Katharine had agreed to make a film for ITN, with Colin Baker, and to do a subsequent studio interview with Nicholas Owen, the court correspondent.

'I wanted people in Britain to be more aware of what was happening on their doorstep,' she told *Hello!* magazine, the regular chronicler of royal good works. 'Most people think overseas charity and development work is all about starving children in Africa and India, as are those images we usually see on television. But people jet off to their holidays in Greece and sit on beaches within swimming distance of this region and have no idea of the acute problems confronting the emerging countries of Eastern Europe.'

It was not one of Katharine's most successful broadcasting ventures. Suggestions that the lost children of Macedonia – condemned to become the detritus of humanity – might be helped by love, cuddles and being allowed to wear their own clothes sounded almost facile in the face of the awful scenes of deprivation. In the subsequent interview, Katharine sounded stilted and nervous. Nonetheless – and to her credit – she had contrived to focus attention on a previously unacknowledged horror. Pictures of her kneeling next to the stricken children inevitably invited a comparison with the informal images of Diana's Angolan landmine campaign, undertaken in the months before her death. In a conscious or subconscious emulation of the Princess, Katharine wore black jeans, black plimsolls and a blue denim shirt; ideal garb for the job but a stark contrast, nevertheless, to the beautifully pressed designer outfits she had stipulated for her charity visits to India and Africa.

It is certain that for someone as conscious of clothes and of appearance as Katharine, the shift in style represented more than an economy-driven shift from glamour to practicality. Her *Tatler* covergirl pictures, a decade before, had carried the message that she – labelled as a broken woman – was a vibrant and beautiful survivor. The Duchess of the nineties was rebranding herself as a careerist who cared nothing for image. The new uniform – on one occasion, tee-shirt, combat trousers, flip-flops and a copy of the homeless magazine the *Big Issue* – signified a move away from royal constraints.

Early in 1998 a senior BBC executive in Northern Ireland – someone who had never met the Duchess before – was introduced to her at the finals of a Young Musician of the Year competition. Katharine had for years regarded the province as her stamping ground. As patron of the Royal

Ulster Benevolent Fund, she had visited many times to offer her brand of comfort to the victims of terrorism. But despite her familiarity with the country and her love of music, she appeared, on her visit to the competition, to be simply one more royal on parade. 'She looked as nervous as hell and terribly grand – surrounded by flunkies,' said the television executive. 'There was no real conversation, beyond royal small talk.'

Some months later, the same executive was invited to Elton John's concert at Stormont Castle in Belfast, following the ratification of the Good Friday agreement, marking the cross-party consensus for a peaceful solution in Northern Ireland. The Duchess of Kent, a notable Roman Catholic whose links with the province had chiefly encompassed the protestant community, was there in an informal capacity as an invitee of Mo Mowlam, the Secretary of State for Northern Ireland. The television executive who had met her six months previously and who was placed in the next seat failed to recognize her neighbour, whose jeans and bomber jacket contrasted with the smart suits of the other guests. And still, the face seemed familiar. 'Who are you?' she asked eventually. 'Is it Honor Blackman?'

'No,' said Katharine, laughing. 'I'm the Duchess of Kent.' This time she showed no trace of nerves. Instead she was joking and relaxed, happy to acknowledge that she regarded herself as a novice in the arena of Northern Ireland politics but ecstatic that a settlement had been reached. The television executive was struck by the vast contrast between the stiff royal, poised but uneasy, and the happiness of the informal Duchess; delighted by the peace and delighted, too, simply to be able to let her hair down at a pop concert.

Royalty is not known for its chameleon qualities. As the

House of Windsor struggled towards evolution in the run-up to the millennium, few of its leading members, barring the teenage Prince William, offered any personal symbols of modernity. Charles, destined to be a post-millennial monarch, continued to favour kilts and socks – regalia of a bygone age – and even Prince Harry attended World Cup football matches in collar and tie rather than the England strip coveted by his peers. At a time when the monarchy had been warned it must revise, when the old certainties were disappearing and when even the right of the royal Dukes – the Duke of Kent included – to sit in Tony Blair's new-look House of Lords was under question, there were greater issues to face than those of dress code. Even so, the unchanging external face of the royal family appeared to symbolize a certain stubborn immutability – an unwillingness or an incapacity to reinvent itself.

Increasingly, it appeared that the Duchess of Kent was one of the few royals correctly to read the signs of change and to adapt to a modern age – not only in matters of presentation but in recognizing that the cult of the regal figurehead, totem of an unquestioning respect and adulation that royalty had lost or forfeited, was dissipating. It seemed to her that to be a royal patron was no longer always enough. The cult of work was one of the touchstones of a new era. The gospel of endeavour, for the Blair government – and, in particular, the Chancellor, Gordon Brown – constituted something close to a new religion. Katharine was determined to tap into it.

Since her appearance to promote Age Concern in Martyn Lewis's film, she had done little for the charity, largely because of her frequent illnesses. In 1998 she told its head, Lady Sally Greengross, that she wanted to do more and to go beyond her caring image. In other words, she no longer wished to be royal patron, preferring the role of president – a job that would involve what she called 'real work'.

Greengross agreed the shift of direction with Katharine. At the time of writing the arrangements had not been finalized, but – with the single proviso that the Duchess of Kent was fit enough to take on a demanding workload – the plan was that Prince Charles, a supporter of Age Concern's work, should take over Katharine's patronage, while she would replace Howard Davies as president. Davies, for his part, would continue to chair the Millennium Debate of the Age and the employers' forum on a mixed-age workforce; initiatives designed to combat ageism in the workplace and in society.

This plan constituted a singular coup for Katharine. If the scheme was executed, she would be replaced as patron by the heir to the throne. She would take over from the former deputy governor of the Bank of England and a man of undoubted intellect and acumen. She stipulated that she wanted to be a 'real president' – launching conferences and being the voice, as well as the face, of Age Concern. She would, assuming the plan succeeded, confound all those courtiers who had ever doubted the stamina or the intellectual depth of the Duchess of Kent.

In addition to her Age Concern plan, Katharine now had her one-off television campaigns and an enduring active commitment to those projects that had always meant the most to her – Unicef, Macmillan Cancer Relief, of which she is also president, and working with the homeless of Westminster. There remained, of course, a portfolio of other commitments – Leeds University, the Royal Northern College of Music, private visits to community projects she supports in the North of England and a string of additional patronages.

But her new interest in Age Concern was significant. The Duchess of Kent, in her mid-sixties – beautiful still, and modern in outlook – was not only a compassionate carer dedicated to bettering the lives of the elderly. She was also an icon to those of her generation. Even those courtiers cool about her charms claim that, in terms of charisma, she is the royal who will one day inherit the role of the Queen Mother – a transcender of old age and an exemplar for all ages. It was doubtful whether Katharine would welcome such a mantle. Though hardly a republican, nor was she an aspiring royal dowager in the traditional mould. Hers was a half-way solution, symbolized by her appearance in Hyde Park on the last night of the 1998 promenade concerts – eschewing the royal box to stand in the midst of a crowd singing 'Rule Britannia'.

Katharine, by now, was not only moving away from the confines of a royal existence. She was also distancing herself from her own past, defined, in the public's mind, not only by depression, sadness and ill-health but by the tableau of a saintly duchess, purveyor of comfort to the poor and needy. Both images were intertwined; both linked to Katharine's personal suffering. Her stepping back from the hospice movement and her new wish to become a hard-edged social commentator rather than a dispenser of china angels to the dying did not imply any lessening of compassion on her part. Rather, she was eager to find more practical solutions to her own problems and those of others. Her decision to cast around for TV work and a wider public profile began (as she had no doubt hoped) to cause a *frisson* in some quarters – notably among the closest friends of the Duke of Kent.

Whatever the Duke's own view, some of those who cared most for him detected, in Katharine's attitude, an attempt to marginalize him. Although admitting no flaw in her marriage, the Duchess confessed publicly that there had, as in any relationship, been ups and downs. This anodyne version of events was scarcely new to the Duke's friends, who were more upset by an assertion that they had different interests. Her passion was music, she said. Her husband's hobbies lay elsewhere. Given the Duke's expertise on opera, a subject on which Katharine had never been well-informed, this remark was taken by Edward's coterie as a calculated and public snub by a woman suddenly, and in their view, rather dangerously eager to air her own opinions.

In the words of one of the Duke's closest friends: 'It is as if she is trying to airbrush him out.'

CHAPTER THIRTY-TWO

Locked in a Nightmare

T HE MARRIAGE OF the Duke and Duchess of Kent was always programmed to fail. Not that its collapse could necessarily have been foreseen. At a time when a lifetime guarantee was expected to attach to royal unions, the prospect of marital breakdown was barely entertained. Even among those who initially had grave doubts about the wisdom of the marriage – notably the Duke's mother, Marina, and Katharine herself – the presumption would have been that the partnership could be made successful.

But a fairytale ending was never an option. Even the Duke's friends, men eager to highlight Katharine's shortfalls, agree that she – over-sensitive and under-trained – never had a chance of settling contentedly into the life she had chosen. To succeed, as an old-style or even a modern royal bride, demanded a cocktail of compliance and durability that the Duchess, independent and frail, did not possess. A royal existence, stuffy, formal and anachronistic, was never going to be the milieu of someone whose good qualities – empathy and spontaneity – were suited to a kinder and less structured world. The Worsleys, like the Spencers, hardly rated as trailer trash. Their families were older than the House of

Windsor, and their blood more blue. Pedigree notwithstanding, Katharine had been brought up as a lonely and relatively
unsophisticated country girl by an adoring father who
decreed that she must always have the best but who could
not, in the end, procure it for her.

The paradox is that if Sir William Worsley had been less
ambitious to craft a perfect idyll for his only daughter, she
might never have married the Duke of Kent. A 'good county
marriage' – one friend's definition of Katharine's own wish
– would have spared her the rigours of royal life and its toll
on her personal happiness . There was never any chance that
the private and the public could be disentangled. The royal
arena was the Duke's natural milieu. A descendant of the
Romanovs, he was also the torchbearer for his dead father –
the son of a King – and the child of Marina, Duchess of
Kent, whose pedigree and grandeur ranked as formidable
even among the highest echelons of royalty. There was no
prospect that Edward could break out of this loop, nor any
sign that he wished to.

If Katharine could not adapt herself to his world, then
the marriage would be pushed to breaking point. The last
rites were effectively administered to the Kent union late in
the 1970s. Katharine's abortion and stillborn child were not
the cause of its demise. Instead they were the accelerant
shifting the relationship from discontent to the partnership
described as hellish by one of the Duke's best friends. 'The
Duke and Duchess,' he says, 'are locked in a nightmare.'

No woman could fail to shudder at the horrors Katharine
endured. Her abortion, undertaken at the behest of doctors
and with the blessing of the Anglican Church she later
spurned, affected her so profoundly that she never spoke of
it again. The stillbirth of her son demolished any last vestiges

of happiness and health. 'After that, it was as if her whole body was breaking down,' says one friend.

There is strong evidence that the Duke of Kent, unschooled in emotional and mental breakdown, did what he could to assist; even if his temper and impatience rendered his efforts almost useless. When his marriage problems were at their height, he sought counsel from a trusted churchman – the royal parallel to a troubled husband asking for guidance from Relate. Since many of the circumstances leading to the collapse of the marriage were of the Duke's own making and given that he had a vested interest – the Queen's approval – in keeping it on the rails, that action is not necessarily laudable. Even so, the Duke of Kent is not the villain of this work. To turn Katharine's story purely into a chronicle of innocents and aggressors would be too simplistic.

On one level at least, the Kents' history is a fable of how bad marriages – particularly those set in the context of the warped family values espoused by the House of Windsor – destroy lives. The union of the Duke and Duchess of Kent was the ultimate marriage of convenience. He was, in the eyes of the Worsley family, a convenient catch. She was, despite Marina's reservations, a convenient bride: pretty, well-bred and suitable. It was convenient for the House of Windsor that the marriage should drag on, long after it had lost all meaning and long after it had become apparent, in palace circles, that the Duchess of Kent had disobligingly gone against royal protocol by mutating into an inconvenience: difficult, disturbed and distraught.

Why did the marriage continue? Beyond all the reasons already rehearsed here, only one man – a close associate of the Duke for many years – advanced a factor no one else had mentioned. 'He loves her,' he said. But demonstrating love, or even defining it, is not a Windsor forte. 'Whatever that is,' Charles said, when asked, at the time of his engagement to Lady Diana Spencer, whether he was in love with her.

If untroubled love ever existed in the Kent marriage, it was both ephemeral and doomed. The Duke was brought up in an environment where he, like all royal males, received little guidance in how to bestow love. Katharine, the cherished daughter, was schooled by her father to expect that love should be bestowed on her. Under any law of supply and demand, that imbalance augured badly for a lasting relationship.

Countless stereotypes fit both the Duke and the Duchess. He is the ill-tempered autocrat and distant husband or, alternatively, the humble public servant and a dutiful father who single-handedly held his crumbling family together. She is the saintly crusader, the unselfish comforter, the spiritual dreamer. Conversely, she is the mother-in-law from hell, the boss of nightmares, the wife conniving at her husband's unhappiness and humiliation.

The truth is an amalgam of all of those. Corrosive marriages, made more claustrophobic by the lack of individual freedoms imposed by a royal existence, do not engender beautiful behaviour. In Katharine's case, the tragedies she suffered and the resulting depression are the great exonerating factor. Few of those who knew the real Duchess were able to, or chose to, distinguish between mental strain and bad behaviour.

The fact that she was damned for problems far beyond her control helped to prompt the emergence of the unreal Duchess, an effervescent carer whose public brilliance never offered a hint of the vacuum in her private life. If Katharine had confined herself only to this schizophrenic existence – with all its implicit falsity – then she would have been driven mad. But the Duchess of Kent is not a manufactured queen of hearts, and her life has not been programmed to two precise and artificial heat settings: cold in private, warm in public.

The measure of the Duchess's genuine compassion lies in the work that, over the years, has gone largely unrecorded, not because no television camera is on hand but because she wants to keep her allegiances private. Hundreds of women facing tragedy have been quietly assisted by Katharine's intervention. In the late seventies, Pat Seed – a Manchester woman diagnosed with cancer and told that she had six months to live – announced that she would first raise half a million pounds for a new hospital unit. The Duchess visited her constantly and encouraged her to persevere, promising that she would officially open the department. Shortly before she died, her project completed, Seed described her as 'one of the most compassionate ladies I know'.

In the early nineties, Katharine, as patron of the Anthony Nolan Bone Marrow Trust, met Fran Burke, a computer systems specialist from Warwickshire who had been told, shortly after her second wedding anniversary, that she had leukaemia. While still waiting for a bone marrow donor who might save her life, Fran shelved her chemotherapy treatment in order to have her two children: Matthew, born in 1992, and Sebastian, one year younger.

As Fran fought for her life, Katharine stayed in constant touch – writing every fortnight to ask after her progress. After a donor was found and Fran's leukaemia went into remission, she publicly hugged the Duchess, explaining how her friendship had helped her survive. 'She has supported me for the last three years,' she said. There are countless other stories of Katharine's enduring attachment to the suffering; an involvement far more durable than the on-the-hoof comfort normally dispensed by well-meaning royals with a job to do and a tight schedule to observe. The popular notion is that Katharine – who finds her personal tragedies too harrowing, even now, to confront – draws some consolation from the comfort she is able to bestow on others. While that is no doubt true, one of her oldest friends believes that there is a wider dimension to her compassion.

Lady Lothian – author, journalist and founder and organizer of the prestigious Women of the Year Lunch (where Katharine, affectionately addressed as Dok, is the most popular royal speaker) – believes that the Duchess of Kent is a healer. In other words, according to Tony Lothian, she has a capacity, far beyond empathy, for affecting the lives of the very sick.

That is not to suggest that Katharine is a worker of miracles; although Father Vladimir Felzmann, organizer of her Lourdes visits, believes that she is. Rather it is to suggest that the role of spiritual healer, with all its mystical, quasi-religious connotations, suggests a level of involvement intense enough profoundly to affect the Duchess as well as those whom she helps. Pat Seed, the dying Manchester cancer patient whom Katharine befriended, explained to Tony Lothian that 'the Duchess always left people feeling happier, safer, not frightened. She made the dying die more easily.'

Seed was particularly struck by Katharine's effect on a young cancer patient only hours from death. Unsure whether to ask her to see the girl, she asked eventually if the Duchess would mind. In Tony Lothian's account: 'After her visit, Pat went into the room and saw that the girl seemed cured. She wasn't, of course. She was expected to die, and she did die. But, for a few hours afterwards, she was wholly better. Pat was convinced after that that the Duchess was a healer. I've only previously seen one healer. She gave so much. She tried to get inside the illness and pray it away. It interested me – whether people really can have some effect in an in-between dimension. It exhausts them, and I think with the Duchess of Kent, that has been very noticeable.'

Some will believe in spiritual healing. Others regard it as no more than claptrap. Yet others may choose to see the difficulties experienced by the Duchess of Kent merely as the symptoms of depression. Certainly depression has played a vast part in her story. But Tony Lothian's central point is that there is a wider dimension in which the consolation Katharine delivers, her own suffering notwithstanding, has a profound and draining effect on her. That personal catharsis may offer a key to the Duchess's character and to her difficulties. The exhaustion and withdrawal which overcame her as soon as she stepped through her front door were always more debilitating than normal tiredness, even allowing for the fact that the Duchess was frequently depressed or unwell.

It is possible that Katharine herself became frightened of her gift – if it is a gift – or at least of the effect it had on her. Her later, happier years, in which she refocused both her style and her career, coincided with her new distaste for involving herself with those nearing death. They were, as she said simply, better left to die with their loved ones.

And who, for the Duchess of Kent, are the most beloved? Grown apart from her brothers and estranged from her husband, she failed also – largely through illness – to conform to her own dreams of perfect motherhood. Despite, or perhaps because of, her overwhelming love for her elder son, George, she has never achieved a close relationship with her daughter-in-law, Sylvana. Helen, a source of great support to her mother, may owe her normality in part to the fact that her childhood was less anxiously overseen than those of her brothers. Nicholas, the last child and the one inevitably most deeply involved in Katharine's blackest years, endured a long battle against illness. Both the Duke and the Duchess sought out the best medical advice, accepted that their son would have to spend long periods in hospital and hoped for his recovery. At the time of writing he is, according to friends, improving.

Ill-health continued to haunt the Kents. In 1998 Tim Taylor, Helen's husband, was diagnosed with Hodgkin's lymphoma, one of the rarest but must curable forms of cancer. Tim, aged thirty-three and with two toddler sons, had a six-month course of chemotherapy at the Royal Marsden Hospital. He emerged from the treatment having lost all his hair but with every indication that he would be among the majority of sufferers who make a full recovery. By the time of his illness, Tim had opened his own art gallery, with an inventory of works worth £4 million. Assisted by Helen, who worked as company secretary, he had earned himself a reputation as one of the country's most promising young entrepreneurs.

Although he was quickly able to return to work, and although doctors assured him that he was clear of cancer, his illness represented yet another serious blow to his parents-in-law and, in particular, to Katharine. Fonder of Tim than of Sylvana, she had to endure not only anxiety on his behalf but also the awareness that no branch of the family seemed immune from ill-fortune. Accustomed to her own and Nicholas's chronic suffering, she had naturally never expected her ambitious, successful, happily married son-in-law to succumb to a grave illness. In both her private and her public life, it seemed that the Duchess of Kent was surrounded by sickness and by sorrow. This surfeit of anguish proved too much even for someone so attuned to the needs of the suffering. It was around the time of Tim's diagnosis that she declared her decision to rein back on her work with the dying.

The Kents' family troubles, however grave and however exaggerated by illness and by the demand that they should maintain an impeccable royal façade, are hardly unique. On the contrary, they are emblematic of the problems encountered by thousands of normal families. But the marriage of the Duke and Duchess of Kent was never intended to be a mirror of the difficulties faced by ordinary people. Watched by three Queens, bedecked in her veiled diadem and 273 yards of silk gauze, Katharine Worsley walked up the aisle of York Minster in 1962, a symbol of romance and a bride of fairytales. And afterwards she wept in her bathroom; terrified already by the future she faced.

Behind her, other women waited: the future Princess of Wales and Duchess of York, babies then, but fated, like her, to be trailed up aisles, glorious and admired in a nation's eyes and, in reality, cannon-fodder to a dysfunctional House of Windsor and to the divorce courts. Even if Katharine Worsley suspected that Diana's life might shadow her own, she could scarcely warn her of the danger. She could, and did, learn from the royal family's problems and tragedy.

When the Duchess of Kent married, the monarchy was adored and untroubled, a paradigm of perfect family life. Three decades on, such mythology was in ruins. A public that had immoderately lauded its royal family and invested it as the guardian and exemplar of beautiful conduct had turned against it with equal ardour. Scandal and divorce had wrecked its lustre. The death of Diana had robbed it of its allure. In a hasty operation to regain credibility, the Windsors lurched from mystique to populism. On one weekend in August 1998, the Queen's Rolls-Royce got stuck in a drive-through lane of the fast-food burger restaurant, McDonald's. On the same day, her Labour Prime Minister, Tony Blair, departed, in a plane of the Royal Flight, for his holiday in the fifty-room mansion of an Italian prince.

The contrast illustrated the royal family's struggle – sometimes desperate and occasionally absurd – to appear in touch with an increasingly sceptical populace. Katharine Kent, meanwhile, had never been out of touch. Although she had certainly acquired some taste for grandeur and the perks of the job, she remained at heart a Yorkshire woman – someone perfectly accustomed to cooking her own meals and buying her own groceries. As Simon Lewis, the Queen's new 'spin doctor', sought out the popular pulse for the monarchy, Katharine was frequently spotted alone in Watlington – the nearest town to her tiny cottage – shopping for weekend food, with a copy of the *Daily Mail* under her arm.

At a time when fringe royals – her family included – were regarded by the public as dispensable, she remained as popular than ever. Unsullied by royal crises, she was also able to rise above them. Effortlessly ordinary, she had slotted easily and gratefully into the less glamorous life she had always yearned for. As the House of Windsor scrabbled for approval, she was becoming the blueprint of the modern royal: independent, hard-working, humble and fulfilling the demands outlined by the focus groups to which the royal PR machine now paid such careful heed.

For Katharine Kent to have found a niche is a singular achievement. Her marriage has been spectacularly dreadful. At one point her life was comprehensively wrecked. She has overcome problems familiar to many women – chronic depression among them – while helping to assuage the suffering of others. Whatever their difficulties, she and her husband have side-stepped scandal and public acrimony.

Naturally, there has been a high tariff to pay. One adjective is used constantly to describe both the Duke and Duchess of Kent. They are lonely. For Katharine, the solitary child and emotionally needy adult, the coldness of her existence could have proved unendurable. Her survival mechanism was to look outwards: to offer love to, and receive it from, others who would sustain her. The dying, the sick, the homeless, schoolchildren in Africa, orphans in the Balkans and the destitute in India – all of these have been less her caseload than her lifeline.

There is no doubt that Katharine Kent could have been a tragic figure, comprehensively damaged by problems exacerbated by life in the royal domain. Instead she chose to counter-balance private difficulties with a public role defined by love and warmth. Maudlin and sentimental as that may sound, it represents a considerable achievement. In personal terms, Katharine contrived to make sense of a broken life. In presentational terms, she offered an example that went beyond cloying images of conspicuous good works. In an age when the myth of the royal family imploded, the Duchess of Kent remained an exemplar of what royalty was once deemed to be and sought to become again. She was someone who gave more than she took.

CHAPTER THIRTY-THREE

Victim or Survivor?

T HIS BOOK HAS attempted to offer a straightforward portrait of a troubled life. Its conclusion is that, for all her travails, the Duchess of Kent has succeeded, sometimes against great odds, in reshaping her existence. There is a more oblique way of interpreting Katharine's life. To portray her more as a victim and less as a survivor would not be difficult.

Following Diana's death, feminists moved to annex the Princess as their newest icon: a woman sacrificed on the altar of an atavistic and patriarchal royal family. Under this theory – one that bears some links to Katharine's story – there were three stages in Diana's evolution. First, she was a helpless pawn, recruited on grounds of virginity and breeding potential by a husband who did not love her. Second, she was a freedom-fighter, triumphing over the Windsors to assert her independence and, by implication, that of all women. Last of all, she was a victim again, hunted to her death by those, the tabloid press included, who sought to undermine her.

One problem with this interpretation is inconsistency. Authors – notably Beatrix Campbell, who railed against 'the Windsors' corporate complicity in the deception of this woman about her destiny' – were reluctant, in her lifetime, to hail her as a feminist at all, let alone a high priestess of women's rights. Another flaw is the constant portrayal of Diana as a modern Artemis, pursued beyond endurance. Indisputably, she was hunted. But she was also able to manipulate the media with a skill that wholly eluded the Windsors. On a matter of fact, she died not because of her harsh and dysfunctional in-laws or because of press hounding. She was driven to her death by a speeding drunk. Even so, both Diana's fate and the story of the Duchess of Kent offer a grim lesson on how the House of Windsor treats its recruits.

Both were the lightly educated, beautiful daughters of ancient families with impeccable royal connections. Both were 'tidy' virgin brides who allowed high expectations to overrule their grave doubts about marrying into royalty. Both became, partly as an antidote to their miserable marriages, 'queens of hearts' and carers whose empathy endeared them to the British public. Both outshone their seemingly charmless husbands. Both suffered depression and loss of self-esteem. Diana became a self-confessed bulimic, while Katharine went through periods where she scarcely ate. In the account of one friend of Katharine's, the Kent marriage differs from the Wales model in the lack of a Camilla substitute. In a *fin-de-siècle* royal family beset by divorce and unhappiness, no two people are more alike than Diana and Katharine. That cloning of problems – more than a matter of chance – is significant for the uncertain future of the monarchy.

Traditionally, males of the royal blood have flaunted their mistresses and shamefully abused their wives. George III's ill-starred marriage to Caroline of Brunswick culminated in her fightback, under which Whigs, Radicals and the social excludees of the time banded together in her resistance movement. That revolt, in the view of Beatrix Campbell, marked the entrée of sexual politics into the royal domain. On that principle, Diana – and Katharine too – would be neo-Carolinians, fighting their corner in a system barely altered by the passing of centuries or the ascension of female monarchs. (The Queen, in Campbell's analysis, is an upholder of the patriarchy and, like Margaret Thatcher, an honorary man.)

But the demeaning of those outsiders who marry into the modern family firm is not gender-specific. Mark Phillips, the divorced husband of the Princess Royal, was rechristened Fog – a nickname denoting wetness and thickness. Even Philip, scarcely a role model for the downtrodden and diminished, once declared: 'I am nothing but an amoeba.'

Nor is it fair to dismiss the royal male simply as the anti-hero of Victorian melodrama. As Ben Pimlott wrote, in a review of Beatrix Campbell's and Julie Burchill's books on Diana: 'Charles appears as a stage villain, a sort of Sir Jasper figure, tying innocent young women to railway tracks – variously to be denounced, despised, laughed at.' While undoubtedly a husband of nightmares and a social improver of dubious record, it is hard to paint Charles as an unloving or uncaring father.

Nor, as this book has tried to emphasize, would it be right to see the Duke of Kent as a harsh manipulator, wilfully conniving at his wife's unhappiness. Greatly on the debit side, his alleged 'roving eye' is said by a leading churchman to have distressed his wife earlier in their marriage. It is probable that the compact under which the marriage continued contained a promise by him that this alleged behaviour would cease. It is likely that, in later years, he attempted to help her, to the narrow limits of his ability, through her problems. In the eyes of the Duke's friends – admittedly the most partial of sources – he, as well as she, is the lonely victim of a cold marriage.

That is not to take the side of royal men, moulded by upbringing and by education to be emotionally illiterate, domineering and, however unwittingly, destructive. Given that background, it is unsurprising that the sad marriages of Diana and Katharine imply a pattern, rather than mere coincidence. The tally of modern royal divorces – including three out of four of the Queen's children – implies less a pattern than an epidemic. Leaving aside the still to be tested marriage of Prince Edward and Sophie Rhys-Jones, the issue is not only that marriages are not conducive to women's happiness; although that is certainly true. It is that they are not conducive to anyone's happiness.

The emotional vacuum existing at the heart of the monarchy goes beyond a failure to meet glossy perceptions of happy families. It may be central to whether it survives or founders. The revolt after Diana's death – when the Queen remained at Balmoral and no flag flew over Buckingham Palace – was prompted less by the Windsors' past coldness to Diana than by their frigid response to those who mourned her. Here was evidence of a family so dysfunctional that it was incapable of offering any succour to those who needed support. Many years before, the Queen had wished to help the Duchess of Kent but found herself at a loss to offer any comfort because she simply did not understand emotional breakdown. The cold-shouldering of Katharine and Diana was only a microcosm of a wider problem. Comfort and understanding, the touchstones of a normal relationship – with one person or a nation – were, as Diana's death proved, simply missing from the repertoire.

As the millennium approached, the fear that Diana's

death instilled in the House of Windsor evaporated. The brief flutter of widespread republican sentiment was a short-lived spasm, useful to the Queen, in that it prompted her to become more accountable and more in touch while remaining sanguine about the future of the monarchy. But the danger still threatening the monarchy will not be dissipated purely by the opening of books, pruning of budgets and the inclusion of a royal visit to a burger bar or a pub.

The public, having buried its fanciful notion that the royal family – all evidence to the contrary – had a monopoly on virtue, will nonetheless expect a minimum standard of behaviour. The monarchy, meanwhile, remains a frigid and claustrophobic institution, demanding of absurd deference and unrealistic obeisance. In pre-millennial Britain, a journalist may speak to a Chancellor of the Exchequer or a Foreign Secretary with relative ease and on first-name terms. Even lesser royals, through their courtiers' design, if not their own, are to be cloistered away and treated as minor deities.

Such spurious dignity is not only anachronistic. As long as such a system prevails, it is hard to see how royal relationships will survive. Women, and men, may continue to be parachuted into artificial lives, severed from the real world and caged in an existence increasingly at variance with a modern age. That is the fate that befell both the Princess of Wales and the Duchess of Kent.

It would be false to draw too many parallels between the lives of Diana and Katharine. In the weeks before her death, there was no overwhelming evidence that Diana had resolved her traumas. Unless one believes – and the evidence is scant – that she planned to marry Dodi Fayed, she would have been destined to remain in a sort of limbo. Katharine Kent, by contrast, had deliberately slipped out of the royal spotlight, eager to do more work in broadcasting and charity while repositioning herself as a quasi-private citizen. Diana, however informal her style, was the mother of a future King. Katharine – her children's lives deracinated from royal duty – is one of the last of a breed.

Katharine's journey to self-fulfilment was a long and painful voyage, made possible only by the fact that, ultimately, her map references were different from Diana's. The Princess, who had palpable evidence of her husband's infidelity from the start of her marriage, countered with friendships of her own, usually with men – notably Major James Hewitt – who had no capacity to offer her happiness. Katharine, spared an 'overcrowded' marriage, yearned not for a substitute partner but for someone who could replace the man she had loved the most: her father. The replacement figures she chose were icons and guides – men like Cardinal Hume and Nelson Mandela. Where Diana sought to loosen the restraining bonds, Katharine opted to tighten them, choosing Catholicism expressly on the grounds that it would offer structure and rules. Although she was religious, Diana's solutions were temporal. While Katharine loved the material world – shopping, clothes and make-up – her last refuge was in the spiritual.

It is difficult to overestimate the importance of Catholicism in Katharine's life. As her friend, and fellow Catholic, Tony Lothian says: 'I believe the need for spiritual strength is the key to her whole character. She was very lonely without it; she is a very lonely character. The Catholic discipline gives her an inner framework. So does her music. I remember watching her singing in the Bach Choir and watching this transfixed face shining out from all the other faces when she sang the St Matthew Passion. Music and religion are, for Duchess Katharine, very related.'

Where Diana was funny, Katharine is serious. That is a more important distinction than it sounds. For much of her married life the Duchess has been denigrated by courtiers eager to brand her as less clever and cerebral than her husband, not wholly up to a serious job. Against that patronizing murmur, Katharine has sought to prove herself as career woman as well as a carer. The signs are that she is succeeding. 'She is not reinventing herself,' says Tony Lothian. 'She is telling the truth about herself at last.'

In other words, Katharine was casting off the stultifying grandeur of royalty – along with the luxuries she once demanded but which never made her happy. Her lodestars – music and religion – have done more than sustain her. No one will ever know, for she does not speak of such things, quite how close she has been to the abyss. But the scope of her breakdown, depression and personal happiness leave open the possibility that, but for the consolation she obtained from her own beliefs and from helping others, her story might have concluded as tragically as Diana's.

Instead, as the monarchy struggles to render itself more modern, more relevant and more kind, she has emerged as a role model for a family that, through its inimical structure rather than through any deliberately malign intent, colluded at her unhappiness. There are those who will see the Duchess of Kent's fate – to remain locked in a deeply flawed marriage – as the worst of penances. Most people would argue that to be condemned to spend a lifetime in a ruined partnership is far worse than separation or divorce. A few might view the private struggle of the Kents more optimistically: as a beacon of hope in an age of disposable relationships.

Michael Mann – the former Dean of Windsor and spiritual adviser to the Queen, and the man who counselled the Duke when his marriage was unravelling twenty years ago – is of the latter camp. 'I actually think they are an example of a family that has gone through hell but has maintained the marriage. George is happily married. Helen is wonderful, with a wonderful family. Nicky is much better than he was. The Kents have come out on top. They are a very good example of a family that has had to fight its way through a slough of despond and come out on the other side.'

To paint the Kent marriage as any sort of idyll would, nevertheless, be absurd. To suggest that the Duchess has wholly banished the demons of the past – depression, loss and loneliness – would be to mislead. For her, once the perfect royal bride, the promise of happy-ever-after outcomes was never more than empty packaging. That does not make her emergence from breakdown and despair less remarkable. Rather, it is a testament to a woman of persistence and courage; a victim, certainly, but also a survivor.

In 1998 the Duchess of Kent presented the Wimbledon ladies' trophy to Jana Novotna. Twice before, Novotna had failed, weeping, after her first defeat, on Katharine's shoulder. 'You will win in the end,' the Duchess told her with absolute assurance. Delivered by any other royal patron, this would merely have been a comforting platitude. Offered by Katharine it was something more. The Duchess of Kent perfectly understood the lonely path from despair to resurrection. She had travelled it herself.

Bibliography

George V, Kenneth Rose (Weidenfeld and Nicolson, 1983)

King George VI, Sarah Bradford (Weidenfeld and Nicolson, 1989)

The Kents, Audrey Whiting (Vintage, 1985)

Marina, Sophia Watson (Weidenfeld and Nicolson, 1994)

HRH Princess Marina, Duchess of Kent, James Wentworth Day (Robert Hale Ltd, 1962)

Princess Marina: Her Life and Times, Stella King (Cassell, 1969)

'Chips': The Diaries of Sir Henry Channon, edited by Robert Rhodes James (Phoenix, 1996)

The Duchess of Kent, Helen Cathcart (W. H. Allen, 1971)

Katharine, Duchess of Kent, Valerie Garner (Weidenfeld and Nicolson, 1991)

Fighting Fashion, Helen Storey (Faber and Faber, 1996)

Elizabeth, Sarah Bradford (William Heinemann, 1996)

The Royal Family at War, Theo Aronson (John Murray, 1993)

A Year Lost and Found, Michael Mayne (Darton, Longman and Todd, 1987)

Dear Bill, W. F. Deedes (Macmillan, 1997)

The Secret World of Opus Dei, Michael Walsh (Grafton Books, 1989)

Diana: Her True Story – In Her Own Words, Andrew Morton (Michael O'Mara, 1997)

Diana, Princess of Wales: How Sexual Politics Shook the Monarchy, Beatrix Campbell (The Women's Press, 1998)

The Brotherhood, Stephen Knight (Grafton Books, 1985)

Who's Afraid of Freemasons?, Alexander Piatigorsky (The Harvill Press, 1997)

With the Greatest Respect, John Barratt with Jean Ritchie (Sidgwick and Jackson, 1991)

THE WORSLEYS OF HOVINGHAM

Sir Robert Worsley Kt = Alice Tildesley

Robert Worsley m. Elizabeth Gerard

Thomas Worsley m. Catherine Keighley

Thomas Worsley m. Elizabeth Wood

Thomas Worsley m. 1 Alice Holcroft
(*d.* 1664)   m. 2 Penelope Egerton

Thomas Worsley m. Mary Arthington
(1649–1715)

Thomas Worsley m. 1 Mary Frankland
(1686–1750)   Great granddaughter of Oliver Cromwell
    m. 2 Anne Robinson

Thomas Worsley m. Elizabeth Lister
(1711–1778)   (*d.* 1809)
Built Hovingham Hall

Thomas Worsley   Edward   Rev. George Worsley m. Anne Cayley
(*d.* 1774)   (*d.* 1830)   (*d.* 1815)   (*d.* 1854)

Sir William Worsley m. Sarah Philadelphia Cayley
1st Bart   (*d.* 1885)
(1792–1879)

Arthington m. Marianne Hely-Hutchinson
(1830–1861) (d. 1893)

Sir William Cayley Worsley
2nd Bart
(1828–1897)

m. 1 Harriet Philadelphia Worsley
(d. 1893)
m. 2 Susan Elizabeth Phillips
(d. 1933)

Sir William Henry Arthington Worsley m. Augusta Mary Chivers Bower
3rd Bart   (d. 1913)
(1861–1936)

Lucy Vaughan Morgan m. Sir John Brunner, Bt
(d. 1941)

Sir William Arthington Worsley m. Joyce Morgan Brunner
4th Bart   (1895–1979)
(1890–1973)

Sir William Marcus John Worsley   m. Hon. Bridget Assheton
5th Bart
(b. 1925)

George Oliver

John Arthington

Katharine Lucy Mary
m. H.R.H. The Duke of Kent

By permission of English Life Publications

Index

Index

Index

Index

Index

christening 17–18
comparison with Diana 52, 64,
      78, 80, 86, 133, 158, 194–5,
      208, 234, 257, 283, 286,
      441–6
as Controller Commandant of
      WRAC 123, 135
conversion to Roman Catholicism
      120–23, 187, 245–6,
      262–76, 277, 278, 289–301,
      403, 445
at Coppins 98–101, 103–5
and Diana's death 387, 392, 393,
      413
drug dependency 182–6, 279,
      308, 353
early years at Hovingham Hall
      32–4, 48, 51, 59, 83
eating habits 241, 244, 279, 308,
      363, 388, 441
and Edward's sixtieth birthday
      party 306–8
engagement to Edward announced
      87
engagements diary 368–70
fashion sense and love of clothes
      102–3, 107–8, 119–20, 189,
      207–9, 217, 256–8, 283–4,
      322–3, 325, 330–31, 357,
      380, 383, 420
and father's death 139–41, 145
feminist view of 440–42
gardening, love of 100, 236
at George's wedding 215–16, 252
at Helen's wedding 254–6
honeymoon 11, 95–6
in Hong Kong 110–12, 114–15
and HRT 259, 261, 353
at Hull University 336–40
illnesses and operations 109, 147,
      259, 366

abdominal surgery 179
anaemia 148
depression 54, 156, 164, 174,
      175, 181–8, 217, 282, 285,
      291, 353–4, 361, 366, 377,
      427
Epstein-Barr Virus 2, 228,
      315–16, 333, 335, 336,
      362–3
gall-bladder operation 157
German measles 141–2
hernia operation 188
ME (myalgic encephalomyelitis)
      (diagnosed) 2, 308–11,
      335–6, 340, 345–6,
      348–55, 360–64, 416
mental illness 158–61
neck problem 179
nervous breakdown 109, 116,
      160–61, 164
ovarian cyst 180
in India 108, 199, 314–24,
      325–7, 332–3, 334–5, 337,
      345, 356–7, 362, 395–8,
      423
interview for YOU magazine
      326–33
in Jordan 221–2
lesbian tendencies alleged 379
as miracle-worker 293–4, 434–5
and modernization of royal family
      417–18
mood swings 186, 217, 279, 328,
      377
Mountbatten on 131
and move to Crocker End House
      235–6, 252, 305
and move to York House 138–9
music, love of 39, 53, 58, 63, 72,
      78, 82, 119, 156–7, 260,
      341, 428, 445–6

Index

Stuart, Lois 24
Studd, John 259, 352–3
The Sun 102, 249, 390
Sunday Mirror 365, 366
Sunninghill, Berkshire 408
Surrey, University of 368
Susan (at Helen House) 192

Tanzania 239–40, 314, 326
Tatler 257, 260, 423
Taylor, Cassius 382
Taylor, Columbus 287, 382
Taylor, Lady Helen *see* Windsor,
    Lady Helen
Taylor, Michael 249
Taylor, Tim 238, 248–9, 254–5,
    274, 382, 436–7
Tennant, Henry 210
Teresa, Mother 395–7
Thames Valley police force 236
Thatcher, Margaret 227, 311, 404,
    442
This Morning 415
The Times 94, 127–8, 369–70
Tomkins, Lucy 320, 325, 422
Tonga 123–4
Toronto 82
    Stockingtop ranch 188
Townsend, Group-Captain Peter 84,
    113, 165
Trollope, Joanna 223
Tully, Mark 315, 317
Tupou, King of Tonga 123
TV-am 416
Twelfth Night (Shakespeare)
    50–51

Uganda 107–9, 110, 114
Unicef (United Nations Children's
    Fund) 1–2, 87, 137, 221–3,
    229–30, 239, 285, 314–16,

326, 334, 341–5, 355, 357,
    374, 426
United Nations 343
United States of America 149
Ustinov, Peter 232

Vanbrugh, Sir John 11
Varanasi 317
Victoria, Princess 99
Victoria, Queen 11
Victoria Eugenie, Queen of Spain 89
Victoria and Albert Museum,
    London 416
Victoria and Albert (TV series) 382
Vienna 157
Vogue 252, 257
Voluntary Service Overseas 422

Waddington, Leslie 248
Wagner, Richard, *Das Rheingold* 158
Walker, Catherine 252, 255
Walkinshaw, Mrs Colin 249
War Graves Commission 284, 369
Waterman, Fanny 227
Watlington 438
Watson, Sophia 44, 127
Wavell, Field Marshal Lord 62
Way Ahead Group 393
Wedding List Company 251
Weinberger, Caspar 225–6
Wellington, New Zealand 341
Wellington (school) 233
Wessely, Simon 354
Westminster Abbey 114, 310, 394
    Children of Courage 311
Westminster Cathedral 289–90, 296,
    298–300, 307, 377
    The Passage 266, 289, 304, 418
Westminster, Deanery of 309–10
Westminster School 232, 233, 234
Wheeler, Gordon, Bishop of Leeds